CARMILLA

THE RETURN

A VAMPIRE NOVEL BY

KYLE MARFFIN

THE DESIGNIMAGE GROUP, INC.

Copyright ©1998 Kyle Marffin

ISBN: 1-891946-02-1

THE DESIGNIMAGE GROUP, INC.

Printed in the U.S.A.

10 9 8 7 6 5 4 3 2 1

To those I love, and the one
I love most, for support and inspiration.
And to Joesph Sheridan Lefanu,
for whose immortal creation,
Carmilla,
I am forever indebted.

*Excerpt From Joseph Sheridan Le Fanu's
1872 Novella: Carmilla*

*(Taken from Laura's own manuscript,
as provided to Dr. Hessellius)*

"You have heard, no doubt, of the appalling superstition that prevails in Upper and Lower Styria...of the vampire.

For my part I have heard no theory by which to explain what I myself have witnessed and experienced other than that supplied by the ancient and well-attested belief of the country.

...Formal proceedings took place in the Chapel of Karnstein. The grave of the Countess Mircalla was opened; and the General and my father recognized each his perfidious and beautiful guest in the face now disclosed to view. The features, though a hundred and fifty years had passed since her funeral, were tinted with the warmth of life. Her eyes were open; no cadaverous smell exhaled from the coffin. The two medical men...attested the marvelous fact that there was a faint but appreciable respiration, and a corresponding action of the heart.

...Here then were all the admitted signs and proofs of vampirism. The body, therefore, in all accordance with the ancient practice, was raised, and a sharp stake driven through the heart of the vampire, who uttered a piercing shriek at the moment, in all respects such as might escape from a living person in the last agony. Then the head was struck off, and a torrent of blood flowed from the severed neck. The body and head were placed on a pile of wood, and reduced to ashes, which were thrown upon the river and borne away.

...In the particular instance of which I have given you a relation, Mircalla seemed to be limited to a name which, if not her real one, should at least reproduce, without the omission or addition of a single letter, those, as we say anagrammatically which compose it. Carmilla did this; so did Millarca.

It was long before the terror of recent events subsided; and to this hour the image of Carmilla returns to memory with ambiguous alternations - sometimes the playful, languid, beautiful girl; sometimes the writhing fiend I saw in the ruined church; and often from a reverie I have started, fancying I heard the light step of Carmilla at the drawing room door."

Laura _____

PART ONE

CHAPTER ONE

Barbara knew she was going to die.

She knew it. Not just in some offhanded way, the way everyone knows that something called death lies vaguely, and comfortably far away in the safely distant future. Not in the way that the old and the sick might see death's approach in their wrinkling skin or their stiffening limbs.

No, Barbara knew she was going to die *soon*. She'd seen it coming for days now. Or should have, at any rate.

She knew she was going to die for sure. At any moment. Tonight. Right now, maybe.

And that was a different kind of knowing altogether.

It was knowing you were going to die just as you stepped through the elevator doors, and your foot felt nothing more than cold drafts blowing in the empty shaft below.

It was knowing you were going to die as you watched the trigger pulled, smelled the powder burn and actually saw – for a brief half-second – the bullet burst right out of the barrel straight for your head. Or heard the chair tumble to the floor beneath your dangling feet just as the noose started to cut into your neck.

It was knowing – damn sure knowing – she was going to die.

And there probably wasn't a single thing she could do about it.

But if only –

"But I thought you loved me," she cried, her naturally shrill voice cracking even higher than usual. "You said that you loved me!" It wasn't a statement, more a question. A wet burning in her eyes flooded over into real tears now, but it only made her feel more foolish. And all the more certain of what was inevitably going to happen.

Her question dangled in the air. Her tears didn't even get an answer. Still sobbing, she shuffled away from the silent figure standing far on the other side of her bedroom. Barbara kicked off her shoes, sent them flying across the floor. She plopped down on her bed and curled up in the blankets, clutching her arms tight around her. Then she tucked her skinny legs underneath herself. They were dark as licorice twists in their torn black tights.

"I thought you loved me." Barbara's words were almost lost in the pillows and blankets. "You loved..."

"No."

The word slashed like a knife, sharp, and slicing right out of the shadows that ringed the corners of the bedroom.

A dark figure glided out of that gloom. Glided across the room, towards Barbara's bed. Glided right into the dim halflight seeping out of the lamp on the nightstand. The feeble lamplight bounced off the figure, just barely illuminating a pallid face, but hardly able to distinguish a black shirt and dark jeans from the deep shadows.

Mean looking black boots made surprisingly little sound as they stepped across the floor, closer to the light, where the figure knelt beside Barbara's bed.

"No, Barbara. I never told you that I loved you. Never." It was a peculiar voice, a deep, almost magical voice. It made Barbara's sobs quiet for a moment. "No, that's only what you wanted to hear. What you wanted to believe."

Barbara's tears stopped, lulled by that soothing voice, not by the cruel words. A delicate touch, a gentle hand stroked all light and cool on Barbara's shoulder. Cool, clear through the old, worn bathrobe and the carefully ripped t-shirt Barbara wore beneath. Cool, when the hand rose to her hot, red, tear-stained cheek.

Barbara curled around to the edge of the bed, closer to that familiar touch, closer to that magical voice. She wiped the last of her tears away with her fingers, their stubby nails chewed short, but painted black nonetheless. She stared glassy-eyed *at that face* – those dark, dark eyes hovering just inches from her own. She searched for some glimmer of hope there.

But those eyes didn't stare back. They just looked beyond her, back into the shadows dangling around the room, back out the bedroom window, out into the dark, moonless night.

"But, you made me *believe*," Barbara said. "You made me!"

Cool hands still stroked Barbara's cheek. A long, delicate finger traced along Barbara's skin, wiping a last, glistening tear off her cheek.

"Yes, perhaps I did. But I shouldn't have."

Barbara screamed.

She slapped the pale hand away and leaped right off her bed, then stomped around the bedroom. She snorted, shook her head, paced back and forth.

Finally, she stopped. Turned, and scrambled back to the figure still kneeling beside the bed. Barbara fell to her knees too, whispering, "But, we did – things." She looked around the dark bedroom with anxious eyes, as if someone might hear her secret. "I wouldn't ever – I wouldn't have let you...we wouldn't have done those things if I didn't think you really loved me. You knew that." She grasped the dark figure's shoulders and pulled them closer. "We were making love, weren't we?" Barbara whispered hoarsely, feeling the tears welling up behind her eyes again. *"Weren't we?"*

The dark figure just stood up with a sigh, and walked right past her. Floated noiselessly across the room and over to the window. Back away from the lamplight, back to hide in the shadows.

Barbara slid down on the floor, letting the tears flow again. She heard the window ease open. Felt a cool breeze blow in. It was thick with the scent of autumn leaves, all freshly fallen on suburban Hinsdale's tree-lined streets.

But Barbara wasn't paying attention. She was mumbling. "I wouldn't have done it, you know. I don't know what you think, but I wouldn't have. No way." Her whisper grew steadily louder, more raspy, then almost hysterical. "I mean, I'm not – not...you know. I'm not like *that*. Not really." She looked up from the floor and watched the shadowy figure start to pace back and forth by the open window. "But you were different. You know, *different*? Different from anyone else I ever met. Special, you know? So it seemed alright. It *was* alright, wasn't it?"

"Barbara, I –"

"You promised me things!" Barbara crawled across the floor, not caring how pathetic she looked, how embarrassed she felt. "You promised me things, promised to take me away from – *here*. Away from this crummy old house. Away from my goddamned old uncle. Away from – everything!"

She crawled all the way to the shadows by the window. She clawed her way up the firm legs planted there, dug her fingers into the black denim, holding on even when those legs shifted and tried to walk away.

"You promised to take me away with you," she bawled. "Forever, with you. Forever and ever."

The wind rose a little stronger outside, and the room began to grow colder. The curtains flapped at the windowframes. A handful of brown leaves blew right in the open window and fluttered across the floor. Looking up, Barbara could just catch a glimpse of that face, that beautiful, pale face, framed by a long, wild mane of dark, almost black hair. It whipped around all crazy in each breeze.

"Please," Barbara pleaded, clawing her way further up those black jeans. "Please – take me!"

More silence.

Barbara's only answer came from the wind whining outside. She let go and slid back down to the floor in a heap. Whimpered helplessly there for a moment or two, then slowly got up and stumbled back to her bed, crunching leaves underfoot as she shuffled along.

At the edge of the bed, Barbara turned back. She unfastened her robe. The cold wind tugged at it and blew it wide open. The robe slid off her shoulders and crumpled around her feet.

Shivering now, Barbara pulled her t-shirt up over her head and tossed it aside. The cool breeze made the hair on her arms stand up, made goosebumps rise across her skin, made her little nipples harden. Barbara touched them, peeking out from behind lashes all thick with black mascara, peeking back across the room, where the shadowy figure watched her intently. She rubbed her fingers over her breasts and down her belly. Trembling, she slipped her fingers under the waistband of her black tights, toyed with it for a long moment, then slowly peeled the fabric down her legs and wiggled them off her feet...all the while, still peeking back across the room. All the while, watching for some reaction.

Naked now, Barbara stood there by the bed, silhouetted by the dim lamplight, her hands outstretched plaintively.

"Please? You promised."

"I can't."

Barbara's brows knitted together. Her jaw clenched. "Then – I'll tell."

The figure stiffened visibly. Barbara could see it all the way across the room, clear through the dark shadows.

"I will," she said. "I'll tell. I'll tell about us. I've kept track all along. I kept a diary, you know, and I'll tell about *you.*"

The dark figure took half a step towards her. Then stopped.

"Tell who you will, Barbara. No one would believe you. You're not even sure yourself."

"Then damn you," Barbara sneered. "Damn you straight to hell!"

Out of the shadows, that pale face revealed a smirk. Then it melted away, back into the darkness. "I don't think you really mean that, Barbara.

Anyway, it's a little late for *that* particular curse, isn't it?"

"Please?"

"Barbara, I can't..."

"Please?!"

"...and I won't."

That was it.

Barbara was sure.

Sure she was going to die.

The figure strode forward now, a tall, slender girl, icily radiant, darkly beautiful. The girl's long, dark hair almost seemed to glisten, even in the dim light. Her pale skin seemed to light up, all translucent like polished ivory.

Barbara lay back down on the bed, watching the pale girl approach, watching her ease onto the edge of the mattress. Barbara looked deep into those dark, beautiful eyes – determined, *desperate* to find something. *Anything*. Just a chance, just a glimmer of hope that this could all be one more of their peculiar, morbid games, those dark, sinful games they'd played here in this same room, right here on this same bed late at night after her old uncle had gone to bed.

She looked for some hope that what she sensed was coming – what she *knew* was coming – could somehow be changed. She'd take it all back, everything. The threats, all of it – just pretend like it never happened. Then everything would go back to the way it was, the way it had been for weeks now. She searched those eyes...

But there was nothing.

There was only sadness lurking there. Or hunger. Or death, most likely. Yes, Barbara looked into those dark eyes and saw death staring back at her.

Her own.

"No, precious," the magic voice cooed. Barbara opened her mouth to protest, but was silenced by the touch of one slender, long nailed fingertip on her trembling lips. "No, Barbara. Just lie still. Give in to it."

The wind was cold on Barbara's naked flesh. She shivered, but more from the icy touch of those cold hands stroking her lips, her cheeks, her throat. Cool fingers traced long, lazy circles around her breasts, then across her stomach and below. Barbara moaned, helpless, and squirmed deep into the sheets when the ice cold touch lingered below her belly, danced like fluttering wings in the warm moistness between her legs. She closed her eyes, surrendering to the sensations, while cool, red lips followed that same delicious path down her chest and beyond.

Barbara started to rock her hips on the mattress. Biting her lips, she closed her eyes to lock out the sight of those two dark jewels staring back at her from down across her own swaying hips. The pleasure was growing, and Barbara couldn't help but give in to the inevitability of it all, couldn't slow the quickening breaths that puffed out of her mouth, couldn't keep her thighs from clenching against that luxurious mane of dark hair, couldn't keep the shrill sighs from escaping her lips. The feeling grew more intense, the pleasure rose..."Oh please, don't stop, I –"

But the icy touch did stop.

Barbara's eyes flung open, just as the first real wave of her climax hit, only to see that pale face rise up from between her legs. To see those dark, deadly eyes flame red and even deadlier than ever.

To see crimson lips part, revealing sharp white teeth.

To see the pale faced girl leap forward.

To feel those teeth plunge deep into her own throat.

Barbara gasped – warm, wet pleasure flooding through her whole body, just as a sudden slice of pain seared her throat.

And suddenly she saw herself, saw everything quite clearly. Just as if she was standing across the room, watching two strange figures squirming on the bed, one clothed all in black from head to toe and perched atop another, who looked small and very naked, with dribbles of blood – *her* blood – trickling down her throat and across her breasts.

There was no love, no hope, no magic. No promises, no escape from a lonely and humdrum life. Or at least, not the escape she'd hoped for.

She was a fool, and now she was dying.

Barbara wanted to scream. Wanted to shout for it all to stop right *now*. Wanted to run out of the room, out of the house, to disappear.

But she didn't.

The teeth still held tight on Barbara's throat. Icy lips still clung to her flesh. And Barbara could feel her limbs growing heavier, her body growing weaker as her blood flowed out of her veins.

Outside, the howling wind grew stronger, louder, even as her heartbeat grew fainter. Finally, Barbara couldn't even hear it herself. Not the wind, not her heart – nothing. She was floating in darkness. And then she was gone.

Barbara was dead.

~

The dark haired girl lingered on top of Barbara's body for a moment, savoring the rich warmth in her belly, the heat seeping into her own cold veins. All satiated and woozy, she finally rolled off and tumbled to the floor.

She curled up there and hugged herself, then proceeded to lick her wet, red lips and smeared fingertips clean. She relished the sweet sensation for a minute, then crawled dizzily over to Barbara's dresser.

She rummaged through sloppily overstuffed drawers, flinging shirts and socks and cheap costume jewelry aside. *Where was it?* Sweaters and paperbacks, nylons and CD's all fell to the floor, forming a small pile of Barbara Clovicky's short life around her.

Finally – *there* it was, tucked beneath some comic books and a dime-store makeup case: a thick, dog-eared spiral notebook, the cover plastered with rock band and movie star stickers.

Barbara's diary.

She reached for her own black duffel bag and stuffed it in.

Behind her, Barbara's body lay lifeless and still. It was already cooling in the chilly breeze that poured in through the open window. But Barbara's scent was still strong and fragrant – childlike, but not innocent.

She plunged her hands deep into the pile of Barbara's clothes scattered on the floor. Brought them up to her face, sniffing deeply. They smelled of cigarettes and bubblegum and cheap wine. She rubbed sweaters and stockings and t-shirts all over her face, breathing them, tasting them. Drugs and cheap makeup and junk food and anonymous sex, that's what they tasted like.

Then she let them all fall to the floor. The scent saddened her. Barbara's dead body sprawled out on the bed saddened her. The girl fought back a redstained tear pooling at the corner of her eye, and licked the last traces of bloodscent from the tips of her fingers.

Suddenly, she stopped, one finger still stuck inside her mouth.

"Barbara!" A familiar old man's voice bellowed from outside.

She leaped to her feet, nostrils flaring, sniffing the air.

"Barbara? I'm home." A door slammed downstairs. Footsteps trampled in the foyer.

The girl scanned the room quickly. She grabbed her black duffel bag and flung it over her shoulder. Then she sprang like a cat, clear across the room to the window in one jump.

She perched on the sill, eyes darting all around. Her ears pricked up, actually nudging aside her hair as they listened to the slow, heavy steps trudging up the staircase.

"Barbara, come on out here right now. I want to talk with you. Alone. It's about your – your *friend.*"

She took one last look back into the dim little room, even while the footsteps drew closer, grew louder in the hallway outside the bedroom door.

Barbara lay there, splayed across the bed. Speckles of red blood dotted her neck and her breasts, starkly vivid against her skin, skin that was now drained almost white. Vacant eyes glared back with mute accusations. It made her wince.

Those insistently approaching steps halted just outside the bedroom door. The lock jiggled.

The girl stood up on the windowsill and jumped. She landed in a crouch on all fours, pausing on the patio for just a second to survey the darkness. She listened to the placid sounds of the suburban streets, watched the headlights of a car crossing the intersection at the end of the block. Sniffed the wind once more, then bounded across the lawn, racing down the sidewalk. Behind her, she could hear a bedroom door creak open.

As she disappeared into the night, she also heard an old man's horrible, anguished cry. She paused for a moment when that terrible wail whisked right overhead and was swallowed up by the howl of the rising wind.

"Barbara? Barbara! Oh my God, Barbara –"

And then she was gone.

CHAPTER TWO

Karnstein, Styria
1863

Even before her eyes opened, she knew the sun had set.

It had finally sunk below the thick crown of evergreens capping the ridge that circled the old, ruined village of Karnstein. She could almost *feel* its blinding brightness dim, feel the evening shadows begin to envelope the little valley. Instinctively, her fingers twitched. Her toes tingled, joints flexed. Then her eyes finally fluttered open, and as her muscles grew limber again, she began to stretch her arms, to sit up. But as she did, her head immediately bumped against something hard, something rigid and unmoving.

Stone.

Cold, hard marble hovered just inches above her face, pressing close against her arms and legs. She felt panic well up deep inside, felt the first telltale waves of claustrophobia, felt a brief temptation to scream.

But it only lasted for a moment.

Like it always did.

So she wrestled her arms on top of her chest. Pressed her hands against that cold stone, till it rose a few inches, and a deep, azure blue light seeped in. She pushed harder. The heavy marble slab ground forward, finally tumbling to the floor. The crash still echoed in the dark while she slowly sat up, gripping the sides of the cramped, cold stone box, waiting for her head to clear.

Yes. Yes, of course, she remembered now. Remembered everything, while she squinted into the darkness.

There – on the floor – a cracked skull grinned back at her, half buried in a carpet of dust and dried leaves, surrounded by a scattered heap of broken bones and rags.

Yes, she remembered.

She remembered stealing into this very tomb late last night. So late, in fact, that the eastern sky was already brightening into purple along the horizon.

Yes, she remembered.

She remembered fleeing through the forest, dashing through the empty village, racing through the old cemetery, with the growing dawn already searing the back of her neck. She found this mausoleum, hidden so well behind a long row of overgrown hedges. She remembered fiddling with the rusted lock on the mausoleum's heavy door while the sun began to lick at the treetops behind her. Remembered the flash of fear before she finally kicked the door in, remembered the whining, screeching sound the door made when it swung open on long unused hinges, a puff a moldy dust exploding in her face. She'd quickly scanned the chamber and picked the tomb furthest to the rear. Broke its seal and frantically heaved the marble lid aside. A brittle, brownish skeleton lay there, its decayed burial gown stretched over the caramel colored bones like cobweb strands. But there was no time for ruminating on the dead. Or for ceremony. The old bones were hurled out, then she leapt into the stone coffin, sliding the heavy lid back in place as best she could.

"Safe again," she'd whispered to herself, even as her limbs stiffened, and her eyes closed. Sleep overtook her then.

And now...now it was evening once again.

Now she stretched her aching back. Smacked her dry lips. Stretched her arms till they felt limber again, then bent over to massage rigid legs. Her deep, dark eyes blinked till they focused completely.

Once the stiffness was finally gone and she felt alert again, she climbed out of the tomb. One muddied slipper touched the floor, kicking up a cloud of dust. With evening calling, the musty stench inside the old mausoleum no longer seemed comfortably protective. Now it was just stifling, dirty, and dead. Her nostrils twitched at the scent of the cool night breeze lurking just outside the door. She shuffled across the mausoleum in a halo of ancient dust, and stepped out into the night.

She just stood there on the steps for a long time, with her face turned into the breeze, letting the cool, evening air blow through her long, blackish hair.

Beyond the hedgerow lay the rest of the Karnstein village cemetery – overgrown, ignored, untended. Cracked grave markers poked through a thin layer of early evening fog. Scraggly bushes quivered in the breeze, tickling tombstones. She pranced off the mausoleum's steps, swirling the gray fog with her long, dirty skirts and tattered rag of a cloak.

A weed infested pathway meandered through the graverows, past the crumbling walls of the cemetery's old chapel, its stained glass windows shattered or missing, the empty windowframes reminding her of the blind sockets in that grinning skull she left on the mausoleum floor. The chapel walls were scorched black with soot: fires set by misguided and overzealous hands over the years.

Ahead lay the deserted village of Karnstein.

And above the empty buildings loomed the tall and imposing towers of Castle Karnstein itself. The spires thrust up into the sky just like black, grasping fingers – taller even, than the tall pines that ringed the entire valley – groping for a dark heaven that was forever closed to all the fortress' namesakes.

She wandered through the village's houses and shoppes, each one empty and lifeless. The forest was creeping right into the town square, with saplings sprouting from the cracks in the streets, bushes taking root in empty doorways. Not a lamp in a single window, not a light to be seen anywhere, and none had been lit in the old village for over fifty years. It was every bit as silent as the graveyard behind her, except for the snap of a branch, the crackle of dried leaves dancing in the breeze, the mournful echo of a nightbird's call from some vacant house.

But for all the desolation and decay, it *was* home, after all.

The ground rose as she followed the deserted streets, past the finer houses that once clung proudly to the feet of Castle Karnstein. The 16th century monstrosity dwarfed even the grandest manor below, and its sheer size suddenly made her feel very small. And very alone. Her cloak billowed in the breeze as she passed through the castle's fallen gates, up its cracked stairs, and plunged through the open doorway.

The main hall was deserted. The rooms were all empty, the floors thick with years of accumulated dirt and debris. Doorways and windows were invisible behind layers of flapping cobwebs. Here and there a broken piece of furniture lay on its side, a shattered goblet or cracked piece of bric-a-brac jutted up out of the dirt and leaves. The walls were bare, except for a rusted shield here, a bent lance there, a notched sword dangling from a mantle. She ran her fingers over the cold stone walls, each mortar joint whispering faint sounds of days and nights long past.

She climbed a winding staircase. It rose above the main hall and circled up into the tallest of the castle's spires. Gripping her coarse and dirty skirts in her hands, she raced up the steps till she reached the last landing.

Just ahead was the entrance to the Karnstein family chapel, once graced by visiting clerics from Graz and bishops from Vienna. But the pews were all overturned now. The statuary and icons were gone. Faded shapes marked the spots where the stations-of-the-cross had hung.

The chapel had been deconsecrated long ago, and that suited her just fine.

She crossed the empty sacristy, approaching a large, ornate door. Across its Gothic arch, the once proud Karnstein name was artfully carved in both German and Cyrillic scripts.

She paused there for a moment, noticing that the door was half opened.

But there was no sound, except, perhaps, the wind moaning through the broken chapel windows. No sounds, at least none that her keen hearing could detect. And *her* ears could locate a heartbeat in the darkness, a half-held breath in a thunderstorm. So she stepped towards the doorway to the Karnstein family crypt. Reached her long fingers for the door handle.

And then she screamed.

Screamed a high, piercing wail that shook the stones in the chapel walls and blew the few remaining pieces of glass right from the windowframes.

She jerked her hand away from the door handle. Steam sizzled off her flesh. Red sparks danced along the edges of her fingernails.

"Sacrilege!" Her beautifully pale face twisted into purple anguish, her magical voice bellowed like a lion's roar. Dark eyes flamed red, glancing from side to side in fury.

And fear.

"Who dares?"

But no one answered.

The chapel was empty.

And more memories flooded back, easing the searing pain in her hand.

Of course.

A strong wind gusted into the chapel, edging the half opened door aside. And the fiery red faded from her eyes as she looked into her ancestral family crypt.

Crosses scribbled in white chalk on the walls. Litanies scrawled on the floor with black paint: *Vampiris Mortis. Strigou, Beware! Hell for the Wampyr.* There was more. And worse.

She sniffed the air cautiously, her long, thin nose wrinkling like a dog's.

Salt water.

Oil.

Holy Water.

Another scream rumbled up her throat, bursting through her red lips in a deafening explosion. She screamed and screamed again. But there was no fright now. Not even pain. It was a scream of rage. A scream of defiance.

"Damn you!" she roared. "Damn you all, with your crosses and your church and your filthy self-righteousness." Her screams echoed throughout the small chapel till they escaped out the shattered windows, rocketing into the night sky, where even the moon and the stars appeared to shudder.

"Damn you," she shouted again, staring straight up above now. "You close Your Golden Gates to me. Will you take away my only place here on earth as well?" She turned back to the crypt. "Damn you," she said again, but it was only a whimper now.

She couldn't enter.

Never again, for all she knew.

Her home, her refuge for over one hundred and fifty years, since the days when the Castle still teemed with busy folk and family and smiling faces. Closed to her now.

More cautious now, she inched forward, the cloak clutched tight around her. She leaned in through the doorway, careful not to touch the door or the arch itself. Even so, her head ached, her nostrils burned and her throat constricted from the consecrated odors clinging to the stone and metal.

There – just inside – in the shadowed recesses of the vault. There, she could see it. A tall, black marble dais. But it was empty, vandalized, painted over with crude crosses and arcane symbols. She could barely make out the inscription on its plaque:

Countess Mircalla Karnstein
1693 – 1713

The letters were blotted out by a still-wet splash of black paint. At the foot of the dais, her coffin lay on its side. The polished ebony still glimmered, the plush oriental silk lining still shined. Skilled craftsmanship marked it as the handiwork of a bygone era, and age hadn't dimmed its beauty.

But sacrilege had.

The coffin was smashed into pieces, the lining was shredded, stained with brownish patches of dried blood. Round white wafers were scattered across the broken wood, still simmering along their edges, just like eggs frying in a skillet.

She shook her head, and turned away from the vault. The dust clouds swirled even higher around her as she stomped out of the chapel.

~

Her plan had worked, it seemed.

Hastily hatched, yet in the end, it had succeeded. But success – relative as it seemed now – may have been due less to her own cunning than to the superstitious fears of her tormentors.

Oh yes, they'd closed in again, just as they always, inevitably did. She knew they would come. Expected it, of course. But it would have been nice to have stayed for just a while longer. She'd grown so very, very tired of roaming, of being alone.

The weeks spent in quiet comfort in Laura's schloss had been so pleasant. Why, there were even times, in the young English girl's innocent company, that she'd nearly forgotten about her own peculiar...needs.

And Laura?

Well, Laura was really quite special.

Just thinking about her, just picturing that naive, angelic face, just imagining her playful, lyrically British voice, just remembering the wasted longing that lurked in that young heart...it brought a tear to her eye.

But it was simply not to be She should have known better.

Inevitably, Laura's father grew suspicious. Found his daughter's friend a bit...unnatural. He brought in that doctor from Graz, then the old General, and that wily Moravian, Vordenburg, and they certainly knew just what was afoot.

Bureaucrats, priests, all the others. Despite all her cunning, all her stealth, all her dark magic – so carefully groomed over these hundred and fifty years – when all was said and done, they always had the upper hand. And with the protective mantle of the Church, any sort of deviltry was allowed.

Fleeing from Laura's schloss last night, she'd roamed the countryside for hours. It was deep in the forest that she chanced upon the lonely woodcutter's cottage, and there in the loft found his young wife asleep on the coarse sackcloth and hay.

She took the girl in her sleep – swiftly, silently, drinking deep but without passion. Then, with the girl's limp body over her shoulder, bundled in the bloodied sackcloth bedding, she crept back through the woods.

Back to Castle Karnstein.

Back to her tomb.

She lay that woodcutter's wife in her own sleek, black coffin.

From an empty vault in the chapel, she retrieved some of her own clothes. Stripped off the girl's nightshirt and bedding wrap, then redressed her in a once elegant ball gown, cloaked her in a hooded velvet cape.

The peasant girl still lived, barely. Blood trickled freely from the wound on her throat, and that blood was quickly smeared across her face and the cloak to disguise her broad face.

Yes, in a Karnstein cloak and gown, in the chapel's dim light – yes, the resemblance just might be enough. If nothing else, she could always trust in her pursuers' fears to cloud their vision.

With night's precious hours speeding by, she tossed on some old clothes – townsfolk clothes – nothing too rich, or too poor. Scooped a handful of precious stones and gold coins into a velvet pouch, in case she had to make her way in the mortal world for a time.

From the chapel doorway, she took one last look at her tomb. Heard the girl's faint breaths. Smelled the pungent aromas of the peasant's blood, all ripe with the scent of farm foods and healthy, hard work.

The woodcutter's wife would just have to do.

And evidently, the charade had worked.

Laura's father, all of them, they'd been fooled. The priest, the clerics, the officials, all duped by a woodcutter's wife masquerading as the Countess Karnstein.

They came back in the daylight, no doubt. Trembling their way up the magnificent staircase, quaking with fear through each darkened hallway. They came with their crosses and their axes and their wooden stakes, their Holy Water and their wafers and their high-minded purposes.

How smug they must have looked when they peered through the chapel's gloom into that black coffin. Smiled with fierce bravado at the pretty, dark haired girl nestled inside.

Then the sacred butchery would begin: a cruelly pointed stake clenched in sweaty, trembling hands over an innocent breast, until the mallet came hammering down, plunging the wood into soft, pliant flesh...perhaps splattering the gentlemen's fine clothes and the priests' fancy vestments with blood and bits of gore. Then, cutting off the head – surely that was more grisly than any of them anticipated? Then finally carrying the body away somewhere to be burned, to hide the evidence of their holy sacrilege.

But through it all, *she* had slept.

Slept fitfully, cramped into some lowly burgher's mausoleum. But safely, nonetheless.

It wasn't likely to be the last night she'd sleep in a shabby bed, she supposed. The future seemed a bit uncertain at the moment.

—

Nearly two hours passed while her slow pace took her no more than a few leagues down the old forest road that led east from Karnstein.

Every so often she heard a low, mournful howl echo from somewhere deep in the woods. The further into the forest she went, the closer the sounds were. Sometimes answered by others, till an entire chorus rang through the trees.

Soon enough, she detected pairs of bright, greenish eyes flashing from behind the tree trunks, following along with her at the same, deliberate pace. But even her ears couldn't trace any footfalls. Not a single cracked twig or crunched leaf. So she closed her eyes and imagined big paws loping along behind the trees. If she slackened her pace, they slowed too. If she quickened, they sped alongside.

The wolves' stealth matched her own.

Finally after another half an hour, she simply stopped. Those green eyes blinked back at her from between silhouettes of tree trunks. There was a barely-there brush of fur, a rustle of a leaf. And a large, gray male wolf stepped out onto the road. It paced back and forth in front of her path.

She spun around at the soft sounds of more footfalls behind her. A dark, black female leaped out of the trees. The two animals circled her warily, sniffing the air.

She sniffed back, and the animals' ears instantly flattened back on their heads.

Slowly, she extended her hands, palms out, and the wolves crept closer. They sniffed her fingertips, then their ears eased back up and their black lips lowered over their fangs. She ran her pale fingers through the thick fur on their necks, and the animals dropped down flat on the road. The female looked back to the trees and barked.

At once, the whole pack scampered out of the woods.

The pack circled her in a kind of dance, nine wolves leaping in the air, nipping at her cloak, dodging and sniffing her skirt and her hands.

Finally, the large male halted. He closed his eyes, raised his huge head and let out a triumphant howl. The others sat back on their haunches and joined in, creating a wild symphony that sent every deer and rabbit within earshot scurrying for cover.

And the dark eyed girl joined in as well, her throat magically singing that very same, mournful, wild call.

When they finished their song, the wolves looked to her with expectant eyes.

"*Nein,* I don't command you. No one could, or should. You may join me, if you wish. I'd like the company." She swept her dirty cloak around her, swirling the fog that clung to the gravel road. It mingled with the steam puffing from the wolves' muzzles. "But come quickly now, if you will. The night wears on. Look, the moon is already high in the sky, and ready to begin it's descent."

She turned and continued eastward down the road, and faster now.

The moon *was* traveling fast. Too fast. How odd, she thought, that whole years – an entire century – could hold so little meaning, but the night's few precious hours could be so dear.

An hour or more later, the trees began to thin alongside the road. The strange caravan crested one more hill and then looked down on a little valley. At its center perched a small schloss. Light poured out of its windows.

The wolves whined and milled around at her feet, sniffing the air nervously. She glared at the pack's leaders.

"Stay, if you prefer, but I have business there." She whipped her cloak out with a dramatic flourish and headed down the path to the house. The night was short. There was no time to calm the animals. The wolves skulked at her feet, huddled in the folds of her skirts, and reluctantly followed her down to the schloss.

The place was rife with man-scent. Just a forgotten petty-baron's keep, these days it was leased to foreigners – Englishers, who found its Alpine roughness charming, no doubt.

She could hear voices drifting out of the open windows, echoing across the little valley. The sweet aroma of burning pine logs wafted out of one corner room. She could picture them all in there, seated by the fireplace in Laura's father's study. Perhaps he sat in his easy chair, nodding off to sleep with his pipe gone cold and a half filled brandy glass on the table beside him.

"What nightmares dance in your rational little English mind tonight, sir? I wonder," she whispered to the open window. "Dreams of shaman's chants? Of stakes and axes, butchery and pyres? Dreams of blood, innocent blood, spilled blood, wasted and congealing on my chapel's floor?"

The wolves still clung to her skirts as she ambled around to the other side of the schloss. "Rest, Englisher," she murmured. "Rest tonight, because the horror will never leave you. Perhaps the old world wasn't the place to bring yourself and your gentle daughter. Best you'd taken your foreign service pension and retired instead to the streetlamps and drawing rooms of London. Where the dead stay dead. And the living need only fear the taxman and green-grocer's bill."

Back on this side of the house, a wide balcony jutted out of the vine covered walls. Even without focusing her mind, she could *see* right into the room above. Feel the richness of the furniture, the soft touch of the rugs ringing the huge, canopied bed.

And she could hear the delicate breaths escaping from angelic lips somewhere in that tangle of silk comforters and puffy pillows. Could picture the long lashes lying all lush and curved like a doll's, lying across the cheeks that had been drained steadily paler for weeks now. The cheeks that were already regaining their natural rosiness after only one night. She could almost feel the satiny touch of long, golden hair, hair shining just like the sunlight she couldn't bear, all carefully brushed and spread across the plump pillows.

She could hear the rustle of silken sheets sliding up and down over Laura's breast with each breath.

She could sense these things so very clearly because she'd seen and touched each one herself, on previous nights, during those happy weeks spent right here in this schloss, in Laura's close company.

Laura.

Did the naive English girl lay up there dreaming sad dreams of loneliness and loss? Or was she twisting and turning in nightmares about fiends masquerading in pale, fair faces?

Was Laura dreaming of the *wampyr?*

A request to the wolves to stay silent was ignored; they kept whimpering. The request changed to a silent command, telegraphed with dark eyes that suddenly flamed fiery red. The wolves cowered as she took hold of the ivy vines clinging to the schloss' walls and quickly climbed up to the balcony.

Quiet as she could, she crept closer to the French doors to Laura's bedroom. They were closed to keep the cool autumn breeze outside. And whatever else the household now feared might lurk in the darkness. She looked through the glass, and hugged herself close to quell the aching inside. Her dark red lips parted, whispering, "Laura." And inside, the figure on the bed stirred.

She reached for the doors, ready to burst inside, ready to whisk Laura away from the humdrum routines of a boring country life, from a bland and vapid future married off to some visiting English dandy, cursed to bear fat and stupid English children in some tidy English flat, doomed to watch old age creep over her flesh while sipping tasteless English tea. She reached for the door, ready to fly in and bestow her special kiss one last time. Reached for the doors, flung them open and stepped in.

And stopped just as abruptly.

Stopped, and stuffed her fist in her mouth to stifle a scream.

Her feet burned like raw hellfire. Steam hissed from the soles of her muddy slippers. A trickle of blood seeped out of her mouth, still clamped down on her own hand.

That cursed water again. The doors, the floor, all doused with it.

Only now did she see the silver crucifix clutched in Laura's sleeping hands.

Only now did she notice the votive candles flickering away on the dresser, the collection of Orthodox icons and Catholic statuary lining the bookshelves.

Now she saw the bundles of garlic and wild roses festooning the chaise and heaped around the bed.

She spun on her burning heel and leaped off the balcony, her cloak spread wide like giant wings.

The wolves waited nervously below, and began to bark when she landed among them.

Suddenly, a lamp lit in the servants' quarters, just a few windows down. A door opened in the stables across the lawn. Voices spilled out into the darkness.

She looked back up at the balcony. "Oh Laura," she sighed. But now the whole schloss came to life, footsteps crunching gravel, lanterns crossing the yard, voices calling from the doorways.

She turned to the pack churning at her feet. "Away, my children!" she cried, then they fled through the darkness before anyone saw them.

She disappeared into the forest and the night, with the wolves howling at her side.

CHAPTER THREE

Hot water blasted out of the shower nozzle and sprayed all over Lauren Vestal's face while she quickly lathered up the bar of Ivory soap.

She hated rushing, preferred long, luxurious showers that practically drained the whole apartment building's hot water tanks. But she was late for work. *Really* late this time, so she could barely squeeze in a good dousing... at least, by her standards.

A stray drop of soap worked its way into her eye. She plunged her face deep in the spray to wash it away and blindly groped the shower caddy for her trusty bottle of shampoo-and-conditioner-in-one. Lathering it up thick in her shoulder length, blondie-brown hair, Lauren thought she heard something, and turned the water down a notch to listen.

No. Nothing. Probably just the radio.

Wait, there it was again.

Damn. The phone.

She rinsed double quick, shook as much water off as she could and reached for her bathrobe. The phone kept ringing. 'This better be important' she thought as her feet slapped damply across the floor to her small apartment's kitchen. She dashed the last few steps, stretching for the phone on the wall next to the refrigerator. "Hello?"

"Well, good afternoon, princess. What did I do, wake you up?"

"Dad!"

"The phone must've rung twenty times." Johnathan Vestal's friendly voice crackled back at Lauren through static and roaring background noises. "It's nearly 1:30 in the afternoon. Out late last night?"

"Hardly, Dad. Say, where the heck are you? I can hardly hear you." Lauren pulled her dripping hair out from under the collar of her robe and ran her fingers through it to shake the water out. "Don't suppose I could call you back? I really want to talk, but I was in the shower and I'm still soaked."

"Sorry, kiddo. Better stay on the line and I'll make it quick. I'm on a plane. Your old man's calling from about 20,000 feet up somewhere between Boston and Richmond."

Lauren hopped up on the kitchen counter and dangled her legs back and forth to air dry them. She grabbed a dish towel from the sink and rubbed it through her hair. "Thought you reserved those expensive airphone calls for your clients. I'm honored."

"I'll ignore that, kiddo. So, what's with showers in the middle of the day? Don't they ever make you work at that job of yours?"

"Odd hours in retailing, Dad. I work 2:30 to closing on Thursdays." Her hair felt better now, just damp, so she tossed the wet towel back in the sink. "Fact is, I'm running really late, so I'm a little pressed for time myself."

"2:30, huh? I should have such hours." Lauren could detect a hint of parental disapproval in his voice, right through the static. "Spend all that time in those fancy schools just so you could attack helpless shoppers and spray perfume all over them?"

Lauren chuckled, even if she was annoyed. "Dad, you know perfectly well that I don't spray perfume on anyone. I'm just a plain old clerk. 'Ladies apparel' at Bloomingdales, nothing more. I'll keep you posted when the big offers for someone with my qualifications come rolling in."

"Oh, come on honey –"

"Sorry, Dad. There's just not a lot of calls for Masters Degrees in Fine Arts from the University of Chicago. You're thinking I'd be running an ad agency by now? Managing my own art gallery?" She laughed, a self-deprecating, good natured laugh. Lauren wasn't ashamed about how she earned her keep in the two years since she'd gotten out of grad school. Because she *did* earn her own way. She'd rubbed shoulders with enough intellectual snobs in the hallowed halls of U. of C. to know that a lot of them were doing worse.

Well, some anyway.

Lauren's laugh lit up her naturally attractive face, animating features that hovered just on the pretty side of plainness. She continued to run her fingers through her damp hair, trying to keep it from turning into a tangled mess while it began to dry. "Look Dad, you can hassle me all you want about career plans next week on vacation." The static on the airphone connection cut in and out. "I can't wait to get back up to the lodge." The static was really loud now. "Did you hear me, Dad? I said I can't wait for our vacation next week. Is everything all set? Did you get the lodge opened up? Boy, it wasn't easy getting time off after only working in the store a few months. My boss –"

"Honey, that's one of the things I called about." His tone changed completely, the lightheartedness evaporated. Even through the static, Lauren knew what was coming next.

"Oh no, Dad. Don't tell me."

"I'm sorry, Lauren. It can't be helped. I have to be on the road most of next week. Maybe even longer. This is a big project, and it's really coming to a head. There's just no getting out of it. Believe me, I tried."

Her whole body slackened with disappointment as she slumped off the counter to the kitchen floor. "Oh *come on*, Dad. We've planned this for ages. I haven't been to the old place for so long. And I haven't seen *you* in months."

"I'm sorry, Lauren. I tried to rearrange things, but it just wouldn't work out. But look, just because I can't get away doesn't mean you can't still have that vacation. Why don't you go anyway? Take a couple of your egghead friends with you and relax a little."

"Dad, I –"

"No, really. You deserve it. No matter how much I tease you about your job, I know perfectly well how hard you work."

"But Dad, it wasn't just the vacation. I wanted to spend some time with *you*."

"I know, honey."

Lauren felt a wetness around her eyes. Just a drop falling from her wet hair? Whichever, she wiped her cheek on her sleeve. "We ought to stay closer, Dad. I mean, it's hard enough without a mother. Don't make me feel like an orphan."

"I'm really sorry, honey. Look, you probably should get your butt off to work. We've gabbed long enough. And I'm running up one hell of a bill on this airphone." He switched right back to his more usual, upbeat tone. "So, I'll give you a call tonight from my hotel in Richmond, and we'll talk some more, okay? And you plan on taking that vacation. That old cabin's just going to go to waste if you don't. I'll talk to you later, sweetheart."

Lauren couldn't hide her disappointment even if she wanted to...and she wasn't sure she wanted to. "Okay, Dad. But you call me tonight for sure. I'm not letting you off the hook this easy."

"I will, Lauren. I promise."

"I should be home around 10:30 or so."

"Alright. I'll talk to you then."

Lauren was back up on her feet, ready to hang up the phone. "Hey, wait a minute!" she shouted. "Are you still there? You said that was *one* of the things you called about. What's the other one?"

"Oh, well maybe I've given you enough bad news for one phone call. I can save it for tonight."

"Oh no you don't, mister! I don't want to be wondering all day. What's up?"

"Well, you know that the Clovicky's were going to stay over at the lodge with us for a couple of days, right? Turns out they won't be able to."

"No offense, Dad, but that doesn't exactly break my heart. Guess it doesn't matter now anyway, since we're not going. Just out of curiosity, why aren't they coming? I thought the Colonel and you had it all planned."

"It was all planned, Lauren. But the fact is, well...this is really strange... *Barbara died.*"

"Died? What, how? When?"

"It's a long story. A strange one, at any rate. The fact is, I'm not quite sure myself, Lauren."

"Dad, what do you mean?"

"I'm not exactly clear if Clovicky told me she *died*, or if she was..."

"Was?"

"Well, was *murdered.*"

"Murdered? Are you kidding me?"

"No jokes this time. Sad business." His voice trailed off a little. "Look, I really have to go, and I'm sure you do too. We'll pick this back up tonight."

"Okay, but don't you dare not call me tonight."

"I will, I will. I promise. And don't you forget. You're going up to the lodge, young lady. No matter what. Bye."

The sound of the radio drifted in from her bedroom. *'And that was Tori Amos with her latest, at half past the hour on your alternative rock station, Q102.'*

1:30! Her robe went flying to the floor as she dashed back to the bathroom to get ready.

—

Lauren's bus thumped across potholes while she stared out the window.

The tall rows of Chicago high-rises lining the west side of Lake Shore Drive were starting to cast shadows across the bus' path; the autumn sun had already begun to slide behind them, even this early in the day. On her left, white caps crashed on the breakwaters lining Lake Michigan, churning the water into its fall and winter grey coloring, with only a few stray joggers to take in the view. Lauren desperately wished she was out there curled up with a thermos of hot coffee and a good book or her sketchpad, instead of letting a bus bounce her all the way downtown, and to the store.

But after all, work was innocuous enough.

She took the job at Bloomingdales to help pay the bills while she worked out just what she wanted to do with her life. Not that her father wasn't always ready with a check anytime she wanted it. But she *didn't* want it, and was determined to make her own way once school was behind her.

Despite four years of college – art major and philosophy minor – and two years of grad school (art again), the job at Bloomingdales was the perfect way to stall. At least till she figured out precisely what she was really after. There weren't any marriage proposals to clutter things up. For that matter, there hadn't been many dates for a little longer than she cared to admit.

Yes, this job is perfect for now, Lauren thought to herself as the bus rolled past the Diversey exit ramp and swept by the Lincoln Park Zoo. Sure, the hours were long on some days, and customers could find truly imaginative new ways to redefine rudeness, especially the gold-carded dilettantes in their designer labels and expensive perfumes. But it wasn't 9 to 5, and it didn't tax her brain much to keep sweaters stacked neatly, or the blouses hung straight, or the panty hose packages lined up in a row.

The bus finally pulled off Lake Shore Drive and crept its way through Michigan Avenue traffic. The Bloomingdales building loomed just a few blocks ahead. But she knew it would take a while to cover even that short distance in the downtown madness.

Lauren thought about her father's cryptic call. She really hadn't been thrilled that the Clovicky's were going to visit up at the lodge, even if it was only going to be for a few days. It would have cut in on her chance to catch up on things with her father, and that was precious time. But the Colonel was just about her father's oldest friend, though she never understood the attraction. And Barbara? Well, Barbara had just gotten weirder over the years.

But, dead? Murdered maybe? Getting home tonight and taking her father's call couldn't possibly come soon enough.

Walton Street was the next stop – her stop. Lauren gathered up her purse and jacket and headed for the door. The bus slammed to a halt as a taxi tried to cut it off, and Lauren popped out the doors. She started off at a brisk pace westward on Walton towards the store's employee entrance. 2:27 – she'd be *just* on time, despite everything.

She punched in, tossed her coat in her locker and headed through the back offices towards the store. A door opened on her right as she sped through the hallway, and Lauren smacked right into it. Peering around the door was Janah, the department supervisor, who instinctively checked her watch.

"Just in time again, I see."

"I'm punched in, Janah. 2:32, you can check it. I'll owe you two minutes."

Janah blustered past her, hurrying off to somewhere in her self-important style. "That's fine, Vestal." She kept on talking at Lauren as she walked away. "Why don't you get right to work on stocking those new imported sweater displays? It's been a real zoo in there today."

Lauren continued heading the other way, towards the doors to the store.

"And Vestal, let's not forget our name tag tonight, shall we?" Janah disappeared into the offices.

Lauren plucked her name tag out of her pocket and pinned it to her sweater as she hit the sales floor. And there she plunged right into the sweaters, as instructed. The afternoon lull dragged along, then turned into a madhouse around 6:00, when the office buildings up and down Michigan Avenue emptied out, and everyone seemed to head straight for Bloomingdales, and straight for Lauren's counter.

Finally after 8:00 the crowds thinned out, and for once there wasn't a soul at her counter. Lauren leaned back against the tangled heap of sweaters, eagerly scanning the aisles, hoping to see Janah marching around somewhere so she could get permission to leave for at least *one* of her two missed breaks.

Sure enough, there was Janah, stomping through cosmetics, barking orders to salesclerks.

"Vestal, what a mess. I certainly hope it didn't look like this all night." Janah talked while she walked, her eyes already buried back in her clipboard.

Lauren surveyed her demolished racks. "No, I, uh –"

"Well, never mind now. Look, Jeff called in sick tonight, and Tracey had to leave early, so why don't you be a dear and see what you can do over in legwear?" Janah disappeared down another aisle on some vitally important mission.

"Sure, Janah," Lauren sighed, though her boss was already five counters away. Lauren totalled out her register, dropped the key in the drawer and headed over to the legwear department.

Rounding the first counter, she slipped on some kneesocks scattered across the floor. Her heart sank at the sight of anklets and gym socks dangling off of racks and countertops, snakepits of stockings tied up in knots and lolling like streamers over the register, ripped open cartons littering the floor.

"Thanks, Tracey," Lauren muttered, shoving a mound of torn packages and balled up panty hose aside to clear the counter.

But at least the evening rush had died down here too. Just one middle aged woman aimed Lauren's way, arms full of merchandise. As Lauren keyed in the cash register, the woman reached her counter, let the heaps of packages tumble out of her arms and then proceeded to stack them into neat little piles.

"And will that do it for you tonight, ma'am?"

"Yes, that's it for now, honey. Now ring each of these piles up separately, would you please?"

Lauren glared at the stacks: twenty or thirty cartons, easy. Each a different size and style and price.

"Separately, ma'am?" This was going to take a while.

"Yes, honey. Is that okay with you?"

"'Course, ma'am. Anything you like."

Lauren plunged in, scanning the codes and ringing each package up, one at a time. One eye on the register, and one on the nearly empty department.

There was just one other customer, a woman lingering an aisle over. A young woman, Lauren guessed, though her back was mostly turned Lauren's way. A girl, actually. Twenty, maybe. With a thick mane of dark, almost black hair. The full, shiny kind you saw in all the shampoo ads.

"That's this stack then. That'll be $32.41 with tax." Lauren made change for two twenties and proceeded to the next pile, wishing to herself that she could sport a head of hair like that girl there had. Maybe a dramatic dye job was just the thing to add some life to her colorless blonde-no-brown. *Sure.*

The dark haired girl was dressed all in black: leather bikejacket hanging on her like it was two sizes too big, faded black jeans. She wandered down the hosiery aisle, spiralling half a turn towards Lauren's counter, and revealing a sliver of shockingly pale skin, doubly white against her dark clothes.

"That will be $29.87 for these, ma'am."

The girl intrigued Lauren, the way she browsed, but didn't appear to be intently scanning the rows of packages the way most customers did –

always hunting for a particular size, a certain style, that special shade, and usually in a hurry. No, she was...

"$19.44 for these here, ma'am. Thanks."

No, it was more her appearance than her behavior that caught Lauren's attention. Even though her face was hidden behind that wild tussle of dark hair, Lauren could tell she was pretty. No, not pretty — beautiful, almost unnaturally so.

But her clothes looked so dirty. There was mud spattered on the long sleeves of her leather, grey dust smeared on her jeans. Yet, as Lauren watched the girl's long, pale hands with their delicate fingers idly dancing across the packages, they seemed clean enough, and tipped with long, perfect nails.

"And that will be $50.85 for this last pile, ma'am." Lauren's customer impatiently handed over more bills. "Thank you, ma'am."

Finally the dark haired girl turned all the way towards Lauren. Weirder still, she wore dark sunglasses. Not just dark — *opaque* black sunglasses. In the store. In the evening.

Lauren handed change back to her customer, who was plainly getting annoyed with the half-divided attention. The fact that Lauren miscounted and gave her an extra five dollars wasn't mentioned.

One aisle over, that dark haired girl stared straight at Lauren. Or so Lauren guessed. Those sunglasses revealed nothing. Lauren stared back.

The sunglasses lowered. Their eyes locked.

"Now, could I have these in gift boxes, honey?"

Lauren was mesmerized by those eyes. She'd never seen eyes like those before. She could have swore they...sparkled. But it had to be a trick of the store lights glaring overhead.

No. Those eyes were dark as the lake on a moonless night, but they sparkled for sure.

"Sweetheart, *I said* could you put these in gift boxes, please?"

"W-what?" Lauren said. "Oh. Oh, I *am* sorry. Gift boxes?" Lauren tore her gaze away from those eyes, *those eyes*, just as the dark haired girl slid her sunglasses back up her long nose. They were gone now. The eyes were gone. But the girl still hovered there, just an aisle over, and presumably still staring at her. In fact, Lauren *knew* she was still staring at her. Should could *feel* it.

"Excuse me," the customer snorted, looking closely at the nametag pinned to Lauren's sweater. "Lauren, is it? Well, Lauren, I want these items in gift boxes. Say, are you sure you're okay?"

"Oh, yes. Yes, I'm sorry. Long day, you know?" Lauren looked back down at the piles of packages on the counter. "Gift boxes? For *panty hose*, Ma'am?"

"Yes, that's right."

"For *each* of these?"

"Yes, is that a problem?"

"No. No, of course not." Lauren dug under the counter for a stack of gift boxes and a ream of tissue liners. She proceeded to assemble the folding cartons, laid in tissue and plopped a single sale-priced panty hose package in each.

Lauren looked back up. That girl was still standing there, rooted in that very same spot. But now she had a handful of hosiery cartons in her hand. She held them up plainly, then stuffed them inside her jacket. Then she zipped it closed.

Then she smiled.

And that smile sent a chill right down Lauren's spine. She actually shivered, just like a cold wind had blown right down her back.

It wasn't a happy smile. It wasn't a cruel smile. Not even a snotty one. It was a *knowing* smile. A look that said 'I know you, I can see right inside you.'

And it scared her.

"Look, just put the rest of those boxes in the bag," the customer snarled. "I'll take care of it myself." She scooped up her packages.

"I'm sorry, ma'am."

No use. The woman was already stomping away in a huff. Lauren turned back to the girl across the aisle.

But she was gone.

Where? She stuffed merchandise in her jacket, she was shoplifting!

Lauren raced out from behind her counter and looked up and down the aisles. She couldn't see her. Then as a family of four cleared the aisle a few counters down, she saw the girl striding right out the front entrance, out into the Michigan Avenue night.

Lauren raced after her, not sure why. Why not just call security? What was she doing? Did she really care if someone filched a few pairs of nylons?

Lauren burst through the front doors just seconds behind her. But the girl was gone, lost in the crowd trundling by on Michigan Avenue.

Lauren scanned down the sidewalk both ways. The glare of a thousand streetlamps and headlights lit up the street. A chilly wind blustered right off the lake. Lauren shivered – from the wind this time, she was sure. But maybe...maybe still just a little from the thought of those haunting, piercing, knowing eyes. And that smile.

That smile...

~

When the bus rolled to a stop on her corner, Lauren was still wondering – *why hadn't she reported the incident?*

She flicked the lights on in her apartment, locked the deadbolt, tossed her jacket on a living room chair and kicked her shoes off, all in one continuous, fluid motion. Heading into the small kitchen, she turned the gas on under the kettle for coffee.

10:45. Dad should call soon.

Her room was a mess, just the way she'd left it this afternoon. With her face washed clean and the money and charge card carbon grime scrubbed off her hands, Lauren changed into her robe and a clean pair of socks. She paused in front of the mirror, and her face stared back at her looking haggard, her eyes drooping, but that was just from work.

Lauren stared at her eyes in the mirror, and for a moment they seemed to become *those* eyes. She blinked, and they were gone. But she couldn't help turning around, just to make sure no one was there.

The sound of the kettle whistling sent her scampering back to the kitchen.

The coffee was scalding hot. Three heaping spoonsful of instant, dark and strong and just the way she liked it. Lauren replaced the kettle on the burner and turned the gas down. It still sang weakly. Finally, the phone rang, drowning out the whistle.

"Hi Lauren, sorry I'm late."

"Hi, Dad." Cradling the phone on her shoulder, she carefully negotiated her way to the living room, balancing the full, steaming cup and stretching the phone cord just shy of its limit. "I hoped you wouldn't forget to call." She eased herself onto the sofa and slowly set the cup down on the end table beside it. Lauren reached behind her and deftly flicked the latch on the window behind the sofa. She slid it open. A draft of cold air blew right in, fresh and sharply damp from the Lake just across the street, and only a few stories below. "You know, I really miss you, Dad."

"I miss you too, Lauren."

There was a long pause, and both digested all that had changed over the years since Lauren's mother died. Selling the big old house in the suburbs, Lauren going off to college, and then grad school, her father moving with his business to New York but mostly living on the road, plunged headlong into his career to make up for his own emptiness. But there had been happier times. Maybe there could be again.

Finally, Johnathan Vestal took charge and broke the silence before either of their eyes misted over. "So, you sound exhausted. Bad day?"

"No more than any other." The pleasant image of her father rolled before her eyes – ensconced in some hotel room with his wingtips beside the bed, his tie undone and his sleeves rolled up, sheafs of files and businessy-stuff splayed across the bed and making Lauren miss him all the more.

But it was suddenly replaced by the image of those haunting eyes. They appeared from behind dark sunglasses sliding slowly down a long, well shaped nose...and that arrogantly all-knowing smile of deep red lips framed by pale cheeks.

"No, not a bad day, Dad. Just a weird one, I guess."

"Well then all the more reason for you to listen to your old man and continue with the vacation plans without me. But we can get back to that later."

Lauren raised her mug to her mouth and blew ripples across the steaming coffee. "Right. So, what's all this you started on about Barbara Clovicky? Dead? Murdered?" She took a sip from the mug, but it was still too hot, and she set it back down on the endtable.

"You got me, Lauren. You want to talk about weird, I'll tell you weird."

Lauren tucked her legs underneath herself, fluffed up one of the big, puffy throw pillows strewn across the couch and leaned back as her father continued.

"I called the Colonel a while back, just to check in. You know, confirm that everything was all set like we planned – him and his niece popping up to the lodge for a couple of days while you and I were up there. I know you weren't too tickled about them coming, but after all, he's an old friend, and you know how much he liked to go fishing up north."

"I know," Lauren sighed. "I know."

"Well, I think he was eager to go this time to get Barbara away, not just to dunk his pole. He didn't say it in so many words. Lauren, you know how close mouthed the Colonel could be. But I got the impression that Barbara was just getting to be too much for the old guy to handle."

Lauren made another attempt to sip her coffee – still hot, but just right, now. "Dad, I can imagine. That was a pretty tough situation for both of them. A teenage girl moving in with a retired uncle. And a retired military man at that."

"Well, Lauren, what else were they going to do? His only sister killed in a car wreck. Good-for-nothing deadbeat of a dad skips out right after. You know, I have a little experience myself with trying to raise a teenager alone."

She smiled, remembering those early days after her mother had died, and her father's attempts at being both mom and dad. But it was a bittersweet smile all the same. "Hardly the same, Dad. *You're* special."

"Thanks," her father said. Then he chuckled. "Yeah, I guess the old guy is a little rigid."

"A little what?" she snorted. "Dad, the man was a dictator. Positively fascist." They both laughed then, picturing Colonel Clovicky's regimented style completely unchanged from his long years in the military. "Now no disrespect, I mean, in light of what's happened, but Barbara was one strange kid."

"Now that you mention it, Lauren, what exactly was with her? Did you ever look her up like I asked you to?"

"Yes sir. I did the dutiful daughter thing, just like you 'suggested'. It was right after graduation from grad school. I called ahead and got the Colonel – stiff as ever, even on the phone. He invited me over right away. Fact is, he sounded genuinely happy – no, *relieved* to hear from me."

"And?"

"And, I went over one Friday night. Headed back to suburbia for a visit, the plan being maybe Barbara and I would go do something together." Lauren took another sip of her coffee, uncurled her legs and stretched out on the sofa with her feet perched on the opposite armrest. "Let me tell you, it was a strange evening. I mean, it was obvious right from the start that Barbara wanted no part of me or this little get-together. That the Colonel was probably forcing her to go out. Dad, when she first came downstairs, I just about choked."

"Why?"

"She'd changed so much. Sure, she always was just a little 'Addams Family' weird, you know? And I suppose when her mother died, and her father split, she just got, well – *darker*. Hey, I can relate to that." The cold wind streaming in the open window blew through Lauren's hair and fluttered at the edges of her lightweight robe. She reached for the afghan draped over the back of the sofa and slung it over her legs. "But now she'd really gone off the deep end. All these creepy black clothes, two pounds of eye makeup, punky hair, clearly into this whole doom and gloom scene."

"So, what did you two do?"

Lauren almost laughed, thinking back to just how silly she felt that night. "Well, I was still expecting the old Barbara. Face it, I hadn't seen her in a few years, since her high school days, I guess. Sure, she was weird, but still your basic teenager, right? So, I'm thinking maybe we head to a mall or catch a movie, stop somewhere for a pizza after."

"Not what Barbara was up for, that it?"

"Check. As soon as we get in my car, she lights up a cigarette and gives me directions to some club back in the city. She had fake I.D.'s, the whole routine. It was one of these really creepy joints, all this brooding gothic dance music, everyone dressed in black from head to toe. A real scene. She just danced all night and drank. And drank and drank. She pretty much just left me there while she was hanging on all these different guys." *And girls*, Lauren thought to herself, but didn't mention it. "But the funny thing was, I didn't get the feeling that the real 'in' crowd wanted anything to do with her. That's probably the most depressing part of it all. She seemed so desperate to fit in, to make this scene. But she *didn't*, despite all the clothes and the makeup and the whole decadent act. It just seemed so...pathetic."

The wind blew colder now, and more insistently, so Lauren snuggled a little deeper under her afghan and gulped a big swallow of her coffee. In on the wind rolled the sounds of the waves hitting the beach outside, mingling with the honking horns and engines revving down on Sheridan.

She heard her father sigh on the other end of the line. "That doesn't exactly clarify anything. Just makes the little I know as confusing as before."

"So, tell me."

"Like I said, Lauren, I had called the Colonel to firm up our plans. I was doublechecking, because when I'd first suggested the idea, he seemed hesitant about Barbara coming along. Said she wasn't feeling well lately, or something like that. When he told me about the problems he'd been having with her, I figured drugs right away –"

"My first guess too," Lauren cut in.

"So Barbara's ill or *something*," her father continued. "But, he also said something about a friend Barbara had staying with her. It was all very vague, but he obviously didn't like this person, maybe was blaming her for Barbara's behavior. And, stranger still, blaming her for Barbara being ill. Or something like that; frankly, he wasn't all that clear, which isn't like the Colonel at all. Then, when I check back in this week, he's talking like a crazy man. The trip's off. Barbara's dead. He starts raving about this friend of hers, and how *she* did it, *she's* responsible. How he'll get her if it's the last thing he does. Just crazy talk."

Lauren sat up on the sofa. "So which is it, Dad? You think she was sick and died, or she *was* killed, or what? You think this girlfriend killed her?"

"Frankly Lauren, I have no idea. I've checked the Chicago papers, but couldn't find a thing. He hung up on me one time. I've tried to reach him, but there's no answer."

"Wow," was all Lauren could say.

"'Wow' is right. There's a slim chance I might have a short layover at O'Hare early next week. Just a few hours. Maybe I can track Clovicky down and get together. We'll see."

"Dad, I don't know what to say."

"Bad business, Lauren. Really sad. Makes me worry about you – alone in Chicago."

"Well don't, Dad. Just because I was an art major, don't think that I'm a flake. You should know I'm about as level headed as they come." She paused. "I'm not Barbara."

"I know, honey. Well, on to cheerier topics. Like your vacation."

Maybe it was the hassle of the obnoxious customers at work today. Maybe it was the cramped walls of her tiny apartment and the exhaust fumes and car noises filtering in the open window. Whatever it was, Lauren was wavering. She knew it. "But Dad, the whole point was for us to get some time together."

"That doesn't matter, Lauren. If you don't go, you'll regret it. You've got the time off from work, take it while you can. Who knows, maybe I can rearrange some things, and surprise you over next weekend. No promises. But I might."

"Oh, that'd be great, Dad. Okay, I know I said I wouldn't go if you weren't going. But maybe you're right. Guess I can still take a little fatherly advice, right?"

They chatted for a little while longer, happy just to be talking with each other. Johnathan Vestal detailed a few simple instructions on where to get the lodge's keys, how to open up, and so forth. He tossed her some more of that fatherly advice to drive careful, watch out for deer crossing the road after dark, to stay away from strangers.

Lauren hung up the phone and crawled out from under the afghan. The sounds of the waves outside sounded nice and soothing, but she flicked off the lights and padded off to the bedroom. As she climbed into bed, her eyes were already closing into a deep sleep.

Sleep that was going to be haunted by dreams of twinkling dark eyes and wicked smiles.

And outside in the chilly autumn night, the wind blew cold off Lake

Michigan, churning the water along the beach and crashing waves against the breakers. And it blew cold on the pale skin of a beautiful, dark haired figure who shivered, not from the wind, but from her own numbing coldness, deep inside.

The figure had stood there, virtually immobile along the shore for an hour or more now, staring up at the tall apartment building. And when one particular lighted window went dark, she turned away, black boots silently walking off into the night.

CHAPTER FOUR

Lauren's 9:00 AM to 9:30 PM Friday schedule was always grueling. So when her dinner break finally came at 6:00 P.M., she'd already logged what anyone else would have considered a full day's work. And there was still another three and a half hours to go.

But so far, at least, the day had been as uneventful as it had been long, and that was just fine with her. That, and the fact that Friday was Janah's regular day off, which made the long hours tolerable.

Today Lauren was back at her usual sweater counter: a few displays of pricey pullovers, a ring of glass counters stuffed with fancy imports and an ever changing sale rack or two. She locked her register drawer, waved to Jeff and Tracey a couple counters over, and headed out of the store on her dinner break.

Dusk was already giving way to darkness in the mid-autumn sky, and a cold wind whipped down Walton Street, chasing away any last remnants of Indian Summer sunshine. Lauren headed west towards Rush Street to run some errands and to pick up a few essentials for her trip tomorrow.

She returned promptly at 6:45 and stashed her purchases in her locker. *'How come you're not here to notice when I'm actually on time, Janah?'* she thought. Peeling open a package of gourmet chocolate chip cookies, she sneaked a nibble or two on the way to her counter, careful to lick her fingertips clean before she dared to handle any of the precious merchandise.

The store was fairly empty. And why not? It was Friday night. Everyone must have better things to do than shop? Home to husbands and wives and families. Getting ready for dates, or out already – plunging into pizzas and beer, lining up for movies, jostling for tables in crowded singles bars. Herding into galleries and clubs, having fun, excitement, romance, sex...love.

Lauren snatched another bite from the gooey chocolate chips stashed behind the register, then reluctantly turned to still another pile of rumpled sweaters. Straightening their sleeves, fixing their tags, she wondered how many of those same women she'd rung up today would have *their* sweaters smashed warmly against them in tight embraces later tonight? How many of those same sweaters would be slowly tugged up and over their best 'going out tonight so it better match my panties' bras? How many of them would be curled up in front of fireplaces tonight, fumbling in the back seats of cars tonight, leaning against high-rise patio railings tonight while some handsome face and gentle but firm hands reached under those sweaters, sending little shivers clean up their spines and right back down between their legs?

How many?

"I'll take these."

A hand, a long and slender hand, an incredibly, unnaturally pale hand plopped down on the pile of sweaters right in front of Lauren.

Her eyes raised slow-motion slow from the stack of sweaters, at first riveted on the winter white paleness of the hand and its long fingers tipped with nails that gleamed like pearls. Her breath stopped short in her throat, and her legs began to tremble ever so slightly. She nervously brushed her bangs away from her eyes so they could focus on that hand. On the scuffed-edged cuff of a black leather bike jacket, and on up the long sleeve and over the shoulders, there – to that face.

That face.

That same face from last night, that same face that crept into a long night of dreams, dreams she couldn't remember clearly, and when she tried to, they left her almost – what? Scared?

Or, embarrassed?

That face...perhaps a little too thin, too gaunt, too pale, like fresh snow, but even more vivid, framed by that thick, long dark hair. Up close it was brown, no, black; it was hard to say, the overhead lights played like fireflies on each strand. There were those same dark opaque sunglasses, just like last night. And that mysterious mouth, richly red like a sticky-sweet cordial in a fancy tinted glass, with full lips, pouty lips, lips that curved just now into a barely-there smile.

"Excuse me, Lauren. Are you feeling quite well?"

Lauren couldn't muster a response.

"Perhaps I spoke too softly before," the girl said. "I said, I will take these sweaters here."

"I'm sorry...I –"

That voice.

It wasn't normal, just wasn't natural. It was like music. Like a flute. Or a cello. Or a harp. Or all of them at once. It hung suspended in Lauren's ears just like she had headphones on, and all the store's white noise faded clear away.

"Really Lauren, are you sure you're all right?"

That voice didn't say 'are you alright?.' The hair on Lauren's arms rose, her cheeks flushed red. Because the voice didn't *say* what it *said*, not really. She heard it probe and soothe all at once, saying *I know you, Lauren Vestal. I knew you before you were you, and I'll know you forever. Be my friend under the moonlight. Come dance with me in the graveyards. Speak with me through the long night. Sleep with me under the sweet cool earth.*

"Lauren, you really don't look well. Shall I call for someone?"

It was a struggle, a massive struggle, but Lauren tore herself free, shaking her head furiously to clear out the lilting, luring sounds of that voice.

"I'm sorry," Lauren finally replied. "Wait – how did you know my name?"

The dark haired girl cocked her head and her smile broadened, revealing hints of glaringly white teeth. The hand that rested on the sweater pile raised towards Lauren and tapped on the name tag pinned to her blazer. "Why, it's right here on your coat for anyone to see, silly." The hand lingered there a long moment, then fell away, slowly brushing across Lauren's jacket, sure to detect the pounding heartbeat inside.

Lauren looked down. "Oh, right. I always forget that it's there." She was still disoriented. "Now, you wanted – uhm, what was it again?"

"I said that I will take these sweaters here, Lauren." The girl lifted the pile of sweaters in her arms.

"These? *All* of these?" The stack of imported sweaters was worth a thousand dollars at least. "But what size, what –"

"Size? Oh, I don't know, really. What size do you suppose I would be?" She stepped back, turned and did a pirouette right there in the aisle.

Lauren shot glances up and down the aisles, but no one took any notice of anything at her counter. "A medium, I'd guess?"

"Medium? Doesn't that sound mundane? Well, I will take a 'medium' then."

"Wait, which one?" This was all too weird. "Which style, which color?"

"You choose one that you like."

Lauren fumbled in the pile. "Well, uhm, this white V-neck is really nice." She held it up. "Let's see, it's a silk and wool blend, imported from Austria."

"Austria?" The girl seemed amused. "How perfect. Then that one will do just fine. I'll take it." She reached for the sweater.

'She'll take it?' Lauren thought. She looked down at the price tag dangling from the sleeve. $350.00. *Not* on sale. Then she gave the girl's clothes another once over – her scuffed black boots, the black jeans dusted with dried mud along the knees and the cuffs, the beat up leather jacket.

She'll take it?

"Look, this sweater is one of our very best. It's $350.00. Before sales tax." Even hidden by those sunglasses, even veiled by that wild main of dark hair, Lauren could tell by the small patch of forehead and the knotted brows that a perplexed look fell over the girl's face. "Maybe I could show you something...else, maybe something a little less –"

"Oh, I am sorry." The girl slung her large shoulder bag around and rummaged inside. "I just can't seem to stay acquainted with all of the different customs anymore."

Yes, there was more to her voice. The magical tones were laced with some sort of an accent. Not much, just a hint; almost more in the formal way she spoke. German? Something Slavic? Or maybe a little of both. But whatever it was lurking at the edges of her words, it was hypnotic. Lauren could've laid right down on the counter there, closed her eyes and just listened to that voice all night long, like a private symphony.

"I try to keep abreast of proper protocol, but things seem to change so fast these days," the girl said. She pulled her hand out of the bag, clutching a wad of crumpled bills, and laid them on the counter. Fifties, hundreds, a thousand dollar bill. There had to be two thousand dollars spread out there.

"No, you don't have to pay me yet. I just thought..." Lauren saw more money peeking out the girl's bag, partly revealed along with the tips of several flat, shrink-wrapped cartons, Bloomingdales logos decorating their corners: the hosiery packages filched the night before. The girl stared back at her now, waiting.

"Well, wouldn't you like to try it on first?" Lauren asked. "It's not returnable if it's been worn."

The girl smiled. "Try it on? Oh yes, that would be lovely. You have a place...?"

"Sure." Lauren leaned out over the counter and pointed. "The dressing rooms are straight down the aisle that way."

"But would you be kind enough to show me?" There it was again. The words said one thing, the voice said so much more. "Uhm, sure. If you like." Lauren stepped out from behind the counter, sweater in hand.

"Follow me."

Feeling a little light headed, and not sure why, Lauren led the scruffy, pale girl to the dressing rooms. She pulled back the curtain on one of the cubicles, and the girl slid past her. "There's a mirror over –"

"Oh, I won't need a mirror, thank you," the girl said while she unzipped her jacket. "Just tell me what *you* think of it."

Lauren leaned against the cubicle doorway, holding the curtain open with one hand and the sweater with the other. She watched as the girl let her bike jacket and duffel bag tumble to the floor.

She wore nothing underneath. No shirt, no bra, nothing.

Lauren had to stifle a gasp when the girl turned around in the tiny room to face her. The girl's skin, just like her face, was nearly white. Not a sickly, bleak albino white, but more like fine marble...creamy lustrous marble statuary come to life right here in this cramped dressing room. And just like marble, her flesh seemed almost translucent, veined with pale pink and blue across her flat belly and the swell of her breasts.

Lauren stared at those breasts now. She should've been uncomfortable, should've been embarrassed, should've just turned and walked right away. But she didn't. She just stared. They were small breasts, almost girlish, like a fashion model's, if it wasn't for the unnatural color of the skin.

Lauren wanted to touch them.

Her hand slid off the curtain.

"May I have the sweater, please?"

Lauren tore her eyes away. Now she knew she was blushing. She felt her cheeks tingling. "Oh. Sure. Sorry, here."

The girl slipped the sweater over her head. "Please don't be embarrassed, Lauren," muffled its way out from inside the wriggling sweater. Hands poked out of the sleeves. "Do I make you feel uncomfortable?"

"No, I...I was just –" Lauren stammered. The cubicle felt small, cramped and cell-like all of sudden. Lauren backed out of the doorway.

"No, wait."

Was it a plea, or a command? No matter, that voice had to be obeyed. The girl squeezed past Lauren and pulled the curtain closed.

"You haven't told me what you think of the sweater." She stepped back from Lauren and pulled her long black hair out from the loose collar, shaking it free and back into place. "Does it suit me?" She stepped closer. Closer still, backing Lauren against the opposite wall with a thud.

Lauren's heart was pounding so loud she was sure the girl could hear it too, sure that the whole store could hear every single beat.

But the room was deadly silent, except for Lauren's breaths. The girl's pale fingers traced their way up the sweater's neckline and brushed aside her full mane of hair, revealing her long, elegant throat, ringed by a slender black velvet choker – at its center a small, ornate red and white cameo. The black hair, the sunglasses, the choker ribbon, the unnatural redness of her lips and the luminescence of the cameo, all against that alabaster white skin – none of it looked quite real. It was like a preciously beautiful hand painted antique photo magically come to life.

"Your choker," Lauren murmured. "It's beautiful."

"Yes, it is, isn't it?"

Lauren squinted at the tiny profiled bust on the cameo. "The woman – someone special?"

"Yes. Yes, she was." Again Lauren *felt* the girl's eyes from behind those opaque sunglasses, and this time they were melancholy...sad.

"Her name was *Mircalla*. She died a very long time ago."

Lauren reached out slowly, tentatively for the cameo. She touched it.

And for a moment, the tiny little dressing room faded away, and in its place was a huge ballroom, filled with elegantly coiffed and powdered lords and ladies prancing back and forth to the lilting strains of a quartet's minuet.

But everything quickly faded right back to the cubicle, cramped and small with the girl inching nearer, leaning closer till her hair mingled with Lauren's, and their breasts nudged. They stared at each other silently, eyes locked, knees brushing, noses but a fraction away.

The curtain slid open. "Hey Lauren, are you okay in there?" Lauren jerked away.

Tracey poked her smiling, nosy face inside. Just as she did, Lauren could've sworn – for just a second – that the dark haired girl's lips curled into a sneer, that she unleashed a hiss.

"Oh, sorry," Tracey fumbled. "I mean, excuse *me*, Lauren. I just wanted to see if you were okay."

"We were...I was..." Lauren stuttered an answer. "I was helping her with her sweater." She slid past the dark haired girl.

"Uh-huh. Whatever," Tracey giggled.

Lauren raced out of the dressing room and back onto the sales floor. The sudden assault of lights and the Muzak slapped her in the face like a wet rag. She dashed towards her counter.

Tracey leaned back into the cubicle as the pale faced girl grabbed her jacket, her bag, turning to glare daggers at her. Tracey backed away to let her pass.

The girl caught up with Lauren just as she slid behind her counter, the glass case between them like some sort of protective fence. "Lauren, I hope

I haven't caused you any trouble."

Lauren just turned away. She couldn't look at her. No, she could too. She *had* to look at her. "Look, just what is your story?" Out of the corner of her eye, Lauren could see Tracey returning to her hosiery counter and grabbing Jeff, then the two of them bursting into giggles.

"I don't know you," Lauren said "You look like some kind of down and out street kid, but you pull out this wad of cash. You stole some stuff last night – you did, I saw you. But you *wanted* me to see you. I don't know why, but you did. And then you're coming on with all this, this weird...*thing* now. Why?"

"I apologize," the girl answered, all contrite. "I've been, well – naughty, I suppose. Perhaps I was trying to get your attention."

"Well, it worked. You got my attention. So what do you want from me?"

The girl pulled off her sunglasses and brushed the hair back from her forehead. She reached across the counter and took Lauren's hand.

Lauren pulled hers away like she'd just been stung.

"I'm sorry, Lauren. Truly. I shouldn't have bothered you." Lauren's defensive posture softened just a touch. "Perhaps you remind me of someone, Lauren. Someone I knew a very long time ago."

"Look, it's okay. I guess." Lauren glanced down the aisle. There was Jeff and Tracey leaning over their counters, eyes riveted to the scene, straining to hear and all ear to ear grins. "So, do you still want the sweater? Here, at least let me remove the tags for you." Lauren grabbed a pair of scissors from beside the register and reached for the sleeve.

The girl backed away. "That's quite all right. I'll take care of it myself."

"No, don't pull on them, you'll tear –"

But the girl pinched the plastic tags in her long fingernails and they went fluttering to the floor. Then she reached in her bag, pulled out another wad of bills and laid them on the counter.

"Okay, hold on and let me ring this up," Lauren said. "That'll be, let's see...$378.00 with tax."

But the girl had already turned away and was slipping back into her jacket.

"Hey, wait. Your change. This is way too much."

"Quite alright. I will return tomorrow evening." The girl hiked her bag up on her shoulder and took another half step away. "You can give it to me then."

"But we're closed Saturday nights," Lauren said. "And I don't work Saturdays. Anyway, I won't be in for awhile. I'm going on vacation. Come on, take your change."

The girl stopped. "A holiday? Oh, really? How nice for you. Some place exciting, I hope."

"Well, not that it matters," '*So why am I saying it?*' "But I'm heading up north for awhile. Michigan. You know, the U.P.? Watersmeet, Michigan. Come on now, let me get your change."

The girl slid her glasses back on, but before she did, her eyes revealed intense interest. "I trust you'll have the company of good friends? Family, perhaps?"

Lauren finished ringing up the sale and deposited the right amount in the drawer. It left several hundred dollars change. "No, actually. Just by myself."

"Well, nonetheless, enjoy yourself." The girl turned and walked down the aisle. "Perhaps we'll see each other again."

"Hey, really now, let me give you your change."

"Consider it a settlement of accounts for last night's little caprice."

"Huh?" Lauren looked back down at the bills. "This is way too much!"

"Then keep it." The girl was already passing wide-eyed Jeff and Tracey behind their counter.

"I can't keep this."

"Then return it to me when you see me."

"But what if I don't –"

"Don't worry, Lauren. I'm quite certain we'll meet again."

Lauren glanced down at the money again, then over to Jeff and Tracey watching her with wide smirks plastered across their faces. Back down the aisle, the girl was halfway to the front doors.

"Hey," Lauren called. "What's your name at least?"

The girl stopped, half turned her head back over her shoulder. She looked like she was about to answer, but instead, she just smiled that same strange smile and strode out of the store.

CHAPTER FIVE

The girl zipped her black leather jacket up tight to her neck, not so much to keep out the cold – after all, she was always cold. No, it was more to hide her new sweater's bright splash of white. It made her too conspicuous, made it too difficult to blend in with the shadows.

But blend in with the shadows she did, lurking in the dark stairway of a bank building on the north side of Walton Street.

She watched Bloomingdales employee entrance across the street, staring intently as she had for an hour now. People finally started to file out, smiling, eager young men and women hailing taxis, counting coins as they ran for the bus stop, tramping off arm in arm to cafes and parties and nightlife and freedom.

And then, there was Lauren, standing on the sidewalk now, pulling her jacket collar up around her neck to keep out the cold. The girl watched Lauren turn down Walton, apparently oblivious to all the 'good night's and 'have a good time's from the other clerks hopping into autos or walking off the other way.

So the girl stepped out of the shadows and followed a short distance, behind but still across the street, watching Lauren wrestle with an armful of bags, fumbling in her purse for busfare.

The girl ducked into another doorway when Lauren reached Michigan Avenue and took her place in line at the bus stop.

"Go now, Lauren," the girl murmured. "Go home and sleep well. I'll send no dreams to disturb you tonight." Soon enough a bus pulled away with Lauren's bewildered face staring blankly out the window. "We'll meet again soon." The bus disappeared up the ramp to Lake Shore Drive.

The girl hovered in the shadows for a long time after Lauren was gone. Finally, with a sigh, she stepped onto the sidewalk and wandered up the street.

At the corner, the whole world came alive like a carnival: Rush Street, which linked with Division Street, the hub of Chicago's nightlife district. It was lined on both sides with restaurants and taverns spilling people out onto the sidewalks. Music pounded out of open doorways, right along with the pungent smells of too much smoke, too much liquor and the telltale scents of too much desire sought after with too many lies.

She ambled along on Rush, peering through windows at desperate faces pressed against the glass, prowling bodies lounging along brass railings and downing drinks beneath potted plants, sweaty eager boys and needlessly coquettish girls all primped up in their strange, synthetic looking clothes. They gyrated on crowded dance floors to annoying music that sounded just like the repetitious drone and clang of forges and millstones to her sensitive ears.

She continued north to another block just like the last – pausing once or twice to consider as whores beckoned from the alleys and hustlers whistled from the hoods of their cars.

The noise, the lights, the crowds, they were all so different from everything she was familiar with. Home? Home was an ocean away, and forever closed to her now. This strange country was home, now.

But there was no place for her in this world, she thought. No more fear of divine retribution. No good or evil, no superstition. No fear of perdition troubled these modern minds, only the fear of a lost commission, an hour's overtime uncredited, a discounted toy unbought. Fear of a cheap drink from a spray nozzle left undrunk. Only vapid, silly fears of missed opportunities for a surreptitious squeeze of a thigh or a breast on the dance floor. *That* was fear for these stupid, happy faces. No fear of the dark; no fear of nameless terrors that lurked in haunted forests or crept out of graveyards.

She felt silly.

She felt out of place. An alien, an anachronism – strangely innocent by comparison.

She turned off Rush, and the street looked quieter here. Darker and lonelier. It suited her.

By the next corner the sidewalks were nearly empty. She halted in front of the windows of a small club, tucked unobtrusively in the first floor of an old hi-rise apartment building. Old as anything could be in this city, she thought to herself.

It looked dark, it looked friendly. She went in.

It *was* pleasant inside; pleasant and soothingly dark. There were no sudden blasts of light and sound when she first opened the door. The music was just loud enough so that you could listen to it if you wanted to, soft enough to hear your own thoughts if you preferred. The decor was as unassuming as the outside, all well worn hardwood floors and faded white stucco walls.

She slipped atop a bar stool a few seats away from anyone else. A young bartender looked up from a drink mixing guide. "What can I get you?"

"A glass of wine, please."

"Red or white? Oh yeah, or pink?"

She smiled. The choices were so simple, and so bland. "Red, please."

He hustled away. She noticed that instead of reaching for a plastic spigot or a giant cardboard cask, he actually uncorked a fresh bottle.

"That'll be three dollars."

She pulled a crumpled bill out of her jacket pocket and laid it on the bar.

"Thank you. You may keep it."

The boy unraveled the twenty dollar bill. "Thank *you*!" He returned to his drink mixing guide.

She opened her duffel bag, pulled out two books and lay them on the bar. Unzipped her jacket and slipped it off, setting it on the empty stool next to hers. She took a small sip from the wineglass, a *very* small sip, and flipped through the two books.

The wine tasted good. Too good, perhaps. Even this little bit. She took another sip, just enough to wet her lips and the inside of her mouth, barely enough to swallow. Just a sip, just a taste, a small glassfull savored throughout an entire evening was her limit. Even that could leave her faint headed and dizzyingly drunk. More could find her violently sick for days.

She flipped through the crinkled pages of a dog-eared spiral bound notebook. It was Barabra Clovicky's diary, scribbled throughout with Barbara's childlike, nearly indecipherable scrawl. Randomly scattered on the blue lined pages were the passages she was looking for, written just weeks – even days – before Barbara's death.

Then she turned to the other book, oversized, paperbound and filled with brightly colored maps. A U.S. travel atlas, and a complete puzzle to her. Though she'd been in America for many, many years – probably for longer than anyone in this bar had even lived – the geography still baffled her. Individual states were as big, or bigger than entire principalities, larger than whole countries in the endlessly shifting borders of her own homeland.

So, where exactly was this *Michigan*?

Was it a town? A county? A state, a region, or just a *place*? She ran her finger hopefully down the table of contents. Ah, there! Michigan. Pages 47 through 50. She turned to those pages, and there it was: a large state shaped just like a mitten, straight across the lake from Chicago.

No, wait.

She turned the page. There were *two* Michigans. An entirely different one perched on top of a place called 'Wisconsin'.

Two Michigans?

She waved the young bartender back over.

"Ready for another?"

"No, thank you. This is just fine for the moment. But I was wondering if you could help me?"

"Sure. What can I do for you?"

"I'm trying to locate Michigan in this mapbook. But it would appear that there are *two* Michigans. Can this be?"

"Not American, are you?"

"No, I'm not."

"Well, let me see." He leaned over the bar and looked at the map. "I'm from L.A. myself. Never was much for geography either." He continued to scan the map, determined to help her not look too dumb. "Oh yeah, right. See, Michigan is split into two parts."

She stared at the map, puzzled. "Does the 'U.P.' mean anything to you?"

"U.P.? Hmmm, let me see. Yeah, sure, the U.P. The Upper Peninsula. Yeah, I think some buddies of mine went fishing up there this summer. That's this part of Michigan here." He pointed to the map. "Here, above Wisconsin."

She needed to be certain, he didn't seem particularly bright. "That's peculiar, isn't it? Two totally unconnected parcels of land, but one state?"

The boy leaned against the back bar and smiled a dopey smile. "Hey, don't ask me. Like I said, I'm from L.A."

"As you say. Then I don't suppose you would know where I might locate *Watersmeet*, Michigan?"

"Nope. Sorry. But if it's in the U.P., it's gotta be there somewhere." He pointed back at the map. "Doesn't look like there's too much going on in that state, does it? Shouldn't be too hard to find."

"Thank you very much. You've been very helpful."

"Sure I can't get you another?"

"No. I'm quite fine for now. Thank you again."

The boy wandered off. She gazed intently at the map, searching for

Watersmeet.

The bartender was right. It seemed to be a remote, unsettled looking place. No large cities. No towns that she'd ever heard of. Large green tinted areas covered much of the state, marked as National Forest land.

Her long finger slid back and forth over the map...Ironwood, Wakefield, Marenesco, *there* – Watersmeet. A tiny little dot of a town at the intersection of two roads: Route 45 going north and south, Highway 2 going east and west. Right in the middle of a green patch of forest. The Ottawa National Forest.

Now, how to get there?

"S'cuse me, gorgeous."

A pudgy hand dropped onto her shoulder. "What's a hot lookin' babe like you doing all alone? And wasting your time *reading* in a bar?"

She turned to face a stocky, middle aged man swaying on drunken legs. His paunch tugged at the buttons of his shirt, providing a convenient blotter for the beer that kept dribbling off his chin while he guzzled from his bottle. She looked down at the hand that still rested on her shoulder.

"So what're you reading, beautiful?" He reached past her and grabbed the notebook. "You a writer or something?"

She pulled the tablet out of his hand.

"Jesus, how can you read anything with those shades on?"

She'd forgotten all about them. She reached up to remove the sunglasses, but was interrupted by his loud, self-satisfied belch. The man slammed his emptied bottle down on the bar.

"Please leave me alone now, and move on." She said it simply, without menace.

Yet.

"Hey, come on honey. You're way too pretty to be stuck in this dump alone. Nothing is happening here. What'ya say you and me shoot up to Division Street and find some real action?"

"Thank you, no."

"Oh, come on." His fat little hand still retained some traces of summer suntan, revealing a pasty band of white flesh on his ring finger. He tried to slip his arm around her shoulders.

She tensed – ready to spring. In a moment his arm might be snapped like a twig.

"Hey buddy, I don't think the young lady is interested."

Fatman wobbled back around and slurred, "Huh? What the –"

She spun on her stool to face another uninvited guest. But this one was taller, younger. Handsomer. Elegantly dressed.

"I said, I don't think she's interested. Why don't you move on?"

The fat drunk sized up the other man and concluded it was time to retreat. "Yeah, uh – right. Whatever." He waddled over towards the door. "Bitch," he muttered under his breath before he stumbled out on to the street.

"Sorry about that guy."

"Thank you," she replied, consciously letting her voice adopt a lighter, more vulnerable tone. "But it really wasn't necessary. He was quite harmless."

She looked the fellow over. A tall, good looking mid-thirties, perhaps. Neatly combed light blond hair. An expensive looking business suit, crisp dress shirt and floral tie. He smelled of expensive cologne, and held a short glass half full with what might be whiskey on ice. And this one didn't try to hide the bright gold band on his finger.

"Well, you never know. Sometimes guys get out of hand."

She smiled coyly. "Are you apologizing for your entire gender?"

"No, I –"

"Well, thank you again, nonetheless."

"So, can I offer you another drink? On behalf of men in bars everywhere."

"That's very kind. But I still have this one."

He took a sip from his glass, with a slight grimace when the liquor eased down his throat. "That's a beautiful accent you have. German?"

"No. *Styrian.*"

He looked puzzled.

"It's a province of the Austro-Hungarian Emp–that is, it is in Austria."

"Ah, Austria. Beautiful country."

"You've been?"

"No, but I've meant to."

"How nice."

"So, *are* you a writer?" He gestured towards Barbara's diary.

"No, just some notes." She scooped up the tablet and the atlas and stuffed them back into her duffel bag.

"Well, my name is Charles. Yours?"

She thought a moment. "Millarca."

"Mee-lahr-cuh. Now that's an unusual name."

"It's a very old name. It has been in the family for centuries."

"So Millarca, do you often read in dimly lit bars with your sunglasses on?"

"I have very sensitive vision." She slipped the sunglasses off and looked him in the eye.

Charles flinched a little. "Well, they're very beautiful eyes."

"Thank you."

"Millarca, you could sit here at the bar by yourself and let every sleaze in Chicago hit on you all night. Or, you could join my wife and I at our table." He stepped back and pointed towards a booth tucked away in a dark corner of the bar.

Wife?

"That's my wife, Gail. Over there."

Her keen eyes pierced the smoky haze and shadows, back to the corner booth where an attractive woman sat nursing a glass of white wine.

Like her husband, she appeared to be in her mid-thirties, wearing a crisply tailored light grey suit, her ears, neck and wrists glittering with expensive looking jewelry. Her pretty face was lightly made-up, with big doe eyes and a short shock of styled, frosty blond hair. Fidgeting with her glass with one hand, the woman anxiously tapped a long cigarette into an ashtray with the other. Long legs crossed and uncrossed under the table.

"So, join us?"

She looked from Charles, to Gail, back to Charles. The wife smiled weakly, shyly from her dark corner booth. Charles beamed. The pale faced girl thought of a cocktail, for some reason.

"I'd be delighted," she said, hopping off the stool.

CHAPTER SIX

The big, sky blue Lincoln Town Car pulled into a high-rise condo's lower level garage, with Gail and Charles sandwiching the beautiful, dark haired waif snugly between them in the front seat.

Back in the bar, they'd all laughed at Charles' bad jokes, and he patted the strange girl good naturedly on the back, then slapped her thigh. Then left his hand there.

And she'd just smiled.

Charles and Gail weren't prepared for her to be quite so agreeable. Almost eager.

No one else had ever been.

Now the trio made their way through the cavernous marbled and pillared condo building lobby, and waited for a sleepy eyed doorman to buzz them in. Stepping onto a softly lit elevator, Charles punched twenty seven, and they rocketed up to an equally plush hallway.

"Well, here we are," Charles said as he opened the door and stood aside to let the girl enter. "The den of iniquity." He dropped his keys on the foyer table. "Let me take your things, Millarca." She slipped off her bike jacket and handed it to him along with her duffel bag.

Charles vanished while she wandered into a large living room. The lights had been left on, casting a soft glow across expensive, slickly modern furnishings: cream colored leather sofas and chairs, sleek enameled tables, one whole wall a floor to ceiling window with a breathtaking view of the downtown skyline on the right, and the dark expanse of the lake on the left. Gail sauntered into the room and stood by the window.

"Anyone for another drink?" Charles called.

"I'll have a scotch, Charles," Gail answered, her voice preoccupied.

"Straight up. In fact, make it a double, dear."

"Millarca?"

"No, not just yet."

"One double scotch, coming right up. Why don't you two ladies get better acquainted."

Gail fidgeted with the cuffs of her grey suit, fussed with its collar, slid her foot in and out of her pumps. Finally, she left the window, ambled over to the wide entertainment center stretched all along one wall, shooting sideways glances at the scruffy looking, dark haired girl, avoiding her even darker eyes. Gail scanned the maze of panels and buttons, punched one, and some innocuous new age music wafted into the room.

Not at ease, not at all at ease with the strange girl still standing there so unnaturally still, Gail plopped down on one of the cream colored sofas. She picked up her grey, suede purse and rummaged through it. Perfectly manicured nails, painted a soft pink, clicked among the contents.

Gail squinted to see in the moody, dim light. She reached over to the endtable. Flicked on a lamp. Harsh, bright light flooded the room.

Gail looked up at the girl.

And then she gasped and dropped her purse on the floor.

Fancy cosmetics, pricey fountain pens, fine leather datebooks – all her costly, precious junk spilled out on the plush carpet. But Gail didn't care. Or didn't notice. She just stared at the girl.

She was so pale.

So very, very pale. It wasn't really visible back in the dark club, or by the eerie dashboard light. Not even under the elevator's soft overheads. But here, now, in this harsh lamplight, the girl looked nearly as white as that white sweater she wore.

The girl approached.

Gail reached down, scooped up the spilled contents of her purse and lay them on the marble and cut glass coffeetable with trembling hands.

The girl turned off the lamp.

She sat down on the sofa.

"Are these what you're looking for?" She reached for Gail's alligator cigarette case and her gold lighter. Slid a long Dunhill cigarette from the case and offered it to Gail.

Gail hesitated, then wrapped her lips around the cigarette, pulled it from the girl's fingers, flinching when she felt the icy coolness of those pale fingers brush her lips. The lighter flared, and Gail sucked in a deep drag, blowing out a cloud of smoke.

"Say," Charles called out from the kitchen, "How're you two ladies doing in there?"

They exchanged glances, but neither answered.

Gail puffed nervously on her cigarette. She felt warm. Uncomfortably warm. Perspiration dampened her palms and soaked the underarms of her tailored white blouse. Her feet ached inside the sharply styled grey suede pumps. The grey suit jacket felt constricting, stifling. She got up from the couch and hurried back to the window, cranking it wide open and letting a cold blast of autumn air wash across her face.

Gail turned back from the window.

Turned to face that dark haired girl. Standing right there now, right there next to her. Just staring at her with those cold, dark eyes. Gail raised the cigarette to her mouth with a shaky hand, but the girl grabbed her wrist, slid the cigarette from her fingers and flicked it out the open window. They just stood there, only inches apart, for what seemed like hours, like days, like...

Impulsively, Gail reached forward and kissed the girl right on the lips.

"So I see you two *are* getting acquainted just fine."

Gail jerked away, backing right into the window.

Charles strolled into the living room. He handed a glass to his wife, and she gulped down the two shots worth of scotch and let it burn its way down her throat. Charles plopped down on an easy chair, all coy smiles. "Did I miss anything exciting?"

Gail's face flushed red. But the dark haired girl glided over to the sofa, eased into its plush cushions, smiling as she flicked her long, blackish bangs off her forehead.

Gail cleared her throat. "Charles, I need another drink. Would you –"

"Oh, why don't you get this one yourself, darling?" They glared at each other. But Charles didn't move. Gail stomped off to the kitchen.

"So Millarca, do you like our condo?" He waved his hand a little drunkenly around the room.

"It's a wonderful view."

"Yes. It is, isn't it." He drained his glass, the ice cubes clinking on his teeth as he sucked out the last drop. "You and Gail seem to have hit it off."

"Actually, we barely spoke to one another." She looked him in the eye, and it made him squirm, made the thin veneer of his urbane seduction routine evaporate, leaving him feeling just a little silly, just like a fumbling fourteen year old clumsily fingering the clasp on a training bra in some basement make-out party. Charles slammed his empty glass down on the table.

"Take your clothes off, Millarca."

She uncurled herself off the sofa and stood right in front of him. Tugged her sweater over her thick mane of hair. Unbuckled her belt, slid it out of her jeans and draped it round Charles' neck. He stared at her, dry mouthed and speechless, stared at her beautifully small breasts, her long swanlike neck, her shimmering ebony hair. Her ivory colored skin was so damnably pale; she was so thin.

Sick?

AIDS?

Junkie?

Those thoughts vanished once her fingers unsnapped the waistband on her jeans, slowly unzipped the fly, each notch of the zipper teasing in his ears. She peeled the front of her pants back, revealing a flat belly, a shadowy tuft of soft dark hair creeping out of the vee of the zipper.

She looked away from Charles, looked across the room. Gail leaned against the wall in the hallway, watching them. She was breathing fast and hard, with one hand clenched tightly around another scotch, the other thrust deep inside the front of her skirt.

The pale girl smiled at Gail, smiled back down at Charles. It made him shiver.

The girl hefted her leg up to the chair, landing her booted foot on his lap. Charles tugged the boot off and flung it across the room, then did the same with the other. The black jeans slowly unraveled over her hips, down her long, thin legs. She stepped out of them.

Charles and Gail both gawked at her queer, unnatural appearance, her utterly flawless white skin. She stood there so shamelessly, no confusion, no nervousness, no veiled regret playing across *her* face while she toyed with the black velvet choker circling her throat.

She was radiant.

The mood music clicked off on the stereo; the room grew heavy with silence.

Finally Gail spoke. "I think...I think..." She sounded distant and confused. "I think I'd better take out my contacts."

"Yes, dear," Charles said. "Why don't you do that?"

She disappeared down the hallway, and Charles turned back again in the chair to face the pale girl. With her scruffy bike jacket, her dirty jeans, her clumsy boots and the bulging duffel bag all gone, she didn't look like the easy prey he'd first pegged her for. A part of him wanted to run from the room, to grab his wife, to flee out of the condo in fear and shame.

But here was this girl, inches away and so mysteriously beautiful he was afraid to actually touch her, afraid to utter a word or the spell might be broken, and it would all just be another dream, just another one of the pathetic vignettes he mustered up in his mind when he half-heartedly humped in and out of his wife. If he moved, if he even breathed too loud, would the girl disappear? Would he wake up on the couch, channel surfing the late night cable shows with Gail snoring beside him?

The girl raised one leg, perfectly straight, like a ballerina, the foot stretched and beautifully arched, poised inches from his chest.

She tucked her foot inside his shirt and tickled through a thick mat of curly hair. She raised it further, slid her little white toes along his neck, over his chin, across his cheek, and lightly up to his trembling lips.

Then she backed away.

Charles pulled himself out of the easy chair. He headed down the dark hallway, hoping the pale girl was following. If she was, he couldn't hear her. All he heard were muffled splashes of water from behind Gail's bathroom door. That, and his own breath heaving in and out of his chest.

He stepped into the bedroom, a black and silver crazy quilt of deep shadows and reflected skyline lights sparkling in through the windows. Charles heard the faucets squeak off in the bathroom. He heard the toilet flush, the vanity doors slam shut. He could hear Gail, but he couldn't hear...*her*.

He couldn't hear her, but suddenly he *felt* her, just like a cold breeze sneaking up behind him and sending a shiver down his spine. He turned, and there *she* was. Charles gulped, and the sound echoed in the silent bedroom. He knew *she* could hear it, because he watched her red lips curve into a smile. He ignored the lock unclicking on Gail's bathroom. He just stared at those red, red lips, not even listening to the familiar sound of his wife's feet padding toward the bedroom.

"So" the girl asked, her low voice all tolling bells and broken glass in his ears. "Is this what you wanted when you approached me this evening?"

He could barely make his mouth form words. "Y-yes. Yes, it was."

That crimson smile curved wider. "Yes. Of course it is, Charles."

The scent of fresh perfume invaded the room.

Charles blinked, the pale girl turned, and there was Gail, leaning against the bedroom door. Her eyes were wide and glassy, scrolling through confusion, anticipation, lust, jealousy, shame.

Gail's frosted hair was just brushed and curling around a face colored with fresh makeup. The grey suit was gone, and now the room's patchwork of shadow and light glistened on her white slip, defining the curves of her body under the fabric. Gail trembled visibly. Her shoulders quivered, and a slender strap on her slip eased down her arm, leaving one full breast half exposed and heaving up and down with each pensive breath she took. Her stockinged feet shifted back and forth, pawing the plush carpet, the nylons making subtle, shimmery sounds just like her breaths.

Gail said nothing.

She just stared.

The pale girl smiled Gail's way, then turned back to Charles. She slid his suitcoat off, let it fall to the floor. Sidling up close, she pressed her cool, naked flesh against him. She unknotted his tie. She slid her hands inside his shirt and tore it open, sent the buttons flying across the room.

Charles grunted.

"You believe that you have seduced me, don't you Charles?" She unbuckled his belt, unzipped his pants. "You really thought that you charmed me in that tavern, I suppose?" His pants slid down his legs and bunched around his feet. Charles' hard, red erection poked through black silk boxers. "Oh my," she sighed again. "Oh my, my, my. Men never cease to amaze me. Or amuse me."

But Charles wasn't even listening now. The girl slid down his body, dragging his shorts with her, letting his erection bob in her hair and slap across her face.

"But you *can* have me Charles." She edged towards the bed. "I'll let you take me." She leaned over the footboard, her rear hiked up in the air at Charles' waist.

Charles remained motionless for a long minute. Some momentary confusion flashed across his sweat-soaked face. His lips dried at the sight of those two pale mounds bent over the footboard, a shadowy secret cave of dark pleasure lurking in the valley between them.

Finally he leaped forward, before this moment could escape him. He tore his socks off and clumsily stepped out of the pile of his clothes. His penis touched, just *touched* the tight curve of her cheeks, and he yelped.

It burned him with a cold fire, hot and icy all at once. But her flesh jerked back to meet him, to envelop him, swallow him whole.

Gail crept over to the bed, ignored for the moment. She sat down on the edge of the mattress, watching the pale girl's eyes, that same wicked smile painted on those red lips. Those dark, dark eyes just followed her, expressionless, even while Charles bucked at the girl's behind. Gail crawled closer across the bed, closer to them.

Charles thrust hard, harder, harder still, banging the frail looking girl's face into the mattress.

She stifled a giggle while his grunts and moans rang in her ears. At the very last possible moment, she unflexed her muscles, released him from her icy flesh, and wriggled out from under him.

"What the – ?" Charles' knees buckled. He could barely work a breath into his throat. "Oh no. Don't stop now...don't –"

But she slid behind him anyway, held him up with thin strong arms, ran her cold fingers through the hair on his chest, clawed his shoulders with her long, sharp nails. Her hands slid down his chest, down his stomach, traced her fingertips along his shaft.

On the bed, Gail twisted herself into the blankets. She stared at this – this *girl* – clutching her husband from behind. Gail almost wanted to reach out to him, to touch him, to take him inside herself. She squeezed and unsqueezed her thighs. She ground her hips deep into the twisted comforter and sheets. Her rocking grew more frenzied; the mattress quivered, the box springs squealed, the whole bed quaked while she watched the dark haired stranger grip her husband's member in both hands, watched those dark red lips smash kisses across his back, over his shoulders...

Up his neck...

To the side of his throat...

Gail's rocking stopped abruptly. The shaking bed came to a standstill. Her eyes grew wide.

Wider still.

She watched the girl flick her long hair aside. Watched those dark eyes sparkle, watched the black irises glow flame red.

For real. Glowed a bright, burning, fire red.

A scream welled up deep down in Gail's throat, a frightened scream of utter disbelief. But one glance from those glowing eyes, and it just froze. Froze and dissipated behind her lips, creeping out like some pathetic, scared little bleating noise instead. Charles never even noticed.

The girl's head inched back from Charles' throat. Her ruby lips curled back to reveal sparkling white teeth, the two canines all pearly and horror-movie sharp.

The girl lunged and those vicious teeth plunged deep into Charles' throat, just as his first shot of semen burst.

His eyes flung open, still in ecstasy for a moment, but discoloring quickly with the first sensation of sweet, savage pain tearing through his neck.

Gail still twisted on the bed, watching, sobbing, terrified and aroused at the same time, while Charles finally began to struggle, while his lips started to open in a scream. While a small, but strong and pale hand let go of his still spurting shaft and clamped down tight across his mouth.

Charles' body finally untensed, loosening into the girl's embrace. His scared, little boy eyes fluttered closed. And all that was left was the sucking sounds.

The sucking sounds...and the trickle of blood, thick and black in the shadows, dripping from the girl's mouth, pooling on Charles' shoulders and dribbling down his naked chest. She propped him up like a mannequin, like some twisted, hellish Pieta, but with her lips still clamped tight on his throat. His breath grew more labored, more faint...more sporadic. Finally, she pulled her mouth away, all wetly red and glistening, and let go of his body.

Charles fell to the floor with a sickening *thump*.

Gail trembled on the bed, whimpering.

The girl smiled. Smiled with dark red blood – *Charles' blood* – smeared across her lips and chin. Her eyes still glowed, but softer now, a pale yellow cat's eye color surrounding deep red centers. And slowly, agonizingly slow, she climbed up over the footboard and onto the bed, crawled across Gail's trembling legs, long fingernails shredding Gail's nylons and sending cold shivers through Gail's body with her dry-ice touch.

She slithered on top of Gail.

Perched there, she wiped a finger across her own blood stained lips. Held it up over Gail's face. "Can you smell it, Gail? *Geblut*. Blood, Gail. Charles' blood. Your husband's blood."

She dragged her finger across Gail's lips, staining them with a slash of red. "Would you like to taste it? You would, wouldn't you? Scared, doomed as you are, you still would." She laughed. It was a dark, sarcastic, chilling laugh.

She straddled Gail's thighs. *"Sterbliche!* Fool of a mortal," she hissed, leaning in close to Gail's terrified face, the coppery bloodscent thick in the sliver of air between them. "And just what were you and your husband going to do? Use me? *Me?!* Kiss me, lick me, poke me, fuck me, then stuff some money in my pockets and throw me out?" The girl's eyes flamed blood red again, and this time, Gail knew what was coming. Long, cool fingers peeled Gail's slip away. The blood-smeared mouth lowered to Gail's breast and those teeth plunged deep into her flesh. Gail smiled and moaned and cried, all at the same time, and the throbbing wetness between her legs welcomed the savage bite.

Finally, the girl sat up on her haunches, still straddling Gail's legs. She blew a kiss to Gail's closed eyes, then rolled off and lay down on the edge of the big bed.

She was filled quite to bursting. Replete and all blooddrunk. It would be nice to just lay here for awhile and rest, to enjoy the sensations of her body absorbing the new blood. But the night marched inexorably on. There were things to do.

She rolled off the bed and headed for the bathroom.

—

After a long, hot shower, she rummaged through their closets and dresser drawers. She picked through Gail's clothing for something new to wear and some things to take with. Slipped on a fresh pair of Gail's brand new blue jeans. Took a pair of soft white socks to cushion against her boots. But she wriggled back into her own white sweater, the new one she bought from Lauren earlier that night. She hugged it close to her skin and sniffed the cuffs, scenting Lauren's touch on the yarn.

She dumped her duffel bag out on the bedroom floor, and a jumbled mess scattered across the carpet: some torn and muddied t-shirts, underwear, all soiled with blood. One stray sock with its heel worn bare. Pencils and pens, a small velvet pouch bulging with flawless diamonds and gems. The travel atlas and Barbara Clovicky's diary, some loose change. A little pink stuffed toy bunny, several thousand dollars in crumpled bills, and the three packages she'd stolen from Bloomingdales. A few dog-eared paperbacks with gloomy gothic covers, and one well-worn hardcovered book, the title "*In A Glass Darkly*" barely legible in scuffed and faded ink. A long and lethal looking hunting knife was its bookmark.

She stared at the pile wistfully; it wasn't very much of an inventory for so long and eventful a life.

Gathering up her old clothes, she tossed them down the kitchen garbage chute. Then she repacked her bag on the kitchen table, neatly for the first time in months.

It was time to be moving on.

She got her bike jacket out of the hall closet, grabbed the big jangling ring of keys that Charles had tossed on the foyer table, then slipped them in her pocket. As she pulled the oversized jacket on, she wandered back to the bedroom.

Charles' naked body lay there, now nearly as pale as her own. He was splayed across the floor by the footboard, with splashes of blood drying on his chest and staining the plush carpeting. His face was locked in a curious expression, a mixture of serene satisfaction and frozen terror. She nudged his limp, flaccid penis with her foot; it recoiled and shrunk back into the wreath of dried semen stained hair.

A little twinkling wind-chime of a laugh fluttered past her lips.

To mortal ears, the room was deadly still and silent. No honking horns, no revving engines or annoying late-night city sounds made their way twenty seven stories up.

But to her acute hearing, the darkened bedroom was alive – if only barely – but alive with the sounds of weakly beating hearts, of faint and labored breaths, alive with microscopic bodily engines frantically regenerating desperately needed blood cells to replenish Gail's and Charles' halfempty veins.

She knew precisely when to stop.

This foolish pair didn't deserve to die. No, they'd live. They'd wake hours or days from now, all sore, weak and feverish. Their dreams would be filled with demons and desire for days and weeks and months to come. The telltale teeth marks might fade, but the searing pain would linger.

And when they gazed vainly in the mirror, the marks might reappear, though only in their reflections. *Her* own image cast no reflection in the glass, but the marks of her deadly handiwork often appeared to her victims' eyes there. She didn't try to understand why. Searching for explanations to everything was a habit peculiar to these modern times. *She* simply accepted magic for what it was.

Magic.

Perhaps it was heaven's way of reminding the lucky survivors just how perilously close their path had strayed near the gaping jaws of hell. "Sleep, children," she purred. "Let your bodies heal. I can't promise that your souls will do the same." A sad look darkened her face. "Mine never will."

The night grew short. Dawn's glimmer would appear on Lake Michigan's horizon in a few short hours. By then she hoped to leave this wretchedly modern city and its jaded inhabitants far behind.

She slung the strap of her dufflebag over her shoulder and headed for the door, one gloved hand toying with the jangling keyring in her jacket pocket.

Now, which were the keys to Charles' big blue Lincoln?

PART TWO

CHAPTER SEVEN

Lauren's bright red Escort compact buzzed along on Interstate 94, its little four cylinder whining in protest as she prodded it up to seventy.

She reached over and hit the search button on her radio. Still another Chicago station was beginning to fade out. The digital display raced across the dial until it stopped on a country & western station, so she hit the button again and watched the display flip way back down the dial and finally settle in on the middle of one her favorite Pearl Jam songs – staticy at first, but growing clearer as she continued northward, and closer to the station's Milwaukee broadcast tower. She sang along loud and happily off-key, drumming the beat on the console.

Exiting at Racine, Lauren pulled into a roadside coffeeshop. She had a hankering for a big, hearty breakfast and that's exactly what she ordered. After two days in a row of missed meals and junk food snacks, Lauren devoured every single bite. Then back on the road around ten, still with 340 miles to go. But once she left the Milwaukee expressways behind, the scenery changed.

And after Interstate 94 flowed into U.S. 41, she finally felt like she'd left the city behind. The six lane interstate dwindled down to a four lane divided highway coursing through the Wisconsin dairyland. Lauren was no big fan of farm country, but in today's mood everything looked picture postcard perfect: the shiny aluminum barns and silos, the giant combines turning over the leave behinds of the season's second corn crops, the polished silver milk trucks cutting across the highway...every bit of it.

Around noon she passed Oshkosh and exited onto Route 45, a winding, twisting, hilly little two lane highway that would just about take her to the lodge's doorstep. Route 45 wound its way through the heart of Wisconsin, playing connect-the-dot with one tiny farming town after another. With each town she passed, the landscape changed. The rolling hills sprouted forests, the sprawling dairy farms shrank into small potato fields carved out of the sandy, rock filled soil, each one bordered by miles of trees.

Back in Chicago the first splashes of autumn color had just started to peak; leaves had only been falling for a week or two. But this far north, *colorama*, as the locals dubbed it, was already fading. Here and there Lauren spotted a patch of bright yellow or orange or fiery red. But the further north she went, the maples, oaks and elms gave way to dense bunches of tall pines – spruce and balsam and arbor vitae, mingled with white barked birch.

Wittenberg, Birnamwood, Antigo. Antigo was the last 'big town' on her route, the real gateway to the northwoods. Lauren stopped for gas there. With the Escort's tank topped off, and her own emptied, Lauren grabbed a big twenty ounce coffee and a bag of cookies for the remainder of the drive. A state trooper hovered two cars back, so she cruised out of town at an anemic twenty five, slow enough to take in Antigo's big old country style houses decorated up for Halloween, all pumpkins, haystacks and wreaths of colorful indian corn.

Now into her last hundred miles, even the farms were few and far between. Thickening walls of evergreens flanked each side of the road, shiny blue lakes and little rivers sparkled where the trees gave way.

The last cookie disappeared into her mouth and the remainder of the coffee went cold as she sped through the resort town of Eagle River, where the streets were lined with souvenir shops and sporting goods stores. The gas stations and parking lots were crowded with anglers eager to get in their last licks before fishing season ended, and hunters heading for the woods hot on the trail of whatever game was in season.

Finally she hit Land 'O Lakes, a small burg straddling the Wisconsin-Michigan state line. Her car passed under the *Say Yes! To Michigan* archway, flanked on both sides by old depression-era WPA vintage carved Indian head signs. Those same signs dotted the roadside every few miles, pointing to turnoffs for campgrounds and waterfalls and lakeside parks.

Just another ten miles now, and she'd finally be in Watersmeet.

Lauren knew it was just her imagination. Always had been. But it seemed that the moment she crossed the border into the Michigan U.P., the forest just sort of 'took over'. Maybe mother nature didn't pay attention to man-made boundaries like state lines, but she'd always felt that the trees seemed older, denser, the lakes deeper and clearer, the wildlife more – *wild* here than below in Wisconsin. And the fact was, she liked it that way.

Liked it just fine.

Her father's instructions were simple enough: look up Cy Houlder for the keys to the cabin. That was the one distasteful part of the trip. She couldn't stand the old creep. Never could.

Cy had been the caretaker for the previous owners of the lodge. When the Vestals bought the place, Cy just seemed to come right along with the deed.

No figuring why, but Lauren's father sort of took to the old coot, letting him do odd jobs around the place. Just minor repairs: fixing a loose board on the deck, plugging a leak in the roof, laying a new post for the pier after the winter ice mangled a piling. Cy lived deep in the backwoods in a ramshackle old trailer, trapping a few furs, doing a little guide work when he wasn't on a drinking binge, hunting and fishing in season and off for a lot of his food. He should have been one of those colorful country characters, and presumably that's just what he was to Johnathan Vestal.

But not to Lauren.

Oh, Cy seemed harmless enough back when she was just a kid. A little gruff maybe, but always good for a story or two about the good old days, the Indian reservations or a rampaging bear.

But later, by her teens, Cy didn't seem so harmless anymore. Then she could read the look in his eyes a little differently, and it always worked out that Cy was hovering around for no good reason when she was out swimming, or sunbathing on the pier. Cy was old back then. He had to be positively ancient by now, Lauren thought to herself. He didn't really do any chores around the lodge anymore, just held onto an extra set of keys so he could get in to air the place out in the spring. For that, Johnathan Vestal slipped him a couple hundred each year. But there was no way around it, she'd have to make the trek to Cy's trailer to get the keys.

The Escort crested a particularly high hill, and there, ahead at the bottom, U.S. Highway 2 cut east and west across Route 45.

There it was, Watersmeet.

It was late afternoon when she rolled into town. Quick enough, she saw that Watersmeet had changed a lot in the few years since she'd last been here. And not for the better.

'Downtown' had never been much to look at. Now it was even less. The little storefront post office had been government downsized into the bigger facility in Iron River, thirty miles east. The Red Owl grocery store was closed, its windows boarded up. The small two-story hotel hadn't been open as long as she could remember anyway, but on the other side of the street the Mocassin Cafe was a garage now, and Jorgei's Live Bait & Tackle was just gone, nothing more than spread gravel and yellow weeds to mark its passing.

The whole town was only a couple of blocks long even in its heyday. There was nothing else further north, just the small Ojibwa Indian Reservation – a depressing tract of pre-fab public housing units surrounded by rusted out hulks of cars and broken refrigerators turning into weedbeds in the back yards. Years of talk of opening a casino on the reservation were evidently just that: talk. Lauren circled town quick enough, staring at nothing.

Nothing.

Watersmeet was just one more town that fell on hard times after the railroads and the copper mines left. One more northwoods town fending off the encroaching forest and trying to scrape by on vacationers from Chicago and Milwaukee. People just like the Vestals.

Lauren turned the car around and headed back to the intersection of U.S. 2. It looked almost prosperous here, with a long, low grey aluminum sided building sprawling across the northwest corner. '*The Moose*' the sign said. She pulled into the pitted and puddled gravel parking lot and slid her car in between two rusty pickups.

The Moose: gas station, grocery and hardware stores, laundromat, coffeeshop and tavern in one. Even live bait and game registration, in season. All strung together in an eyesore of a building a hundred fifty feet long. Lauren needed some groceries. She went in.

A sullen looking teenage boy lounged behind the cash register, never bothering to look up while she grabbed one of the three shopping carts.

Hardware and sundries on her right, groceries on her left. The cart squeeked down the empty aisles.

She had the place to herself, except for the cashier. But voices drifted through the wide doorway on the far left side of the store. Loud voices, and a lot of swearing. She stood up on tiptoe and peeked over a dusty stack of cereal boxes. There was a combination coffeeshop and tap room beyond the doorway, and a nice little argument was brewing up inside.

Lauren filled her cart up quickly and didn't pay much attention to what she grabbed. She still needed to get that key from Cy Houlder, and wasn't in the mood for exploring the forest backroads after dark.

Rolling her squeeky cart up to the register, she couldn't help but eavesdrop on the conversation filtering in from next store. It sounded like things were really heating up in there now.

"*Goddamn it, them sons-a-bitches in the DNR got you all brainwashed with a pack a lies. I'm still telling you, let those furry devils back in and you can kiss all your deer hunting goodbye. Maybe small game too."*

"No, you've got it all wrong. As usual. Look, I'm tired of trying to explain this logically. It worked in Minnesota. It worked in Wisconsin. Other states too. And it will work here. Besides, they belong here. More than we do, maybe."

The cashier reluctantly set aside his copy of Playboy and rang up Lauren's groceries. A loaf of bread, some baloney, chips, dip, soda. A couple bottles of wine, assorted junk food. Meanwhile, she continued to listen in next door.

"That so? Well then you just tell me what everybody's going to do when there's no more hunters coming up anymore. No one shopping the stores. Hell, those goofs from Illinois and Milwaukee are about the only way we can make a buck or two anymore."

That voice – it sounded familiar to Lauren's ears. A little older. Maybe a little more hoarse.

Cy Houlder?

"I'm telling you, and no lie. You keep bringing them goddamn green eyed monsters in here and you can be for goddamned sure I'm setting my traps with poison bait."

"Now Cy –"

So it *was* him.

In fact, even the other voice sounded familiar too...younger, friendlier, but...

"No, I mean it," Cy continued. *"My Remington twelve gauge'll make short work of them."*

"Cy Houlder, these timber wolves are a federally protected species. You kill one, even by accident, and you'll be facing a $5,000 fine. Probably jail time too, if the DNR proves you did it on purpose."

"No one'll get $5,000 outa me. Hell, I ain't got $5,000. So mark my words –"

"No, Cy. You mark my words. Don't cause any trouble. I won't be able to help you out. Now I've argued about this enough. I've got to make a pit stop and get back to work."

"Okay, okay Steve."

Steve? Lauren craned her neck, but couldn't see clearly into the tap room.

"That's $46.10, lady." The clerk stood with his hand out.

She dug into her purse and handed him three twenties. After he tossed her things in two paper sacks, she took her change and headed over to the doorway. Bulging bags in each arm, Lauren peered inside.

The coffeeshop and tap room were really just one big room, with a low divider separating the restaurant area from the bar. The restaurant side was half a dozen mismatched tables and chairs and a six stool counter, all empty. The tap room wasn't much fancier, just a long, narrow room lined with fake brown wood paneling. A plain formica counter for a bar, flanked by eight wobbly looking stools. And right up front on the first stool perched a grim looking, wiry old fellow: Cy Houlder himself.

His rough hands curled around a loaded shot glass that he poured into his beer. If it wasn't so unthinkable, Lauren would have sworn Cy wore the very same old clothes he had on the last time she'd seen him, and that was years ago. A faded flannel shirt and grey work pants tucked sloppily into rubber wading boots, a worn out baseball cap, sun bleached into an unidentifiable color was cocked on his head. It was a size too small, so greasy looking tufts of white hair squirreled out at all angles. Cy's days-old scraggle of a beard looked white now instead of grey, and taped up eyeglasses rested on his big, red nose; those were new.

Cy knocked back his boiler-maker and scowled at her.

"Yeah? What're you looking at, girly?"

"Mr. Houlder? Cy Houlder?"

His skinny, ugly old puss just screwed up even uglier with a suspicious look. "Yeah? What's it to you?" He glanced back down at his empty glass. "You another one of them tree-huggers come to bitch at me about that doe got caught in one a my traps? 'Cause if you are –"

"No, Mr. Houlder." Lauren set her two bags down on the bar. "I'm Lauren Vestal." She scanned his bloodshot eyes for a hint of recognition, but they just looked tipsy and confused. "Johnathan Vestal's daughter – Lauren."

It took a moment, but finally a wide smile cracked his grizzled old face, tobacco browned lips opening to reveal teeth the color of caramel mixed with soot. "Johnny Vestal's girl? Little Laurie Vestal, well I'll be goddamned." He took another quick peek at his glass and turned around to the bar. "Hey Nate – lookie who's here. It's Johnny Vestal's kid, all growed up. Pour her a cool one on me."

"Oh no, thanks, Mr. Houlder. It's been a long drive and all, I –"

"Oh, come on. You're a big girl now. You can have a little drink with ol' Uncle Cy."

Lauren's posture stiffened. "No, *really*. Thanks, though."

"Yeah, your dad dropped me a line about you two coming up round this time. Where's he at? Over in the store? I'll bet he's waisting more good money on some goddamn good for nothing fishing lure, ain't he?"

"No, I'm up here by myself, Mr. Houlder. My dad just couldn't make it."

It looked like Cy's brain was working triple overtime digesting that bit of news. "What's that? By yourself? All alone up at that big old lodge of your dad's?" His gaze wandered all up and down Lauren like he was taking inventory. She shoved her hands in her jacket pockets and pushed it closed tight around her.

"Well, how long you up for?"

"Maybe a week," she said. "Maybe a little more. I'll have to see."

Cy slapped his grimy hands hard on his knees. "Well then, I best come by and chop you up some firewood. Gets mighty cold at night, this time of year and all."

"Nice of you to offer, Mr. Houlder. But I'm sure I'll be just fine. Really."

"Suit yourself." He toyed with his empty glass. "Hey Nate, set me up again, willya?" Then he turned back to Lauren. "So I suppose you want me to drive you up to the lodge? Open it up for you? Been a while since you been up there."

"Actually, Mr. Houlder, I just wanted the keys. My dad said I could pick up the extra set from you. I was just headed up to your trail –, uhm, your *place* now to get them."

"Oh, the keys, huh? Hell, I don't know if I even got 'em on me. Lemme see, now." He started patting his pockets. "So how'd you know I'd be in The Moose anyway?"

"I didn't. I just stopped in for some groceries, and I thought I heard your voice."

"Yep, ol' Cy's singing does carry don't it? Scared off more'n one bear just by hollering." He chuckled, patting down his pants and shirt and making a big show of looking for the keys. "No surprise you heard me. I was yelling up a storm, goddamn right I was. It's just that son-of-a-bitch Steve Michaels riles me up so about him and his Department of Un-natural Resources."

So, it had been Steve. Steve Michaels.

A door swung open at the back of the bar, and there he was right on cue, Steve Michaels, tall and good looking as ever, wiping just washed hands on his jeans. "Say, Nate," he called over to the coffeeshop counter, "the hand dryer is broken again."

"Lookie there, Laurie," Cy cackled, "there's Steve now."

As Steve walked up towards the front of the tap room, recognition slowly lit up his face.

"Lauren?"

"Steve?"

"What are you both, goddamned stupid?," Cy said. "'Course, Steve, it's little Laurie Vestal. Up here on vacation. All by her lonesome."

Lauren held out her hand. "Steve, it's been a long time." Steve Michaels hesitated a second, then wiped his hands once more across his jeans for good measure. They shook hands warmly, lingering.

"Five years, Lauren. It's really good to see you. What are you doing in here?"

"Well, like I was just telling Mr. Houlder here, I was picking up a few things in the store before heading up to his place to get the extra set of keys to the lodge. And I thought I heard him in here in the – uhm..." Lauren looked around her while she paused. "...in the bar. Thought I might save a trip out of my way. I'd like to get in before dark."

Cy Houlder gave his shirt pockets one last dramatic pat down. "Sorry, girly. Don't look like I have those keys on me."

Steve winked at Lauren and leaned around Houlder. "Cy, looks to me like you've put away one too many of those boiler-makers." He picked up a giant keyring laying there on the bar, right next to Cy's empty shot glass and a crumpled pack of Lucky Strikes. Steve jangled them in front of the old man's face. "They're right here, Cy."

Houlder's scowled. "I knew *they* was there all the time. I just don't think them Vestal keys are on that ring."

Steve grabbed two keys wound together with rusty wire and a plastic luggage tag, *Johnathan Vestal-Birch Lake* printed boldly on both sides. He untwisted the keys from the ring and tossed them to Lauren.

"Thanks, Steve," she said, catching the keys with one hand. "Really." Lauren gathered up her groceries and turned for the door.

Steve followed close behind. "Hold on, Lauren. I'll walk out with you."

They headed out to the parking lot, leaving Cy Houlder to help himself to another shot. He downed it quick and sighed, a dark, disgruntled look furrowing his bushy brows.

Outside now, Lauren pointed at the embroidered patches on Steve's parka. "So, you work with the DNR now?" They strolled across the gravel, stopping next to her Escort.

"Yep." He helped Lauren load her bags in the overstuffed hatchback. "I tried college first. Just the junior college over in Minocqua, nothing fancy. But it wasn't for me. So I signed up for a training program with the DNR. Went full time four years ago." Steve scrunched the groceries in between her suitcases.

Lauren slammed the hatch shut. "What were you and Uncle Creepy arguing about in there?"

Steve smiled. "Oh, Cy's harmless enough. He just gets all worked up over this timber wolf reintroduction program the state's been working on the past couple years."

"Wolves? Up here?"

"Well, there are now. We've taken loners from Minnesota and Canada, rehabbed some injured animals. We're relocating them in the Ottawa National Forest."

"Great. Used to be I just had to worry about bears. Now wolves too."

"Actually, Lauren I wouldn't give them a second thought. Wolf trackers can spend months just trying to catch a glimpse of them in the wild. They're pretty instinctive about avoiding humans. The fact is, you should consider yourself lucky to see one. Bear or a wolf, they'd catch your scent and be long gone before you even knew they were around." He leaned half a step closer. "Say, but what about you? I've bumped into your Dad in town a few times, he mentioned that you went on to grad school. Did you stick with art? You always were a real good artist."

It had been a long time since anyone had complimented Lauren on her artwork. There certainly hadn't been encouragement in school. *"Good's* kind of a relative term back in Chicago. Let's just say I'm doing something else right now."

"Now that sounds interesting, Lauren. I'll have to find out more."

She laughed. "Oh, not as interesting as you'd think." When she opened the car door, she looked up at the sky. "Well, it'll be dark soon, I guess. I better get going."

"Guess you'd better, Lauren. Suppose I should, too. I still have four more feed stations to check before I can call it a night."

Awkward silence hung in the cooling air between them. Both searched for the right thing to say. Steve went first. "So, Lauren, if you're going to be up for a few days, maybe we could get together? Catch up on things?"

She smiled with relief and slid into the Escort. "That would be real nice, Steve. I'd like that."

While Lauren started her car, Steve backed away towards his dark green DNR van. "Great. Well then, I'll give you a call. Maybe we can have dinner or something, after you're all settled in."

Lauren nodded, smiling, and pulled out on to U.S. 2. *Steve Michaels.* How about that?

They'd met one day completely by chance back when Steve was

part-timing in the bait and tackle shop in town. Friendship blossomed into something more, and it lasted through her high school years, and right into college. But eventually school and work took over. Then Lauren's mother died, and going to the lodge just wasn't much fun anymore. There were just too many memories. Oh, there were a few long-distance phone calls. A few cards and letters back and forth between Chicago and Watersmeet. Then they just drifted apart. But, it would be hard to forget Steve. Not just because he was always so genuinely, inexplicably and sincerely nice.

And not just because he was ruggedly good looking. Lauren smiled slyly to herself, thinking how a few years hadn't changed that one bit.

No, it was because Steve Michaels had been Lauren's first.

The first, and that's one fellow a girl wouldn't forget, no matter how long the distance or how many years slipped by.

Her Escort disappeared eastbound down U.S. 2, Lauren's last glance in the rearview mirror reflecting nothing more than a setting sun, turning the sky a bright orange behind a horizon of black, silhouetted trees. Ahead, the road climbed a hill towards a sky that was already purpling into early autumn dusk.

CHAPTER EIGHT

"This is Unit Two, calling in, H.Q."

Romilla Township Sheriff's Deputy Tony Hambly squirmed in bored discomfort. His police cruiser was parked on the narrow grassy median dividing the four lanes of U.S. 41, and he'd been there almost an hour now. And though his radar gun was on the whole time, he hadn't nabbed one single speeder.

Hambly watched the steady flow of cars heading north through Wisconsin from Milwaukee and Chicago, all of them at an annoyingly safe fifty-five. All those plump pickings of out-of-town stickers and Illinois plates should have been good for at least two or three tickets before sign-out time. But Tony Hambly was either too new to the job, or just not bright enough, to realize that his shiny blue and white Crown Vic cruiser with the big rack of Mars lights on top was plainly visible for two miles either way.

He tried the radio again. "Unit Two – I repeat, Unit Two calling in."

For the last few minutes the setting sun glared back at him from the rearview mirror like a big orange searchlight. It was just a few minutes shy of five o'clock, and he was more than ready to close out his Saturday day-shift...ticketless or not.

Sally was waiting back at home with promises of a special dinner, pork roast maybe. With those little oven-browned potatoes the way he liked them. And maybe if the mood was right, and there wasn't anything really good on the tube, *and* if the kids would cooperate and hit the sack on time for once, then maybe, just maybe, he and Sally might squeeze in a little private time. Before he had to get up for the dreaded 5:00 A.M. to 11:00 P.M. Sunday shift, that is.

And if memory served correct, Sally'd gone shopping up to the mall in Fond Du Lac this week. And wasn't that a Frederick's Of Hollywood bag he saw in the bottom of the trash last night? Maybe...

"H.Q.? Come on in, H.Q. This is Unit Two."

Just static.

"Chief, come on, already. This is Unit Two calling in."

"Alright, alright, Tony. What's your big hurry?" Finally. Hambly turned the key in the ignition, ready for the okay to head back in.

"H.Q., this is Unit Two. It's 17:00. I'm heading back to the station."

A chuckle crackled back through the static. "Seventeen hundred? Tony boy, you really have to get all that junior college law enforcement crap out of your head."

"All right, Chief."

"Let's just say I know it's five o'clock, and you're ready for home and supper, right?"

"Check, Chief."

"So, how'd you do this afternoon, boy?

Hambly was afraid the chief would ask. "Not too good, Chief. One speeder earlier this afternoon out on County K. Just five miles over the limit."

"Yeah? And lately?"

"Sorry, Chief. That's about it. Nothing in the last hour."

"Come again, Tony?"

"Uhm, that's no speeders in the last hour, sir."

"None? What the hell...where are you at, boy?"

"On Route 41. About a mile and half, maybe two miles south of the wayside."

There was a pause on the other end while the Chief pictured Hambly's location. "A mile and a – what the hell are you doing there? You might as well put a billboard on the roof of your car...*Cop Ahead – Slow Down.*"

"Chief, I –"

"For Chrissakes, boy. You got two viaducts, half a dozen tight curves and umpteen billboards along 41 inside our jurisdiction. Hell, you can hide like a crease on my wife's wrinkled old ass. We're not going to get the station remodeled this year on one pissy little five miler an afternoon."

"Yes sir."

"All right, Hambly, you can head in. But check out the wayside on your way back. Been some calls about kids drinking and carrying on there the last few weekends. Like to nip it in the bud before it gets to be a habit."

"Will do, Chief. Unit Two out." *That's just great*, Tony thought as he pulled out onto 41. Now he'd have to head back to town the long way. By the time he checked out the wayside one more time, got back to town, changed back to civvies and sped home, Sally's dinner could be good and cold. And that wouldn't be a good way to get her in a friendly mood for later.

The Romilla wayside was just up ahead: a sprawling roadside picnic grove with clean bathrooms, petwalks and lots of parking – for the station wagon and camper crowd, it was heaven. For the local police it was a nuisance.

The wayside looked nearly empty.

A lone trucker stood by his Peterbilt, enjoying the last of the red-orange sunset and cupping a match in his hands to light up a cigarette in the wind. As Hambly's cruiser pulled up the wayside drive, the trucker hopped into his cab and roared off. The squad slowed to a crawl, passing the only parked car.

That *same* car.

Officer Hambly had been through the wayside three times today, and that same light blue Lincoln Town Car was parked in this spot each time. He hadn't given it a thought before. Older folks sometimes catnapped in the wayside. Or someone could have been off on a picnic or a hike in the country. But it was getting pretty late for anything like that now. With the sun drooping below the horizon, the sky grew darker by the minute.

He paused behind the Lincoln and turned his spotlight on the car. Roast pork and Fredericks Of Hollywood or not, Tony decided to give the Lincoln a closer look.

He parked the squad a few spaces over and left the engine running. The autumn air felt crisply cold when he got out. He zipped up his jacket, hiked up his holster and walked over to the Lincoln.

It looked innocent enough.

Illinois plates. Valid registration. City of Chicago sticker on the wind-shield. Even an Illinois Clean Air Approval label beside it.

Peeking in through the driver's side window, Tony could make out a travel atlas on the passenger side of the front seat, opened to the Wisconsin map. The keys were in the ignition. The doors were locked.

Thump

The deputy's hand automatically shot to his holster.

Thump, again.

Thump – the sound came from inside the trunk.

Hambly felt the hair rise on the back of his neck, and a cold sweat break out on his palms and his face.

Thump

He backed away from the car, unsnapping the strap on his holster.
Thump

The pounding continued. It was definitely coming from inside the trunk, and getting stronger, louder. Scenes from half a dozen gangster movies scrolled through Hambly's head. A stolen car dumped up here in the Wisconsin farm country? A kidnapping? A mafia hit?

He backed around to the rear of the Lincoln. The car rocked up and down with each *thump*. The deputy left a good twenty feet between himself and the bucking vehicle, but he was close enough to see that the trunk lid was denting from the *inside* with each *thump*.

Hambly's shaky right hand curled around the grip on his Browning 45. The gun cleared the holster.

There was one last, loud *thump*, and the trunk sprang open. Hambly's pistol fell clean out of his sweaty hand and went spinning across the asphalt.

"What the –" he mouthed, but no real sound actually came out. Tony was so scared, he didn't even think to pick up his gun.

A small slip of a girl sat up in the trunk.

She slid one blue jeaned leg over the bumper. Her black booted foot just dangled there idly.

"Oh, excuse me, officer." She ran a hand through her long, dark hair, then shook it out, the wavy locks shining under the dim light from the trunk's interior lamp. "I thought I was alone."

The deputy stood absolutely still, his feet frozen to the ground even if his knees were beginning to shake.

The dark haired girl casually yawned. Smacking her lips and blinking the darkest eyes Tony Hambly had ever seen, she preened just like a cat, and then slung her other leg out of the trunk. "Officer," she said, in a curious sounding voice, "Would that be your pistol over there?"

His eyes followed her arm and the long, pale finger pointing to his Browning. "Jeez!" he hissed under his breath. Hambly shot a look at the woman, then over his shoulder to his idling cruiser, then scrambled for the gun. He didn't holster it.

"What the hell – Miss, are you okay? What in the world are you doing in there?!"

It was getting dark so very fast. He could barely see her face, even with the trunk light. The cool night breeze blew her long hair around so much it obscured her features. But he could see her eyes, and they sure didn't look scared. Not the way a crime victim's eyes should look, like a frightened animal's, all wide and dazed and terrified. For that matter, they didn't look like a suspect's eyes should either. You could almost always see the guilt in *their* eyes, see the lies forming right behind the pupils.

At any rate, that's what Tony had been told.

No, dark as it was, he'd have to say her eyes just looked *amused*.

"Miss, what are you doing in there?"

The girl leaned her head out from under the trunk lid and nonchalantly looked up at the darkening sky. "Actually, officer, I'm not entirely certain. I suppose I locked myself in here by accident."

Tony kept his distance. He holstered his gun, but he didn't strap it in. His right hand hung close to the grip, poised and ready like a gunslinger's.

"Miss, have you been involved in a crime? Did someone kidnap you, lock you up in there? Do you need a doctor?" She hopped lightly out of the trunk. "Ma'am, why don't you step away from the car? Are you sure you don't need some help? How long have you been in that car? All day? It's been here all day, I know that for a fact."

"Well, I suppose I have, officer." She turned around and leaned back into the trunk, reaching for something.

Hambly was too scared to worry about overreacting. He whipped out his gun again. Both hands held the weapon this time, straight out in front. "Alright now, Miss. Take your hands out of the trunk – *Now!* I want you to back away from the vehicle, with your hands clasped behind your neck."

She turned around, all harmless and innocence. "Whatever for, officer? Have I done something wrong? I was only reaching for my bag." She took a step towards him.

The deputy stepped back. "Look, I don't know what your story is, but until I find out, I want you away from that trunk, your legs spread and your hands on the side of the car where I can see them. Now!"

The girl just shrugged and wandered over to the side of the Lincoln.

"Hands stretched out, I mean it!"

She nodded, those dark eyes starting to look a little exasperated, and placed her hands on the side of the car.

"You have some ID?"

"*I-D*? No, officer. I'm afraid I don't."

"Well, just stay right there while I call this in. And don't move."

Hambly backed towards his cruiser and flipped on the Mars lights as he slid in. Nervous hands slid the pistol on the dashboard while he fumbled with the radio.

But the chief didn't seem to share his concern. "You got *what*, boy? Look, don't be bothering me with this kind of crap. You got some doper in the wayside, bring her in. Your wife'll kill me if you miss supper another night."

"Chief, you don't understand. There's something really weird about this, this – girl. I want immediate backup out here. Maybe you should send a paramedic unit too."

"Hold on, son. Aren't you overreacting just a bit? Abramson's not even back from gassing up Unit One yet. And you know he needs to stock up on some of Lottie's bismarks before she closes. And I'm sure as hell not coming out there."

"Chief –"

"Hambly, why don't you just give me the plates first, and I'll see if they're on the hot sheet before we go calling out the Marines. Okay?"

"Okay. Right. Let's see, it's Illinois, Thomas – T, Abel – A," He squinted to see the numbers on the plates. The girl was just leaning with her back against the car, staring up at the sky. Hambly leaned out the window and shouted, "You! I said legs spread, hands on the side of the car!" She waved back to him and smiled. Her grin sent a chill right down Hambly's spine.

"Chief, that was, uhm – Thomas – T, Abel – A, uh, uhm, Kangaroo – K, –"

"Kangaroo – K?! Son, just what the hell did they teach you in school, huh? Why don't you settle down. You'll wet your pants, you're so nervous. Just *read* me the damn numbers, will you?"

"Right. Right, that's Illinois, T-A-K-6-4-8."

The girl still lounged against the car. She hadn't assumed the position, and didn't look like she was about to either.

"Well, Hambly. Nothing on the hot sheet."

"Chief, I really want –"

The chief's voice assumed a commanding tone. "Boy, what you're going to do is this. Just hold your suspect or victim or whatever the hell she is right there. Now you're a big old fellow, aren't you? No little female's going to get away from you, is she? Soon as Abramson's back from Lottie's, I'll send him right over. Meanwhile, I'll run the plates in the computer and see what we get."

"Yes, sir."

"Now son, don't go shooting anybody, promise?"

"Yes, sir."

"And I'll call Sally and tell her to put supper back in the oven. Goddamn, if she isn't going to kill me."

The radio went dead. Hambly grabbed his revolver off the dashboard and slid it back in his holster. He stepped out from the cruiser.

The girl was gone.

He ran up to the Lincoln, ran clear around it two whole times. Looked all around the wayside. Nothing. She was definitely gone.

Romilla Township Sheriff's Deputy Tony Hambly headed back to the cruiser with a bad feeling brewing in his stomach. The Chief was going to skin him alive for this. And so was Sally. He'd be lucky to make out with a cold pork sandwich now.

And Frederick's Of Hollywood, well, just kiss that goodbye.

~

It wasn't magic, not really.

By the time the officer was out of his vehicle and searching for her, she was already a hundred yards away, lost in the shadows of a thicket ringing the wayside. And by the time he returned to his car, she was far, far away, cutting due north through a farmfield.

So, Charles' and Gail's fancy automobile was lost. Just as well. She'd driven before, of course. She just never liked it. Automobiles had annoyed her since they first appeared on the cobblestoned streets of Graz. Noisy, smoky, clanking, smelly things, they only got worse over time. More power, more speed, more buttons, more gadgetry, more everything.

She meandered along the side of the road as it wound through the rolling farmland. The slender little sliver of a not-quite new moon wouldn't rise yet, not for another hour or two. She was good with such things: sensing the path of the moon and the stars, gauging the sun's arrival by the coloring of the sky. Just now, a few stars began to twinkle between the breaks in the clouds, each looking brighter, clearer and bigger out here in the country than anything she'd seen for quite some time back in the city.

Unfortunately, she had absolutely no idea where she was. She could point herself north easily enough, but other than that...

Charles' and Gail's automobile had taken her a good hundred and fifty miles before dawn broke. She had waited too long, been too eager to cover more miles Friday night. But one hundred and fifty miles still left a long way to go; two or three hundred more, by her guess.

She continued north along the backroad for an hour. A few cars passed, but none noticed her. Or if they did, they found her unnaturally pale reflection in their headlights a bit too Halloween-scary this late in October.

Still another half hour of walking, of listening to the light tread of deer in the farm fields on the side of the road, raccoons and weasels scurrying through the brush, the wind gently blowing autumn leaves from the branches. She raised her jacket collar up to her ears, not that it would help. It was cold out, but at least her insides still felt warm from last night's feast.

She hoped it would last.

Headlights loomed up from behind.

A brown pickup truck slowed at her side.

"Little lonely out here, ain't it?

"No." She maintained her pace while the truck inched along with her. "I'm just walking."

The driver looked puzzled. "So, you want a lift, or not?"

"Yes, thank you." She stopped. "That would be very nice."

The pickup eased to a stop a few feet ahead. The driver reached over and opened the door.

"So, where you heading?"

She tossed her bag in and climbed up after it. "North. Just north."

The truck pulled away with a rustle of fallen leaves, its tailights glowing like two red eyes in the darkness.

CHAPTER NINE

About seven miles east of Watersmeet, Lauren turned off U.S. 2 onto a rough and narrow, thinly blacktopped road. It wound continuously upward in an endless series of tight curves for another mile and a half, where her headlights danced across a thick gauntlet of pines standing sentry on each side of the road. The wall broke periodically to reveal shallow little minnow ponds and rough gravel roads, some no more than pitted tire tracks gouged through the forest. They were hunter's trails into tree stands, or supposedly secret paths to favorite honey holes. Some were old logging trails long overgrown. Cy Houlder's trailer lurked a mile or so down one of those roads, and Lauren was glad that she wasn't prodding the little hatchback down one right now.

Abruptly, the blacktop ended and the Escort skidded as it's small tires grappled with the sudden switch to gravel. Another mile now, with the road still rising steeper. Off to her right she could spy pitch black holes behind the trees, and she remembered them well enough: sharp dropoffs, sometimes fifty or even a hundred feet deep, rolling down into treacherous deadfalls spiked with fallen timbers and dried tree trunks.

She came to a fork in the road. There was the familiar wooden sign her father had made out of an old piece of birch – *Vestal*, with an arrow pointing right. She followed the arrow, leaving the gravel road to continue its winding path all around the lake.

The Vestal road dropped down steeply through the trees. Dark as it was, she could detect the glitter from quieting waves on the lake below and to her right. Rounding one last turn, her brights shined on the broad open lawn surrounding the lodge.

To anyone else's eyes it probably would have looked dark and lonely and foreboding: a big, black silhouette of a cabin, outlined two stories tall against Birch Lake, with wide decks edging both the first and second floors. The road ended in a circular drive just outside the front door. In the twilight, and with all its windows shut tight and the shutters closed, with no warm, inviting light pouring out, it *did* look a little remote.

But to Lauren's eyes, after so many years, it looked...it looked just like coming home.

She pulled the car up into the drive, shut it off and got out.

Absolute silence.

It almost felt like her ears had plugged up. They adjusted to the silence very slowly, just the same way eyes adjust to sudden darkness after the lights have been turned off.

Lauren just stood next to her car and looked around, listening. And bit by bit, she could begin to detect subtle, little sounds.

The brush of evergreen boughs swaying in the cold autumn breeze at the edges of the lawn. Down below, Birch Lake's waves lapping at the sandy shore and the old wooden pier. Nightbirds and bat wings fluttering along the lodge's eaves. A few stray crickets that were defiantly holding out against the cold weather's descent. A little twig crunched under the paw of some scurrying animal, and the soft landings of dry leaves onto the ground below.

It wasn't silent at all. It was alive, overwhelmingly so. It was like... magic.

Lauren clambered up the front porch with an armload of bags. She felt around in the dark for the lock, juggling the bags and her keys, and finally got it open.

It was pitch black inside.

She could hear her father's voice in the back of her head, *"Wouldn't hurt you to keep a flashlight in the car, Lauren. Never know when you'll need one."*

She set the bags down just inside the door and carefully inched her way through the front hallway with short little baby steps, arms stretched out in front of her. Feeling along the wall, she bumped into a little table and knocked over the lamp resting on top, but she caught it before it went reeling to the floor. She felt along the lamp, down to its base, along the cord to the plug. Then along the wall until she felt the socket, and wrestled the plug in.

The hallway lit up with a warm and pleasant glow.

She'd have to plug in all the lamps, and there were quite a few. The lodge was built long before electricity made its way into the backroads of the Ottawa National Forest. Cold, blue gaslights and fragile kerosene lamps were the mainstay then. When it had been wired for electricity, no overhead lights or wall switches were installed. All these precious little lamps were quaint, but they sure made nighttime arrivals a clumsy affair.

Lauren loaded herself down with suitcases and bags and headed upstairs. Round eight o'clock, she was more or less unpacked. Essentials stashed in the bathroom, hanging clothes in her closet and the rest stuffed into drawers. She could neaten it all up tomorrow.

Maybe.

If she was in the mood.

Tomorrow. *Mañana.*

Vacation.

She was surprised to find her old room untouched, the furniture just where it had been, even the same comforter across the bed.

It had been a long day stuck in the Escort's cramped seats. Lauren kicked off her loafers and wiggled her toes free. She peeled off her clothes. The seams and rivets of her jeans and the skinny straps of her bra left little red tattoo marks on her legs and her shoulders. A quick shower sounded good, but she just scrubbed the travel grit from her face and her hands, stuck her blondie-brown hair in a ponytail and tossed on a well-worn pair of grey sweats.

This morning's hearty breakfast was just a faint memory now. Soon enough she was headed into the living room with a baloney sandwich clenched in her mouth, a bag of chips tucked under her arm, a cold glass of milk in hand, an apple stuck in her pocket.

The living room fireplace was all set up. In no time, Lauren was sprawled out on the big leather sofa, warming her feet by a blazing fire of sweet smelling pine and birch logs.

The old lodge looked even better than she remembered, all warm and familiar with its knotty pine log walls glowing a golden ochre under the flickering fire light. Every stick of furniture, each picture and knickknack and memento brought back pleasant memories of happy days gone by. The aroma of fallen leaves lingered in Lauren's nose, triggering recollections of nights just like this, nights filled with twilight walks in the woods, hand in hand with her mother. Of evenings out in the battered old john-boat fishing with her father, or fighting off sleep with a mug of creamy hot chocolate cupped in hands grown tired from a long, hard day on the beach.

Of necking with Steve Michaels on this same couch, before a warm fire that smelled just like this one.

Lauren set the emptied milk glass on the endtable with a contented sigh. This would really be a great vacation after all, she thought as the fire burnt down. "Thanks Dad," she said out loud, her words echoing off the log walls. She dragged her tired frame off the sofa, shut off the lamps and headed up to bed.

Yes, it was really going to be great.

As she climbed in under the comforter, Lauren couldn't think of a thing that could possibly ruin what was bound to be a wonderful week.

Of course, she couldn't hear Cy Houlder whispering a curse when the last lamp went dark in the living room.

And she didn't see him creeping around the shadows out on the deck, straining for a peek at her through the windows.

—

Some two hundred and fifty miles south of Birch Lake and the lodge, a brown Chevy pickup bounced along a dismal, bumpy Wisconsin backroad. Inside, the dashboard's green lights cast a ghastly color across the beautiful face of a deceptively young looking dark haired girl.

All she really wanted right now was a quiet and uneventful ride north, just to ease back in the seat and feel the cold wind on her face, just to gaze out the window at the growing number of stars above and the rising hills speeding by in a blur on each side of the road.

But from the very moment she first stepped into this truck, she *knew* – knew in her bones – knew that something very bad would occur. She didn't know what, or when, exactly. But something...

The truck careened around a tight curve, and the half dozen empty beer cans rattling at her feet rolled noisily to one side of the floor and then the other.

With a fleshy hand tipped with dirty fingernails desperate for a trim, the driver upended his own can over his mouth. The beer foamed at his lips and suds caught in his longish mustache. He let loose a self-satisfied burp and crunched the aluminum can in his fist, like it was some great show of strength. "So? We been driving for half an hour. Are you going to talk or anything?"

He glanced at the slim and silent figure on the cracked vinyl seat beside him, watching her hug the passenger door. He was going to toss his crushed can onto the floor at her feet, then thought better of it and flung it out the window.

"What would you like to talk about?" she replied, watching his big t-shirted belly double up into folds when he reached down between his legs to wrestle another beer from the twelve pack on the floor.

"Hell, I don't care. Just don't seem right to hitch a ride and then sit over there all quiet-like. I'm not going to bite you, y'know."

She smiled to herself.

"Your car break down or something?"

"Something like that, yes."

"Uh-huh. You said you were heading north. Like where, exactly?"

"Oh, just as far north as you plan on traveling tonight."

His jowly face seemed to be hard at work on trying to figure her out. He kept one eye on her and one on the wavering patch of road lit up in front by the truck's headlights. "Yeah, well I'm not so sure where I plan on stopping tonight."

They drove on in silence for a few minutes more. She tried to fix her mind on his, but she could make no real connection. She wasn't a mind-reader, after all. It took a victim's compliant touch to reveal their soul, their longings, to induce her dark magic to work. But all she could detect here was what she saw for herself: a pig of a man, fattened on too much beer and too many greasy hamburgers, desperately in need of a change of clothes and a good bath. Driving a truck as dirty as he was. It wasn't just the cans rolling around at her feet. It was the thick grime on the inside of the windshield. The oily stains ground in to the door and the armrest. The smelly old t-shirts and holey socks stuffed behind the seat. The sad and empty eyes in the faces of the naked women cavorting on the dog-eared pages of the sex magazines poking out from under his seat.

There was an aura of evil inside this truck, as tangible and thick as the fog welling up in the night-shrouded fields outside. It was a vapid, mean-spirited little evil of a little mind with tawdry little desires and noxious little fantasies.

"You talk funny, you know that?"

"My accent? And here I thought I'd done away with it by now."

"Nah, you talk different. You're not from around here, are you?"

"No, I am not."

"Back east, huh?"

"Well, in a way. Yes, from 'back east'."

"Yeah, I could tell."

"You're very perceptive."

"Huh?"

"Nothing, really."

He finished his beer and sent another can flying out the window. She was spared the manly show of strength this time. And spared the fetid aroma of another belch.

"So, what's your name?"

She cocked her head in thought for a moment. *"Marcilla."*

His brow knitted over her answer. They made the furrows on his forehead wrinkle deeper, dragging thin strings of his greasy hair down half an inch. *"Mahr-ceel-uh?"* He pondered that a moment, then chuckled. "You just make that up right now?"

"Actually, yes." She smiled coldly. "And what is your name?"

He thought for a minute. "Stan. Just call me Stan."

"And did you just make that up also?"

"Yeah, I did."

If she knew anything about human nature, she knew that soon enough his pudgy, dirty hands would begin inching across the seats to rest on her leg or to grab for her breasts. Or those silly magazines would be offered to her. Or the beer. Or something. But the notion of this lout touching her, of his unwashed hands soiling her creamy white flesh, of his foul-smelling breath nearing her lips...*No.* It simply would not be.

So she just stared out the open window, watching the nightime scenery flash by.

Never expecting to be surprised.

Not expecting to feel something hard and cold and metallic suddenly push through her hair and come to rest on the back of her head.

She didn't expect to slowly turn and see the short muzzle of a pistol pressed there against her cheek.

"Well, Marcilla, or whatever the hell your name is, bet you didn't expect this."

Out of the corner of her eye she could see the gun barrel glowing green under the dashboard light. It was all rank at her nose with the smells of oil and sulphur. "No, I certainly didn't. But perhaps I should have. And so, what now, Stan?"

"Yeah, that's right. That's it, bitch. Just keep it up with the little smart-mouth routine. You got some lip, you know?"

The barrel pressed harder against her cheek. She could grab it from his hands quick enough. Perhaps she could make him turn the gun on himself and blow his chubby little head clean off, if she really put her mind to it. Perhaps. But she wasn't particularly interested in having his brains splattered across her new clothes, or in having the truck smash into a tree. "Patience, child," she cooed to herself.

The truck slowed, till it just crawled along the lonely backroad, then it turned onto a narrow rutted lane, bouncing over the gravel shoulder. Fatman Stan's hand bounced along with it, but the gun barrel stayed pressed against her cheek. He flicked off the lights and rolled to a stop down the dark lane.

"Okay, slide over this way. Come on, Come on Get out of the truck."

She did as he said. But once outside, Stan looked unsure of what to do next.

With the headlights off, the rolling farmland was cloaked in absolute darkness. At least it was to *his* eyes. To hers, just the glimmering stars overhead let her see the anxious sweat beading up on his jowls, see the dull sheen on the dark gun barrel.

"Alright, here, stick your hands out, sweetheart." He grabbed her wrists, one after the other, and positioned them outright in front of her. "Like that, right."

With one pudgy hand, its fingers looking just like overstuffed sausages, he undid his belt and slid it out of his wide pants. Awkwardly, with only one free hand, he looped the leather around her wrists, his waistline providing more than enough length for several loops. Then he threaded the leather through the buckle, cinched it tight and grabbed the dangling tail like a leash. "Come on, you." He pulled her roughly away from the truck.

A few steps ahead, he gave her a hard shove. She fell to her knees, but fought back the growing fury, still considering...

He dropped the belt. Her strapped wrists fell in her lap. "So, smart mouth, not so talkative now, huh?" The gun slid along her cheek, down below her nose, right to her lips. "What, do you think I'm stupid, or something? Some hot butt like you's going to be thumbin' on County K at night, right." The cold steel wormed its way past her lips and clinked against her teeth.

"Sure. You know and I know you were just out hitching to get laid. You just didn't expect to come across *me*, did you?" The barrel pressed insistently against her teeth. She parted them, and let it ease right into her mouth.

"See! See, you like it. I knew it. I knew the minute you got into the truck." He unsnapped his pants, fumbled with the zipper. The grimy slacks fell to his ankles. She winced when she saw that he wore no underwear, when she saw his free hand heave up the big roll of his belly, where a miserable little wick of a penis uncoiled like a newborn snake.

"Well, you like sucking on that .22 so much, let's see if you can use those lips for something other than smarting off."

He gripped his member in his big paw. It almost disappeared into the fleshy folds of his hand. "Let's see you wrap those lips around a real barrel, baby." He leaned in closer. Dark as it was, she could see drool forming along his lips.

"Yeah, you use that mouth for something other than fancy yappin', and maybe I'll be real sweet, maybe kill you nice and quick."

Enough.

There was a temptation to see if her teeth could simply crush the barrel, but instead she just spit the little pistol out of her mouth.

She raised her strapped hands, raised them up slow, and maybe in the dark, maybe to *his* eyes it almost looked like this girl was actually going along with it, that she was reaching out for *him*.

Or maybe it was so dark he couldn't even tell that the hands kept on rising, past the dark shadow of his hidden crotch and his jiggling belly, rising right up in front of his face.

Maybe he couldn't even see those pale hands flex, or the veins rise or their muscles expand. Couldn't see those hands push apart.

But he could hear it alright.

He could hear the thick leather belt that was wound three, four times around her wrists – hear it snap, hear this slender wisp of a girl split the belt just like it was paper ribbon.

The tattered strips of leather hadn't even hit the ground, but already her hands shot up, gripping his neck, pulling that big hulk of a body down, down towards a grinning, leering pale face that seemed to glow all pink and orange and red from the fire that suddenly flamed in her eyes. Her head shot forward like a cobra's strike. Fangs clamped down so hard and so deep on his thick neck that even her plain and human-looking front teeth dug far into the flesh.

This was no dark kiss of coldly sensual passion. This was the killer thrust of the wolf's jaws, the lioness dealing a deadly blow. His carotid artery and jugular vein both split wide open. His windpipe smashed instantly, stifling any hope of his thin, girlish scream from ever escaping. His eyes bulged in utter disbelief as he felt his blood gush into her mouth.

The blood tasted foul, rancid.

And instantly, she *knew* him.

Knew this wasn't the first time, no, not the first at all. Knew that he'd been cruising back roads and byways night after night, hunting for lonely hitchhikers and women stranded with flat tires. Knew that the same pathetic little worm of a pecker – this same one that was quickly shrinking into the folds of his belly right now – had been shoved into screaming, helpless women and girls too many times to even count. Knew that his little pistol had been pressed hard against other pretty heads before, and that it had left fair hair and frightened faces clotted with blood when it was finally pulled away.

She knew him, alright.

She knew him and it made her sick.

She wrestled her fangs from his throat, and pulled away. Spit the sour blood out of her mouth, gagging. It was so shamelessly, needlessly, vapidly *bad* that it stung her teeth and gums.

The blood flowed from his shredded neck like an open faucet. His knees were already giving way under his great weight. His flabby arm raised with the gun still hung limply in his hand. He tried to point it towards her.

But she grabbed that flailing limb in a flash, and *crack,* his humerus bone snapped like a twig. Some sort of a slightly audible squeel creaked out of the gaping hole in his throat, and the pistol fell to the ground. His arm jiggled helplessly along with the rest of his twitching body.

Short seconds later, *Stan* flopped down into the sandy dirt too, and his big fleshy bulk quivered a few last times before it grew completely still.

And completely dead.

His taste was still rank in her mouth. She stared at the lifeless hulk on the ground, and spit out the last of his foul blood onto his corpse.

Wiping her mouth on her sleeve, she kicked a bootfull of sand at his body before heading back to the truck. By the interior light she could plainly see little spots of splashed blood on her sweater – the lovely and precious white sweater she'd bought from Lauren just last night. It was ruined, but she couldn't part with it.

With the fat man's corpse cooling behind her in the night air, she stripped, standing next to the truck. The breeze felt refreshingly clean on her skin. She tossed her blood stained jeans into the brush. Wiped her jacket and boots off as best she could. She saved the sweater though, folding it carefully and returned it to her bag.

Feeling better in a new pair of jeans and a fresh shirt, she emptied the cab of his belongings, the beer cans and the magazines and hamburger wrappers and soiled old clothes – everything. Just bundled them up and tossed them at his lifeless body.

She started up the truck, flipped on the lights and pulled back onto the road.

The dashboard clock said it was nearly ten o'clock now. First she'd have to figure out exactly where she was. Then get back on a main road north. Another map would help. There were still many miles to cover till she could reach Michigan and Watersmeet.

CHAPTER TEN

Lauren checked her watch before she put the dog-eared menu back between the napkin holder and the mismatched salt and peppers shakers. Almost noon. If the waitress would quit gabbing with those two camo-suited hunters and finally look this way, maybe she could get her order in. The menu said plain enough, 'breakfast served till 12:00'.

Finally the two men zipped up their olive and brown patterned jumpsuits, grabbed quivers and giant bows and left. The waitress scanned the diner once they were gone – empty except for Lauren sitting at the counter. She headed over Lauren's way, looking annoyed. Maybe it was supposed to be her break time.

"You taken care of, honey?"

Lauren cocked her head to look around The Moose diner. "No, I'm not." Some phantom waitress was supposed to be waiting on her?

The waitress slipped around to the service side of the counter and flipped out her pad. "So what can I get you?" She took a pen out of the pocket of her pink shift and leaned into Lauren's face.

"Well, coffee for a start. Black, please. And I think I'll have an order of french toast, and –"

"Sorry, honey. No breakfast after twelve."

"But, it's only –"

"Says so right on the menu. Look we have to clean the grill for lunchtime."

"But it's only five to."

The woman rolled her eyes and looked increasingly bored. "So, what's it going to be?"

Lauren grabbed the menu again. It didn't take long to pick something

else. The Moose didn't have much of a selection. "Okay, make it a BLT.
And I'll still take the coffee, please." The embroidery on the waitress' pink
uniform shift read *Annie,* and to Lauren's eyes, Annie didn't look any older
than herself, maybe just more tired, a little more used up. Her coffee
came in a melmac mug that looked as worn out as Annie. Some flatware
appeared on the counter. Lauren had been 'yes-ma'am-ing' customers long
enough to cut the girl some slack. Annie slouched behind the counter
while she refilled the coffee-maker, once pretty legs looking awfully tired
in their support hose, feet dragging in white sneakers when she disappeared
into the kitchen.

Lauren barely had time to think about how late she'd slept in this
morning. Annie was back in a wink, sliding a plate down on the counter
and disappearing again with, "I'll get you a refill."

The sandwich was okay, but the chips and pickle on the side had that
suspicious look, like this wasn't the first plate they'd been dumped on.
Miss Smiley pink dress never even returned with a check. Lauren gave her
a few minutes while the coffee cooled in her cup next to the half-eaten
sandwich. Eager to get going on a day half gone, she checked the price on
the menu, added the tax in her head (ringing up sales at Bloomie's was
good for something) and left a perfunctory tip.

12:30, and the Escort was buzzing north out of Watersmeet. Lauren
had no particular plans, just a day without work, her sketchpad, her
camera and her watercolors rattling around on the passenger seat.

A couple miles north of town she cut off the highway onto a gravel
forest road that looked vaguely familiar. Sure enough, it was a backroad the
family had taken many times on lazy sightseeing drives and roundabout
routes to some of Dad's lucky fishing holes. She pulled over alongside
an old timber bridge spanning the Ontonagon River, and whiled away a
pleasant hour making some graphite sketches of the noisy, white water
swirling around the boulders and bridge footings.

Then on down the road again, till she came across the Buck Lake boat
landing, where a beautiful autumn vista of the blue water and its islands
spiked with wide cedars fighting the wind beckoned to her. First the camera
came out, its whirring motordrive sounding rudely mechanical in the quiet
forest. Watercolors next; Lauren dashed off half a dozen color sketches before
the light changed and the blue water went grey.

With the shadows already lengthening, and the sun well on its way
down the sky, she moved on. She continued on down the road as it snaked
alongside the Ontonagon to Bond Falls.

There she raced against the shadows groping their way down to the falls. She sat Indian style on a huge granite and iron ore boulder jutting out over the thundering falls, and knocked out a group of charcoal drawings.

With the sun ready to sink below the treeline behind her, she checked her watch, surprised to see that it was almost four o'clock. Lauren packed up her things and headed back to the car.

These forest roads might curlyque their way back to Birch Lake for all she knew, but it wouldn't take much to get lost, especially now with the sun drooping fast and the trees turning into opaque black walls all around her. Lauren retraced her route and ended up back in Watersmeet. She pulled into The Moose's parking lot, hoping she might see Steve's green DNR van there.

It wasn't.

Lauren popped back in anyway.

The Moose was empty again, except for Annie the waitress, still working, or still there, at least. Annie never lifted her nose out of a romance paperback while Lauren took a seat at one of the tables. Camera bag, watercolor kit and sketchpads all unloaded noisily. Annie looked up, half smiled and ambled over.

"Back for more?"

"I guess."

"Hey, sorry about earlier, you know, breakfast and all. I guess I could have rustled up some french toast for you."

"It's okay."

"Well, I really had a long morning, and –"

"And a lousy afternoon, looks like," Lauren added.

Annie's grin widened. "Got that right. So, what do you want? It's on me."

"Any coffee on?" Lauren asked, unzipping her jacket.

Annie looked over her shoulder. "Sure, but I wouldn't recommend it. Been sitting on that burner for a few hours. Must be cooked to mud by now." Annie didn't know just how strong Lauren liked her coffee. "How's about a nice hot chocolate instead? I was just going to have one myself."

"Sure." Lauren said, eyeing up some chocolate chip cookies lined up on a tray by the register. "How are those cookies?"

Annie was fixing up the hot chocolate behind the counter. "No fair asking. I made them myself last night. Go on, help yourself."

Lauren grabbed her things, took a handful of cookies and a paper napkin and moved to one of the stools by the counter. Annie set two steamy mugs out. "Marshmallows?"

"Why not? I'm on vacation. Who's counting calories?"

Annie dropped some marshmallows in the mugs and came around to Lauren's side. "Mind?" she asked, looking at Lauren's stack of cookies.

Lauren nodded from behind her big mug and slid the cookies between them. Melting marshmallows bobbed at her lips. The hot chocolate was good – rich and creamy and made with real milk, not just some powdery instant and water.

"Annie's the name." The waitress pointed at the name stitched on her pink shift while she dunked a cookie in her mug. It disappeared in one bite.

"Lauren." They shook hands.

"Pleased to meet you, Lauren. To be honest, pleased to meet anyone, this time of day. It gets pretty lonely here round now. But that'll change soon as the locals file in for dinner."

"I can imagine."

"You're here on vacation?"

Lauren nodded.

"Well, good for you. Kind of late in the season, though. You missed all the fall colors. Hunting?"

"Nope. Just relaxing, getting away from the city."

"So, you're an artist maybe?" The waitress gestured towards the sketchpads and camera.

"Mmmm, sort of. I guess."

"Well, can I peek?"

"They're not much. Just some sketches."

"Oh, come on." Annie reached over and slid the pads in front of her mug. "What do you think I'm going to do, laugh at them?" The waitress flipped through the sketchpads and spread out the drawings and watercolors on the counter. "Pretty nice. That one there, you must've been hanging way off that rock pile on the second bank at Bond Falls when you did that." She leaned in close over another. "Yeah, I really like this one, too. Buck Lake, right?"

Well, that was encouraging, Lauren decided. At least someone could recognize the subjects.

Annie held two up side by side and brought them close to her face, examining them in detail. "Yeah, real nice." She laid them back down. "Real nice, all right. You shouldn't be so shy about your stuff, kiddo."

Lauren could feel her cheeks flushing red, embarrassed, but pleased at the same time.

"So," Annie said, raising an eyebrow, "who's you're friend?"

"Sorry?"

"Your friend. The girl you drew in all these pictures."

Lauren looked closer at the sketches and watercolors. "What girl? I wasn't drawing any girls."

"Sure, *this* girl. She's in each one." Annie pointed. "Here, on this one of the old wooden bridge over the river. See, you drew her in a kind of shadowy spot between the trees. And this one here, you got her sitting on the shore of that big island in Buck Lake." The waitress turned and winked. "Man, I hope she wasn't really posing for you – well, *naked* like that. Kind of a cold day and all."

A ringing started in Lauren's ears.

Her pulse started to race, her chest began to pound while Annie continued, "And on this one, she's just sort of leaning against the rocks across the falls. She sure is pretty. Always wished I looked..."

But Lauren couldn't really hear Annie anymore. She was too dumbstruck. Too confused. She felt dizzy, felt like the drawings were ready to start swirling around on the counter and the whole room would follow.

She scooped the sketches back into the pads and grabbed her coat and things. "Um, I'm sorry Annie. I have to be going. Right away." She slid off the stool.

"What's the matter, Lauren?" The waitress followed behind. "What did I say?"

But Lauren was already out the door and racing across the lot. She just tossed her things inside and started the car up. Annie watched from the doorway, wondering what she'd done wrong now, as the Escort's lights flicked on and it peeled out of the parking lot with a spray of gravel and sandy dust.

A chilly wind blew the dust away. It blew up Annie's short sleeves and snaked right up under her pink uniform. She shivered and went back inside.

～

An hour later, Nate Stambaugh scurried out from behind The Moose's bar just in time to catch Annie slipping her jacket on. She'd almost made it to the door.

"Annie! Annie, where you going, sweetheart?"

She jockeyed for a good escape route between Nate's bulk and the doorway. "No way, Nate. Don't even think of asking. I said I'd work till five thirty. It's almost seven now. I'm splitting."

Nate did his best to make his naturally gruff voice sound halfway charming. "But Annie," he pleaded dramatically, "who's going to wait the tables? You know I got no one else since Sue quit nights." He reached out to her, but Annie slipped away. Juggling trays of burgers and hash and eggs in The Moose had left her nimble as a fox.

"Too bad. I've been telling you to hire someone."

"But Annie –"

"No, Nate. I've been on my feet since six this morning. You know *six a.m.*, Nate...two hours before you've been waltzing in lately. Call your wife. She still remembers how to wait on a table."

Nate's chubby cheeks drooped. "Oh, come on, Annie. You know Dora'd never."

"Dora'd *never* nothing. She worked tables just fine till you two got hitched. Ask me, you were better off when she was still a waitress."

Nate grabbed Annie's arm, and maybe a little too hard at that. "Yeah, well, I didn't ask you."

"Right." She wrestled her arm free and pushed open the door. "That's it. I'm out of here."

"Annie, I can't handle the diner *and* the bar."

As she stepped outside, cold air came blasting in on Nate, enough to make him retreat a step or two.

"Nate, for chrissakes, it's Sunday night. Nobody comes in Sunday night."

He chewed that over for a moment. "Yeah, maybe you're right." Annie headed out into the parking lot. "Hey Annie, you'll be here in the morning, won't you?"

"Sure Nate, sure. Six sharp, like always." Disappearing into the darkness, she spun on her heel and called back, "Just make sure that good-for-nothing brother of a cook's here too. I'll serve it, but I'm sure not cooking that crap too!"

The wind slammed The Moose's door closed in Nate's face.

Annie crunched across the gravel lot, hiking her jacket collar up around her ears when she felt the cold wind.

The parking lot looked pretty lonely. A couple old geezers were still knocking back a few Sunday night shots in the tap room, but that was about it. Probably no one in the grocery store. The laundromat was empty – and why not? What could be more depressing than doing your clothes in The Moose's laundromat late on a Sunday night?

Nothing.

Annie knew. She'd done it often enough.

Seven p.m. on a Sunday, in beautiful downtown Watersmeet. Nothing open but The Moose. No place to go, nothing to do.

Maybe just as well there wasn't anything going on tonight, she supposed. Had to get up bright and early, five thirty tomorrow morning, and haul herself back into work. She was dog tired. All she wanted to do was to head home, get out of this ugly pink uniform, kick off these shoes and prop her feet up in front of the TV.

Of course, it would be better – could've been – if she'd held on to Tommy. Tommy Walsh had been something to come home to, at least. Just to help her out of this shift, maybe massage her aching feet before she fell out on the couch.

But it was no good wishing. Tommy'd been gone for two months now. Off somewhere in Minnesota, on a mining job, he'd said. And who could blame him if this empty little burg and the ugly plastic walls of her trailer couldn't hold him. Maybe if she hadn't ridden him so hard when he was out of work...

But man oh man, Tommy could do it all night long, and whether Nate or Sue or Nora or anyone at The Moose knew it or not, Annie liked it that way – all night, and as often as she could get it, no matter how hard a day she'd had.

She groped in the dark for her car keys. Seven o'clock, and it was totally dark already. Winter was coming on fast, this year. A long, lonely Watersmeet winter.

Annie watched a pickup truck hesitate on Route 45, then pull in to the parking lot. Its headlamps lit her up like a searchlight.

She squinted back at the truck to see if she recognized it, but couldn't see much at all in the glare of those high-beams. But thanks anyway, she thought to herself. The lights were just enough to help her pick her car keys out from the charms and doodads and other keys on her ring.

She unlocked the rusty door of the old Dodge van, Tommy's party van.

He'd left the keys and a couple hundred dollars on the kitchen table when he split. Half the van was held together with bondo and baling wire, and the engine wasn't likely to last through another U.P. winter. But Tommy had done up the inside real nice, with brown shag carpet strips glued to just about every square inch, and a monster set of speakers bolted down in back. Too bad she couldn't afford any CD's.

Annie climbed in the van, anxious to get it started and the heater going. Damn, it was getting cold early this year.

The overhead lamp had burnt out long ago. And wouldn't you know it, that pickup that just pulled in the lot shut its lights off. She fumbled along the dashboard in the dark till she found the ignition.

The old Dodge's sixer grumbled and groaned, sludge-thick oil and carbon-coated plugs getting ready for one more try. Annie pumped the gas pedal.

Nothing.

The engine turned slowly with awful grinding noises, but it just wouldn't kick in. She tried it again, flooring the gas and just letting the starter whine till it finally said 'the hell with it', turned over uselessly a couple more times, and froze.

With a backfire bang, a puff of grey smoke blew out from under the hood.

Now what? Too cold to walk all the way home. And if she asked for a ride in the bar, it was a sure bet that either Nate would have her helping out for free till closing, or she'd be wrestling with one of those old coots all the way home to her trailer.

Annie hopped out of the van and slammed the door shut with a curse. She popped open the hood and looked in at the dirty maze of hoses and wires. It wouldn't do any good; even if she knew the first thing about motors, the closest things she had to tools were a bottle opener and a nail clipper.

She leaned her elbows on the top of the grill, head scrunched in her balled fists, and swore under her breath. A cold breeze shot a sudden shiver down her spine.

"Can I be of any assistance?"

"Huh?" Annie jumped and spun around.

A woman stood there. No, more of a girl, maybe. Hard to tell in the dark. Long dark hair. And the kind of thin, pretty face that always made Annie jealous. The kind of pretty face that Annie always...

She looked familiar, but...

"You seem to be having trouble with your machine."

She talked funny, Annie thought. Sort of foreign.

"Guess I am. You know about cars?"

The girl chuckled. Her laugh had a chilling, ice-clinking-in-a-glass sound. "No, I'm afraid not. I wouldn't be of much help in there." She gestured towards the engine compartment.

Annie looked at the dead hunk of dirty metal. "Well then, guess you can't help."

"But perhaps I can take you somewhere?"

"Oh, I don't think –"

The girl laid her hand on Annie's. It was colder than cold, colder even than it was outside, it seemed. Annie whirled back around to face her.

The girl didn't move her hand. "Annie? It *is* Annie, isn't it?"

"Yeah. But, how'd you—"

"Annie, it's already quite dark. And I'm sure it will be much colder still as the night wears on. Are you certain you wouldn't like a ride home?"

Annie looked suspiciously over the girl's shoulder, over at the pickup truck. Dark as it was, she couldn't see much. But it didn't look like anyone else was in the cab. And it *was* a pickup, so there wasn't much room for anyone to hide behind the seats.

Another gust of wind whipped through parking lot. It shot right up Annie's skirt. Her rental trailer was a good hour's walk away. And if she didn't peel off these support hose and this rotten uniform soon, relax just a little before hitting the sack and going back to work tomorrow...well, she would just go batty.

"Well, I don't know. You think you'll be heading my way?"

The girl smiled.

Annie decided there wasn't any particular reason not to trust her. If this girl was some druggie, or was going to try and roll her, she could have done it already. It was dark and lonely enough in the parking lot. Anyway, she'd been tossing drunks and loudmouths out of diners and bars since high school. What kind of trouble could this skinny little thing cause?

"Sure. Why not? A ride would be great."

The dark haired girl kept Annie's hand gripped tightly in her own, leading her across the parking lot to the brown pickup. "Come, then," she said, still smiling, and Annie shivered again.

CHAPTER ELEVEN

Lauren's eyelids grew heavier by the minute.

She sat there on the living room couch with the remnants of her second night's baloney sandwich dinner on the cushion beside her. Dinner was dressed up tonight with a glass of wine, and then another, that half empty glass tilting now in her tired hand.

She stared at the fireplace, where the birch logs were down to orange embers. Stared without blinking, waiting for the wine to lull her to sleep.

It was best just to stare at the fire. That was better than looking down at the coffee table. Better than looking at the watercolors and the sketches spread out there. Better than looking at that sleek, black haired, naked figure that appeared in each of the pictures.

Lauren couldn't even recall thinking about that peculiar girl, the one who troubled her last two days in the store. The one who somehow crept into her dreams. And she certainly didn't remember drawing or painting her.

But there she was.

Lurking in each sketch, each drawing, each painting, hiding behind tree trunks, peering out from behind bushes and half-hidden across the water. She hid inside Lauren's artwork the same way she lingered in the back of Lauren's mind. And just thinking about it made the little hairs rise on the back of her neck.

Lauren yawned. Best to just knock off for the night. A good night's sleep, a fresh start in the morning, that's what this vacation needed to get back on track.

She dumped her dishes in the kitchen and topped off her wineglass.

Sloshing as much wine as she sipped, she headed upstairs to the bathroom. Scrubbed her face and hands, brushed her teeth, combed out her hair...waiting, just waiting the whole time for that face, that girl's face, that eerily pale and dark eyed face to appear in the steamed up mirror. Waiting...

But there was nothing in the mirror. Just her own tired eyes staring back at her. Peaceful, undisturbed sleep, that's all she needed.

The treks through the Buck Lake woods, along the Ontonagon up Bond Falls all took their toll. Her legs ached as she pulled off her socks. She winced from sore muscles when she climbed out of her jeans. "No more dreams tonight, please," she said out loud, as if that could make it happen.

One last gulp, and Lauren emptied her glass while she took her jeans and socks to the closet. She dropped them on the floor and yawned again, then tried to wrestle her bulky white cableknit up over her head. Tipsy or tired, it was no use. She let the sweater flop back down in place. Back beside the bed, she started to wriggle out of her black tights when still another yawn contorted her jaw, stretching so far this time that her ears rang when it ended.

The ringing faded and she gave the tights another tug.

No, there was ringing all right. But it wasn't her ears.

The phone rang downstairs.

Rang again, jarringly loud in the silent cabin.

Lauren dashed out of the room and clomped all clumsy to the living room. Ten rings, she counted them as she leaped through the last of the fireplace's dim light and grabbed for the phone.

"Hello?"

"Lauren? Are you okay?"

"Steve! Hi. Sure I'm okay. Why?" she said, all out of breath.

"Well, you sound funny."

Lauren climbed over the back of the sofa and fell into the cushions. "Oh, sorry," she puffed. "I just ran from upstairs to catch the phone."

"Sorry I called so late, Lauren. I didn't get you out of bed, did I?"

She slipped a throw pillow under her head and crossed her black legs on the opposite armrest. "No, not at all. What time is it, anyway?"

"After ten. Sorry."

"Steve, we're not sixteen anymore. Anyway, back home I'd be lucky to be out of work by this time."

"Well, there you go. Guess we're both workaholics. I just got in myself."

Steve's voice was deep and soothing, a warm sound that made her feel good, helped her to ignore those drawings still scattered on the coffeetable a foot away. "Working on a Sunday, huh? So at least I'm not the only one who gets stuck doing that."

"Lauren, I can't remember my last Sunday off. Can't remember my last day off, period. This whole wolf reintroduction program has to be completed before winter sets in. And the DNR hasn't added any extra staff, so we still have to do all our regular jobs."

"I can't wait to hear more about what you've been doing, Steve. It all sounds so interesting."

He chuckled. "Does it? I guess it is. Sure better than banging a cash register in one of the tourist traps. I think I'd go crazy doing something like that."

Lauren felt her cheeks redden. "I bet you would. I ought to know."

"What do you mean?"

"Never mind, Steve."

"Well, okay. But you still owe me a lot of catching up, Lauren. I want to hear about college, and grad school, and what you're doing in the big city, all of it. Now *that* sounds interesting to me."

"Oh, you'd be surprised. Life in the big city's not as exciting as you'd think." Lauren glanced down at the drawings on the coffeetable. The pale faced girl stared back at her from across the waterfalls, from behind a tree. Then that same face flashed in her mind, hypnotic eyes and knowing smile, inches away from her own in a claustrophobicly small Bloomingdales dressing room. She bit her lip and the image faded. "Well, maybe it is. Or maybe life in the city's just weirder. But then, I suppose weird can follow you anywhere you go..."

"Lauren?"

"Look, don't mind me." She conjured up a picture of Steve, all broad chested and outdoorsy handsome. "I'm celebrating being on vacation. Broke out some wine and everything. And if you remember, I get soused pretty easy."

"I remember," Steve said, his voice heavy with nostalgia. "At least you could wait to let *me* ply you with drinks."

"Steve, Steve." Lauren pulled her legs off the armrest and coiled them underneath herself. "I don't remember you ever having to *ply* me with drinks."

Steve was quiet for a moment. The same memories of first love found, and then lost, rolled around in both of their heads. "Well, anyway Lauren, I'm sure anxious to see you. Actually, I thought I might bump into you today."

"Exactly how do you 'bump' into someone up here? Everything's just so – so, *big*. I forgot how the woods seem to go on and on."

"Yes, they do, don't they?" he said. "But my crew worked most of the afternoon right near your place. Over by Sun Lake. You know, just past Lake Marion? It's right alongside U.S. 2."

"Oh, sure. I must have driven right past you guys on my way back to the lodge. Too bad I missed you. So what are you up to there?"

"We were setting up a monitoring station. Radio receivers that can track the wolves wearing transmitter collars. Not all of them, just a few key animals."

"How'd it go?"

"Well, we didn't finish. The guys were ready to mutiny after dark, so we had to call it quits. We'll finish up tomorrow morning."

"So, *my crew*, Steve? You're in charge and everything? You really do have a lot to tell me about." Not that she actually heard anything, but Lauren sensed he was beaming. She could picture him and his proud smile. And she liked it. A lot. "So, when are we going out so we can actually get started on all of this 'catching up'?"

"Well, about that, Lauren..."

"Steve...?"

"Well – see, the fact is I'm working a pretty rough schedule these days. No choice really. I don't expect to get any real time off for quite awhile."

Lauren had heard this kind of routine before. But she didn't expect it from Steve Michaels. Really didn't. She could feel herself tensing up, her grip tightening on the receiver, her free hand growing impatient and nervously flicking at a stray piece of lint on her tights. "Yes, *and*?"

"And, I really wanted to see you, that's all. But if we get together, it will have to be pretty late. The way things are right now, I could be working every night this week."

She heaved a sigh of relief, and didn't care if Steve could hear it either. "Is that all? We can't get together until late?"

"Well, I didn't –"

"Steve Michaels, you ass! I don't care what time we get together. I know it's been a long time, but I have a newsflash for you: I don't have a curfew anymore. So when do you want to meet?"

"How about tomorrow night?"

"Tomorrow night would be great. I'd tell you to come over right now, except I'm only half dressed and I'm feeling sort of drunk." Lauren tried to imagine how his face looked now.

"I'll be right over."

"Just kidding, Steve. But seriously, tomorrow sounds good. What do you have in mind?"

He had his plans ready. "Well, I'll be working around Sun Lake all morning. But in the afternoon we head down to the Wisconsin border waters, and we'll be there into the evening with a few guys from the Wisconsin DNR."

"Okay, I've got your daytime itinerary, so what about getting together?"

"I'm getting to that. After we finish up there, my guys can go home, but I'm supposed to head back with the Wisconsin group to their office for a quick wrap-up meeting. That's in Eagle River. Could be pretty late by then – maybe eight, eight-thirty. So I thought, if you don't mind, that is, why not drive down to Eagle River tomorrow evening and we can meet down there?"

"Sounds good to me. I hoped you weren't going to wine and dine me in The Moose. I tried it today. Fine cuisine. Sweetheart of a hostess."

"Oh, Annie? Well, that's The Moose for you. But it's still off-season, you know. And a weeknight at that. Not too much to choose from, even in Eagle River. Do you remember the White Pine Inn?"

Lauren rolled the name around in her head. There were so many 'White Pines', 'Cedar Boughs' and 'Balsam-Aires' up here.

"I'm sure you've been there, because I know I've heard your father mention it. Just east out of Eagle River, on Route 70. It's one of those big cabin and condo resorts on the chain. Supper club's right on the water..."

"Sure, sure, I know the White Pine." She didn't. "What time?"

Steve thought it over one last time, quickly tracking through the timetable he'd been rehearsing. "How about nine o'clock? I'm sure the kitchen will close at ten, but I bet we can squeeze in dinner before they shut down."

"Nine o'clock is fine, Steve."

"Great. I'll see you then, Lauren."

"Okay, Steve. See you then."

"Well, I guess it's goodbye, till tomorrow night."

"Steve?"

"Yes, Lauren?"

"Steve, I'm really...that is, I'm just glad you called. I mean it."

"Well, Lauren, you knew I –"

"No, I knew you'd call, of course. I don't mean that. I just mean, it's really nice to talk to you again. Things have been kind of weird for me lately, and this vacation didn't exactly get off to the right start today. But, I think everything's going to be fine now. Just hearing from you made it all a lot better."

"Glad to hear it, Lauren."

"See you tomorrow, Steve."

She reached over the back of the sofa and cradled the phone. Swinging her legs off the cushions, she winked at those drawings on the table in front of her, as if to say, 'No, I'm not going nuts, and *you* don't phase me one bit'. She bounded back upstairs.

Lauren lit the kindling in her bedroom fireplace and had her pillows all propped up against the headboard, just the way she liked. The fire caught quick, lighting up the knotty pine walls a cozy ochre-orange.

She was content with the crackling fire, content to let her eyes grow heavy watching the flames' reflections dance across the walls, content and snugly warm under the comforter, even content with the lightheaded wine buzz. She was ready for sleep, and even ready for dreaming, because now her dreams would be about Steve, and tomorrow night.

～

And she did dream of Steve.

At first.

As fast as sleep overtook her, the dreams hovered close behind. She dreamt of Steve, just as she hoped she would...of the first time he held her hand. Of their first kiss. Of the first time they made love, her first time ever, and his as well, she was sure. Right here in the lodge, just down the stairs, there on the living room sofa.

But in the dream, there was none of the awkward adolescent shyness that had really been there. No fumbling, no fingers caught in zippers or tangled in bra straps, no shoe laces that wouldn't come untied. No little bite of pain when he first entered her.

In the dream, it was all soft-focus, movie-perfect, all romance and passion, and Steve was a tender, expert lover, and she was beautiful, no tan lines, no sweating, no creaking cushions, no embarrassed rush to get dressed after it was over.

But then, the dream changed.

Steve's face blurred. His body shifted, softened, went all pale and cold to the touch. He melted like ice in the sunshine, narrow hips widening, hard buttocks softening, broad shoulders narrowing. His flat chest rose with two soft mounds that brushed against her breasts. Muscular legs dissolved, went smooth and cool and wrapped around hers like velvet snakes.

And it wasn't Steve pulsing all firm and erect and warm inside her anymore.

It was fingers now, fingers all over her body. Long, cool fingers stroking her breasts, teasing her nipples. Pale, long nailed fingers crawling like spiders across her belly, through her mound of soft hair, plunging inside her.

The face dissolved, disappeared. The short, wavy brown hair darkened, went long and wild, with thick bangs draping over a shifting forehead.

The face blurred, all spectral and indistinct, till two points of red light glowed in the murky whiteness, and a new face formed inside the frame of dark hair...a thin face, a beautiful face.

A girl's face.

Delicately white, ghostlike, and perched just inches over Lauren's own. The red lights became feral eyes smoking beneath arching black brows. The mouth was all red and shiny, its tongue licking smiling lips.

The face lowered, the mouth drew closer, barely touching Lauren's lips. A delicate brush at first. Then a kiss – soft, and tentative. Then hard and passionate, mouths parting, lips crushed together, tongues lolling about behind their teeth.

Lauren's hands gripped the pale, smooth skin of the back arching over her. She squeezed her muscles hard on the cold, probing fingers, and pushed up into that soft palm on her breast.

It was better...it got better and better still. It was better than – better than...

Lauren's eyes flipped open, waking to a pressure mounting and warming between her legs. That pressure, mounting pressure, insistent and intense pressure, waking to find her own hand tucked underneath her tangled sweater, her own hand stuffed deep down inside her tights and dancing, gently dancing precisely where and how and in that special way that only Lauren herself knew.

She was awake now, but she didn't stop, couldn't stop, till her legs kicked back the comforter, till her head pressed back into the pillows and rocked from side to side and her breath puffed like steam. Till she bit down on her lip and tasted the tangy flavor of her own blood, till the dream evaporated and she slid right into a noisy, panting climax. Slowly she slid one weak hand out from under her sweater, slid the other out from under the waistband of her tights.

Finally, Lauren just lay still on the bed, her legs sprawled, her arms limp at her sides. Her breath slowed to normal and her flushed skin cooled.

She didn't feel embarrassed. Not even a little.

She felt *scared.*

She sat up in bed. "Who are you?," she cried. "Why are you doing this to me?"

But dreams don't answer. She pulled the comforter up and lay down into the pillows, begging the night, or the wine, or her tears or *anything* to drag her back into a deep and dreamless sleep.

It took awhile, but finally her eyes closed, and sleep came.

But just like the night before, Lauren never heard, never saw, never even noticed the skulking figure in the shadows on the deck outside.

And Lauren *would* have been embarrassed, would have been mortified if she knew Cy Houlder's grizzled old hands happily played shake the stick inside his grimy pants out there on the deck, grunting like a rutting buck while he watched her through the window, till he was done and he lowered his arthritic old frame down the deck's stairs.

But even Cy himself didn't know that another pair of eyes stood sentinel over the Vestal lodge tonight.

Red, glowing, knowing eyes watched from the shadows of the trees ringing the lawn. Watched and duly noted Cy Houlder's slinking escape back down the road to his heap of a car.

And those burning eyes remained there, watchful and guarding.

CHAPTER TWELVE

The forest just watched, like it always did.

But it didn't care.

The forest only watched, content to observe the slender crescent moon struggling through thickening patches of dark clouds above, watched the pale moonlight settle on the lodge's roof and its decks. Settle on Cy Houlder's bony shoulders as he scurried off the deck and across the lawn. It watched his wiry frame scramble across the driveway and down the road.

Watched, but didn't care.

And even if it didn't really care, perhaps it *did* notice the pale, black haired figure lurking in the trees by the lawn's edge. Because *she* wasn't of the forest, and she wasn't of mankind, and she wasn't of the earth. And the forest didn't know about heaven or hell. So, perhaps it noticed her glowing eyes, eyes focused so intently on the lodge. Observed that slender figure steal silently through the trees, following Cy Houlder, keeping carefully behind him all the way.

The forest watched, even if it didn't really care.

The forest didn't care, because it was busy with its own affairs. As it always had been. As it always would be.

Because even as old Houlder reached his rusty station wagon, and fired up its engine and backed the car away another hundred yards before turning on the headlights – even as the pale, dark haired girl watched him pull away, the forest only watched, because it had its own affairs.

The forest only cared about old Houlder when he stomped through the woods with an axe slung over his shoulder, or when he was weighed down with iron jawed traplines, or sliding another shell in the breech of his gun before an off-season hunt. *Then* the forest noticed Cy Houlder, and remembered him.

But for now, the forest didn't care that his alcohol-glazed eyes never noticed that brown pickup truck parked off in the darkness on one of the side trails along the Birch Lake road. Didn't care that he headed back to his old trailer as quietly as his clanking, pinging, out-of-tune engine would allow.

Didn't care that the old man never looked back in his mirror – because if he had, Cy might have seen the slender figure following close behind, glowing dark red under the glare from his broken taillights. Just flitting between tree trunks like some ancient wood sprite, following until she saw where the old man turned off, and marked the spot carefully in her mind. Followed, until she stopped in the middle of the road, stopped dead in her tracks – and perked up her own ears just like the forest's animals did. Flared her white nostrils the same as they all had, and sniffed the air.

And then she smiled.

She smiled at the sound of the timber wolves' song.

Smiled and hugged herself, because that howling chorus was finer music to her ears than any symphony.

—

The howling crescendoed, then faded, but the sound still rang in her ears. It rang with memories: memories of her homeland, of the Styrian hills and woodlands, of the forests nipping at the walls of Castle Karnstein.

The deep Michigan woods rose right up at the edge of the road. She crept through the trees, stealthy as any other forest predator. Fast-forming frost slicked the ground. Walking was slippery at best, treacherous even, and she stepped carefully around the sharp edged tree-trunks and dry thickets spiking up from the gully bottoms.

There – just ahead, in a small clearing on high ground, there in a tiny break in the thick press of trees.

There they were, alert and sniffing the air warily. One large grey and white she-wolf pacing nervously, her lips pulled back and her fangs bared. Her dark furred mate searched the edge of the trees. Two others, smaller, younger, yearlings perhaps, lay on the sandy ground, vigilant nonetheless.

The girl stepped through the trees and into the clearing.

The two yearlings leaped to their feet, and the pack formed a line in front of her. Hackles raised, jaws snarling, ears drawn back in a sign of ready aggression, they tensed – ready to spring.

But the large she-wolf's ears lowered a notch, her jaws slackened a bit.

She sniffed the air even more intently, and her green eyes revealed a mix of curiosity and perhaps, embarrassment. Embarrassment at having been surprised. The other three eyed the dominant female, ready for a signal.

The girl stepped forward, with no fear on her face. She smiled at the pack, revealing her own gleaming teeth, every bit as sharp and predatorial as theirs.

She crouched and held out her hands to the animals.

"Guten Abend, mein kinder." She asked for permission to join them. *"Darf ich mich zu Ihnen setzen?"*

The animals cocked their heads at her voice, so magical, so calming, it spoke to something deep inside, something instinctive, spoke somehow of kinship and sisterhood. The foreign words didn't matter. Human words never did. It was her voice that mattered.

The large she wolf stepped forward, slowly inching her paws one in front of the other till her muzzle steamed right in the girl's face, and the animal's deep green eyes locked with the girl's own red ones. They stared at each other like that for a long time. Then the wolf raised her head and barked, and all at once the whole pack joined in, barking, and circling around the girl.

"Thank you, my children, for granting me leave in your land." Her voice made the fur on their ears tingle.

The wolves leaped, played and rolled at her feet. She laughed out loud, a hearty and sincere, unabashed laughter that rippled like ice water. It was the first time in a long time, a very long time, that she laughed so happily.

She sat down on a large boulder at the edge of the clearing. It was veined with flecks of copper ore that sparkled in the dim moonlight. "Come, let me meet you all," she said. The wolves lined up before her.

First, the large she-wolf, head held high befitting the leader of the pack. But the animal willingly accepted the girl's cold, gentle hands on her head. "Ah, *Die Konigen*, the Queen Mother. I'm honored, your grace." The girl ran her long fingers through the animal's fur. They caught on a collar; the wolf chafed as she fingered it. "And what is this? Do not upset yourself, mother wolf. The mortals always leash the predator. They always cage whatever is noble and free, whatever they do not understand. Perhaps in your case, they meant well." She pinched the nylon strap in her sharp fingernails and sliced it open. Removing the radio transmitter collar, she looked it over, then casually crushed the metal transmitter, with no more effort than if she was crumpling a wad of tissue. The broken pieces fell to the ground. "No matter. Now you shall be free."

Next came the alpha male, a charcoal grey, muscular animal, eyes glowing like burning jade in his dark face. *"Der Konig,"* the king, she said solemnly, bowing her head slightly to please the vain male. "Your eminence." The wolf bowed back to her, then strutted to her side, preening.

The two yearlings jostled playfully to be next, so she grabbed both and hugged them close. Full grown to look at, but still young at heart and friskily playful, the two wolves rubbed their matching grey muzzles against her neck and licked at her face. *"Der Prinz,"* she gushed amid her own laughter, "And *Die Prinzessen*, I presume. Pleased to make your acquaintances."

There they stayed for quite some time, while the moon fell behind the clouds and the night air grew colder by the minute. She talked to the pack, and they were totally enraptured by her magical voice, whether her words were in English or old Austrian.

She told them tales of the rolling woodlands of her homeland, of the vast and ancient Styrian treestands and the snow capped Alps looming behind them. Of wolfen brethren from across the ocean and from centuries past. And they listened.

"Would that I could join you tonight, my friends. I long to glide through the trees with you. To scent the prey, to chase it down. I long for that magic moment just before the kill...to look in the victim's eyes and read its acquiescence, to give thanks for its noble gesture of submission." She rose from the boulder. "But the deer blood doesn't fortify me, as it does you. Though its taste is sweet."

The wolves got to their feet anxiously and circled her. All but the Queen Mother, who stared off into the woods and sniffed the air.

"Perhaps another night. Indeed, I may wish to introduce you to someone special, very soon. Another guest in your forest, though I think perhaps she is no stranger. I trust you'll welcome her as you have welcomed me."

The large she wolf barked to the pack. The night was flying by quickly. Deer scent was strong in the wind. It was time to hunt.

The wolves disappeared into the forest, into the night.

She watched them prance away. But Der Konigen, the Queen Mother, paused as the pack filed by, then trotted back to the clearing. She stopped at the girl's feet and bowed her great furry head low, as if to say *'Thanks, and well met. Thank you, for removing the man-collar.'* Then the wolf whirled around and followed after her pack, speeding to retake the point, making no more noise than the wind as her large paws bounded away.

The girl smiled. A truly contented smile. All was well.

She left the clearing and made her way back to the hidden pickup truck. And the forest watched. But it didn't care.

CHAPTER THIRTEEN

Monday morning arrived late at Birch Lake. Or, at least its arrival was hard to detect.

Clouds rolled in Sunday night and brooded overhead now, all opaquely grey. The sky looked heavy with moisture, the only question: if plummeting temperatures would bring a cold autumn rain, or an early season's snow?

The gloomy looking morning didn't help Lauren's mood. Showered, dressed, her bed made, Lauren took last night's empty wineglass downstairs, the latent alcohol odor reminding her of Steve's call..and of her dream. Looking outside, her breath fogged the kitchen window and just made the yard and the trees outside look even greyer and gloomier. She cracked open the back door and was slapped by a gush of cold damp air, but she ventured out anyway and brought back an armload of firewood for the living room.

Once she dumped the logs by the hearth, she found those drawings and watercolors still cluttering the coffeetable. The drawings were good. Damn good. The fact was, she probably hadn't been doing enough artwork in her spare time, at least not since school. There was always some excuse. Work. A date. Out with friends. A book too good to put down, one last run through the late night TV channels. Always something.

But, how...*why* did that peculiar girl's image worm its way into each picture? Why couldn't she remember painting that figure, drawing that face?

Lauren stuffed the drawings in a big sketchpad and tucked it behind a bookcase.

Cold or not, she had to get out of here. She tossed on her jacket and cap, wrapped a scarf around her neck before heading out to the car.

With the defroster clearing the windows, Lauren watched the wind whip Birch Lake into a frenzy. It blew from the west, but shifted from the northwest every so often, kicking up white caps that raced towards the opposite shore. Swarms of fallen leaves scattered across the lawn and down to the beach. She rocked inside the little car with each gust. Then a mist began to fall. Not quite rain, just a warning of more inclement weather lurking up in those dark clouds.

Out on the highway, she passed a green van pulled over at Sun Lake. DNR emblems decorated the van's doors. Lauren scanned the lakeshore, eager for a glimpse of Steve tramping through the reeds. But the lake looked deserted. Just more grey waves and windblown branches.

The Escort continued west to Watersmeet.

The Moose's parking lot was packed. Ten-thirty: coffeebreak, presumably.

The tap room was empty, its lights off. All the action was in the little diner, and it was bustling, with every seat taken. The sullen looking teenage boy that ran the grocery checkout line on Saturday was bussing tables today, looking like he'd rather be just about anywhere else right now, doing just about anything else. A pink-smocked waitress angled her way in between tables with trays of breakfast plates wobbling on each arm. And there was the big fellow who tended bar when Lauren was in before – Nate? Nate rang up receipts at the cash register and barked orders without looking up from the keys.

"Dora! You got orders piling up back in the kitchen. And get some refills going on the coffee, will you?!"

The waitress shot him a warning look. "This is the last time, Nate. I mean it. You better hire another waitress fast, 'cause I'm not subbing like this anymore!" She plopped plates of hash and eggs at a table, then whisked past Lauren.

"For Chrissakes, boy, grab the coffeepot and do some refills, willya?" The teenager grumbled his way back to the counter and fetched the coffeepot. "Decaf too, boy! Decaf too."

Greasy aromas sifted out of the kitchen to tickle Lauren's nose all the way by the register.

Nate looked up from the cash drawer. "Don't suppose you ever waitressed, honey?"

Lauren shook her head. "Nope. Sorry." She looked around the hectic coffeeshop. It looked like a good day to grab a donut at a gas station down the road. "Don't think I'd want to start today either."

"Don't blame you." Nate punched in another receipt. "Goddamned Annie, doesn't show up this morning. Then has the gall to phone in an hour ago and tell me she's sick. Who the hell's she think she's kidding? Her van's parked right where it was last night, right out there in the parking lot."

Lauren spotted one stool emptying by the counter. She tasted ham and eggs in her mouth. Changed her mind. "Well, sorry."

"Yeah, who's she think she's kidding?" Nate grumbled. "If I know her, she's probably shacked up with somebody. I'll crown her when she show's up tomorrow. And she *better* show up tomorrow."

She backed away from the counter, but Nate wasn't watching her anymore. "Yes, well, good luck," she said, ducking out the door while Nate barked a fresh round of orders.

The weather went steadily downhill after she left Watersmeet.

Slick roads got slicker, and after the dashboard thermometer dropped below thirty two, the sheen on the pavement turned into ice.

Lauren spent the day cruising trinket shops and tourist traps in the little burgs straddling the Wisconsin-Michigan line. It was just the kind of thing she and her mother used to do on cold, gloomy days, even if Johnathan Vestal always begged off, preferring to snooze by the fireplace, or even to risk a good case of the sniffles and have another go at the walleyes, ankle deep rainwater in the johnboat or not...*anything* but a day of 'shopping'.

It felt more like the first week of winter, but the souvenir stands and antique shoppes were done up in their Halloween best, with Indian corn wreaths on their doors and haybales in front of their windows, jack 'o lanterns on the counters and torn-sheet ghosts dangling from their eaves. By the time Lauren windowshopped her fill and pointed the Escort back towards Watersmeet, the falling mist turned to sleet. And her little compact didn't carry much weight for traction on icy roads.

She played with the radio while the overcast skies darkened from their already grim grey into almost black. Evening was descending early. It was all Lauren could do to concentrate on the road. She didn't pay much attention to the weather report: *a wide front swooping down off Lake Superior already blanketed northern Minnesota and the northwest portion of the U.P. with an unexpected early season's snowfall. Hazardous road conditions predicted for the night. Warnings to stay off the highways for anything but essential travel, and no clue on the final path of the front.*

One near spinout on a tight curve, and she stopped fiddling with the radio, kept both hands on the wheel, and her eyes glued to the road. All the same, when she made the final dash up Birch Lake Road, the deadfalls and gullies looming at the edge of the gravel looked double scary, and she wished the Escort was a four wheeler instead. One with a car phone to boot.

~

Lauren made it back around five thirty.

She wouldn't have to leave for Eagle River until eight, slick roads or not. But she was anxious, surprised to find herself feeling just like a nervous high school kid primping before a dance.

She fiddled and fussed, pawing through the closet and the dresser and muttering to herself the whole time that she didn't bring a thing to wear. Showered again, shaved her legs, fought a losing battle with the blowdryer and her unruly blondie-brown bangs, then fussed some more with eyebrow tweezing and nail polishing.

Still waving her hands in the air to dry the fresh nail polish, she had another go with her clothes, laid some things out on the bed, concluded they were all ugly as sin, and was ready to torch the whole lot.

Back in the bathroom, she wiped the steam off the mirror and added a little more grey eye shadow, flounced on some more blush. With a dab of red lipstick, Lauren gave up, staring back at a face that she suddenly decided she'd grown tired of. A nose that was a little too perky, a mouth that was a little too wide, everything still a little 'too cute' for twenty seven. But this was as good as it would get.

One more flip through the hangers in the closet, and Lauren slammed the door shut. *You're getting awful nervous for one little date with an old sweetheart, kiddo.*

Nervous? *Hell, yes.*

Lauren cinched up her robe and headed down to the kitchen. Maybe just one glass of wine to relax her? Just a few sips. It wouldn't do, wouldn't do at all to get drunk tonight.

At least, not yet. It was still a long drive to Eagle River, and the roads wouldn't get any better.

She poured out a chablis and wandered into the living room, sipping at her glass. The wind howled up a storm outside, knocking around at the shutters and whistling at the glass. She glanced out the living room windows. The lodge's lights shined out onto the lawn, where freezing rain now turned into snow flurries. But that was okay, Lauren thought to herself. A light dusting of snow could be charming, could make dinner with Steve in a cozy northwoods chalet all the more romantic. And if there was anything more to follow after – maybe there would be – if there was anything more to follow, then fine. A little snow falling outside would be a wonderful thing to wake up to if she found herself snuggled up under a warm blanket with Steve Michaels. It could happen.

Lauren gazed out the window and took another sip of her wine. The lodge windows illuminated the flurries drifting through the sky, making them sparkle like diamond dust. The lawn was lit up nearly all the way down to the lake, where she could just make out the wind blown waves rocking the pier. And there on other side of the pier...

Something moved out there.

The lights from the lodge made it almost all the way to the beach... *almost*, but not quite. But through the filter of the falling snow, despite the dense shadows cloaking the beach, Lauren thought she saw something, something *else* moving by the pier. Not just the boat.

There – there it was again.

Lauren pressed her face against the cold glass and strained to see more clearly. There was something...

Her wineglass dropped to the floor in a crash of broken glass.

Lauren thought she might scream, but all she managed was a gasp.

It was *her*.

That girl...the girl from the store, the girl from her dream. It was her.

Lauren could just make out her dark silhouette, that exact same figure that crept into yesterday's drawings and watercolors. That girl stood in the water by the pier. Just a few yards out from shore, knee deep in choppy water.

Naked.

Naked, even though it was well below freezing out there, and snow-flakes whipped themselves into a frenzy in the icy winds.

Naked, and – and, *bathing?*

Yes, it looked like she was taking a bath. Washing herself in Birch Lake's frigid waters. In the dark. With the snow falling on her hair.

The girl looked up from the water, and whatever light made it down to the lake caught her upturned face now. Lit it up all moony pale, big dark eyes glinting with a hint of red. Those eyes locked on Lauren's, saw her there standing inside the living room window. That red slash of a mouth twisted in that same odd, knowing sort of grin that Lauren had seen that first night – Thursday night, back in the store. Seen in her dreams since.

Shaking, Lauren pulled her face away from the window, then dropped to her knees, carefully cupping broken pieces of glass in her palm. She peeked back over the windowsill.

There was nothing by the pier.

No one in the lake.

Nothing.

Trembling fingers checked the lock on the window. Lauren raced to the front door and checked the locks there too. Then back to the kitchen, where she did the same. The lodge was locked up tight.

She dumped the broken glass in the trash and returned to the living room, stepped around a puddle of wine and little slivers of glass. She looked back out the window.

Still nothing.

As if there ever had been anything out there.

Lauren clutched her robe tight around her. She slammed the blinds down and pulled the drapes closed over them.

Nothing.

Of course she couldn't see anything out there. Because there hadn't *been* anything out there. Couldn't have been.

Could there?

A naked girl, casually taking a bath in frigid lakewater, at night, in the beginnings of a possible snowstorm. A girl who couldn't possibly know that Lauren was way up here – *or come to think of it, she could know, couldn't she?* – but surely couldn't know exactly where...Birch Lake, out of all the countless lakes up here?

Sure.

Right.

And Cy Houlder worked for the CIA, and Steve Michaels was really a space alien and they were going to make her CEO of Bloomie's when she got back from vacation. Sure.

"This is crazy," Lauren hollered to the empty living room. "This is crazy-crazy-crazy!"

Let some shrink put a down payment on a another Porsche figuring it all out for her. She'd worry about it later. When she got back home to Chicago. Tomorrow, maybe. But *later.*

She trudged back upstairs, trying to focus on something normal, something that wasn't creepy-dreamy, something that made sense.

Like what to wear?

She finally settled on a black and red plaid wool skirt, topped with a black pullover sweater. She wondered if it was a little too *Seventeen* magazine while she untangled some dark nylons from the snakepit of tights and stockings in her drawer, wiggled into them and decided to stop worrying, period. She found a black bra that looked halfway new, snapped it closed and pulled on her sweater. Then made one more trek to the bathroom for another round with the hair brush and her unruly bangs.

Lauren bounded down the stairs in a pair of chunky black loafers, shiny with almost-out-of-the-box smooth soles. She left all the lights on, grabbed her black leather jacket and stepped outside.

The wind was forming little piles of snow in the corners by the doorway. It already built little white mounds around the Escort's wheels. And its cold fingers probed their way up her short skirt as she dashed across the driveway.

Halfway to the car, she paused and looked back across the lawn, down to the lake. A shiver ran down her spine. But it was just the wind, nothing more than that. The pier still rocked and the waves still slapped against the boat and the shore. But no one and nothing that she could see was lurking there.

Lauren shook her head, laughing to herself as she hopped into the car.

—

Eagle River, Wisconsin was a forty mile drive south from the front door of the lodge. A long way to go for dinner maybe, but with no stoplights, and nothing but forest in between, it usually was only a half hour drive.

Usually.

It was almost nine when Lauren finally slipslided into downtown on empty streets. Apparently everyone else paid more attention to the rotten weather and was already snug in their homes and their rental cabins and motel rooms. She drove right through town under streetlamps haloed in white circles from the falling snow. Out of town, it was all forest again, at least from what she could see through the snow piling up on her windshield. Finally, two slow miles out of town, she spotted a sign. And just past, warm lights glowed from the windows of the White Pine Inn.

Opening the car door, she was shocked by how much the temperature dropped, and just in the last hour. The wind was vicious, and the snow was way beyond flurries now. She ran into the White Pine Inn main lodge, skidding on her slick shoes, then stomping snow off the loafers in the vestibule.

On her left was a small registration desk for the resort itself. A sleeping golden retriever manned the desk, yawning and tucking its big paws in its belly when she let in the cold air. Lauren shook snow off her jacket and continued in to a cozy looking lounge area, all knotty pine and ochre lamplight just like everything else in the northwoods.

The lounge was empty, except for a bartender idly wiping glassware. "Yes ma'am?"

"Mmmm, I'll have a white wine spritzer, please."

"Coming right up."

She paid for her drink, and took a seat in one of the easy chairs by the fireplace. Her skirt rode a little too high up her thighs as she sat down. Lauren gave it a tug and settled back into the soft cushions. But a cold draft nibbled at her legs anyway, and she wondered why she hadn't gone with slacks instead.

The lobby door opened again, let in another icy breeze, and in came Steve right along with it. He stomped snow off his shoes and unzipped a long nylon parka.

"Nice night for a drive, Steve?"

"No kidding. Guess I didn't pick the best night for a get-together, did I?" He rubbed his cold hands and puffed warm breaths into them.

The bartender waved to Steve and brought over a bottled beer. Steve sat down across from Lauren, looking freshly shaved and exuding just a hint of Old Spice. The firelight danced on his brown, wavy hair, sparkled in his brown eyes and on his warm smile. He took a sip from his beer and settled back into his seat, then half rose again to arrange the bottom of his corduroy blazer. "So you found your way all right, I see."

"No problem, Steve. You know, I think I was here once with my family. I just don't remember it being so nice." From behind her glass, Lauren drank him in, noticing how his big hands curled around the beer bottle, how his button down collar shirt looked so crisply clean, how the crease on his jeans drew her eyes straight up his long legs, right to his trim waist.

"You probably just didn't want to tag along with them, Lauren. Might have been a kegger at the Lake Marion beach, or hanging out in town at the A&W, or –"

"Enough, enough," Lauren laughed. "You don't have to bring up my sordid teenage past."

"Well, those were good times."

"You know, you're right," she said, seriously. "They really were. I made some pretty good friends up here on vacations. It's too bad everyone just ends up going their own separate ways." She sipped from her glass.

He nodded. They both stared at each other, both wrestled with lots of things they wanted to say. Steve cleared his throat. "So, hungry? Why don't we get a table before they close the kitchen."

The dining room was half empty, and the few people eating kept glancing up from their plates at the snow piling up outside. Lauren ordered broiled walleye with wild rice. Steve went for a nice thick steak, medium rare. Their before dinner drinks gone, they ordered a bottle of wine.

"Was that your DNR van parked by Sun Lake this morning?"

"Guilty."

"So what were you up to, Mr. Wolf Expert?"

"Lauren, I wouldn't be too quick to call anyone a wolf 'expert', least of all me. I doubt if I could track them if we didn't have some of the animals radio collared. Fact is, that's what I was checking on this morning."

"Something wrong?"

"One of the wolves in that area has one of those collars. But it stopped transmitting last night."

"And that's bad, right?"

"Could be nothing. Worn out battery, some malfunction in the receiver."

"But?"

"But...it could be something else. Like maybe the wolf wasn't wearing the collar anymore. Maybe the wolf is dead."

Lauren waited while the waitress poured their wines. "Cy Houlder?" she asked after the girl was gone.

"Could be. But I really hope not."

"Why?"

"Because if Cy's been messing with the wolves, he's going to be in big trouble. And I don't want to be the one who has to blow the whistle on him. Guys like Cy, well – they're kind of a dying breed. People forget how much of a wilderness the northwoods were just forty, fifty years ago. Power company hadn't laid lines into most of the houses yet. Hardly anyone had a phone. U.S. 2, that was just a gravel road. Outhouses, ice sheds, I'm talking real pioneer stuff."

"Let's not turn him into Daniel Boone now."

"Well, Cy's a part of all that," Steve said. "Him and a few of the other old timers you'll see tipping a few at The Moose. So in a way, I have a kind of grudging respect for him. He certainly knows the woods better than any of the shirt-and-tie administrators from Lansing I have to deal with."

Steve leaned across the table and lowered his voice a notch. "But I've already pulled some traps out from the woods around Cy's place. Big traps, spiked down with poisoned meat." In a real hush now, he said, "No, the only thing I can think of is that Cy's been trying to kill off the wolves we've brought in."

Lauren saw the genuine concern in Steve's eyes. "Did you talk to him about it?"

"Sure. A dozen times. You walked in on one of our 'discussions' in The Moose Saturday. But I don't think Cy takes me seriously. Or anyone else in a DNR uniform."

"I don't know." Lauren winked. "Your uniform had me all impressed." She watched him blush and decided that was just about the cutest thing she'd seen in ages.

"Sorry I changed, then. But to answer your original question, my crew and I were checking the radio receiver by Sun Lake this morning. It was working fine, so..."

"So...Cy Houlder."

Steve shrugged. "I meant to hash it out with him today, but there just wasn't time."

Lauren sipped her wine and felt it warm its way down her throat. "Well, that's good to know. Nothing against your wolves. I mean, I hope everything turns out all right. But if you stood me up for an evening with Cy Houlder –"

"Don't worry," Steve laughed, "I've done time in Cy's shack before. Try being polite while you turn down his homemade deer jerky and cranberry hooch."

Their food arrived, and it was piping hot and as delicious as any over-priced nouvelle-with-an-attitude dinner Lauren ever had back home. While they ate, they talked about good times of years gone by, but not *so* very long ago. Good times that, for tonight at least, suddenly seemed retrievable. Just across the table, in fact.

The waitress cleared their dishes away and brought coffee. Lauren was pleased to find hers nice and strong, and she looked at Steve through the steam rising from her cup, thinking how he was everything she remembered him to be, only better. If that was possible.

"Well, you certainly put a quarter in me, Lauren. But enough about old times. What about you? You still haven't told me all about the glamorous life in the big city."

Lauren glanced away, noticing the snow clinging to the dining room windows and swirling through the evergreens outside. "Not much to tell."

"Oh, come on."

"No, really. You already know some of it. School, that is. After Mom died, I really buried myself in schoolwork. It was just – just easier that way. Maybe that's why I ended up going to grad school."

"And you stuck with art, right? You were always drawing and painting up here, I remember."

She nodded. "I stuck with art. I just don't know if art stuck with me."

Steve's face twisted into a puzzled look.

"Don't get me started, Steve."

He cocked his head, as if to say 'start'.

"The bottom line is, I've always meant to do something – oh, something 'artistic'. But I don't seem to be able to cut it at anything in particular. Maybe I just can't decide what I want to do. Or maybe I'm afraid to try."

"You? I don't believe that, Lauren. Come on, you can tell me. We used to daydream out loud all the time. Remember laying in a boat, drifting on Birch Lake, talking about all the things we were going to do? What *do* you want to do?"

"You mean, what do I want to do when I grow up?" she said. Steve's eyes widened in protest. "No, I know you didn't say that, Steve. But sometimes, that's almost how I feel. I'm twenty seven years old, and I'm still just marking time, just dreaming about things I'll do *some*day."

Lauren fidgeted with her cup, sloshing coffee into the saucer. "I want... I want – " She chuckled to herself. "That's just it, Steve. I *want*. I want everything. I want to do it all. I want to be Michealangelo and Emily Bronte, Amelia Aerhart and Joan Jett, Meryl Streep and Georgia O'Keefe all rolled into one. Maybe a supermodel and a mom while we're at it. I want to do everything. I want to *be* everything." She drained her cup. "I want it all, and I've done nothing."

"Lauren, what's wrong with dreams, and goals. What's –"

She cut him off. "Absolutely nothing, Steve. Not when you're seventeen and laying in your summer boyfriend's arms blowing hot air about how you're going to light the world on fire. But ten years later, well, it would be nice to accomplish *something*. I mean, you have your wolves, and..."

"And who says you're not accomplishing something, Lauren?"

"I do," she said, and a little louder than she meant to. The dining room was almost empty now, but the few people left glanced her way.

"I do," she repeated, softer now, and leaning over towards Steve's damnably understanding face. "You want to know what I do for a living? I'm a clerk in Bloomingdales department store. Sweater counter, first floor. I have an MFA from the University of Chicago, and I'm a goddamned sweater clerk at Bloomie's."

"Lauren, if that's supposed to shock me or something, you picked the wrong guy. I'm from Watersmeet, Michigan. Just having a steady job is a big deal up here."

"Nice try, Steve." She dabbed her mouth with her napkin. "It's not like I set out to be a store clerk. It just happened. I guess I've just been waiting for something else to happen."

Steve locked eyes with her. "Maybe something is."

"Maybe." Then she looked away. "It's all very simple, Steve. I should have been a cat."

He started to laugh, and then realized she wasn't kidding. "A cat?"

"Yes, a cat. I should have been born a cat. You know, nine lives? Because it would take nine lives to do all the things that I say I'm going to do *someday*. Travel, paint, break some hearts, paint some more. Nine lives. That's what it would take. Let's say I'm using this one to plan the next eight." Lauren shoved her chair away from the table. "And on that note, Mr. Michaels, I'm off to the ladies room."

When she returned, the dining room was empty, all except for Steve, still sitting at their table. The lights had been dimmed.

"Think they're trying to give us a hint, Steve?"

"All this reminiscing, I guess we've lost track of time. I don't think they stay open late on weeknights." He glanced at the windows, where the falling snow looked more like a blizzard. "Maybe everyone's anxious to get home while they still can."

Lauren slipped into her jacket. "Did they leave a check already? What's my share?"

"Oh no. This is my treat. That way it's a real date."

Lauren sidled up close to him and took Steve's hand. The Old Spice aroma mixed with scents she could only label as 'man smells', and they were all good. "Sounds fair. But I kind of hate to have our 'date' end so soon." They left the dining room, still hand in hand. "Want to have another drink in –"

The lounge was empty and dark too.

"Well, I don't want tonight to end just yet either," Steve said. "That is, if you're interested, I mean, if – well, my cabin's not too far out of the way back to your place. It's probably a mess, I've been overhauling my snowmobile and I have parts all over the place, and –"

"Steve, shut up and kiss me."

Lauren smiled and gave him a hug. She stood up on tiptoe, her heels slipping right out of the clunky loafers, and planted a kiss on Steve's lips.

They couldn't see each other's face in the darkened lounge. But they could hear each other's breathing, and they could feel each other's heart beating.

They kissed again, arms locked tight, thighs and chests pressed hard into the other, their lips smashing together, roaming, then parting, so they could taste each other, and the taste on their tongues was sweet and familiar. Even after all these years.

Lauren pulled away and caught her breath.

"Lauren, I –"

She landed a finger on his lips.

"Come on, Steve. I'll follow you."

CHAPTER FOURTEEN

Lauren tailgated Steve's Cherokee all the way to his cabin. If he'd tapped the brakes, she would have kissed his bumper in a blink. But the only way she could see through the blinding snow was to keep her eyes riveted on those two red taillights just ahead, those two spots of red glowing through a curtain of white.

Those two spots of red, glowing...

They burst in the door of Steve's cabin in a flurry of shivers and stomping feet. The snow billowed right in with them, a puff of icy smoke blowing at their backs.

There wasn't much talking now.

None at all, in fact.

They tossed off their coats. Steve brought a bottle of brandy from the kitchen while Lauren surveyed his cluttered living room, stacked with outdoor magazines and fishing tackle, a card table and folding chair dinette spread full of disassembled engine parts, pieces and thingamajigs from his snowmobile.

Steve opened the brandy and poured two glasses. They drank to chase away the blizzard's chill and then fell into a warm embrace. Standing there between the living room and the kitchen, between the nightlight over the stove and the living room's shadows, they kissed again, tender at first, then once more and long and hard this time, hands roaming and bodies pressing.

They paused, eyes locked and glassy, their breaths steamy and audible in the quiet cabin. Steve led Lauren to his bedroom, her feet making wet, squishy noises inside the snow-filled loafers. The bedroom was dark too, the opaque wall of falling snow outside the window reflecting nothing to lighten the gloom. Lauren kicked off her soggy shoes and stubbed her toe on something as Steve maneuvered her to his unmade bed.

They kissed, they hugged, rolling around in the tangle of sheets and blankets, wrapping their legs around each other and pausing just long enough between long kisses to catch a breath or to look in the other's eyes.

He tugged at her sweater and it popped off her head with a sparking crackle of static electricity all through her hair. Lauren reached back, unzipped her skirt and slid it down her legs, feeling that familiar warmth growing stronger down between them. She reached for Steve's belt and smiled up at him, undoing the buckle, unsnapping his pants and slowly sliding down the zipper. She ran her hands inside. Steve shivered, and a little moan rumbled in his throat.

They kissed again, more urgent now, and the rest of their clothes came off, fumbling and anxious, shirt buttons catching and jeans clinging, bra straps tangling and Lauren's nylons rolling, rolling, rolling, slowly peeling down her long legs into black rings around her ankles, Steve's lips retracing their way back up her thighs. She kicked her legs till the stockings finally fell off her feet and went fluttering to the floor with the rest of her clothes.

Naked now, she took Steve in her arms, felt his whole body all warmly, smoothly on top of her. His touch was tender, but his body was all lean and hard from years of northwoods living and outdoor work. And his real hardness rose up from between his legs, probing at her belly and the velvety tuft of blondie-brown hair below. She reached for him, held him, caressed him, guided him into her, to where she'd been wet and warmly ready before they'd even gotten all of their clothes off, almost before they'd made it to the bed. She let out a soft sigh of pleasured contentment as he entered her, as he slid in slowly and tentatively through her moist and glistening hair, deeper then, past swollen folds of flesh, a little more still, and they were suddenly rocking together on the bed, and Lauren wound her legs round his back and held him tight.

It had been so long, so very long. Not just since the last time they'd made love together, her and Steve. No, it had been too long since she'd made love to anyone. It felt so good, so very good. She clenched her thighs around him, dug her heels into his legs. Pressed down against the mattress with her hips, pressed down on his sliding and his thrusting to feel that hardness just where she wanted, just where it felt the best, the very best, where it felt so, so good, so very good, and it wouldn't take long now, not long at all.

Lauren felt her face flushing, her whole body flushing as the pressure built in her belly and then cascaded across her breasts and arms and into her toes and her fingers and especially down deep between her legs, till she cried out with raspy, breathy sighs and murmured 'oh's, and came and came and...

Steve slowed and watched her climax grow, peak and then subside. He moved patiently, gently, listening to her breathing ease. But she rolled him over onto his back and straddled him, her moist warmth embracing him until his face got all funny and dreamy looking and his eyes clenched tight and he grunted and sighed and she felt him go all pleasurably sticky-warm inside of her. She kept on rolling her hips, slower, slower, slower still as he faded out. Then Lauren fell back into Steve's arms and they lay there all spent for a long while, just listening to each other's heart beats, and the howling wind outside.

Finally Lauren raised herself up on one arm and looked down at Steve's half-closed eyes and contented face. "I suppose this is a hell of a time to ask, but are you seeing anyone special, Mr. Michaels?"

Steve shrugged. "Not me." He lifted his hand to her breasts.

Lauren playfully brushed it away. "Seriously, Steve."

"I am serious. I've dated some. There've been a couple of people over the past few years. But nothing ever came of them." He lifted his hand back to her breasts. "Maybe knowing someone like you made it tough. Maybe I kept comparing."

They kissed again. "And what about you, Lauren? I didn't exactly ask, either. You can't tell me that there aren't a million guys lined up at your door back in Chicago?"

Lauren shook her head and smiled. "Hardly."

"Come on."

"No, really. Same as you, I guess. There were some guys, sure. And then, well..."

"Well?"

"Well, what?"

"Well, who else?"

"No one else, really. No one else that mattered. Just dates. Flings. Crushes. And not much of that lately, to be honest." Steve's insistent fingers sent tingles down her chest and below. She arched her breast into his hand, toyed with the soft hair on his chest. It was too dark for him to see it, but she had a far away look in her eyes. "No one else."

"You sound like you're leaving someone out. Got a husband minding the ranch back home? A fiancee you're not mentioning? A real bad relationship? Something like that?"

"No, nothing like that at all, Steve. I was just thinking about something.

Okay, about some*one*. But it's not –"

"Not what?"

Lauren pulled away and rolled over, her back to Steve. She pulled up the blanket, suddenly feeling cold, uncomfortable, and starkly naked. Staring out the window, a peculiar and pale face crept into her mind. "It's nothing, Steve. Really, nothing. It's just...*no*. I don't want to talk about it."

"Well, good. I don't want to talk about him either. Tonight, I want you all to myself."

Lauren looked back over her shoulder at Steve, at the shadowed silhouette of his broad shoulders and his hard chest rising with each breath.

They made love again. And after it was over, they fell asleep just the way they finished: Steve cradled up against her back, and Lauren staring out the window at the blowing snow. Listening to his steady breathing until her own eyes grew heavy and she dozed herself, her last waking thought a silent prayer for sleep without dreams...no dreams, please, not after tonight, not with Steve asleep right here beside her.

～

Steve woke up and checked the clock radio on the nightstand. The glowing LED numbers blinked 4:30.

If there was any moonlight, the falling snow blocked it out. The room was just one, big bluish-black shadow.

He reached over for Lauren, but the bed was empty.

"Lauren?"

"I'm here, Steve." Her voice just floated around in the inky darkness.

Steve sat up. "Where are you?"

"Right here, by the window."

Her voice sounded distant. Steve strained his eyes to focus better. He could just barely make out her form by the window. She stood there half dressed, leaning against the curtains and staring outside.

"Are you okay?" He got out of bed and carefully stepped through the darkness to her side.

"Look at the storm, Steve."

Moonless or not, the night sky was whitened and filled with a raging, blowing sea of falling snow. No flurries now, and much more than just *snow*, it was a full blown storm, and accumulating fast. There was a foot on the ground if there was an inch.

"Wow, when did all that happen?"

"It's *been* happening. I couldn't sleep, and I didn't want to wake you.

I've just been watching the snow build up out there. Looks pretty bad."

Steve came up close behind and wrapped his arms around her. Lauren settled in to them, leaned her head back against his chest.

"I've seen a few pre-season snows," he said. "But this – it sure doesn't look like October, does it?"

"October? Oh, right. Happy Halloween, Steve."

"Huh?"

"Happy Halloween. It's Tuesday. Halloween."

"Oh. Same to you." He tightened his arms around hers, his hands cupping her breasts. "You know, we could get snowed in." He almost sounded hopeful.

But Lauren pulled out of his arms. She stood close, almost touching, but not quite. She pressed her face against the cold glass and just stared outside. "I don't know, Steve."

"Maybe later in the day the plows will clear the roads. But now..."

"Now?"

"Well, you wouldn't go out in that, would you? In that little tin can of yours? You barely made it here."

"Don't knock my baby. Anyway, I don't want to hang out here all day while you're chasing wolves in the snow. No, I think I'll chance it."

"At least let me drive you. The Jeep's a lot safer."

"No, I think I'll be okay."

"Lauren, it looks pretty bad out –"

"I said *no*," Lauren shot back, a little too curt, more so than she meant to. Softer then, and taking his hand, "I don't want to be stranded up at Birch Lake without my car. And you never know how your day'll go. Really, I think I can drive in this just fine. We get snow in Chicago, you know."

"Lauren, I don't think –"

"Oh, come on. Don't go all big brother on me. I'll be fine." She let go of his hand and stepped away into the dark room.

"Wait? Now? You're going *now*? It's only 4:30. Wait till it's light out."

"Why? It doesn't look like it'll get any better out there. If you ask me, it's going to get worse." She felt her way through the shadows to the bathroom.

Steve looked back out the window. "Maybe," he called. "At least there won't be any other traffic to watch out for." Then more to himself, "That's for sure."

In the bathroom, Lauren splashed her face with cold water. She barely had half an hour's sleep, just waking and watching Steve for a long time, till she finally got out of bed to stare at the storm by the window, where she wrestled with imaginary faces floating in the snow, and a nagging voice in the back of her head that kept prodding her to go back to the lodge.

They groped around in the dark and dressed in silence.

"So, you're really ready for this, Lauren?"

"Sure, why not?"

"Nothing. Just making conversation." Steve half buttoned his shirt. "Lauren, are you sure everything's all right?"

She looked around for her loafers. "Of course. Why?"

"Because you sound kind of – kind of 'not here'. Are you sorry we did this?"

The plaintive tone in Steve's voice got to her. She hugged him and gave him a peck on the cheek. "No, why would you say that?"

"I just want to be sure you don't regret anything. I want to make sure that this was as good for you as it was for me."

"Oh come on, lover, you were great. Couldn't you tell?" That didn't come out like she wanted it to. It was almost as if someone else put the words in her mouth. She slipped her feet into cold, damp loafers.

"Lauren, I don't mean it like that." Steve grabbed her hand, pulled her back into his arms. "What I mean is that I hope you're as happy as I am that we got together again. To be honest with you, I was a little nervous that this evening wouldn't work out. But it did. Or, I *thought* it was all working out."

"Steve, everything *has* been wonderful. Honest. I never really thought I'd see you again. And even after all this time, it's just been – well, just like old times. No, even better."

"Then, what –"

"Steve, nothing's the matter. I just couldn't sleep, and I got to thinking about different things, and it got me a little down."

"You should have woke me up. We could have talked."

"No. I couldn't. It's not something I'd be comfortable talking about. Not yet, anyway." She gave him another quick kiss. "Anyway, you just looked so damned cute when you were sleeping, I didn't have the heart to wake you."

"Okay. For now," he said. "But you're not off the hook yet. I think there's something you're not letting me in on."

"And I'm sure I will. We've got the rest of the week to let you pick my brain."

Steve guided her back to the living room, turning on the lights as he did. "Don't imagine there'll be many trick or treaters tonight," he said. "Not going to be much of a Halloween for the kids this year."

"Well, I didn't pack my costume anyway."

Steve helped Lauren on with her coat. "Man, are the guys going to have a laugh on me."

"About what?" She looked for her purse.

He poked at a coil of cables on the card table. "Who thought I'd need my snowmobile before Thanksgiving?"

"Oh, this will probably all melt by the weekend and it'll be Indian summer again."

Steve followed Lauren to the door. "Sure you won't change your mind?"

"Steve –"

"Please stay. You can drive back in the –"

"Steve, I'll be fine. Really." She opened the door and the snow leaped at her, icy cold and sharp, like broken glass on her face.

Steve watched Lauren climb through the drifts to the Escort, already covered over in a smooth, snow sculpted white. "You call me when you get to the lodge," he hollered over the wind. "I'll stay up."

Lauren waved back and nodded as she climbed into her car and started it up.

Steve watched the red compact slide half sideways down his driveway. "I know I'm going to regret this," he mumbled before he closed the door.

～

Lauren spun the radio knob, finding static everywhere. Finally she caught a station out of Rhinelander, all fuzz and crackles and barely audible over the wind whistling at the Escort's windows.

The news wasn't good.

"*...one for the record books all right. We have reports of 14 inches on the ground in Bessemer and Wakefield, 18 inches at Ontonagon, and gale force winds coming off Lake Superior there. Iron River, Crystal Falls, both reporting 16 inches. Like we've been saying all night, the National Weather Bureau has issued a winter storm warning. It's that old arctic express acting up again, just a little early this time, though. We're stuck under a broad front that stretches all the way from northwestern Minnesota to the north shores of Lake Michigan, and windy as it may be, it isn't moving out of here very quick. Stay tuned after this commercial break, and we'll have Chief Pembine from the Onieda County Fire Department with some updates on all those power outages we're hearing* *about. And more news on school closings for later today...*

It was after 5:30 when she made out the faint outlines of the Birch Lake Road sign. Hitting the brakes, the Escort slid right off onto the shoulder, and right into a deep drift. The engine revved, gears shifted, she rocked back and forth, until the car struggled its way out of a two foot mound of slick, wet snow, tires spinning furiously all the way.

Almost morning, sunrise barely an hour away, and the eastern sky should have been brighter. Maybe it was, Lauren thought, just hidden somewhere behind that impenetrable ceiling of dense, grey clouds and that blowing, swirling wall of dusty, flaky white. It could have been the dead of night or high afternoon, and it still would have looked pretty much the same. Lauren coaxed the Escort onto Birch Lake Road.

Though she couldn't see them, Lauren knew the road dropped off into those killer deadfalls just a few feet on either side. One ill-timed spin now, just one fishtail that she couldn't whip out of, and she'd flip into a fifty foot hole, swallowed up in the darkness and buried under the snow in no time. Oh, they'd find her after the spring thaw. Sooner, if this early season surprise melted away before winter's real arrival. Small consolation.

"Damn," she cursed out loud. "Why didn't I listen to Steve?" She flicked on her brights, thinking they'd make it easier to see through the blizzard.

But they didn't.

The brights didn't make it easier to see the road.

Didn't make it easier to see anything at all.

Didn't make it easier to see –

Lauren screamed and slammed on her brakes.

She regretted jamming her foot down the second she did it. The wheels locked. The Escort skidded then and pivoted sideways.

Two blinding, yellow-white lights burst out of the falling snow, thirty yards ahead and barreling right for her.

But there was nothing – absolutely nothing – Lauren could do. She flung the steering wheel to the left, then right, but her car just whipped around sideways on its own, and the blinding lights from an oncoming vehicle zeroed right in on her door, and kept on coming.

One second she looked at the lights through her windshield.

The next, she threw her hands up to shield her head as they glared in her side window.

And then, there was the roar of an engine, and the crunch of hard metal ramming her door, shattering her window and spinning the Escort into a three-sixty. It slid and bumped through piled snow, till the little car came to a stop against a drift.

The impact knocked the wind out of her. Lauren gasped for air, pulse racing, head pounding, her ears ringing from the warning bells and buzzers from her dash board. It all only took a few seconds, no more, but before she had a chance for any damage control, a loud *thump* reverberated from outside and behind her.

The other car.

Lauren twisted in her seat belt, but she couldn't see a thing. The side window was holding in place, but the glass itself was shattered into an opaque honeycomb. All she could see out the rear window was the blowing snow.

"Oh God, oh my God," she started chanting in numb fear. Lauren fumbled with her seatbelt, tears welling up in her eyes and making it even harder to work the clasp. She popped it free, tried to open the door. It opened a few inches, then jammed, bent metal grinding against bent metal. The snow whistled in the narrow opening as she rammed the door with her shoulder – once, it budged another couple inches. Again, and it opened a little further. Again, and it swung open with a metallic screech.

Lauren jumped out of the car, and her legs plunged kneedeep in the drift. She squinted back down the road.

Nothing. Just snow stinging her eyes.

No – *something.*

A small, squeeling, steely sound. And hissing, like a teakettle come to boil. And there...was that two little red lights glowing?

Two red lights, glowing...

Shivering uncontrollably, she zipped up her jacket and stumbled through the snow, with the wind slicing at her face and clawing up her skirt. Every step was a chore, each yard was a labor. The wind parted the white curtain for a moment, and a murky silhouette appeared, with two dots of red glowing at one end. A few steps closer, and the shape of a brown pickup truck appeared. It was spun sideways and teetering at an odd angle right at the edge of the road.

Lauren clambered through another drift on her hands and knees and crawled up to the truck.

The front end was smashed from whacking her car. And the pickup had been stopped – and only just – but stopped by a tree poking up right along the shoulder.

The taillights still glowed red, but they were flickering. Steam sifted out from under the crumpled hood and disappeared into the swirling snow. As Lauren approached the truck, metal squealed, scraping on wet wood. The tree creaked backwards, and the pickup's nose dipped down still further.

"Oh my God, oh my God, oh my God,..." The litany just poured out of Lauren's chattering teeth. There were two tons of truck there, leaning half on the road and half off over a pitch dark hole of nothing, with only the tree holding it up. And from the sound of creaking, snapping wood, not for much longer.

Lauren staggered closer.

There was someone inside.

"Oh my God, oh my God, oh my God," Lauren kept repeating. "Oh God, of course there's someone inside, oh my God, oh man, oh man..." She inched forward, shivering hand outstretched towards the pickup's door. She barely touched the handle.

The truck lurched forward, sliding two feet ahead and tipping to a forty five degree angle with another screech of metal and tearing wood. Lauren screamed and jumped back, slipped in the snow and landing flat on her seat. The weakening tree trunk groaned and snapped some more.

"Oh man, oh jeez, stuck in the middle of nowhere," she said to herself, and loud – she could hear herself right over the whining wind. "Ten miles from town, with the snowstorm from hell ready to swallow me up whole, oh man..."

Lauren crawled back to the pickup truck's door. She could see a body inside, a shoulder leaning against the window, a head slumped over the steering wheel.

It looked vaguely familiar.

She grabbed the door handle. The truck shifted again. But just a little this time. So she pressed the knob, gently tugged at the handle, gently like she was touching a ticking time bomb.

The door unlatched. She opened it a little. A little more. The truck didn't move. She tugged harder, and the door opened all the way.

The body inside spilled out into Lauren's arms, knocking her back down in the snow. Lauren tried to shove it off, brushing long black hair off her face so she could...

Long black hair.

Lauren's whole body shivered and it wouldn't stop. She slid the body all the way off, pushed it over on its back, and stared.

Just stared.

It was her.

And in a way, she knew it would be.

This was no dream now. The wind biting her ears and the snow caking up on her legs was colder than real. No dream...

The girl from the store. The girl in her drawings. The girl in her dream.

The girl didn't move. Lauren reached over and wiped away snow that already flocked the girl's face. She felt like ice. Lauren shook her.

Nothing.

What now? She stood up and looked at the pickup truck, dangling precariously over the edge of the road. That tree was bound to give any minute, sending the truck down into one of those deadfalls. There – another snap of wood, a screech of metal, and the truck slid forward another foot or two.

Lauren turned around, and her breath stopped cold in her throat.

The girl was sitting up, holding her head.

"Oh my God, are you okay? Are you hurt?" Lauren dropped to her knees and grabbed the girl, who was sinking back into the snow. "Say something! Are you all right? Look, don't lay down here. You're going to freeze to death."

The girl's eyes were half-opened slits. She barely looked alive. But her lips were moving. Lauren leaned in, trying to hear over the howling wind. "What? I can't hear you."

"The dawn," the girl moaned. "The dawn."

"Huh? Look, we've got to get some help. We have to try to get to my car."

The girl pointed towards the truck.

"No, your truck's a goner. We'll take my car."

But the girl gripped Lauren's arm, stronger than she would have expected. "My bag."

"Your *what?*" Lauren looked back at the truck. "I'm not going in there!"

"My bag." The girl dug her fingers into Lauren's arm, and it hurt.

"Okay, let me take a look."

Lauren climbed back to the pickup and peeked inside the open door. There was a big black shoulder bag over on the passenger side of the seat.

The tree groaned and the truck slid another foot.

"I'm not climbing in there."

But the girl just stared back. Her eyes might be half opened slits, but they glared at Lauren, somehow a plea and a command at the same time.

Carefully, Lauren put one foot inside. She leaned across the seat, stretched as far as she could, but she couldn't reach the black bag. She raised one more foot inside, stretched her arms to their limit, and slid her fingers around the bag's strap.

The truck shifted.

There was a screech and an awful crunch of metal, and the truck started to slide forward.

"Holy –" Lauren leaped backwards and banged against the door as the pickup slowly slid forward – and downward. Wide, terrified eyes looked out through the cracked windshield, saw the deadfall looming ahead, and then Lauren shoved hard and landed outside by the girl, the black bag tumbling into the snow behind her.

The tree snapped through and disappeared. The pickup slid after it. Banging, crashing and crunching exploded out of the dark hole, and then there was just silence, except for the howling wind.

"I could have gotten killed. For *this*." Lauren kicked the bag. But the girl closed her eyes and lay still in the snow.

"Look, we've got to get out of here. Can you walk?"

The girl shook her head. "The dawn," she said again.

"Right, it'll be morning soon. Maybe the snow will let up."

"The dawn."

"You look like you need a doctor." Were there ambulances in Watersmeet? Lauren had no idea. "We have to call for help. My place is just down the road." They trudged through the snow, back to the Escort, Lauren half carrying the girl's limp body all the way.

Lauren scrambled around to her side. "Okay, baby. Don't let me down now." The car's engine whirred and groaned, but it wouldn't catch. She tried again, but still nothing. The battery was draining quickly, and even the dashboard lights dimmed almost blank. Finally, the engine started, sputtering and coughing, but running. She leaned her head against the steering wheel and sighed a thank you.

The Escort slid and stumbled all the way down the Vestal road. Drifts rose everywhere, and the little compact caught in most of them. When they wound down the last curve towards the driveway, the sky started to brighten. Not a real dawn, just a slightly less murky greyness behind the falling snow. The wide lawn spread out before them, but it was a sea of white, crested here and there with sharp edged snow drifts that looked like white capped waves.

But the lodge was dark.

A big, black hulk of darkness. No lights shined out of the windows, and Lauren was certain she left them on.

The Escort fishtailed into another big drift and came to a stop. It wasn't going any further. "Well, this is it, I think," Lauren said. "Come on."

They were still a hundred feet from the front door, with snow piled deep all the way ahead of them. Dragging soaked and freezing legs through three foot drifts, that hundred feet felt like a mile. The girl was just dead weight in Lauren's arms, but at least she was conscious. Lauren could tell, because the girl kept mumbling, and it still *sounded* like 'the dawn, the dawn'.

Lauren opened the door, dragged the girl in and let her slide down onto the floor. She dumped the black bag next to her and reached for the hall lamp.

Nothing.

"Wait here." Lauren headed into the living room and tried the first lamp she could reach. Nothing. She tried another. The power was out, for sure.

Expecting the worst, she picked up the phone, raised it slowly to her ear, but before it even got there, she knew. She could tell. There was no dial tone. She punched the buttons. Nothing. She returned to the hallway.

"The power's out. The phone too. I don't see how we're going to get any help."

The girl just shook her head.

She looked hurt. Concussion, maybe? Internal injuries? Leaning against the wall, Lauren dripped melting snow on the floor. She kicked off her loafers, dropping clumps of slush along with them. Now she was really scared. She didn't see any visible wounds, no cuts or blood or obvious bruises. But the girl could hardly walk, and just moaned to herself there on the floor with her head hung low and the snow sliding off onto already soaked clothes.

"Well, I don't know who you are. And I don't know how you got here, or how you found me. Or *why*." Lauren knelt beside her. "And if I could, I wouldn't just call you an ambulance. I'd call the cops." *If there were cops to call* she thought to herself. Watersemeet was too small for a police force. So who was there to call anyway? The state police? Were there county police? And wouldn't they have their hands full right now with a surprise snowstorm raging away?

And what could she tell them? *'See, there's this girl. She's been following – no, stalking – no, haunting me, and she... well, I just want you to come and haul her away.'*

Right. They'd haul *her* away. To the nut house.

The girl moaned again, shoving her head deep inside her wet jacket. "The dawn. It is almost dawn. *Bitte, bitte...*"

Not sure what to do, certain she was making a bad decision keeping this girl here, but just as certain that there wasn't any choice, Lauren hefted the girl off the hallway floor and dragged her up the stairs, one slow step at a time.

She got the girl to her parent's room and dumped her on the bed. With the shutters closed and the drapes drawn, it was dark as night in there, and Lauren did more fumbling and bumping than anything as she peeled off the girl's wet clothes. She pulled a blanket over the girl's limp body and left her there.

There was nothing else she could do for now. Eyelids drooping, her whole body aching, she trudged off to her own room. Lauren stripped out of her wet clothes and fell into bed, sleep ready to overtake her the moment her wet hair hit the pillows.

But then Lauren's eyes popped open.

She hopped out of bed.

And locked her bedroom door.

PART THREE

CHAPTER FIFTEEN

Graz, Styria
October, 1916

The long lines of grey uniformed troops marched across the Mur River and wound their way along the narrow Leitner Grassen. They were grim faced ranks, each man's eyes revealing that he knew where he was headed. This was the newly formed 14th Corps, replacements designated to fill in the wide gaps on the Romanian front.

From June through August, the Austro-Hungarian armies steamrolled through the Carpathians and the Transylvanian Alps, butchering Russian and Romanian divisions while they covered so many miles – and so quickly – that supply lines were stretched to the breaking point. But the string of victories ground to a halt in September, and now the Empire's troops were hopelessly stalemated along the southern mountain slopes – in sight of the broad Romanian plains below, but undersupplied, understaffed, and unable to conquer them.

These days, the news from the southeastern front was almost too huge to grasp: 400,000 brave young soldiers captured by the Russians; 600,000 Austrian and German casualties overall. If the news also boasted of over a million Russians captured, wounded or killed, that was small consolation to the legions of widows, mothers, sweethearts and children.

They were all that seemed to remain in the once bustling city of Graz now.

She watched from her third floor window above the corner of Schonau-Gurtel and Leitner Strassen, letting the cool, damp air that wafted up from the Mur bathe her pale face and tease her long, dark hair. She watched the troops disappear into the night with their clatter of iron-cleated bootsoles and wagon wheels and hooves...even the occasional lorry engine.

So much wasted youth, she thought.

So much manhood doomed to horrible, useless deaths in a hopeless struggle to prop up the faded glories of a decadent Empire that had outlived its time. The Styrian Duchy, like the rest of Austria, might have ceded from the war soon after the very first decimating losses of 1915. It was common knowledge that the Emperor Franz Josef himself never wanted to be a part of this vast and unwinnable war. A small, quick campaign to put down the rebellious Serbs and restore national honor, that was all he had in mind.

But it was also common knowledge that the important decisions were no longer made in the Court in Vienna.

They came down from Berlin.

With the soldiers gone, she just stared out into the night, out across the well groomed shrubbery of the Stadt-Augarten just a block away, and northwards along the Mur, where somewhere upriver a churchbell tolled, like a sad farewell to the sons of *Steyrer*, Styria's pride.

That bell sounded just like a funeral dirge to her, and in that, it mirrored the melancholy mood she'd been mired in for weeks now.

Ever since she decided to leave.

A madness gripped all of Europe. It wasn't just here, on the frontiers along the Romanian and Serbian borders. The same, bloody insanity was being waged in virtually every corner of the continent. An entire generation of European civilization was marching into a meatgrinder at the point of a sword, and few could even remember what started it all.

But surely everyone would blame *Osterreich-Magyarorszag*, the Austro-Hungarian Empire. She was certain of that.

But it wasn't only the horrors of war that made her decide to leave. She'd seen warfare before, and not just cheering from the sidelines, cheering or weeping women's good-byes to the soldiers. No, her long, black hair had been tucked up under a cavalryman's helmet before, her breasts bound flat under the coarse wool of an infantryman's tunic. She'd bloodied the great sabre of the Karnsteins when the men of household were gone, shouldered a musket, sharpened a lance.

She'd seen many wars.

No, it was the feeling of dread *this* war gave her. The feeling that all that had once been fair and noble and fine in her homeland, in Europe itself, was dying.

And being dead herself, she simply couldn't bear it.

She closed the shutter and turned away from the window. Her small satchel was already packed and lying beside the bed. A horse waited in a stable down the Keilstrassen. It took five hundred schillings to buy that animal; the army requisitioned every horse last year.

She looked around her little suite. It had been nice to live like a real person for a while. Accumulating things: elegant clothes, fine books, furniture, drawings and photos she'd be leaving on the walls.

She heard footsteps stomping up the staircase. Soon, there would be a familiar knock on the door. It would be *Katzchen,* 'Kitten', come to say good-bye. All the other girls had already said their good-byes, the ones who weren't afraid to speak to the mysterious mistress on the third floor, that is. But leaving Katzchen would be painful. They'd been through so much together, Katzchen and her.

Even if, when all was said and done, they were only whores.

⁓

Barred from her own crypt.

Her ancestral home vandalized, left tainted and unclean. Only the narrowest of escapes from an ugly and quite permanent death. Turned away from Laura's house. And the whole Karnstein countryside pumped up with bravado and out hunting for demons.

She'd fled from the marches of Karnstein over fifty years ago. Fled from the English girl's home in the valley, with the wolves running at her side. Fled from Styria itself.

She lived like an animal, slept in caves and tree hollows, wore her clothes down to rags and then ran naked through the forest night, pouncing on victims whether her thirst needed slaking or not. Seeking forgetfulness in the blood, vengeance against humanity. For seven long years after she leaped from Laura's balcony, she wandered the Empire's wilderness, memory stinging as much as her fingertips from the touch of the priests' Holy Water.

And so it was that she finally made her way west through the new born German Federation, though at the time, she paid no attention to politics and borders, to any affairs of mortals, for that matter.

Down through Germany, and in to France.

France, in 1870.

France, fighting a desperate, losing battle in the Franco-Prussian War. The war that would, in turn, lead to the bigger and more terrible struggle forty four years later.

But *she* found the battlefields in Alsace and Lorriane much to her liking.

Torn throats, gashed wrists, bodies bitten and then bled dry. What horrors were those compared to the ripping and rending and utter obliteration of rifle fusillades, mortar shells and cannonade?

Yet somehow, it all ended there.

Among the wounded and the dying on the moonlit battlefields, she learned that orgies of blood and murder could never diminish her grief, could never make the pain go away, could never erase the memory of the quiet English girl, or any of the others from across so many years. Perhaps that was God's way, His punishment for the lost souls that lived in the darkness between Heaven and Hell...to simply go on. To endure, to continue, no matter how great the loneliness.

In that no man's land on the Franco-Prussian battle lines, she became the Angel Of Death.

She still prowled the battlefields after the sun went down. Still crawled through the trenches, but now she searched only for the doomed. The wounded, and the dying. The soldiers left on the field to die, with limbs blown off, faces missing, stomachs shot open. Crying like children, howling in pain for a bullet to the head, begging for merciful deaths.

And every night, she answered their cries.

There were no more terrified eyes staring back at her when she drank. Now she was their dark nurse, their sister confessor. Now she was greeted with relief. Welcomed. The wounded soldiers knew her for what she was. They saw her glowing eyes, her white flesh, her lips caked with dried blood. But the wounded welcomed her kiss that could make the pain go away, make their fevered minds dream for a last few dying moments of homes and good food and warm beds and pretty girls. They welcomed her like a comrade because they could see that she was damned even more than they were.

It was there on the battlefields that she met Katzchen.

Her name had once been Katrina, but the soldiers called her 'Kitten' and purred when they wanted her. So Katzchen she was, and had been for two years. Since she was fourteen.

One night, Katzchen stumbled upon her as she gave her blessed kiss to a German sentry who'd just been ambushed by a French patrol. The enemy could have killed him, but instead they tied him to a tree and cut out his tongue so he couldn't warn his comrades. He'd hung there gurgling in pain until she found him, and with her kiss, his pain melted away, he was back in his little flat in Munich, reading to his wife while their little daughter played with their puppy on the floor. She kissed him, and drank, and then he was gone, hopefully on his way to heaven, where his savior couldn't follow.

When the French patrol attacked, Katzchen fled the German camp and came upon her just as she wiped the last drops of the sentry's blood from her lips.

They stared at each other in silence for a moment, even though a fierce skirmish waged just a few hundred yards away.

They stared, Katzchen and her, and found some strange sort of kinship in each others' eyes. Eyes that had seen over two centuries of horror and loss, and eyes which had seen several lifetimes' worth in barely sixteen years.

There was no question that Katzchen knew right away what she was staring at: a naked, white girl, eyes blazing red, blood dripping from her mouth, animal teeth glimmering in the colored lights of the soldiers' flares. But Kat just grabbed her hand. "Come on, we must get away before the *Franzosisch* return." They fled, and were together ever since that night.

Katzchen was a whore.

A good whore, considering she was only sixteen, but a whore nonetheless. It was all she knew how to do. So she did it well.

Together, they decided to make a go of it. And for whatever reason, they succeeded.

They returned to Austria. Worked the rough trade along the docks of the Danube. Saved their money, moved to Graz, and set up shop in a dingy hovel by the railroad, grimy workers from the switching yards, ten *groschen* a pop. Added a few girls. Then moved uptown to Leitner Strassen, with a small deposit on a fine three story building overlooking the Stadt-Augarten and the Mur.

They named it *Die Schwarzen Mieze* – The Black Kitty – and it became the richest and most famous brothel in fin-de-siecle Graz.

In time, Kat quit spreading her legs for the customers.

Sometimes, she almost missed it. Almost. But with success came other duties. Procuring new girls (which was never much of a chore – The Black Kitty's reputation proceeded itself, and girls hiked in from the farm-lands looking for a job), bribing councilmen and priests (some of them, their best clients), maintaining the fine furnishings they accumulated, and keeping the accounts. A whore, maybe, but as it turned out, Kat had a flair for business.

As for Katzchen's partner?

Too many questions were discreetly discouraged.

But many of Graz' finer gentlemen – and quite a few of their wives and daughters – paid extra for the exotically pale mistress in the third floor suite, finding her predilection for nipping at their throats nothing more than a wonderfully wicked decadence.

All in all, things had been good for her and Kat.

Until the war came.

~

"All packed, I see."

"Yes."

"So, you really mean to leave."

"Kat, you know I do."

"I know. It's just so hard to picture *Die Schwarzen Mieze* without you." Katzchen sat down on the edge of the bed. "You know, you look exactly the same as you did that night we first met. Over forty years ago."

"Not quite the same, I hope." The dark haired girl swirled her black suede riding skirt and fingered the matching jacket. "Bathed better, and a little more fashionably dressed, at least." She laughed, and removed her wide brimmed riding hat, letting her long hair tumble out.

"True." Katzchen laughed too. "Or more correctly, bathed and dressed at all. You were quite naked then, the way I recall." Kat pulled a kerchief from the pocket of her velveteen dress and dabbed at her eyes. The years hadn't been unkind to Katzchen; nature had simply taken its natural course. Sixty two now, Katzchen was grayer and plumper, though her black market suit and the henna in her hair concealed most of it. She cleared her throat. "But that was a long time ago, wasn't it?"

"I suppose. Time is very relative."

"For you, perhaps. Not for everyone." Kat's eyes followed her friend pacing back and forth in the suite. "Haven't you ever wondered?"

"Wondered? About what, Kat?"

"Why I've never asked you. About yourself, I mean. Why I've never even said...the word."

"The 'word', Kat? *Vampire,* is that what you mean?"

Katzchen's powdered face reddened. "I'll be damned. Forty six years together, and I've never once said that word. And I won't now, either."

"Why? After all this time, I can't possibly scare you. And I can't imagine either of us being offended by...well, by anything."

"It's not that," Kat said. "I was always trying to be polite."

The dark haired girl laughed. She slapped the bedpost with her black gloved hand. "Oh, Katzchen. Dear, precious Katzchen. Only the Empire's most friendly whore would be so considerate." Her laughter subsided. "Seriously, Kat, you've kept my secret better and longer than anyone I've ever known. For that, and for so many, many things, you have my eternal thanks."

"*Eternal* is the operative word with you, isn't it?" Kat glanced at her friend's fading smile, the glint of the white teeth behind the unnaturally red lips. "What I really meant was, haven't you wondered why I never asked you to...well, to 'do it' to me?"

"And now that I'm about to leave, you would like me to?"

Katzchen shook her head.

"I will, you know."

"No. Does that surprise you? I've thought about it, of course. Many times. I know you'll think now that I'm getting old, I regret never asking. Asking when I was young and pretty, like you still are." Katzchen reached out and caught her partner pacing by. She made her sit down on the bed. "I knew what you were from the moment I saw you. It wasn't the filth, wasn't your naked pallor. It wasn't even the blood. No, it was your eyes. Your eyes told me what you were. And right now, when I look into your eyes again, I know that I could never want what you have. Because your eyes show the same horrors and loneliness I've endured. But your eyes also tell me you've lived through so much more, so much longer."

And those eyes began to glimmer with little sparks of dark red. The dark haired girl tried to turn away.

"No, don't look away. I've seen your eyes glow. It's not that," Kat said. "It's how your eyes reveal not only all you've seen, but the knowledge, the certainty, that so much more is yet to come. *That's* what I could never bear."

"Kat —"

"No, hear me out." Katzchen held her hand up. "I want to say these things now, because I'm sure we will never see each other again." She dropped her hand on top of her friend's, the one wrinkled, the other flawless and white as creamy marble. "You and I have been so very close. Not lovers. I know so many of the other girls in our business end up close that way. And I've always assumed you preferred your loving like that as well. But we — we've been *freundin*, true friends. And I just want you to know that no one could ever have been as good a friend to me as you have been."

Katzchen patted her round belly. "You know, I visit the doctor more these days than the milliner. I don't think I will live much longer after you're gone. I enjoy my gin and my cigars and my pastries too much to expect a long life. Anyway, the war may come knocking at Graz' gates soon." Kat squeezed her friend's hand tight. "When you think of me, don't pity me my age. It's I who feel saddened by yours."

"Kat, you don't even know my true age. The fact is, I'm more a product of all that is dying in Europe right now than you could ever imagine. And a part of me thought about dying right along with it."

"You? Dying?"

"Oh, I can die, Kat. The legends and fairy tales and the Church are all quite clear about that." She fingered the wide brim of her riding hat. "I don't know why, but I decided that just because the Empire and all of my links to it are dying, I didn't have to also. I decided to go on, as I always have before. But not here. Not any longer. The Austria I knew will be eradicated when this madness is finally over. That much I'm sure of. And I sense...I *fear* that this war's end won't really be the end. I see...something – something much more horrible for this land, something mortals have never imagined. Something even the damned couldn't conceive of. If it's any consolation, I think you'll have found peace before the final horrors befall Austria."

Kat looked puzzled. "And how will you escape all this horror? Where will you go?"

"West."

"West? Where?"

"Best, perhaps, that you don't know all the details, Kat. Lets just say my route will take me through the Entente countries."

"So? Then where?"

"To the new world."

Kat's eyes widened. "America?"

"That's my plan, yes."

"But surely you realize it's only a matter of time before the United States joins the British and French and the Russians against us?"

"Kat, please. Don't try to play patriot with me. It doesn't suit you."

"But, they'll be our enemy."

The dark haired girl jumped off the bed and towered over Kat. The waifish body seemed to grow as she held her head high, her shoulders back, her chest thrust out, till she stood there all fine and noble like some Wagnerian warrior maiden. "I am a loyal subject of the *Osterreich Magyarorszag*," she pronounced, as if she was swearing a solemn oath. "The last Countess of Karnstein, a sworn liege maiden of the Court in Vienna, grand-niece and ward of Charles Ferdinand of the Hapsburgs, a defender of the Duchy of *Steyrer* and the Holy Roman Empire in the east."

Then she diminished, shrunk, returned to that slender wisp of a pale faced girl. "Kat, don't talk to me about allies and enemies. Our allies today were forsworn enemies yesterday, and will be again tomorrow." She grabbed her satchel off the bed. "I'll go to the west, where my titles will have no more meaning than my memories."

They walked to the door, hand in hand. Katzchen stopped on the landing. "My friend, I know so little about you. But even I know that before you leave Styria, you'll make one last stop, won't you?"

"Yes."

"But you know she may be dead by now."

"She's not dead. That much I know."

Katzchen watched her friend glide down the staircase. On the next landing, that pale face turned back, dark eyes boring into Kat's. "She's still alive."

—

It was a three hour ride from Graz to Karnstein, and at that, with only the briefest stops to rest the horse. Out in the hill country beyond the city, she had to hide in the woods while a regiment passed by, their puttering truck engines with their acrid smoke fouling the night air and steeling her confidence that she'd made the right decision. It *wasn't* her Styria anymore. Change was inevitable. Progress was unstoppable. Perhaps it would be tolerable in a foreign land, especially one as young and rootless as America. Free of centuries-old dynasties, and all the bad blood there was between them, it was an almost mythical land, by all accounts, a veritable Garden of Eden.

And since she was barred from Paradise, America would have to do.

When she finally reached the old forest road, she held the horse's reigns tight. West, the road wound towards the ruins of Karnstein. She sniffed the wind and listened intently for a wolf's howl. But she heard nothing. Perhaps they'd fled this dying land too. She spurred her horse eastward.

An hour's hard riding later, she left the horse to cool itself in the dewy grass outside a familiar schloss she hadn't seen in over fifty years.

She approached the building, felt the bricks and mortar, listened to whatever the walls might have to say. But they told her little: years of neglect, a master long dead, his things sold piecemeal to settle debts, the servants gone when their wages couldn't be paid.

And the house spoke to her about its mistress, the daughter of the household, grown old and lonely before her time. The walls told her how the English girl Laura, roamed the empty halls at night, calling out a peculiar name, how she'd done so for fifty years now.

With her black riding skirts billowing in the wind, the dark haired girl climbed up the overgrown vines clinging to the schloss' walls.

The balcony was buried in piles of unswept leaves and dirt. She inched her way towards the French doors, remembering after all these years the searing pain she felt the last time she stepped through them. Perhaps the Holy Water had been washed away by fifty years of wind and rain. Or perhaps its white magic had weakened over the years.

She peered through the doors, squinting to see through dirty, cracked panes.

There were no wild roses tonight. No garlic bouquets, no crosses or icons littered the room. In fact, Laura's bedroom was nearly empty. The only furniture inside was a bed, covered in tattered, yellowed sheets that matched the faded paper on the walls.

"Oh, Laura, what has time done to you?"

The woman on the bed was a cruel caricature of Laura grown old. Fine golden hair had gone gray, what little was left of it. Rosy cheeks and creamy skin were jaundiced, wrinkled and spotted. Gnarled, arthritic hands clutched a dirty blanket that was stained with spit and blood.

The balcony doors opened. She stepped inside. And as soon as she did, her nostrils immediately flared.

Not at the scent of holy talismans and hosts.

But at the scent of sickness. Of decay and imminent death.

Consumption.

'Tuberculosis', the doctors called it now. An incurable, slow, painful wasting away of a death. The grave's own decomposition begun prematurely in the lungs, without even the patient courtesy to wait for the victim to die.

Laura coughed, sat up in bed, delirious eyes scanning the room. "So," she said, "You've finally returned."

Her voice was brittle, dry, until Laura broke into another coughing fit, leaving a weak looking drop of blood dangling from her lip. "I always knew you'd come back. I told everyone that if I waited, you'd come back to me. Of course, they all thought I was 'touched'."

"Yes, Laura. I've come back." She sat down on the bed beside Laura and took the old woman's hand. How old was she now? Sixty nine? Seventy, seventy one? Age had taken its toll, but disease had done so much more.

"I don't look very fetching now, do I? But look at you, you're still so beautiful. Just like I remembered. I can't remember much anymore, but I remember you."

"And I've always remembered you, Laura. Always."

Laura coughed again. It shook her whole body, shook the rickety bed. She fell into the dark haired girl's arms, rocking back and forth like a baby cuddling in its mother's embrace. "Now you're back, and we can start over. I never feared growing old, you know. Because I always knew you'd come back someday to take away the pain and the loneliness. You'd come back to make things like they were, use your dark magic, the way you always promised me. To make me young again."

The rocking stopped. "Laura, time's played tricks with your memory. I have no such power."

But the old woman wasn't really listening anymore. "Yes, now my hair will be golden again, and my skin soft and velvety. My breasts will grow full again, and you'll kiss them and tease me and we'll run naked under the moonlight again. Now that you're back."

"Laura – Laura, listen to me." But the old woman just kept murmuring to herself. "Laura!"

Laura squinted up at her, focusing glassy eyes. "Who are you?" She backed away on the bed. "What do you want with me? Leave me alone." Laura pulled the blanket up to her chin. "Leave me alone to die."

"But I can help you die, Laura. Peacefully, with only the most beautiful memories to guide your journey."

"No, get away," Laura shrieked. "I know you. I know what you are. Father told me. You're just a ghost. They killed you. The doctor, the priests, Vordenburg, they told me you were dead. They killed you."

"Laura –"

"Vampire!" Laura spat the word out like it was the worst of curses. Then she fell into another spasm of coughing, spitting and choking.

Red stained tears trickled down a pale cheek.

"Get out of my house!" Laura screamed.

The girl paused at the doors, gloved hands clamped over her ears to shut out the sound of Laura's gasping screams, "Go, vampire, go back to hell, go!" She ran across the balcony and leaped right over the railing. Calling her horse, she hopped on and kicked her heels hard into its flanks. The animal galloped across the overgrown lawn, its hoofbeats drowning out any other sounds.

Even the sounds of Laura's last spasm of choking coughs, even the sound of Laura dying, alone in her empty house and her barren room.

Even the sound of Laura's very last gasp, the last word that choked past her bloodied lips.

That last word...

"Carmilla."

CHAPTER SIXTEEN

For the most part, Watersmeet slept through the worst of the snowstorm. The wide cold front that blew southeast out of Minnesota and over Lake Superior was just turning sleet to flurries when Watersmeet closed up shop Monday evening. Everyone was curled up in front of televisions, or bent over newspapers and children's homework by the time the flurries turned into big, wet flakes of snow.

On Tuesday morning, Watersmeet woke up to a pre-season surprise: a foot and half of snow in the low spots, three foot and higher drifts where the wind could manage it. And the white stuff was still falling.

Nate and Dora Stambaugh argued through their pre-dawn showers over whether to open The Moose or not. For once, Nate won, even if Dora harped on him all the way into town. But Nate didn't care much, by then. The whine of his snowmobile engine drowned out whatever his knit face mask, earmuffs and fur-lined hood couldn't.

Cy Houlder woke up around seven, saw the snow, and gave up any thoughts of laying more traps like he'd originally planned to do today. But hell, he still had his snowshoes. Maybe toss out some more of those poison-laced, old deer guts he'd been curing in the shed. He didn't want to let a whole day go by without flipping off Steve Michaels and that whole wise-assed DNR lot. His creaky frame shuffled into the kitchen, knowing perfectly well that the fridge and the cabinets were likely close to empty. He hadn't bought any food, hadn't even been thinking straight for a couple of days, for that matter. That Vestal girl had his mind all crazy, shaking her titties and diddling herself for anyone to see, the goddamn slut. Well, anyone with a mind to go skulking around by the lodge and creeping around on the deck over at the Vestal place, that is. Cy rummaged through the sparse pickings in the old gas Servel with ugly notions of what she'd been up to all night.

Round nine o'clock, Steve Michaels slammed his phone down one more time. He called Lauren all morning, but just kept getting a recording over and over again, *We're sorry, but the number you are dialing cannot be reached at this time; please hang up and dial again.*

The phones could easily be out around the lodge. They seemed to be out just about everywhere east of town, or so he'd been told when his boss phoned earlier. The snowstorm canceled any plans for work today... canceled any chance of even getting to the DNR office, period. It would be mid-day before the county had the main highways plowed proper; tomorrow at best before they even started to think about the secondary roads.

Munching on a days-old danish, Steve stood at his workshop door, where his classic '75 Ski-Doo stared back at him. But uselessly, and in a couple hundred parts spread all over the floor. He dusted powdered sugar off his hands, grabbed a socket wrench and plunged back in, determined to keep calling Lauren every half-hour.

Annie Riordan hung up her phone about the same time Steve did. "Don't know if you're planning on dropping by, Lady Godiva, but if you are, *don't,*" Nate told her. "The Moose is empty as church on the bass opener...storm and all. But you just make sure your little ass is here tomorrow morning, Annie, and..." She looked out her trailer window. There was a chest-high drift right out in front, and the wind shook the aluminum and plastic box right on its cinder block footings. But Annie would have braved the storm. Her van might be buried under the snow back in The Moose's parking lot, but her snowmobile was gassed up and ready to go out in the carport. At least work would keep her mind off of...things. Off of the soreness lingering in her neck and her breasts. Off the peculiar, warm sensation that flooded over her when she touched her throat. Off those strange dreams she'd been having since Sunday night, since that weird girl gave her a lift home...

All across town, down the backroads and deep in the woods, it was pretty much the same.

Calls to delay appointments or to stay home from work. Moms already pulling their hair out, stuck with a house full of kids because the schools were closed, and the kids worrying about Halloween parties and trick-or-treat being postponed, or canceled altogether. People trying their phones every few minutes, knowing perfectly well that no one was likely to bother fixing any downed lines until the storm let up. And worse, those who lost their power, piling up the firewood or better yet, heading over to neighbors' warmer houses for coffee and hot soup.

It continued like that all day. The county plows did their best in a losing battle. They'd clear a path down U.S. 2 or Route 45, then the snow filled it back up, and the wind blew more on top to finish the job. They didn't even consider working the backroads and private drives.

So morning wore into a grey and gloomy afternoon, and afternoon darkened further into a cold and windy evening. But the storm wasn't ready to give up yet.

Not just yet.

⌐

The first thing Lauren noticed when she woke up was just how dark it was.

She glanced at the old wind-up Big Ben on the dresser. 4:45.

P.M., presumably.

She bolted up in bed, but a sudden pounding in her head dropped her back into the pillows. Rubbing her temples, running her tongue around a mouth stale with the taste of last night's alcohol, she wondered how she could have slept the entire day away.

Before she could get her bearings on when's and how's, she noticed how chilly her face and hands felt, and she pulled the blanket tight around her chin.

No, not chilly. Cold.

There were no lights on. But she was sure she'd left all the lights on before leaving last night to meet Steve.

No lights, and it was cold.

That could only mean one thing.

The power was still off.

A shiver quaked through her whole body. Lauren looked down on the floor to where her clothes all lay in a damp pile beside the bed.

And then everything started to dawn on her, everything that had happened.

The snowstorm.

The accident.

The girl.

Lauren leaped out of bed. She grabbed her robe out of the closet before the cold nipped at her naked skin, then dashed down the hallway to her parents' room.

It was even darker in there than in her bedroom. The drapes and blinds were still drawn tight. If there was still any last light outside, it wasn't finding its way in here. She stepped through the darkness towards the bed, afraid of what she might find there. That the bed was really empty?

That it had all just been another quirky dream?

But the bed wasn't empty.

Lauren could barely see, but she felt along the mattress, and there she was. No dream, that girl was still asleep right there on her parents' old bed.

Lauren nudged her, but the girl didn't flinch. She leaned in close to the dark haired girl's face and listened, but she didn't hear a thing. The wind still howled outside, and the shutters were still banging around at the windows, but not so loud that she wouldn't hear the girl breathing.

She reached for the girl's wrist. It hung all limp and cold in her hand like dead weight.

There was no pulse.

Her own heart pounding, Lauren leaned her head down to the girl's chest. Not a sound. She pressed her head down harder.

Nothing.

The girl was dead.

"Oh God, she'd dead!" Lauren yelled, jumping off the bed. "I killed her!"

She backed away from the bed, bumped into the wall by the door, panic welling up inside. "Oh God, she's dead, she's dead. She needed a doctor, she...Oh God."

She tried to get a grip on herself, tried real hard. Lauren backed out of the room and into the hallway. What to do, what to do? She felt her way through the thickening darkness, down the hallway, down the stairs to the living room. Negotiating her way around the furniture, she uncradled the phone, hoping, hoping...

Nothing.

The phones were still out.

Think, think.

Lauren took a kerosene lamp from the mantle, matches by the fireplace. With the yellow lantern glow quivering ahead of her, she returned upstairs.

She hesitated by the door to the room. She wasn't sure she wanted to see her, wasn't sure she wanted to see a corpse lit up in the glare of the lamp.

She peeked around the doorway. Then reached the lantern inside. It cast an eerie and flickering glow in the room, and on the still form across the bed. The girl still lay there.

Lauren set the lantern down and sat down on the bed. She stroked the dead girl's dark hair.

"I'm so sorry. God, I'm so very sorry." She parted the long bangs on the girl's pale forehead. "It was an accident. The storm, and everything – I'm just so sorry. I'm..."

The dead girl's head moved.

Lauren screamed.

She jumped off the bed, and froze against the dresser.

The girl's eyes fluttered open, sparkling red in the lantern light.

Lauren kept backing against the dresser, as if she could melt into it, melt into the wall behind and disappear.

The girl's mouth opened, and the lantern light glinted on her white teeth. She turned her head on the pillow, and smiled.

"Good evening, Lauren."

Lauren's knees buckled.

The girl sat up on the bed. The blanket slipped off her small, white breasts.

"Lauren, are you quite alright?"

Lauren let go of the dresser and slumped on the floor. Her head really pounded now. "You – you were dead!"

"Excuse me? And when was this?"

"Now! Just now. You were dead. You weren't breathing, there was no pulse. I checked."

The girl giggled, her laugh tinkling like falling icicles. "I'm sorry if I frightened you. I'm a very deep sleeper." She arched one dark brow, and her glance speared Lauren. "It would be easier to wake the dead than to rouse me, once I'm asleep. But as you can see, I'm quite awake now." She slid her long, pale legs out from under the blankets and dangled them off the edge of the bed.

Lauren still clung to the dresser, clutching the handles as she pulled herself up off the floor. "But – I thought...oh man, oh man. No, this is too weird. *You're* too weird, you really are."

"Yes, I have been told that before. Or things much like that, at any rate."

"So, are you okay?" Lauren inched away from the dresser, still keeping her distance. "I mean, last night – I thought you were a goner."

The girl's face screwed up. "Last night?"

"Yes, last night. The storm. The accident, crawling through the snow for – I don't know how long. You were just about out cold."

The girl nodded. "Oh, yes. Of course, the accident. We met on the road, didn't we?"

Met on the road? "I'll say we did. You almost went down with your truck."

"Yes, I seem to recall that now."

Lauren stepped just a little closer to the bed. "Are you sure you're okay? You got the worst of it last night. And we both got pretty soaked, and damned near frozen. Nothing broken? Nothing hurts?"

The girl looked down at her arms and legs. "No, nothing, it seems. And you, Lauren?"

"Me? Don't worry about me. I was just so scared. I don't think I've ever been that scared."

"But you are feeling well now?"

"Sure, I guess so. Give me another day and I'll probably be down with the cold from hell. But right now, okay, I suppose." Lauren shivered and cinched her robe tighter.

"Oh, but look – you are shivering." The girl slipped off the bed and draped her arm around Lauren's shoulders. "You must still be chilled inside from your ordeal."

An even bigger chill shuddered through Lauren's body when the girl touched her. The sensation was strange – icy to the touch, but sizzling beneath, like gulping down a stiff shot of iced vodka...cold at first, but burning all the way down.

"No, it's just that the power's still out," Lauren said. "We have electric heat here, that's all. You know, if the power doesn't come back on soon, it's going to get awfully cold in the lodge." She knew she *should* slip away from the girl's arm. *Should...*

"But you have fireplaces, no?"

"Sure."

"And wood?"

"Well, yes. Of course."

"Well then, we simply have to keep them going, and all will be well. Where I come from, people have gotten by on nothing more for centuries. I expect we can manage." She stroked Lauren's hair with her long, delicate fingers.

Lauren was embarrassed by her familiarity, by her closeness, by her pale nakedness. Finally, she did slip out from under the girl's arm. "Look, what is it with you? Seems to me, we still have an awful lot to clear up here."

"Such as?"

"Well...such as, why you're even here to begin with? Such as who the hell you are? And why you've been following – *stalking* me?" Lauren fussed with her robe's collar, clutching it closed over her chest. "You have been following me, haven't you?"

"Are you asking, or seeking reassurance?" The girl's face drooped. "Lauren, do you *really* wonder?"

Lauren backed towards the door. "What I want to know is if you... if you're maybe an axe murderer? I want to know if you're a pycho who hears voices at night telling you that the girl behind the sweater counter at Bloomie's is really Elvis' ghost. No, wait, don't tell me. You're meeting the mother ship at Birch Lake, that it?"

The girl looked puzzled.

"Look, the only reason you're sitting here right now, instead of in a jail – or better, in a padded cell – is because the phones are out."

"Really?" The girl looked up at Lauren, her dark eyes glimmering beneath long bangs. "And if the telephone worked right now, then you would call the police? You are that afraid of me?" She smiled that mysterious and wicked smile. "Would you really, Lauren?"

Lauren turned away. She couldn't fight that haunting face, the way the girl made it all tortured and innocent looking. "I just want to know...I just –"

Those *eyes*, gleaming right through the girl's dark hair. That red, red mouth, all glistening and sinfully curled up at the corners. That pale skin, like an ice sculpture come to life. Lauren wanted to turn away, but she felt compelled to look.

The girl took her hand. "I know how peculiar it must all seem to you. How peculiar *I* must seem to you. As it is, we are stuck here, you and I, and we should simply make the best of it." She raised Lauren's trembling hand to her cold lips and kissed it. Her voice became deep, mysterious, her words lilting with an otherwordly cadence. "I have done you no wrong. I mean you no harm. But my following you has frightened you, I can see that now. And for that, I am sorry. Truly." Her eyes sparked like fireworks – or was it just the flicker of the lamplight? "But surely you aren't completely repelled by my – my interest in you?"

Lauren leaned against the doorway, shoulders slumping. The girl's voice was a narcotic.

"But there's more than enough time to discuss such things." The voice returned to normal. As normal as it could be, low even when sounding bright, laced with that imperious, German accent. "The night continues to grow colder. Blazing fires are what this house needs. Perhaps a nice hot bath for you, little one."

Lauren nodded, still lulled by the voice. Then she shook her head clear, and returned to the real world, where words were just words, and not deadly lures to who knew what or where.

"Well, the hot bath sounds great, but I don't think that's going to be on my agenda. Or yours, if you're thinking of one. It isn't just the lights and the heat that are out." Lauren took the lantern. "The water heater's out too. A cold shower's the best we can do."

"Nonsense." The girl playfully shoved Lauren through the doorway and into the dark hall. "Get a fire going in your room, and I will see if I can get this old hearth here started; it looks like it hasn't been warmed in years. Let us get all the fires going, Lauren. You'll have your bath."

Lauren hesitated in the hallway.

"Go on, Lauren. I'll be with you shortly. Trust me."

Lauren backed towards her room, still looking at the girl's face hovering in the doorway. "One question," Lauren asked. "What's your name?"

"My name?" She paused for a moment. "My name is... Carmilla."

"Carmilla," Lauren said in a flat, American way.

Carmilla smiled and shook her head. "*Car-MEE-luh,*" she carefully enunciated, her voice much richer and foreign sounding, her red lips massaging each syllable.

"Carmilla," Lauren repeated, trying to mimic her, but still sounding flat. "Carmilla."

The girl laughed. "Well, Lauren, pronounce it however you wish."

Shuffling down the hallway Lauren continued to repeat the name, and once she turned into her room, Carmilla started a fire in the long unused fireplace, expertly holding a burning stick of kindling up the chimney to warm the cold air and draw up the smoke. She closed the firescreen and turned to leave.

But she paused, and looked at the dresser mirror. It stared back at her, mocking her with its vacant reflection of the dark bedroom. Frowning, she unhooked the mirror and slid it behind the dresser.

Carmilla followed after Lauren.

CHAPTER SEVENTEEN

Johnathan Vestal checked his watch one more time. His plane landed forty five minutes earlier, so what was holding up the luggage?

6:00 P.M., and the baggage claim area on O'Hare International Airport's lower level was thronged with impatient travelers. Johnathan's plane circled for over an hour before landing. Glancing at the faces around him, he could tell his flight wasn't the only one held up by the rain.

He scanned the overhead monitors for some sign of his flight number's baggage. Nothing yet. Tossing his trenchcoat over his shoulder, he toted his briefcase and laptop over to the banks of payphones.

It took fifteen minutes standing in line before he could dial up the Drake on Michigan Avenue to check his reservations. Then a quick call to reconfirm his Wednesday morning's appointment, and another to his office in New York. Johnathan jotted down phone numbers and notes, and with each swipe of his pen he dashed any chance of popping up at the lodge before the week was over.

He hung up on his office, ignored an annoyed murmur or two from the line forming behind him and tried one more call: Colonel Clovicky.

The last few calls to his old friend were disappointing. No answer at all, or, just brief and depressing exchanges. It had only been two weeks since Barbara Clovicky died, and the Colonel was still wrestling with the tragedy.

By the fifth ring, Johnathan prepared to hang up. Either the Colonel was out, or more likely, brooding in his own private grief. But then he heard "Clovicky, here," that familiar matter-of-fact greeting the old man always answered with.

"Colonel, I didn't think you'd answer."

"Johnny, nice of you to call. Where are you? Sounds like a football stadium."

"I wish. No, just the airport. O'Hare, actually."

"In town, are you? Don't suppose that crazy schedule you keep has any openings in it?"

"Well, as a matter of fact, it does." Johnathan wasn't prepared for the Colonel's upbeat tone, much less an invite. "I've got a meeting in the city tomorrow morning, then back to New York. But I don't have anything planned for tonight."

"Why don't you come over, then? Say, you haven't eaten yet, have you?"

"Airline food? No, sir. I was waiting till I got to my hotel."

"Well, I'm right in the middle of cooking up a big pot of spareribs and kraut. Interested?"

For a second, Vestal thought he could almost smell pork on the bone and baked sauerkraut right through the phone. "I haven't tasted your ribs and kraut since our last fishing trip up at the lodge. I think the smell scared all the walleye over to the other side of the lake."

The Colonel laughed, and it was like music to Johnathan's ears. "Well maybe it did, Johnny, but it probably kept all the bears away too. Grab a cab and get yourself down here. I'll look for you around nineteen hundred."

"Hold on there soldier. Don't you know it's raining outside. I don't even have my bags yet. Better make it 7:30."

It was another hour before he had his luggage tucked in a taxi's trunk. The cab crawled through the rain, southbound on the Tri-State Tollway in a slow-moving sea of red taillights. He flipped through the Wall Street Journal, half listening to the radio.

Apparently the wet weather drenching Chicago was wreaking havoc throughout the midwest. Flooded basements in Milwaukee, snow falling in Minneapolis and throwing flight schedules out the window. Northern Wisconsin, Michigan and Minnesota all blanketed under a heavy, pre-season storm. Foot and half here, two feet there, three feet there, and so on. Travel advisories, icy roads, the whole routine. Chicago's rain and chilly winds were just the southern tip of a nasty weather system that had swept out of Canada and stalled right over the midwest.

Lauren's father made a mental note to call the lodge later to see how bad the weather was up there.

The drive was a slow, snail's pace all the way to the Ogden Avenue exit. The taxi splashed down the tree-lined Hinsdale streets, past heaps of fallen leaves raked up by the curbs, past well-appointed lawns fronting red bricked Georgians and Tudors. Despite the rain, a few determined kids were still trick-or-treating – soggy, but happy.

Juggling his bags, he rang the Colonel's bell, hoping to find the Colonel's old face looking half as recuperated as his voice sounded on the phone.

———

Once the entire pan of ribs and kraut was neatly polished off with a couple of pilsner beers each, Lauren's father and Colonel Clovicky adjourned to the study. Like the rest of the house, the room was littered with old newspapers, magazines and books, a noticeable change from its normal barracks-clean spit and polish. But then, the Colonel seemed changed too. Johnathan watched the old man pour two brandies, noting how white his hair looked, how his craggy face seemed more lined, almost droopy. Clovicky offered him a cigar, which he declined, and the old man took one for himself as he slid a stack of papers off a leather wingback and fell into it.

"So Johnny, what do you think of my stories?" The old man clipped the tip off his cigar.

Johnathan shifted uncomfortably in his own easy chair. "Stories, Colonel? All you've told me are riddles."

"How's that, Johnny?"

"You've been dancing around...*something* all through dinner. Stop being so cagey, and tell me what this is all about. Sounds like spook stories to me. And I'm afraid I don't believe in spooks. Not even tonight."

The Colonel rolled his cigar around in his mouth and fussed with the ashtray and his brandy on the desk beside him. He blew out a blue smoke ring and nodded towards the window, where the wind lashed the rain against the glass. "Pretty good night for spook stories, though, don't you think, Johnny? Being Halloween and all."

"All I know is that your niece is dead, Colonel, and from the sound of things, you think there was some kind of foul play involved."

The old man slammed his glass down on the desk. "Foul play? Johnny, you couldn't even begin to imagine just how foul. If I tell you what I really think, you'd say I was just plain nuts. A regular Section 8."

"More riddles, Colonel. Tell me straight and simple."

"Straight and simple?" Clovicky hefted himself out of his chair with obvious discomfort. "It'd be a lot easier if it *was* straight and simple." He stood by the window and stared outside in silence for a while, intently puffing on the cigar. When he finally spoke, he sounded tired and sad.

"Back when my younger sister died, I was devastated. She wasn't much older than you, Johnny. There was quite a difference in our ages. Now, she was all the family I had. 'Course, who'd have thought her no-good bum of a husband would just up and disappear right after, with my sister's body barely in the ground two months, God bless her."

"And leaving Barbara on your doorstep," Lauren's father said.

The colonel nodded from the window in a halo of cigar smoke. "I don't mind telling you, it was hard. Ten years of retirement hadn't changed me much. I'm a military man, not a parent. Never was much interested in families or children. The army was my family. My troops were my children, I suppose. And Barbara – well, Barbara was one hell of a sullen little thing. But who could blame her? Bad enough her mother died on her so young. But to have her father run out like that? Bad business.

"But if my retirement plans had to change a little, so be it. I took Barbara in, and tried to do my best. I didn't know how to deal with a teenage girl, especially such a moody, ill-behaved kid like Barabara. But I knew I could provide her with a warm bed, food and clothes until she was old enough to be out on her own. I owed that much to my sister.

"But Goddamn, that girl was a handful. The older she got, the worse she got. She was always so determined to fit in, but never seemed to manage it. And always gravitating towards the dangerous crowds. The troublemakers. Trying to be accepted, to get noticed, I guess. I can see that now. But back then, well, it was just one endless argument after another. She was always hanging out with one bad group after another. And you could tell that those other kids never gave a hoot about her. They were just takers. Hanging around so they could raid my liquor cabinet when I was out, filch a couple of bucks from my drawers. The boys – using Barbara...well, you know what I mean.

"It just got worse after high school. She tried college, then just up and dropped out." The Colonel turned back to Lauren's father. "I used to tell her about your girl, Johnny. About Lauren. After all, you'd lost your wife, Lauren had lost her mother, but it didn't seem to effect her, at least not that you could see. *She* went on to college, did well in school by what you tell me. Always seemed like a pretty level headed kid."

Johnathan cleared his throat. "Well, maybe that was a mistake. Maybe telling Barbara about Lauren just made her all the more resentful?"

But the old man ignored him and continued. "Things just got worse after she dropped out of college. She'd sleep all day and be out all night, heading into the city, going out to nightclubs and parties. Coming home drunk, or worse. Never had any real friends, mind you. Just those same sorts of no-good hangers-on. Real queer looking guys, all leathered up and with half a dozen earrings in their ears and their nose and who knows where else? Drugged up girls who'd spend the night and stuff their purse full of food when they left. Things had gotten so out of hand, that it didn't seem unusual when Barbara brought this last one home. Except that *she* just didn't leave. Stayed here quite awhile, in fact. Right up until..."

The Colonel emptied his glass and poured another brandy. "Now, she was a strange one. Stranger than all the rest, in her own way. She just didn't look – *natural*. Unwholesome, you might say. If I told you I thought she didn't quite look human, you'd think I was losing my mind, I suppose. But that's the best way I could describe her.

"But beautiful, Johnny, so bewitchingly beautiful, it could take your breath away. Just the sight of her – why, it made you think things – sinful things, whether you wanted to or not." He stared out the window again, his voice sounding frail and far away. "It's hard to explain."

The Colonel turned back. "Mind you, I barely saw her, even though she was here quite some time. Barely spoke to her, either. And the couple times I did – well, it's almost like I wish I hadn't. With just a look, just a word, that girl could freeze you right down to your bones, make your tongue do flip-flops inside your own mouth. It was scary. Now I've always prided myself on being the most pragmatic, no-nonsense person you could ask to meet. But that girl – she made you think about things. Supernatural things. So why didn't I just throw that hellcat out right at the start, Johnny? Why?" The old man choked on his words, and took a big gulp of his brandy.

Lauren's father shifted uneasily in his chair again, uncomfortable witnessing another man's anguish, unsure what to say. "Colonel, why blame yourself? How could you know that any –"

"No, Johnny," the Colonel shot back. "No, you don't understand. Things changed. They got even worse. Barbara started to look...well – sick. Now, she never cared for sports or anything else that you'd consider 'healthy'. But a while after this *friend* showed up, it got worse. I guess you could say that Barbara started to look more like the other girl. Like this *Carmilla*. At first, I just thought it was their outfits. You know the look, all black clothes and dark makeup, so they look like zombies or something. I suppose it's fashionable.

"But, Barbara just got paler. Acting sick, and sickly looking, like she wasn't eating right, or she'd had the flu. I figured drugs, of course. I knew she did drugs. Or assumed as much, at any rate.

"Finally, I got fed up. I went to talk to my parish priest, Father Bernard over at St. Boniface. I knew most of what he would tell me already. Pray for Barbara's redemption. Hell, I'd been doing that since she first moved in. But when I pressed him, he pointed out the obvious: Barbara was over eighteen, and there wasn't much I could do legally, other than throw her out, or catch her with drugs...that is, if I felt things had gone so far that I wanted the police to get involved. 'Course, I didn't. Maybe I should've.

"But old Bernie's no dummy. He could see I wasn't satisfied with anything he was offering. So, off the record, he gave me some brochures and some phone numbers. Some of those semi-legal 'de-programmers'. I'm sure you've heard about them. They'll kidnap your kid if they're hung up on some cult or in with some bad crowd...hide them away and 'de-program' them."

The Colonel paused for another gulp of brandy. "Well, Johnny, I left the rectory that evening pretty fired up. Hadn't felt that way in a long time, not since the army. It was like the night before maneuvers. I was so determined. Armed with those phone numbers, I'd settle the situation once and for all.

"I'd give Barbara one last ultimatum: the 'girlfriend' moves out immediately. No more carousing, no more screwing around in my house, no more crazy hours, no more drinking, no more drugs. None of it! And she'd have to choose: back to school, or get a job. It would be a yes-or-no deal. And if her answer was no, then I was going to call one of those numbers, and let someone else take over."

The Colonel coughed and sputtered into his glass now. "But what did I find, Johnny?" Lauren's father was shocked to see tears appear on the old man's face. "What did I come upstairs and find?"

Clovicky dropped his cigar in an ashtray and waved Johnathan away when he started to get up out of his chair.

"She was dead, Johnny. Dead as could be. Horrible, bloody dead. Naked, on the bed. Her body was white as a sheet. Blood smeared on her neck and her chest. Holes in her throat, Johnny. There were holes in her throat, for God's sakes!"

The Colonel brought his glass to his lips with a shaky hand. He emptied it, coughed, then mumbled, "My sister's little girl, dead. Placed in my care, and I failed. Failed as miserably and completely as a man can fail. She was dead."

Lauren's father stared at the Colonel's collection of weaponry and army memorabilia adorning the study walls. He inventoried the floor to ceiling brownness of the room, hardwood floors, paneling, wood furniture and leather chairs. He let his eyes roam over anything, anything but the

Colonel himself, while the old man composed himself.

Clovicky pulled a handkerchief from his back pocket and wiped his eyes. He retrieved his cigar from the ashtray and got it going again, then went for a third brandy. "Sorry, Johnny. It's just..."

"No need to apologize, Colonel. But what you're telling me is that Barbara *was* killed. That she was murdered? What do the police say? What's up with the investigation, what –"

"Police?" The old man just smirked as he sat back down in his wing-back chair. "What you'd expect. No leads, not a trace of anyone named 'Carmilla'. Some cult thing, that's their position for now. The investigation's still open. I check in with them every few days. I'm not holding my breath." He rocked the chair back and forth, pausing before he went on. "I've been doing some reading the past couple weeks, Johnny. Been doing lots of reading, actually." He gestured around at the stacks of papers and books. "Finding out all kinds of interesting things."

With the cigar relit, the Colonel surrounded himself in a blue haze again. "Silly things, really. Legends. Superstitions. Old wives' tales. For example, did you know that some folks believe that you can keep a witch from flying just by sprinkling salt on her broom?"

Lauren's father eyed up his old friend suspiciously. *Where was this going?*

The Colonel continued. "Silly, right? Well, some people used to believe things like that. Or, there's some who think you can ward off bad dreams, evil dreams – succubi, incubi, that sort of thing – just by drinking the juice of seven crushed onions before bed."

The Colonel was smiling now. Smiling a little crazy, actually. But his old hands gripped his handkerchief and wound it into knots. "You have to wonder how such ridiculous notions even get started, right? Why, in some places, they actually believe that wrongdoers – now I mean *real* bad folks – well, some people believe that these 'wrongdoers' are cursed. Cursed so bad, that they can't get into heaven. In fact, cursed so bad that the Goddamned devil doesn't want them either. So they're stuck here on earth, forever."

The crazy smile evaporated, and the Colonel's eyes narrowed. He stared hard at Lauren's father. "Now in some legends, in central and eastern Europe, for instance, the worst kind of wrongdoers aren't your everyday thieves and rapists and murderers. No, the very worst kind are the blasphemers and the suicides.

"And according to some of these legends, not only are these evil souls cursed to walk the earth forever, but God is just so ashamed of them, of having created them in the first place, that He won't even let them go by their own names. Their baptized names, you see. So, they're cursed to make up names as they go along through eternity. To sort of, save God the embarrassment." The Colonel puffed away on his cigar.

"Superstitions really are silly, aren't they, Johnny? Salt on a broom. Seven onions." The old man shook his head. "So silly. As these legends would have it, cursed souls can't just make up any old name. No, they have to use each and every letter from their real name. Just sort of jumble them up." He stared hard at Lauren's father. "Like an *anagram*."

"Colonel?"

"Oh but there's more, Johnny, plenty more. It's not like in the movies. Not at all."

"Colonel, what the hell are you talking about?"

The old man leaned forward, his lined face still red where he wiped the tears away. His eyes scanned the room, as if what he had to say was some dark and terrible secret.

Which it was.

"Johnny, don't you see?"

"No. As a matter of fact, I don't."

The Colonel leaned back in his chair, his eyes set hard, his whole face as grim and determined as Johnathan had ever seen it.

"Barbara was murdered, Johnny. She was killed by a vampire."

⁓

The cab ride downtown seemed unusually long. Rain still fell, and every bit as hard as it had during the drive from the airport. It masked the glow of the Chicago skyline as the cab splashed down the Stevenson Expressway.

So, the old man had finally lost it.

Age, raising a troubled child, the shock of her death – evidently it was just too much for the Colonel. But it shook Johnathan right down to his bones to see his old friend end up this way, a man he'd respected all these years, now giving in to crazy, religious superstitions.

Vampire.

The word left a foul taste in Johnathan Vestal's mouth. It conjured up monster movie images, Bela Lugosi and black capes and bats and campy Transylvanian accents. Definitely not the sort of the thing he'd ever have expected to hear from the Colonel. But even a strong man could break under enough pressure.

The cab snaked up Lake Shore Drive and downtown Chicago managed to glimmer through the falling sheets of rain. Lauren's father wrapped up the whole ugly business as neatly and as pragmatically as his own logical businessman's mind allowed. The police and that Father Bernie from the Colonel's church – certainly they were on the right track.

Poor Barbara Clovicky probably got involved with some kind of cult. Drugs and crazy sex stuff, maybe some kind of blood rituals, who knew? Only things went too far.

He settled into his hotel room at the Drake, then dialed up the lodge.

The grisly image of Barbara Clovicky – naked and dead, splayed across her bed with blood smeared on her throat – still chilled him.

The phone rang a few times, then a recording cut in. *'We're sorry, but the number you are dialing cannot be reached at this time; please hang up and dial again.'*

Which he did. Several times, and each time he got the same recording. Till the hotel operator cut in and offered to try for him.

She came back on the line after a few minutes as Johnathan Vestal eased himself onto the kingsize bed, unkotting his tie. Very few calls were making it through. A freak snowstorm, just like he'd heard about on the radio earlier – power lines down, phone lines down, roads snowed under, schools and businesses closed.

Lauren's father lay awake until the wee hours Halloween night, knowing he'd be useless at his morning meeting, but any hope of sleep was doomed by the recurring image of Barbara Clovicky. And by vague worries over Lauren, alone up at the lodge.

A restless sleep finally came around three, as he cursed himself and his misplaced priorities, cursed himself for not making more of an effort to rearrange his business schedule, for not making more time for his daughter. Johnathan Vestal cursed himself for not being up at the lodge by Lauren's side right now.

CHAPTER EIGHTEEN

Birch log bark was already sizzling on the grates in Lauren's bedroom. The fireplace in her parents' room hissed with the sounds of sap boiling out of two big flaming hunks of pine.

But there was no fireplace in the bathroom. The electric baseboard heating units idled along the wall, impotent tonight because of a downed power line. Somewhere out in the vastness of the Ottawa National Forest, a wire coated with too much ice and snow sparked and spasmed under a wind-swept drift.

Listening to the water spill out of the faucet into the tub, Lauren held a kerosene lantern up to the thermostat on the bathroom wall. 62 degrees. Not cold, not by any means. At least not cold in the way that it was bitter, snowy, wintry cold outside right now. But chilly enough, uncomfortably so. And likely to get chillier still.

She stuck her hand under the the faucet. The water was lukewarm, at best. And by the feel of it, cooling by the moment.

With only a few inches of water in the tub, she turned off the hot faucet. That was all the water heater had to give. The rest would be as icy as the waves crashing on Birch Lake's shore.

Lauren unknotted the sash on her robe and slowly, almost reluctantly let it fall open. The chill raised the soft, downy hairs along her belly, hardened her nipples and made her skin tingle. She shivered as the robe slid off her shoulders.

The door opened, just as her robe fluttered to the floor. "Well, Lauren. Here's your hot bath, as I promised." Carmilla stood in the doorway, still naked, still pale, anemic, looking like a spectre with fog licking at her slender frame. She held a steaming pail of hot water in each hand, and walked right past Lauren to set them down beside the tub. "Oh, I'm sorry. Perhaps I should have knocked?"

Lauren quickly slipped her robe back on and held it tightly closed with her arms. "No, I – you just surprised me, that's all."

The dark haired girl winked. "I have been known to do that to people." She emptied the two buckets into the tub, bathing herself in a cloud of steam. "That should do it."

Lauren stood back by the vanity, watching.

"Well, go ahead, silly," Carmilla said. "Get in while it's still hot. I'll fetch some more."

"Where did you get the hot water?" Lauren asked.

"I heated it on the fire, of course. There are two more buckets warming now. I'll get them." She turned to go.

"Wait, warmed them on what fire?"

"Downstairs. In the kitchen."

You've been downstairs?"

"Yes. I lit a fire in your kitchen and your parlor," Carmilla said. "That is all right with you, Lauren, isn't it?"

"Sure. Of course." Lauren backed away as Carmilla brushed past her, and a shiver ran down her back. The strange girl was so close, so...*naked.* Brazenly naked, except for a narrow black choker ringing her neck. It made Lauren uncomfortable. Uncomfortable, but...

"Carmilla?"

The pale girl paused at the door. "Yes, Lauren?"

"Aren't you cold?"

"A little, I suppose. I'm always a little cold."

"No, I mean, aren't you –" Lauren gestured towards her. "Aren't you cold...like that?"

Carmilla looked down at herself. "Oh, I see." She toyed with the velvet choker round her neck, her long, white fingers tracing along the edge of the cameo at its center. Then she backed through the doorway, all sly smiles and twinkly eyes. "Does it bother you, Lauren?"

"It's not that, it's just –"

The girl was out in the shadowy hallway now. "Do I make you feel uncomfortable?"

"No. No, but –"

But Carmilla was gone, disappearing into the blackness of the unlit hallway.

The tub was warm enough now, but the bathroom wasn't. Lauren made quick work of the bath, wincing when she rinsed her hair under the cold faucet. Wiping soapy water from her eyes, she suddenly felt like she was being watched, and glanced over her shoulder.

Carmilla stood in the doorway, that strange smile curling the corners of her red lips.

They stared at each other in silence for a moment.

Then the wind howled at the window, rattling the frosted panes. The sound was enough to break the spell.

Lauren abruptly sat up in the tub, wrapping one arm across her breasts and the other below. "Would you hand me a towel?"

Carmilla's already dark eyes darkened further. "Of course." She handed Lauren a towel, spun on her heel and left in a cloud of steam trails.

"Weird girl," Lauren muttered to herself while she quickly dried off. The air felt doubly cold now on her damp skin. She slipped back into her robe, snatched up the kerosene lamp and dashed to her bedroom.

"Weird weird, weird," she mumbled while she dug through her dresser for some clothes. This whole situation was weird. Too weird. Twilight Zone weird.

She dressed by the fire. Heat washed over her face, her arms and legs, but a damp chill tickled her back, and it made her shiver. That, and the thought of Carmilla slinking naked around the lodge.

Just who was this girl? Why was she here? What was she up to?

Had they met before last week? Sometime in the past? Someone she snubbed at school? A disgruntled ex-Bloomies' clerk? Some nutty customer she'd shortchanged? Why not? Crazy things happen all the time, people were killed for winking the wrong way on the subway platform, or wearing the wrong sneakers to school.

Lauren bundled up in layers of clothing, leggings under sweats, two pairs of socks. One t-shirt, then another, then a flannel, and two sweaters on top of that. The fire looked toasty burning away there in the hearth, but she didn't know how long the lodge could stay warm without the electricity.

She stepped into the hallway, with the kerosene lamp splashing quivery golden shadows on the knotty pine walls. Lauren paused by the half opened bathroom door. It was dark inside. She could hear the shower running.

Lauren shook her head. *What a nut. An ice cold shower, in the dark. Might as well be taking a bath in Birch Lake in a snowstorm...*

The thought froze in Lauren's head.

She backed away from the bathroom and headed downstairs.

Huddled under a blanket on the living room sofa, Lauren went through the motions of eating a sandwich. But her mind was on her 'guest'.

She watched Carmilla standing by the big fireplace. The girl had showered and dressed, and was brushing out her thick mane of dark hair now. She wore a pair of faded jeans and a white cotton blouse, all lace and ruffles and belled sleeves. That was all; no sweaters, no layers, not even a pair of socks. Her small, white feet poked out from the jeans, one foot curled into the rug, and the other raised up on the hearth.

"You're sure you don't want to borrow some of my clothes?" Lauren asked. "You've got to be freezing."

"Thank you, no. I'm grateful that you saved my bag last night, or I wouldn't have anything to wear.

Lauren persisted. "But you can borrow something if you want. Really. My stuff probably won't fit you perfectly. You're a little taller than me, a little thinner, I suppose. But, still –"

"No, Lauren. I'm fine. If I need something of yours, I'll help myself."

Lauren gave up on her sandwich and gulped down a mouthful of red wine. "And you're sure you're not hungry? You really should eat something."

Carmilla finished with her hair and left the brush on the mantle. She smiled. "You're a very gracious host, considering that I am not actually an invited guest. But I don't think I'll eat just yet. Perhaps later."

"Then have some wine, at least." Lauren gestured to the bottle and extra glass on the coffeetable. Carmilla nodded, poured half a glass and took a slow, delicate sip.

"That's it? Half a glass? The way that storm is blowing outside, you might want to consider getting good and drunk just to keep warm."

"No, actually," Carmilla said, languidly strolling about the living room, aimlessly fingering the furniture and knickknacks. "I understand that alcohol is the worst thing to fight off the cold. Lowers the body temperature." She gazed back at Lauren from under her bangs. "Thins the blood, I'm told."

"Well, maybe it does. I'm not an expert drinker." Lauren emptied her glass, and clutched the blanket around her while she leaned over to pour a refill. "But it's warming me up right now." She gulped a mouth-full, but it made her shiver as it went down her throat. She glanced at Carmilla, and saw her smiling. "We'll need more wood," Lauren said. "I didn't bring much in. Who expected *this*?"

"Who, indeed? But, please, since I'm your guest, let me do it." Carmilla floated out of the living room.

Lauren stared after her. "Hey, my coat's hanging –" But the girl was gone. "Carmilla?"

She heard the back door unlatch, and the howl of the wind blow inside.

"Carmilla? Don't you want my coat? Some boots?" *A brain?* Lauren crawled out from under her blanket and leaned over the back of the couch. "Carmilla?" No answer, and nothing to be seen down the dark hallway or in the kitchen beyond. Lauren ran after her.

The back door was open, snow blowing in on the wind. A three foot drift had piled up in front of the threshold. "Jesus, it's freezing out there," Lauren mumbled through chattering teeth.

She watched the door sway with each gust of wind, digging a semi-circle pattern in the snow.

She could just shut it now.

Slam it shut, lock it tight, and her strange 'guest' would be out of her hair.

No.

No, of course not. She couldn't really do something like that.

And wasn't sure she wanted to, either.

Lauren stuck her head through the doorway, feeling icy snow crystals slap her face. "Carmilla!" she called out into the darkness, but her voice was swallowed up by the wind. She called again, but there was no answer. Snow built up quickly around her feet.

"Fine." She shrugged her shoulders. "Freeze to death." She went back to the living room and crawled under her blanket.

After a while, there were noises in the kitchen. Logs tumbled to the floor. Then another load, and another. Carmilla appeared out of the dark hallway with a stack of split birch and pine in her arms, which she set by the fireplace, then glided away with a trail of snowflakes fluttering off her hair and her shoulders. She bustled back and forth from the kitchen and up the stairs, leaving logs by each fireplace. Finally she returned to the living room, dusting off her pale hands on her jeans. Her hair glistened with melting snow. The bottoms of her jeans were soaked.

"That should get us through the night, at least." Carmilla took another small sip from her wine glass, then settled down on the couch beside Lauren.

"You're really determined to freak me out, is that it?" Lauren said.

"What do you mean?"

Lauren kicked off her blanket. "What do I mean? I mean prancing around the house with no clothes on before. I mean going outside in the snow like that. No coat, no shoes, nothing. Look, I didn't risk my neck to pull you out of your truck just so you can die from pneumonia!"

Carmilla shook her head and laughed, a crystal windchime laugh. "Lauren, I told you, the cold really doesn't bother me. I have a very unusual constitution." She tucked her feet up under her legs and ran a long, pale finger around the rim of her wineglass. "I suppose you think it all quite peculiar?"

"Well, peculiar *is* the operative word with you, isn't it?"

"Perhaps. I am what I am. Why not accept me that way?"

"*Accept* you, Carmilla? Things being the way they are, I don't have much choice, do I? But you're not getting off that easy. Try telling me who you really are."

"What would you like to know?"

"Anything. Like, where are you from?"

"My accent betrays me, doesn't it? But you asked me this before."

"I did?"

"Yes, don't you recall? Only last week, in your store."

Lauren's brows knitted tight as she tried to remember. But last week seemed like another lifetime.

"Lauren, as I told you then, I am originally from Styria."

"Uh-huh. And that's where exactly?"

"Styria is a state in Austria. Today, that is. Originally it was a principality of the Autro-Hungarian Empire. But all of that ended with The Great War." She noted Lauren's puzzled look. "What Americans would call the First World War. I am from a small but proud duchy named Karnstein. In fact, you might say that Karnstein is my surname, as names are used here in the west today. Though that was not the case in my – that is, in earlier times."

Carmilla continued to talk, punctuating her words with an occasional nudge of her knee against Lauren's, her hand patting Lauren's hand, her shoulder bumping Lauren's shoulder. There was a magic in each touch, a magic in her voice that tugged at Lauren's senses, that lulled her into another time and place.

"You don't know what to make of me," Carmilla said. "You look at me and you see a skinny girl with dirty clothes. But if you could know the things I've known, seen the things I've seen, Lauren, you'd think differently, perhaps. My namesakes were Countesses of the Hapsburg line. Would you believe me if I told you that I myself am the last Countess of Karnstein?"

Lauren rolled her eyes.

"No, I can see that you don't," Carmilla said. "Yet, it is true. Much that was very old and very fine in my homeland ended with the empire. And the very last of Austria's soul died in the holocaust that followed in the much more horrible war, just a few years later. But these things are unimportant here in America, aren't they?"

Lauren shrugged her shoulders, not sure what the girl was getting at. "If you mean believing you're some kind of royalty, well..."

"Actually, I originally fled to the west to forget my heritage. But it was naive of me to think I could." Carmilla smiled, and her dark eyes took on a faraway look. "Centuries of Karnstein blood flows in these veins. At times, I feel those old days calling me. The Styrian hills and forests call to me. Memories of my homeland, of my old life still beckon, Lauren."

Lauren started to nod along with Carmilla's words, as if they all made perfect sense.

"It has been very long since I have seen home. Much has happened there since I left. Perhaps I wouldn't find it as much to my liking as my memories?"

Lauren's glassy eyes focused suddenly. "Wait, what memories? How long could it be since you've left home?"

"Oh, a very long time, Lauren. A very long time."

"Come on, it can't be that long. You look younger than me. And I'm only twenty seven. How old are you?"

Carmilla seemed lost in thought for a moment, calculating an answer. "On my last birthday, I was twenty one."

"There, see."

And so they talked.

They talked for hours and hours, it seemed. It was hard to tell, because Lauren quickly lost track of time. Carmilla talked of places and things she'd seen. Of histories, of times and places long gone by, but told with such fervor that Lauren felt transported there, felt she was hearing the intimate details of a firsthand account. Carmilla talked about her homeland, of the proud Karnsteins, of the court in Vienna, of the operas and cafes in Graz. She talked about the land itself, of the trees and the ground and the rivers and the stones, of the animals and the birds. She talked about wars and plagues and nobles and dynasties, about hard times and good times and magical things.

And with each word, Lauren felt herself drifting deeper and deeper into the girl's web. She felt hypnotized, drunk, drugged by Carmilla's cool hands and cello voice and the mysterious tales she told.

So she didn't feel awkward or shy when Carmilla asked *her* to tell some stories, and Lauren did because she felt *impelled* to do so, felt commanded to reveal all she could about herself. Lauren revealed dreams and longings and desires just like the ones she told Steve Michaels about last night. But she told more, and sometimes she heard herself say things that she'd never even acknowledged before.

Eventually, Lauren's voice trailed off. Whether it was the wine or some dark magic Carmilla weaved, Lauren drifted off to sleep, curled up in Carmilla's lap.

The tip of Carmilla's tongue slid out across her lips, wetting them so they shined like rubies under the firelight. She leaned down close to Lauren's neck, where the pulse beat loudly just below the skin. Carmilla's breath frosted the flesh on Lauren's throat, and her pearly teeth hovered there.

Her eyes flashed cold fire. She hissed. Then slowly raised her head, closing her lips over her teeth.

"Not tonight. Not yet. But soon. Very soon." And with that, Carmilla lifted Lauren off the couch and carted her upstairs, as if she were no heavier than a china doll.

She tucked Lauren in bed and planted a soft kiss on her forehead. "Sleep well, precious. Dream of me, dream of my world.

Carmilla stoked Lauren's fireplace and returned downstairs.

—

The blizzard still raged outside the lodge's windows, and the turbulent clouds churned in the night sky. But Carmilla burned her dark eyes through the grey pall, till she could sense the stars rotating above, and the moon descending towards the treeline. Two hours, perhaps three, till dawn's arrival.

She sipped from her wineglass, savoring the momentary warmth in her throat. But it cooled too quickly. The nagging chill in her flesh and her bones returned fast enough. She needed...a taste, just a sip, something to warm her.

Annie.

Carmilla left her glass on the windowsill and went to the front door. She turned the knob and let the wind blow it open. The night and the storm lay beyond.

She stood on the porch and sniffed the fresh, cold air. The wind whipped her long hair around her face, and the snow quickly flocked it like powdered sugar. She stared out into the night, stared through the swirling white veils and deep into the darkness. She focused on the sight, the sound, the smell, *the taste* – of Annie. Focused her mind till cold, hungry desire burned in her belly and chilled her mouth and made her teeth tingle. She focused on those sensations, then sent them out into the night like dark messengers that flew over the lakes and careened through the forest till they settled some ten miles to the west and north.

And there inside a rusty metal trailer that rocked and buffeted in the blizzard, Annie Riordan's eyes popped open, and she sat up in bed.

Annie lifted off her electric blanket. Slid out of bed and plodded to the trailer door. It flew open in her face before she even touched the latch. The wind whipped her cotton nightgown up to her hips. Her legs buckled when the cold licked her skin, but Annie felt something else – another touch, just as cold, but burning like dry ice, caressing her thighs and rubbing her belly and kissing her breasts.

She shuffled right past the pile of boots beside the door. Past the parkas and the snowsuit hanging on the hooks there. She stepped right out of the trailer, left the door flapping as she stumbled through a drift.

Half an hour later, maybe more, Carmilla's ears pricked up.

A bright beam of light sliced through the darkness, kicking up a spray of whirling snow along the north edge of Birch Lake. It lit up the edges of the wall of trees and the white caps crashing on the snow covered beach. The light sped closer along with a whining motor sound.

Annie's red snowmobile appeared out of the woods, skimming along at full speed and skirting Birch Lake. Her hair was thick with sparkling snow and ice, blown back off her face and half-frozen into place. Her nightgown was soaked, pressed wet and flat against her body.

The snowmobile spun to a stop right in front of the lodge. With the motor still running, Annie tumbled off, and plodded through the high drifts, clawing her way to the porch, where *she* stood. Stood smiling, with snow dusted arms held out in welcome.

Annie climbed up on the porch, and knelt at Carmilla's bare feet. She looked up with clouded, vacant eyes and a face frozen blue from the cold and the snow. Cracked lips held back chattering teeth, and her whole body trembled inside the wet nightshirt.

Carmilla reached down and raised Annie's shaking body to her own. "Come, let me warm you."

Annie struggled with the ice-coated bow on the collar of her night-gown. Finally untied, the gown slid off her shoulders and bunched around the curve of her hips.

Carmilla licked her lips and leaned towards Annie's neck. She kissed her throat, feeling the pulse inside pounding against her mouth. With a sigh, Carmilla's short, sharp fangs plunged into Annie's flesh.

Finally, she felt Annie's pulse start to slow, and she wrenched her lips from the girl's cold neck. Annie hung limp in her arms, half standing on wobbly legs, with her head flung back, her mouth hanging open and gasping in the cold air for breath. Blood trickled from the wounds on her throat and ran red across her wet shoulder and down her breasts, all the way down her belly, till it stained her white nightgown.

"Go now." Carmilla let her go and backed away. "And thank you."

Annie didn't budge. She mumbled something, but her lips were too frozen to say the words.

"No, you must go now, and rest."

Carmilla disappeared inside the lodge. The front door slammed shut with commanding finality.

Annie still stood there, shivering on the porch.

Finally, some small measure of awareness returned to Annie's eyes. She looked down at the blood on her bare skin and her nightgown. Annie crawled back to her idling snowmobile. She fumbled with her nightgown, pulled the wet fabric back over her shoulders and struggled with the bow. But her frozen fingers couldn't manage it.

Tears mingled with the melting snow on her cheeks. She let out one loud wail, as if her mind suddenly recognized where she was and what she'd done...what she had allowed to be done to her.

Then the engine revved, the snowmobile spun around and sped back along the shore of Birch Lake. Soon enough the motor's whine and the headlight were swallowed up by the snowstorm and the night.

Inside the lodge, Carmilla stood by the living room window, watching her speed away. When Annie was finally gone, even to her eyes and ears, she went upstairs.

Carmilla stood by Lauren's bed. Her eyelids grew heavy. Her joints stiffened, a familiar languidness creeping into her limbs. Dawn approached, even if the storm raging outside was reluctant to reveal it.

Carmilla slid off her jeans. She unbuttoned her blouse, neatly folded her clothes and lay them on the nightstand. Then she climbed into bed and snuggled up close to Lauren.

A smile curled on Carmilla's lips when Lauren murmured in her sleep, and rolled one arm over to her side. She took that arm and wrapped it tightly around her.

Carmilla's lids eased closed, and as the familiar deep sleep quickly overtook her, she whispered to herself.

"Soon."

CHAPTER NINETEEN

Wednesday morning, the blizzard finally ended.

Snow still fell when Watersmeet woke up, but by the time breakfast dishes were cleared and morning showers taken, the sky already looked brighter.

The county plows were at it all day and night Tuesday, leaving the two main highways passable, if still hazardous. With the storm moving on, they finally made some headway. The snow no longer fell as fast, or faster, than they could plow it away, so U.S. 2 and Route 45 were clear by nine. Then the plows took aim at the buried sidestreets and backroads surrounding town.

School opened. A little late and with only half the students showing up, but it opened anyway. Watersmeet's handfull of small businesses unlocked their doors, shoveled off their stoops, and hoped for the best. The Moose, for one, was bustling. Truck drivers were ready to risk just-plowed roads, townfolk ready to chance a drive to work, carless locals stomped in on snowshoes and cross-country skis for groceries. Private plows and tow trucks buzzed all over the parking lot. And everyone was popping in for breakfast and coffee.

Nate Stambaugh had his hands full. Annie Riordan hadn't answered her phone Wednesday morning, and no amount of sweettalk could get Dora in. He needed help waiting tables, to say nothing about the cash register back in the store. A hand lettered sign was taped up by the checkout line, *Bring your purchases to the diner...Free coffee! (Serve Yourself.)*

And Annie Riordan stared at her phone each time Nate called, but she didn't budge. She huddled under a quilt in the trailer's kitchenette, sweat-soaked and shaking with fever and chills. Strong coffee cooled in a plastic mug on the counter, and she took another gulp. Not that she was thirsty. Annie was afraid. Afraid of falling asleep, afraid of the terrifying nightmares full of sin and sex and red eyes and even redder lips, and blood running down shivering blue skin. Annie was afraid of what the next night might bring.

Cy Houlder didn't let the storm phase him one bit. Around the time Nate gave Annie Riordan's number one last, desperate try, old Cy was crunching his way back across the snow to his shack.

Cy's mouth watered while he unstrapped the snowshoes and dropped them by the door. He carried a plump raccoon that had been too curious, poking around one of his wolf traps. The damn trap nearly cut the little critter in two. Head pounding with a cheap bourbon hangover, Cy was sure that the coon wasn't from one of the traps stocked with poisoned bait. At least, he was pretty sure.

The old man set to work firing up his propane stove and skinned the raccoon, grumbling to himself while he worked. He'd been out early, gone to check the traps originally or so he kept telling himself. But his snowshoes clomped all the way to the Vestal lodge.

Houlder dropped gamey smelling coonmeat into a larded up fry pan, and reheated a pot of day-old coffee. He was anxious to get back outside to check some more of his traps and his poison baits, and hoping to find bigger quarry this time. *That* would really put him one more up on that goddamned Michaels punk. And if Steve gave him any more lip about those precious wolves, Cy'd show him. He'd show him alright.

But Cy Houlder wasn't on *Steve's* mind. It was Lauren he was worried about. But there wasn't much he could do about her now.

The phone woke him early. The Gogebic County district manager was rounding up the crews. A DNR four wheeler would be around at 7:00 A.M., and everyone was heading up to the trout hatcheries to chip ice and shovel snow off the breeding ponds. *'I'd pack a toothbrush and a change of clothes if I were you, Steve,'* the boss said.

Steve was still trying Lauren's number when the truck waded through the drifts in his driveway, but all he got was that same damn recording.

~

Lauren slept the day away, waking to the sounds of a fire crackling in the fireplace.

Carmilla closed the firescreen and dusted her hands off on her naked thighs. *"Guten abend, Lauren."*

"What?" Lauren rubbed sleep from her eyes. "Oh, morning."

Carmilla smiled and shook her head. "Hardly. *Abend* is evening. Good evening, Lauren."

"Evening? You mean I slept all day again?"

"I only awoke a short time ago myself." Carmilla sat down on the edge of the bed.

"So you started a fire before I woke up? Thanks."

"Yes," Carmilla said. "It had gone quite cold during the daytime, I'm afraid."

"So the power must still be off."

Carmilla shrugged her shoulders.

"And the phone too, I bet," Lauren said.

"I didn't try your telephone."

"Well, I'm going to." Lauren slipped out of bed and ran downstairs. The phone *was* still out.

Lauren slammed the useless hunk of plastic down, felt the chill in the living room, and got right to work starting a fire. While it caught, she looked out the picture window, where twilight was just settling on a surreal, wintry landscape. It looked like the storm finally stopped. But the wind had carved weird shapes in the snow, layering drifts like desert dunes, sculpting white garden gnomes out of tree stumps, a giant snow-muffin out of her car. The clouds parted in a purple sky, and a few stars began to glimmer. They reflected on the snow, made it glitter, as if the last layer had been sprinkled with gems. She heard the wind churning up Birch Lake's waves, where chunks of ice crashed against the shore.

She returned upstairs. After a quick, cold water bath, she dressed, wondering where Carmilla had disappeared to. Lauren headed back to the kitchen, shivered when she stepped into the room, and started a fire in the woodburner. Dinner was a dismal affair, scrounged up from the dwindling leftovers from her first stop in The Moose.

Carmilla appeared in the kitchen, dressed and running a towel through damp hair. She smiled at Lauren, who sat at the table, eating in the dark. Then the pale girl went to the door and gazed out the window at the back yard, the towel draped around her shoulders now.

"Sure I can't fix you something to eat, Carmilla?"

"No. Thank you."

Lauren polished off the last of a sandwich. "No," she said, washing it down with instant coffee. "Of course not. You don't eat, do you?"

"Lauren?"

"Runs around this ice house naked," Lauren muttered into her cup.

"Sleeps all day. Doesn't eat. Must be how you keep that rosy complexion of yours."

"I'm sorry, Lauren. Are you talking to me?"

"No, not really." Lauren took her dishes to the sink.

Carmilla came up beside her, an innocent smile brightening her face. "I'm restless. Let's have some fun." She pulled the plate out of Lauren's hand and shut the faucet off. "Let's go outside and play."

"Outside? Why? It's freezing out there."

"Oh, a little cold. What of it? There's a beautiful night waiting outside this house. The storm has ended and the clouds have parted. The stars are twinkling on the snow, and the moon is riding high in the sky. Come with me. Come and play with me outside."

That smile.

Those eyes. There was no way to deny her.

"Okay. But we're going to freeze our asses off."

As soon as they stepped off the front stoop, the cold slapped Lauren hard across the face. Just a few feet off the stairs and the snow curved up in a tall, three foot drift.

Lauren bundled up as best she could manage: boots, two pairs of socks, leggings pulled up over tights. Two sweaters, a scarf and her jacket. She climbed through that first drift, and already her fingers felt frozen inside her mittens.

But Carmilla was a dozen yards ahead, sprinting like a deer right on top of the snow. Lauren hadn't watched her dress, but at least the girl had a jacket and boots on tonight, and even wrapped a scarf around her neck. Still, it seemed unnatural: Carmilla's jacket unzipped and flapping in the wind, no gloves on those pale hands swinging at her sides.

And she really just skipped right *on top* of those drifts, the same ones that sucked Lauren's legs down into cold, white quicksand.

Carmilla led the way, laughing and jumping and running across the snow. They skirted the lakeshore, where Carmilla paused and stared out at the dark waves. The water frothed at the pier and lobbed ice chunks on the beach. She sniffed the air, smiled and threw her arms out like wings.

"Isn't it beautiful, Lauren?" The wind whipped her long, dark hair around her face. "Isn't it simply wonderful, so fresh and strong and beautiful? On a night like this, I feel like I could fly." And she almost did, racing along the shoreline with her arms stretched wide, her jacket and hair flapping in the wind.

She circled around and around Lauren in tightening rings. Gliding by, Carmilla stooped to grab a handful of snow. Still circling, she began to pat the snow in her hands.

"Don't get any ideas," Lauren called out, smiling in spite of herself. "I pitched a pretty mean softball when I was a kid."

But Carmilla still patted the snow in her hands, a gleefully wicked smile on her face.

"I'm warning you, Carmilla." Lauren scooped up a handfull of her own. But before she was ready, Carmilla fired. The snowball hit Lauren on the shoulder.

Lauren returned a well-aimed shot, zinging Carmilla right on the side of the head.

But Carmilla was already loading up again, and suddenly a barrage of snowballs shot back and forth, till they both stopped trying to aim, and just heaved handfulls onto each other. Snow in their eyes, snow in their ears, snow in their mouths, they collapsed in the snow, laughing hysterically. Lauren tried to catch her breath. "Oh man, why am I laughing so hard? I can't stop."

"Because it's fun, Lauren."

"Fun? You're nuts, it's freezing. I shouldn't be laughing, I should be shivering."

"But you're not cold now, are you?" Carmilla grabbed Lauren's hand and pulled her up out of the snow. "Come, let's walk in the woods." She set off for the dark wall of trees just ahead.

"Hey, hold on," Lauren hurried behind as best she could. "I'm not going into the woods at night."

"Why not?"

"Because. There are animals in there."

Carmilla laughed. "Well, of course there are animals 'in there', silly. It's a forest. And a very beautiful one at that."

"No, I mean *animals*. Dangerous animals. Bears, badgers – wolves, Carmilla." Lauren caught up and pulled on Carmilla's sleeve, tying to drag her back away from the trees.

"Lauren, don't be foolish. It's winter time. Not by the calendar, perhaps, but winter nonetheless. The bears are going to their dens. Badgers? The gentlest of woodland pets, nothing more."

"So, what about the wolves then? I happen to know for a fact that there are wolves in these woods. Right around here."

"I know, Lauren. I've met them." Carmilla pulled her sleeve free and continued toward the trees.

You 'met them'? Lauren stumbled behind. "Wait up."

They plunged deep into the woods, Carmilla prancing on top the of snow with ease, and Lauren clumsily trudging a few steps behind. "Slow down, will you?" Lauren hollered.

But Carmilla didn't answer. Suddenly she froze, stood absolutely still, with her head raised to the breeze. Lauren's thought it sounded like the girl was breathing awfully hard.

But no, she was – *sniffing.* Sniffing the wind.

"Carmilla?" The girl seemed lost in her own world. Carmilla's head slowly turned from side to side, apparently searching for something. Then she spoke, but for all Lauren could tell, Carmilla spoke to the wind and the trees themselves.

"Mein Kinder," she said, her voice low, even more peculiar sounding in her native tongue. *"Wo ist sie?"* She paused, listening to the wind whine through the trees. *"Prinz? Prinzessen?"*

Lauren peered through the gloom, but could only see the trees silhouetted against the snow.

"Konig? Konigen? Kommen sie hair!" Still, only silence, except for the mournful howl of the wind through the evergreen boughs.

But then the wind's sound changed. It became more melodic, and yet, melancholy at the same time. Lauren strained to hear. She turned to Carmilla. Dark as it was, Lauren could see her pale face.

Carmilla was smiling now.

The howling wind really did carry a different sound. Lauren heard it clearly, and it sent a shiver through her whole body. It was the unmistakable howl of a wolf, blending in with the whistling wind. First one, then another, and still another. A whole chorus of howls, and growing louder by the moment.

"Carmilla –"

"Still, bitte!" Carmilla whispered. "Please, be quiet for a moment."

"Carmilla, let's get out of here. Those wolves are coming, I can hear them."

"Wait, please. Don't be afraid."

The howls subsided. The woods were silent again.

And then Lauren saw them.

Yellow-green eyes glowing from behind a stand of pines no more than fifty feet away. Six bright dots, she guessed, three pairs. The eyes floated in shadowy forms that melted in and out of the darkness as the wolves paced just behind the trees. Lauren held on tight to Carmilla's arm.

"Guten abend, mein kinder," Carmilla said. The wolves still lurked behind the trees, acting like they were ready to bolt at any second.

"Darf ich vorstellen Fraulein Lauren Vestal." Carmilla shoved Lauren

half a step ahead of her. *"Mein Freunde."*

Lauren felt the wolves' eyes riveted on her. "Why do I suddenly feel like the Easter ham?"

"Lauren, hold your hands out, with the palms open. It's a sign that you mean no harm." It sounded crazy to Lauren, but she did it.

"Something is wrong." Carmilla sounded genuinely concerned. "They're nervous tonight."

Lauren measured the short patch of snow between her and the wolves, figuring they'd be on her before she even could turn around. *"They're* nervous?" she whispered. "Carmilla, are you insane? Let's get out of here while we can."

"Nonsense. I am being polite. I have properly introduced you. There's no good reason for their boorish behavior." She stepped forward. *"Kommen sie hair!"* She stamped her foot. "Right now, my children."

The green eyes blinked, and then one by one the wolves stepped out from behind the trees. Lauren jumped behind Carmilla while the wolves silently padded across the little clearing and sat at their feet.

"There now," Carmilla cooed. "That is much better." She reached down to pet the large grey and white animal that sat closest to her. The wolf's ears drooped, and it lowered its head.

"My children, this is my friend, Lauren Vestal. I suspect you have seen her before, even if she was unaware of your presence. She is a gentle creature, and she is my friend. Do you understand?"

The three wolves barked their assent.

"Go on, Lauren. Say hello to them."

Lauren still hid behind Carmilla's back. "Are you crazy? They're looking at me like I'm lunch."

"Lauren, you'll hurt their feelings. They have accepted you. Now greet them properly." She shoved Lauren back in front of her.

"Uh, well – *h-hello, wolves*," Lauren said. The animals watched her intently.

"Oh really, Lauren. Pet them. Go on." She took Lauren's hand and ran it through the thick fur on the first wolf's neck. "You see? They're quite friendly to those they choose to accept." The wolf inched closer to Lauren and nuzzled up against her legs. She had to stifle a giggle. Still nervous, she knelt down beside the wolf and carefully petted it's snow dusted pelt.

"I don't believe it. It's – it's just like a dog."

Carmilla smiled and shook her head. "Hardly. This is *Die Konigen*, the Queen Mother. She is the leader of the pack." The animal beside the

Queen, dark grey and slightly larger, edged around to Lauren's other side and sniffed her face. She flinched at first. Hot steam shot out of its nostrils. Its long fangs glinting so close to her throat made her shiver. But fear melted into laughter when the animal began to lick her cheeks.

"And that is *Der Konig*, the King. He is the Queen's mate." Carmilla chuckled as the third wolf leapt right into Lauren's lap and shoved its big furry head right into her face. Lauren rolled onto her back under its weight while it sniffed at her hair and licked her mouth just like an excited puppy.

"And this rambunctious fellow is *Der Prinz*, the Prince. He is the Queen and King's son, a yearling. And quite the ladies man, it seems."

The three wolves romped around Lauren, sniffing and licking at her, nipping at her mittens and her jacket. Lauren could barely contain herself. Her fear melted away. It was the most magical thing she'd ever experienced.

But then the Queen stepped away and sat beside Carmilla. When Lauren looked their way, the girl and the animal appeared to be – talking. The Queen barked, and the other two wolves leapt off of Lauren.

"Carmilla, what's the matter?" Lauren asked, getting up out of the snow.

"Something has upset them, that much is certain. And, one of the pack is not here."

Lauren dusted snow off her clothes. "There's another one?"

"Yes, *Die Prinzessen* – the Princess. Another yearling." She turned to the wolves. *Was ist los?* Where is the Princess? What has happened?"

The Queen ran to the edge of the clearing, then turned back and looked to the other wolves. They followed her path and silently disappeared into the darkness beyond the trees.

"Die Konigen, was ist los?" Carmilla asked again. But the wolf just whined, and turned to go.

"Lauren, let's follow."

The Queen wolf vanished.

"Where are they going, Carmilla? What's wrong?"

"Hurry now, we must follow." Carmilla grabbed Lauren's hand and pulled her along. They ran into the trees and followed the wolves. Lauren had trouble keeping up, but that small hand holding hers dragged her along. Just when she was ready to beg for a rest, the trees thinned. Up ahead, the three wolves paced back at forth at the edge of the woods.

A wide clearing opened up before them, utterly treeless and painted white with snow blown into crisp edged drifts. After almost total darkness back in the woods, the light sparkling on the snow made Lauren squint.

She stood by Carmilla's side. Then she heard the dark haired girl hiss.

Hissed. She didn't sigh, didn't whisper. She hissed, and the sound made the hair on the back of Lauren's neck stand straight up.

"What is it, Carmilla?"

"Look." The girl raised her hand, pointing her long, pale finger to the opposite side of the clearing. Lauren stared across the glittery snow. There, straight across from them, and maybe a couple hundred yards away...something was moving. It was tiny and indistinct from this far away, but something or someone was there.

The Queen wolf growled.

~

Cy Houlder flicked a cigarette butt into the snow and watched its little orange glow sizzle out. He fumbled around in his jacket pocket for the half pint of Old Grand Dad that usually kept him company outdoors, helping himself to a generous gulp. It was mighty cold, and he'd been outside way too long. It was after seven, he guessed. Should've headed back a long time ago, and now he was a good mile or more north of the shack, with some rough ground to cover on the way back.

He swore under his breath. This had been a rotten day. Stealing a peek at that Vestal girl this morning had just gotten him all antsy and riled up, with no good way to work it off. So he spent the whole day checking his traps, and besides that mangy coon he had for breakfast, came up empty handed. Not a rabbit, not a beaver, not a fox, nothing.

And once again, nothing in any of his *special* traps. The big, jagged steel jawed traps that could snap small game, or your own hand if you weren't damn careful, clear in two. The traps he'd been baiting with old dear guts and opossum meat that had been soaked in his 'special sauce'...strychnine and drain cleaner.

His wolf traps.

It *was* late, but there still was one more trap, and it'd be a damn shame to head home without at least a look-see. He shouldered his rusty Remington twelve gauge and cut north by northwest through the trees.

Right at the south edge of that clearing up ahead, that's where it was. Hooked onto a hefty piece of chain and bolted onto a three foot iron spike pounded deep into the hard, rocky soil. If that trap shut on something, it wasn't going anywhere except to hell...unless it closed so tight that it cut right through.

Cy paused to lift the side flaps of his hat off his ears. And then he could hear it nice and clear in the crisp, night air. A whining, and a whimpering. Shrill, desperate sounds. That, and the clinking of iron chain links.

"Hot damn!" he yelled. Cy's wiry old frame did a little jig right there in the snow. Sure enough, he had one. He really, really had one.

Thirty feet or so in from the south edge of the clearing, *Prinzessen* was crying madly from a fear and a pain like she'd never known before. Her jaws snapped wildly in anger and frustration, long fangs slicing her own lips to ribbons, and frothing up her muzzle with bloody foam.

A steel trap's rusty teeth clamped down on her right hind leg, slicing through fur and muscle, and snapping the bone so her paw dangled uselessly by just a few shreds of flesh. The pain in her leg was horrible. But the fire in her belly was worse. Her stomach and throat and tongue were seared raw from the drain cleaner sauté, and her heart and lungs were starting to weaken from the strychnine.

Prinzessen's strength was fading fast. She couldn't understand what was happening, only that mean teeth bit her leg and foul meat burned in her belly, all ripe with the worst of all odors...man-scent. All she wanted now was for her mother to come and make everything well again, to make the pain go away, to return to the den where it was always warm and snug and her brother was always ready to play.

Cy stepped into the clearing and inched his way closer to the wolf struggling in his trap. He brought his gun around, a five shot pump, all bunged up, rusting, and none too reliable lately. He had it loaded with a magnum shell, two lead slugs, and two more shells, in that order; a little something for any occasion.

The trapped wolf struggled so desperately it never even noticed his approach. But when Cy pumped the first shell into the chamber, the wolf stopped whimpering, and spun around to look at him. Old Houlder stared at yellow-green eyes, all glowing with hellfire hatred for him and any other man that ever toted a gun, shot an arrow or laid a trapline in the woods.

The shell's pellets would make mincemeat out of that hateful face. Wouldn't kill the damn thing, not likely. But it was going to make that son-of-a-bitch cry for mamma, but good. Then he'd pump a big old lead slug right smack in the middle of its chest, and that would put the lights out in those devil eyes for sure. Cy pointed the gun down at the growling wolf, slipped a grimy finger around the trigger, and took aim.

"Wait!"

Cy loosened his grip on the shotgun and scanned the clearing suspiciously.

"Wait, don't shoot!"

The call came from somewhere out of the darkness, maybe to the north. A girl's voice, by the sound of it. It was hard to tell, the way sounds played tricks in the cold night air. Cy's eyes weren't what they used to be, his glasses were criss-crossed with scratches, and the moonlight glaring on the snow didn't help any. But it looked like two figures were heading his way, and mighty quick at that. Quick as the snow would let them, anyway.

Cy leveled the barrel at the wolf's head again.

"Halt!"

A different voice this time. Closer, too. In fact, it sounded like the funny accented word was right in his ear. Cy looked back up the clearing, but the two figures were still only halfway across. *"Halt!* Stop, I command you!"

Cy shook his head. He lowered the gun, squinting at the two figures drawing closer.

But then another sound drifted across the clearing, and it sent a chill right down his back and into his toes.

A wolf's howl. Answered by another, and then another. Soon enough, he saw three dark shapes, low to the ground and loping at full speed, kicking up sprays of white powder behind them. The animal groveling at his feet let out a hopeful whimper.

Three wolves. Two big ones leading the way.

Cy raised the gun again, but this time he aimed straight up across the clearing. Damn it all if it wasn't Johnny Vestal's girl, and by the looks of it, that other slut she was shacked up with now, both of them tumbling across the snowdrifts, and chased by three wolves, seemed like.

He clutched the Remington tighter and sneered. Serve the two whores right if he just left them for dinner for the wolves. "You girlies better hightail it over behind me here," Cy hollered. "Before them devils run you down. Ain't gonna be a pretty sight here in a couple seconds."

Carmilla made it first. She skidded to a stop a few feet in front of Houlder. He forgot about the wolf twisting and whining at his feet, and gazed at her long black hair blowing in the wind, pictured his grimy fingers running through it. Cy's belly did a couple flipflops. He felt his mouth water.

"Prinzessen!" Carmilla plunged to her knees beside the wolf and cradled it in her arms. The animal coughed up blood onto the snow.

"Back off, honey," Cy said. "That devil may be trapped, but it could still tear your arm off. Better let me finish it off." Cy aimed his shotgun at *Prinzessen's* head.

Carmilla glared at the old man. Must be a trick of the light, Cy figured, but for a second he thought her eyes flashed red just like stoplights. A low growl rumbled deep down in Carmilla's throat. But Cy never noticed it over the wolf's whining.

"Carmilla!" Lauren just made it, stumbling through the deep drifts.

Behind them, the pack was no more than fifty yards away now, and bearing down on them fast.

Carmilla stood up and approached Cy Houlder. "Little men with guns. Pathetic little men with wrinkled old wicks gone dry, men that have to torture magnificent creatures, have to kill what they cannot be, cannot have, cannot understand."

Cy took a step backwards. "Now you just back away, sweetheart, or you're gonna get yourself hurt too." No mistaking it now, that girl's eyes were glowing red, or he was snowblind. Cy looked to Lauren. "You tell your friend to back off, or she's gonna get hurt."

"Carmilla, lets –"

Just then the three wolves approached. One glance from Carmilla, and they halted a few yards back. Their eyes burned green with hatred. The Queen Mother growled when she saw *Prinzessen* struggling in the trap.

Cy swung the gun up from *Prinzessen* to Carmilla, then across to the wolf pack, then back down to *Prinzessen* again. "What the – what the hell are you, girly?"

"More than you'll ever know, old man." Carmilla pointed down at *Prinzessen*. "You did this?"

"Yeah. So?"

"And now that you've watched her suffer and cry with pain, you mean to shoot her?"

"Yeah, I'm gonna shoot that little...what's it to you?"

"I think not." Carmilla stepped forward.

But too late.

Cy tugged at the rusty trigger and the shotgun went off. A hundred count of tiny lead pellets blasted into *Prinzessen's* face, ripping the fur right off her head and spinning her body completely around. She let out a short yelp, and then lay still, panting.

Cy pumped the shotgun again and raised it to Carmilla. Behind them, the three wolves poised to leap. *"Halt!"* she commanded, and the wolves stopped.

"Now you just back your skinny little ass out of here, girly," Cy said. "There's a big ol' magnum slug loaded up now, and it'd tear a hole the size of your honeypot right smack in the middle of your pretty little head. I'd hate to put it there, I really would. Much rather shoot that little wolf you're all fired up over. But I'll take you down without blinking an eye, count on it."

Lauren climbed across the snow to *Prinzessen's* panting body. "Oh, Carmilla, she's dying. She's dying." The wolf gurgled a little. Behind them, the Queen Mother whined.

Cy slowly inched the gun away from Carmilla, and pointed it at the trapped wolf. "Back away now, Laurie girl, or your gonna get yourself hurt."

"Don't do it, Mr. Houlder," Lauren begged. "Maybe we can still –"

The loud blast of a magnum shell knocked her on her seat. Prinzessen jumped, and then lay still – a big red hole ripped through her body, smoking blue around the edges with the smell of burnt fur.

Lauren's ears rang from the shotgun blast. The slug had whizzed bare inches from her face.

Carmilla lunged, but Cy's old frame nimbly outdid itself. He dodged her and pumped another shell in the chamber all in one swift motion. Leaping over the dead wolf, he brought the gun up again, pointing the smoking barrel straight at Carmilla's chest.

"I'm not screwing around here. You ladies get your asses out of here and let a man do his job." Cy cradled the stock under his arm, but still kept it aimed at Carmilla as best he could. He shoved *Prinzessen's* carcass aside and slammed his foot on the trap's trip plate. The steel jaws pried open, and the wolf's leg plopped on the bloodied snow. Cy dragged the body out of the trap.

"I mean it, you two," he said. "Get the hell out of here."

Lauren wiped a tear from her eye and stepped away from *Prinzessen* and the vicious looking trap. "Carmilla, come on, let's do what he says. Let's just get out of here."

But the girl didn't move.

"Carmilla, please. Let's –"

Carmilla spun around, and the look on that white face froze the words right in Lauren's throat. Those dark eyes glowed, burned a fiery red, and no tricks of the light this time. Red lips curled back over her gums, showing jaws clenched in fury and grinding together, two menacing looking fangs protruding over the other teeth. She snarled at Lauren and shoved her aside.

Carmilla took a step towards old Houlder.

A twelve gauge's heft breeds confidence. Bravado even, especially when it's trained on a trapped animal or pointed at a little wisp of a girl, no matter what kind of tricks the moonlight played on her eyes. Cy stiffened as Carmilla approached, but she just kept coming. He took half a step backwards.

"Son-of-a-" the old man started to mutter, but he never finished the curse.

He took that half a step – just half a step.

Half a step back and right onto the opened jaws of his own steel trap.

They shut with a *clang*, slicing right through his old boots and snapping bones like dry branches.

Cy screamed bloody murder. "Get it off! Oh my God, get it off of me!"

A dark stain spread out on his pants and dribbled over onto the rusty edge of the trap's serrated teeth. A thick coppery smell filled the air.

It made Lauren's stomach turn butterflies.

It made the three wolves edgy, made their noses twitch and their mouths salivate.

It made Carmilla's dark eyes glow even brighter. She darted her tongue out and licked the edge of her red lips.

Cy flailed at the trap with one hand, the other still clinging to his gun. "Sweet Jesus, get it off! Please, please pull it off of me!"

Carmilla's sneer softened. Her lips eased back down over her gums, curving into a malicious smile. But those two white fangs still glistened in the half-moonlight.

Lauren stood by, absolutely frozen in fear. The three wolves were growling on one side, ready to spring. Cy Houlder screamed away and his shotgun waved wildly in the air. Carmilla drew closer to him...her face, her eyes, those teeth...

"Jesus Christ, get this goddamned thing off of my leg!" Cy just kept on screaming. He kicked at the trap, but that only made the vise-like jaws cut deeper into his leg. Pain clouded his eyes, but he could still see Carmilla approaching, and she had a greedy smile plastered on her face.

"Yeah, that's right, come on bitch. Goddamned she-devil, come on!" He hefted the shotgun up, stuck his finger back in the trigger and started to squeeze.

"No!" Lauren shouted. Fear vanished. She jumped across *Prinzessen's* body and lunged for the gun. The shot rang out just as she made contact.

But it was enough. Lauren knocked the barrel away, and the blast missed Carmilla by a mile.

Carmilla grabbed the shotgun and tore it out of Cy's hands. The old man watched wide-eyed while she smashed the twelve gauge over her knee. With the smell of cordite still hovering in the air, she flung the bent barrel one way, the pump and stock another. The last two shells tumbled out of the magazine and disappeared into the snow.

"Carmilla, come on!" Lauren shouted. "Let's get out of here, now!" She grabbed Carmilla's hand and tugged. "I mean it, Carmilla. Now!"

"Of course, Lauren. We can go now."

"Wait!" Cy screamed. "You can't leave me here."

Carmilla stopped and turned back. "And why not, old man?"

"Don't leave me like this. I'll freeze to death out here."

"I hardly think so."

"Jesus Christ, you gotta help me. I'm gonna freeze to death."

Carmilla took Lauren's hand and walked away across the snow. "No, I don't think you'll freeze to death, old man," she called back. But I do think *Prinzessen's* family here would like a word with you."

Cy stopped struggling for a moment.

"Carmilla – no!" Lauren cried.

Carmilla's eyes narrowed. She turned to the anxious wolves pawing the snow a few feet away from Houlder. The Queen Mother looked deep into Carmilla's eyes.

The words came from deep down in Carmilla's throat, low, commanding and malevolent. *"Toten ihn,"* it sounded like to Lauren.

The wolves understood clearly.

"Kill him," she'd said.

Carmilla dragged Lauren through the snow with her.

The wolves stood up and approached Cy. "N-no," was all he managed. *Die Konigen* made the first lunge for Cy's flailing arm.

"No! N-no-no-no," he screamed, over and over again. *Der Konig* leaped right on top of Cy's chest, and growled into the old man's face, then bit into his shoulder. *Der Prinz* sank his long canines into Cy's thigh, his powerful jaws shredding flesh and snapping the bone.

The old man waited for the searing pain to knock him unconscious. That's what he'd always supposed. That you went into shock – that your body took over and knocked you out, because the pain was just too much to endure.

He'd been cruelly misinformed.

Die Konigen looked up into Cy's crazed eyes, blood smeared across her muzzle. The Queen bared her long fangs, tore aside Cy's jacket, and dug her teeth into his pulsing belly.

Cy had been misinformed, alright.

He was wide awake and feeling each and every bite while the Queen wrestled her snout inside his guts, her head haloed in the steam rising out of his own warm, wet insides.

Carmilla dragged Lauren across the clearing, back towards the woods and the lodge. Screams echoed across the snow and bounced off the trees as they disappeared into the night.

"No! For the love of God, No..."

CHAPTER TWENTY

Lauren couldn't keep up with Carmilla for much longer. Evergreen boughs slapped her face, her boots filled with snow and her mittens fell off as they clawed through the drifts. But there was no stopping. Carmilla's grip never loosened.

"Stop, Carmilla. Please, I can't make it any further." They rolled over one last, tall drift and suddenly burst out of the trees. Birch Lake churned noisily on their right. Up ahead, wind blown snow was painted bright yellow in front of the lodge.

The lodge was lit up. Warm light spilled out of the windows.

"Carmilla, the lights! The power must be on. Maybe the phones are working. We can call for help."

Lauren's legs finally gave out halfway across the lawn. But just as she slid into the snow, Carmilla scooped her up in her arms, and they glided across the drifts, past Lauren's buried Escort, right up the porch and inside.

Lauren stumbled into the living room. "Got to get help, got to get help. Maybe they can still save him, maybe..." She grabbed the phone and frantically punched buttons. "Paramedics. That's what we need. Maybe they can still do something. Got to..." She kept on punching the buttons, harder and harder.

But there was no answer.

"Come on. Come on, answer, damn it. Someone answer the phone!" Hysterical tears started to roll down her cheeks. "Someone, please." Her fingers pounded the buttons. "Answer, damn it. Answer!"

"Lauren —"

"Someone has to save him, someone has to..."

"Put the phone down, Lauren."

"No, we've got to do something. The power's on. So the phones have to work too. The phones *have* to work."

Carmilla tried to draw Lauren into her arms.

"No, Carmilla, we have to –"

"Enough!" The word silenced Lauren, that always soothing voice losing its magic for just a moment.

"Enough now, Lauren." It was Carmilla's voice again, alluring, otherworldly and seductive. "Calm yourself, please. There's nothing you can do, you must know that." Carmilla unzipped her jacket and slipped the scarf off her neck. She stoked the living room fireplace back to life, though there was no more need. The baseboard heaters were clinking with heat and the room was warming already.

"But, Mr. Houlder. The wolves."

"The old man is quite dead by now, Lauren. I assure you. And deservedly so, in my opinion."

Lauren fell into the couch and just sat there, a limp bundle dripping melting snow. Carmilla sat down beside her, helping Lauren off with her jacket and her boots.

"How can you say that?" Lauren asked. "Who are *you* to say that? I know he was a sleaze, but –"

"*Prinzessen.* Majestic, beautiful *Prinzessen.* Carmilla pulled Lauren's legs into her lap. She bushed the snow off Lauren's socks, massaged her cold feet. "Poisoned, tortured – for what? For a pelt? For sport? For food, I would understand. But not petty meanness."

Lauren pulled her legs off Carmilla's lap and leaped off the couch. "Who are you to pass judgment?" She crossed the room. "Who are you to say who lives – who dies?"

The words seemed to hit home. "A very fair question, to be sure. A moral dilemma for anyone." Carmilla slipped off the couch and approached, but Lauren scooted away and stood by the window.

"Lauren, I am weary. Weary to the bone of mortal man's petty, venal little evils."

"Carmilla, *what* are you?"

"Lauren?"

"You heard me. What are you? How could you find those wolves like you did? How could you – *talk* to them? Was I just dreaming out there? Or did this all really happen? Your face – Carmilla, your face. Your eyes...they burned, they – your teeth..."

"Lauren, I –"

"You broke that shotgun like it was a toy. You carried me across the snow like I was a ragdoll. You told those wolves to kill Houlder. You *commanded* it."

"Yes. Yes, I did. I have a sort of – affinity for certain animals. Not all animals, mind you. Just the truly wild. The predators. We have a... a kinship, you might say."

"Carmilla, tell me. Please. What are you?"

Carmilla approached again, and this time Lauren didn't run away. She wrapped her arms around Lauren's waist. Her pale face drew close, and those hypnotic eyes bored deep into Lauren's. "Are you really certain you want to know?"

For Lauren, everything became a blur then.

There was a kiss by the window, just a quick, friendly brush of skin.

But then there was another, with voodoo eyes and ruby lips that were, all at once, icy cool and burning hot on hers, and a soft, velvety tongue probing insistently at her mouth.

Then they weren't at the window anymore, but on the couch, and the kisses were passionate, sexual, and Lauren could feel her whole body tingling, feel her nipples harden, feel the warmth flooding through her inside, feel the urgent moistness between her legs.

But suddenly, Carmilla pulled away and slid over to the other side of the couch.

"Carmilla, what's the matter? This *is* what you want, isn't it? This is what you've been after? So, you've won. Somehow, you've won. You've followed and stalked and seduced – and now you've won. I want you. I want to make love to you. I want to be with you."

Carmilla shook her head. "It's not that simple. It's more of a com-mitment than you suppose."

"Look, I don't know where this is going either. I'm not even sure why it's happening." Lauren reached over to the girl, but Carmilla slipped off the couch. "Anyway, it's *you* that's been doing the whole seduction number on me. So don't start playing coy now."

"I do not think you fully understand yet, Lauren."

"But –"

"One more night," Carmilla said. "One more night, to be certain. Absolutely sure that this is truly what you want. I couldn't bear your remorse."

～

Lauren woke up Thursday, sensing that it was still light out. With the curtains drawn tight over the window, her bedroom was still dark enough. That wasn't it. She just *felt* that it was still daytime. And after waking up in total darkness for two days now, it almost seemed unnatural.

But for some reason, it didn't seem unnatural to wake up naked in bed.

Or to feel Carmilla's cool, pale skin beside her under the blankets.

Carmilla still slept. Slept, that is, in her peculiar way: perfectly still, soundless, without a breath. Lauren gazed at the girl for quite awhile, wondering...wondering. Here, right now, lying close to her in the shadowy bedroom, everything was a dark and magical fairyland, where animals talked and day was night and words opened the door to some half-hidden otherworld. A world she wanted very much to step into, to discover just what lay beyond.

And outside would be daylight, and reality. There'd be Steve – that was nice. And Dad, too. There would be charge cards and paychecks and gas pumps and TV and checkout lines. Wristwatches and bus rides and rent and Bloomie's and Janah and lunchbreaks and timeclocks.

Lauren leaned over and kissed Carmilla's cool, unmoving lips. Then she slipped out of bed and padded off to the bathroom.

The shower was hot, deliciously, scalding hot, searing away Lauren's two day chill. The blow dryer whirring in her ear sounded like a rude intrusion in the quiet lodge. In her placid dreamworld.

But not nearly as intrusive as the phone ringing downstairs.

Lauren slipped on her robe and dashed out of the bathroom.

The phone was still ringing when she ran into the living room. She stopped a foot away and just stared at it. For three nights she prayed to hear that reassuring sound. Now, Lauren was almost afraid to pick the phone up.

But it kept on ringing.

"Hello?"

"Lauren, thank God, you're okay!"

"Steve?"

"I've been trying to get through to you since Monday night, but the phones have been out. Course, you know that. Lauren?"

"Yes?"

"Lauren, are you okay? You sound funny. Is everything alright there?"

"I'm – I'm fine, Steve. Really. Thanks for calling." Lauren started to hang up.

"Wait a minute! Are you sure you're alright? Did you get in okay Monday night? I mean, the storm and all."

"Sure, Steve. I got back fine. No problem."

"I wanted to check in on you. But I couldn't get my snowmobile working, and there just wasn't any way to get around till today. Then I was stuck up at the trout hatchery since yesterday morning. The storm almost ruined all of the tanks. But, boy, am I glad to hear you're okay."

Lauren was listening, but not really hearing him.

"I talked to your father this morning."

"Oh?"

"Yeah, he was pretty worried. He'd been trying to get through to you too. He heard about the storm and all."

"That's nice, Steve." Lauren clenched her fist. She didn't want this right now.

She wanted...

"Lauren, you don't *sound* okay. Are you sure –"

"Yes, Steve. I'm fine. Really."

"Well, look. I'm just about done here at the hatchery. I'll be hitching a ride back home pretty soon. Most of the roads are plowed now. Have the plows been through there yet?"

"Plows? I don't know." She looked out the living room window and saw water dripping off the eaves. A late afternoon sun reflected off the waves on Birch Lake. The mounds of snow were melting. "No, I don't think so."

"Well, they should have been. They may not have gone all the way into your place, but the crews know about old Cy's shack, and they always dig him out."

Hearing Cy Houlder's name jolted Lauren. "Steve, about Mr. Houlder..."

"What, Lauren? Has he been bothering you?"

"No. No, it's not that. Just...nothing." Lauren thought about the Garden of Eden. About a serpent tempting Eve. She thought about crossing a threshold, and the door slamming shut and locking tight behind her.

"Oh, old Cy's alright," Steve said. He's been through plenty of snowstorms. Though no one was really prepared for this one. So early in the season and all. But I hear a new front is moving in. Could be back to sixty degrees in a day or two."

Lauren had nothing to say. She was thinking about Carmilla, lying softly, palely naked in her bedroom upstairs. She was picturing Carmilla in the clearing last night, with that white face contorted in rage, and those eyes glowing. She was hearing Cy Houlder's desperate screams, and the wolfpack's growls.

"Lauren? Lauren, are you still there?"

"Yes, Steve. I'm here. Look, I really can't talk right now."

"Oh." His disappointment was audible and it came right through the phone line and washed all over her ears. "Well, I was thinking that once I got home and cleaned up, maybe I could give Birch Lake Road a try in the old Cherokee. It might make it."

"Steve, I don't think –"

"Or I could borrow one of my friend's snowmobiles. Then I could –"

"No, Steve. Not tonight. I have a lot on my mind. I have to go."

"Go?"

"Steve, thanks a lot for checking in on me, but maybe another night."

"You'll be heading home in a couple of days, won't you? This damn storm ate up a whole big bunch of your vacation. Of our chance to get – reacquainted. I was kind of thinking we could pick up where we left off. I thought..."

But it was like another voice rang all crystalline and wind-chimey inside Lauren's head, calling her name, crowding out everything else. "Steve, I can't think about that right now. I have to go, really."

"Lauren –"

"Please, Steve. Don't come here. I *have* to go now. Bye."

She hung up the phone.

Lauren's stomach tied up in knots. A cold sweat broke out on her forehead. She just blew him off. How could she...

Lauren pulled the robe snug around her. Suddenly, the lodge didn't seem quite so cozy. The real world beckoned, and it didn't seem all *that* humdrum. For a moment, at least, it seemed reassuringly normal, and human.

She headed upstairs.

The dim, late-afternoon light still seeping through the windows was fading fast. Lauren tiptoed past her bedroom. There wasn't a sound from inside. Carmilla was still asleep.

She backtracked down the hall to her parents' room, where she'd left Carmilla that first night. Inside, Lauren flicked on the dresser lamp.

Something looked funny there, something was missing.

The mirror was gone.

She looked around and found the mirror behind the dresser. Looked around some more, saw Carmilla's bag, and emptied it out on the bed. It was as good a way as any to learn something about her peculiar 'guest'.

But the pile on the bed didn't provide any answers, just more questions.

At first.

There were clothes: jeans, shirts, leggings, socks, underwear. There was that same sweater, the one Carmilla tried on in Bloomingdale's last week. It was crumpled up in a ball, and stained with dark, reddish dots across the front.

There was money, lots of it, all wadded up in rolls or crumpled like trash. Lauren counted out four thousand U.S. dollars, gave up, and still there was more. Deutschemarks, Polish Zlowtys, Austrian schillings, some of it obviously very old.

She looked over her shoulder, held her breath and listened. Other than the occasional clank from the baseboard heaters, the lodge was silent. Carmilla must still be sleeping. *Of course Carmilla's sleeping, the sun's still...*

Lauren pushed the thought out of her head before she could finish it.

She opened a black velvet pouch and spilled out a handful of diamonds and gems on the bedspread.

There were several passports, each with a different name, each with a photo of a pretty, dark haired girl, but none of them were actually Carmilla. They looked *like* her, but weren't her.

Pencils, pens, sunglasses, loose change, a pink stuffed bunny. Some dog-eared romance paperbacks. Lauren pawed through the pile and pulled out an old hardcover book, its spine cracked, its pages yellowed, the cover worn and faded: '*In A Glass Darkly*', she could just make out the title. But her eyes were drawn more to the peculiar bookmark: a black handled knife nearly a foot long. She cracked open the book, and a musty, mildewed aroma made her nose wrinkle. There was something written on the flyleaf in a fancy, old fashioned penscript, but it was even more faded than the cover.

She set the book down, her head spinning, her eyes still on that lethal looking dagger, till they settled on three slender, shrink-wrapped packages, Bloomingdale's logos on each one. Last Thursday evening came reeling back – the store, Carmilla, her sunglasses, her creepy smile, slipping these three packages of nylons inside her jacket and sauntering off.

Lauren massaged her temples, her head spinning. She didn't know what she expected to find, but there were no answers here, just riddles and mysteries. She scanned Carmilla's things then glanced over her shoulder to the bedroom door. The hallway looked darker now.

But there was one more item.

A spiral bound notebook, the cover plastered with stickers and doodling. The pages were wrinkled and waterlogged, probably from spilling out in the snow Monday night...Tuesday morning, that is. It looked like some kind of journal. A diary, maybe? Carmilla's?

Lauren shoved the black bag over to the end of the bed, pulled her robe tighter and flipped through the notebook. The first few pages appeared to be written with a marker, and had bled into a crazy, watercolor mess. She flipped some more, till she found some pages that hadn't washed away, and started to read.

With each word, a cold, clammy sweat rose on her skin.

With each line, her fingers started to tremble.

With each page, it became increasingly clear. She was holding someone's last testament.

She was reading the diary of a dead girl.

She was reading Barabara Clovicky's diary.

CHAPTER TWENTY ONE

Colonel!

The man actually expects me to call him Colonel! It's like living with Hitler, for Chrissakes. "Clean your room, go back to school, get a job. Are you drunk again, Barbara?" No, you old fart, I'm not drunk, I'm stoned. I'm dusted. Go croak, will you?

God, I've got to get out of this house.

The next few pages were all smeared ink and water-wrinkled paper. Lauren looked up from the notebook, looked over her shoulder at the door, looked at the window where the late afternoon sun barely lit up the water dripping off of icicles on the eaves.

Her mind raced – why would Carmilla have Barbara Clovicky's diary? Why, unless...

...and that's why I couldn't get into Black Sunday's again, fake I.D.'s or not. But if blowing the bouncer in the john was the only way, then fine. Hell, he gave me some 'blow' of his for free, since he said I did him so good, and I could count on getting in anytime I wanted from now on. As long as I was up for sucking off that fat little stump of his. Sure, whatever.

August 17

Tried all the Rush Street joints, but of course I couldn't get in. But who cares, those places are all just stupid yuppie scum. Right, like I'm gonna shake my ass on lighted dance floors and chug margheritas with some junior stock broker. Sure. Done it, been there. All the chicks are just duked up like Mademoiselle magazine 'Hey-Don't-You-Think-I-Look-Just-Like-Julia-Roberts', puh-leeeze. And they're all just secretaries and two-bit clerks in the department stores anyway. Like that goodie two shoes Lauren Vestal bitch.

Die slut, will you just please?

I remember when the Colonel had her old man send her over. Trying to set a good example, I suppose. There she is with this fancy-ass college degree – no, two – and what the hell is she doing? Spraying perfume or selling purses or panty hose or something at Bloomingdales. Oh, cool, huh?

Hit Metro tonight, and then went to La Mere Vipere. Blew a joint in the alley before I went in. Put an extra twenty on top of the cover charge, so of course the doorman let me in. Money talks, no B.S about I.D.'s. Knocked back the last of my coke in the can. Hard to focus there, because two butches were going down on each other in the next stall. With all that whiz and toilet paper and barf on the floor, and they're doing the tongue polka. Sweet.

But I saw her again.

HER!

This is the third time!

Her?

Lauren shuddered.

September 2

Two nights now, she's come home with me.

At first she brushed me off. Too cool, real attitude. I'd always see her hanging out in the corners of the clubs, like where it's real dark. All by herself, mostly. Guys were always trying to put the moves on her. Chicks too, lots of those tattooed muscle-bound bitches were always hanging around her. But mostly, she just blew them off, just shooed them away like flies, man. Too god-damned cool for words.

So who thought she'd actually want to talk to me? Who thought she'd let me sit at her table, or hang with her by the bar?

We just talked and talked almost till morning, listening to all my Cure CD's, my Souxie And The Banshees, and Bauhaus. You know, for someone so cool and obviously into the whole goth thing (I mean, she's got to be, right? That whole pasty face-black hair-dark eyeliner scene) she's really not very up on music. That's weird, isn't it?

September 6

Dear Diary – screw you. Who has time to write anymore?

It's like she's moved in with me, right here in my room. Well, sort of. It's only been a few nights, so far. But she's staying. Well – not really. She does disappear sometimes. During the night. And she has been gone all day a couple times. And she's like totally screwed up about some things, keeping the room dark and not bothering her when we sleep. But if it works for her, I'm game.

And, we did it.

I mean IT.

Or should I be saying, IT happened. Let's face it, I've had just about every kind of sex you could imagine. Some even I couldn't imagine. But it was just like – 'sex', you know. I mean, nothing happened, nothing good, that is.

Anyway, I usually do it for a good reason, it's not like I'm a slut, like really loving it, ooh-ooh-baby-give-mama-some-more. So maybe I didn't always get off...OK, maybe I NEVER got off...but it didn't always feel bad. OK, sometimes it did feel bad. But screw that, I always got something out of it. Tickets, or a ride, or some booze or some blow. Something.

But if I'd known it could feel like this...

I guessed she liked girls. You could tell. I mean, I've seen her with guys too, but I just guessed she dug girls more. So she's doing this kissy face stuff with me, and I'm just going along for the ride because I want to hang with her and all. But then she starts to do me. And at first I didn't want to bother, not my scene. But then I got off. I came, and I never ever ever felt anything like that before. And I came again and again. God, it was just unbelievable.

September 9

Night after night, it's almost too much for me. We go out half the night drinking and partying, and then come back to my room and just ball all night. She's loves to party, just won't do anything hard. Absolutely no drugs, that's for sure. Which is kind of a drag. And drinking, well – let's just say I can drink her under a table. But that's cool, I don't care.

The Colonel is getting unbearable. Definitely does not dig having a houseguest.

Screw him.

September 15

She's not natural. Not human, man. Not even close.

I shouldn't be surprised, should I? Isn't that why I was following her around in the clubs, trying to talk to her? Because I knew back then that there was something different about her? But she's like every death-metal-video-chick slasher-flick-madonna in the flesh. For real. It's not just the goofy way she talks. At first I thought that was maybe some kind of act or something. I mean, a lot of hip-wanna-be's do that fake Euro-accent thing. Hell, I guess I've done it too. I mean, it's one way to try to cover up the fact that I'm just plain old Barbara Clovicky, drippy nobody who lives with her creepy old uncle in the boonies.

But with her, no man – it's real. She really is from Europe. Austria, she says. Like Germany, I guess. But there's more.

I don't know how to put it into words. She's so positively goddamned beautiful that everyone is happy to follow her around like some panting dog. Hell, I am. Maybe it's her eyes, like she's wearing some kind of secret agent hypno-mascara.

Now this sleep all day, party all night thing – don't get me wrong, that's more or less my schedule too. But I mean, MORE OR LESS, not all the goddamned time. She's really into it. It's kind of cool, kind of scary. Sometimes I think I should ask her to leave. Maybe my uncle is – NO, that's too weird to even contemplate. Like he could be right on ANYTHING.'

The next few pages were stuck together and mostly unreadable. Lauren traced the washed-away writing with her finger, pausing over patches with the words intact. '*...yeah, now I'm wise. Now I think I know what she...'* Then, '*...could it be? Could it really be? The very thing that every one of those arrogant snob son of a bitchin' pretend artists and yeah-baby-I'm-in-a-band types that I've been doing my goddamned best to be friends with – the very thing that every last one of them would think is the absolute most coolest thing in the world is exactly what I've got hanging with me...'*

Two pages later, the only words Lauren could decipher: '*...it happened. No joke. She's for real, and it happened...'*

September 30
She MUST love me like I love her. She never takes too much. She could, if she wanted too. Hell, I want her to take it all. Drink me dry, drink it all, please, please, please, please.

It's gotten so I can't think about anything else.

October 2
The Colonel is getting to be a real problem. He won't let up. Wants her out. Right, like I could make HER leave. Like anyone could make her do anything she doesn't want to.

But this really shouldn't be a problem, should it? I bet she could take care of him. I just bet.

October 5
She did it again goddamn it!.
We were laying in bed talking after I let her drink from me, and she turned the conversation around. Again! Made me talk about that prissy bitch again.

She thinks she's so smart. Thinks with that magic voice of hers that I can't tell when she's manipulating me, but I can.

Why does she keep asking me about Lauren Vestal?

But I know, it's all my fault. That night we grabbed the Colonel's boring-mobile and went cruising downtown, and I had to pull that bone-headed stunt, popping into Bloomie's. Stupid, stupid, stupid, stupid!!!!

I had to show off, didn't I? I'm gonna be Ms. Cool and pocket some stuff. But she didn't care. Didn't even notice. And I stole the stuff for HER!

Then I remembered that stuck up Vestal wimp worked there. So I scouted around and saw her. She didn't see us. At least, I don't think she saw us. Knowing her, she probably would have called security and had us thrown out or something. Lauren really would have called them if she knew I had a couple hundred dollars of perfume jammed down my pants.

And there was Lauren, all dressed up clean and proper and nice, straightening up some sweaters behind a counter. Now there's a real impressive career, right? Minimum wage, and waiting on all these arrogant north shore bitches. No thank you. Hell, I made more in one minute swiping that perfume than she probably made all week.

But when SHE saw Lauren, something happened.

She took her sunglasses off and just stared and stared. I practically had to drag her out of the store. Then all that night she's pestering me about Lauren.

I told her, forget the bitch, she's not for you. Regular straight arrow, all good grades and obey the speed limits and pay your rent on time. Daddy's little girl. But there was no stopping her. She just kept on me about Lauren, and what can I say? When SHE wants to know something, you don't just say 'No'. You answer, whether you want to or not.

Why is she so interested in that bitch? That Lauren's a nothing, a big boring old zero, if you ask me. Why?

October 7

I must really be coming down with something. I can hardly get out of bed. And she's not even around today. Bolted off somewhere just before dawn, and didn't come back. She better come back tonight, after sunset. She better be knocking on my door.

I'm looking in the mirror right now. My teeth still look the same. And I still have a reflection. I asked her about that, like when would I start changing? And she just laughed. Laughed right in my face. Said it doesn't work like that. Okay, so how does it work? I want to be like her. Just like her, forever and ever.

But when I prodded her about the changing, she got all honked off, just wouldn't talk about it anymore. Told me I couldn't possibly know what I was talking about. Not to ever bring it up again.

Man, oh man, I hope she comes back tonight. I'll just kill myself if I scared her off. Maybe I was acting too possessive? How would I know, I'm no good at this relationship stuff. I never really had one. Not a real one.

Anyway, with guys it's a lot easier. If they get all pissy on you, you just stick your hands down their pants, and they're happy. They'll give you anything you want.

God, I hope she comes back tonight.

God? Right, like he's listening to me. He's probably just jealous anyway. Probably all pissed off that something so beautiful exists that He didn't make. And that's she's mine.

Carmilla!!! Please come back tonight, Carmilla!!!!!!

The notebook fell right out of Lauren's hands.

Carmilla.

The name just screamed right off the page. *Carmilla.* The entire time she was reading Barbara's diary, the back of her mind kept telling her – telling her precisely what she refused to admit.

Barbara was writing about Carmilla the whole time.

No, this was impossible. Lauren shoved the notebook away, and looked across the room to the window. The sunlight was gone. The sky was all violet and going dark.

Maybe *everything* was a dream, she thought. Every little bit of it – Carmilla, the snowstorm, the accident, the wolves, Cy Houlder, everything. Maybe if she closed her eyes real tight and wished real hard, she could wake up in her own room, back in her apartment, or behind her sweater counter at Bloomie's. No more walking nightmares, no glowing eyes, no sultry, seductive voices.

No diaries from dead girls.

"Lauren?"

That magical voice. And directly behind her.

Lauren screamed.

CHAPTER TWENTY TWO

"Lauren, what is the matter?"

And there was Carmilla.

There she was, standing by the bedroom door, that dark eyed angel, gleaming in her pale nakedness, all malignant perfection with her long, dark hair dangling around her face, all sin and artistry with those ruby lips, with those opal eyes, with that curious black choker and its red cameo circling her slender neck.

Lauren backed across the bed, slamming into the headboard.

"What are you doing, Lauren?"

"I – I was just –"

"It's all right. Please don't be afraid." Carmilla sat down on the bed, and Lauren tried to slide further away.

"Carmilla – this stuff – all this money, these jewels, the passports. What's it all mean?"

"Mean? They mean...nothing. These are my things. I don't have much, as you can see. Only what I can carry with me."

"But what are you doing with this diary? Is it for real? Or is everything about you just a bad dream?"

Carmilla leaned over and picked up the notebook. She scanned the page Lauren stopped on. "Oh, it's quite real. You've read it?"

"Some."

"Quite depressing, no?" Carmilla flipped through the pages. "I see it's almost ruined. The snow, I suppose."

"Why do you have it at all?" Lauren shouted. "She's dead. Barbara Clovicky is dead! So what are you doing with this thing?"

"If you read it, Lauren, why would you even ask?"

"What *are* you?"

"So, you haven't finished it then? No, you didn't say that you had. Then let me finish it for you."

"Don't," Lauren said, shaking her head. "I don't want to hear..."

"Oh yes, you do. You know that you do."

"*October 8*", Carmilla began. She read slowly. Her accent was more pronounced, more deliberate than usual while she struggled with Barbara Clovicky's spider scrawl.

"*...This is no good. No good at all. She didn't come back last night. What am I going to do?*

She knows perfectly well that I'm leaving soon, and there's no getting out of it. The Colonel's dragging me up to that shack in Michigan. He made it real clear that I'm coming even if he has to lock me in the trunk.

I could stomach that old Mr. Vestal, he's harmless, I guess. But smarmy ass Lauren'll be there, and I don't want to be stuck up there with that bitch. I don't know how, but I absolutely have to get out of this..."

Carmilla looked up from the notebook. "She doesn't seem to have liked you very much, Lauren. I wonder why."

"*October 10*
She came back!

But something's changed. She was, like, way cold. I don't mean to touch, she's always cold that way. No, she was like really cold to me.

I was all over her, but she just pushed me away. Didn't want to ball, didn't want anything. I'm like 'Here, come on, take me, goddamn it! I'll slit my wrists for you, I'll slice my fucking throat for you, just drink! Drink, or I'll kill myself.'

But she was just ice, man, total ice. Just sat there shaking her head. Then she started to cry."

Carmilla paused. "The rest is rather grim. And especially difficult to decipher. There are no more dates on her entries.

"*...I'm so dusted. I can hardly get off the bed. The Colonel came in a little while ago, raising holy hell, but I threw a bottle of gin at him. Just missed his ugly old head. Damn, that was stupid. I could go for a drink right now.*

She hasn't come back. I don't think she'll ever come back now. I wish I was dead..."

"*...Screw that graveyard bitch! Maybe I WILL just slit my wrists. Bet she'd be lapping it up if she could. She'd be sorry. Sooooo sorry.*

But I can play games too. I bet the cops would just love to hear about her.

That'd take care of her nice and neat, the stingy bitch..."

"...I wonder where she sleeps when she's not here? Man, if she's already got that sweet-meat Laurie Vestal bitch shacking up with her in some cemetery I'll do them both. I swear I'll slice and dice Vestal into blood 'n guts confetti..."

"...I'm getting sick, I've been crying so much. Man, it hurts. It hurts so bad. If I knew loving somebody could hurt so bad, I never...
The Colonel's out. At least I don't have him badgering me. Screw him, I wish he would just go away and die. I need her, man. I need her so bad. So why is she holding out on me? Why?
Wait! There's someone downstairs.
There's someone coming up.
Could it be? Oh, Carmilla, please, please, please let it be you. Come through that door and take me away from all of this shit. Come back to me and make everything like I thought it would be.
Please, Carmilla, please..."

Carmilla set the notebook down on the bed. "That is the last entry." She slid off the bed and paced around the room.

"That's it? Just like that," Lauren said. "And then what happened?"

Carmilla glared back at her. "You have to ask?"

"I want to hear it from you."

Carmilla glanced at Lauren, then turned away. She stopped by the window and peeked through the curtains.

"Carmilla, I want to hear it. Tell me."

"What happened then? Then she died."

"She 'died'," Lauren shot back sarcastically.

"Yes, Lauren. Barbara died."

"How?"

"Why must you ask?!" Carmilla spun around, her pale face twisted in anguish. "Why do you insist on asking things you already know? How did she die? I killed her, Lauren. I killed her!"

"How?"

"How do you think?" Carmilla screamed. Her white fingers clawed through her hair. "Could it really be? Could you really not know by now? Have I misjudged you that much?"

"How did you kill her?" Lauren persisted.

But Carmilla wouldn't answer. She looked back out the window, where the moonlight painted her nakedness a pallid blue.

And there she stood, unnaturally still.

"So, you're just not going to answer me?"

"You know the answer," Carmilla said, her voice low and cryptic. "But you refuse to acknowledge it." She opened the window and sniffed the air, stood there without saying anything for a long time. Finally, she said, "Do you believe in fate, Lauren? Do you believe in pre-determination? That the course of our lives has been preordained, and no matter what we may do, everything will follow along certain unavoidable paths, to unavoidable ends?"

Lauren felt the cold breeze sneak into the room. She hugged her robe tighter and tucked her feet under the blanket.

"I'm not trying to change the subject, Lauren. You see, pre-destination was a very popular belief in my time. It is a disturbing notion, if you pause to consider the implications." Carmilla turned around and leaned against the windowsill, the cold wind fluttering her hair into the drapery. "This is not idle, philosophizing. I've pondered this conundrum for ages, believe me.

"Mind you," she continued, "I don't say I've ever reached any conclusion. Yet, it is a vitally important issue. At least, it is for me. You see Lauren, it makes me question if God might actually be the cruelest of all beings in both heaven and earth. Think about it." Carmilla's dark eyes were deadly serious.

"If God knows all things that are, and were, and will yet be, then He also knows that the child still in its mother's womb will grow up to be a murderer. Yet, He suffers it to live. God knows such things, but still the thieves and the rapists and the killers are born. God created the loathsome diseases that ravage the body, He drives the cyclones and the droughts and the earthquakes."

Suddenly, Carmilla leaped across the room and landed on the edge of the bed, glaring at Lauren. "I'm talking about fate. About *doom*. You see, Barbara was doomed."

Lauren shook her head and inched away, trying to melt into the headboard. Carmilla leaned forward, one pale hand outstretched, but she didn't reach for Lauren. Instead, she reached between them and toyed with the pile of her own things, emptied from her black bag and spread out on the bed.

"She was utterly doomed, Lauren. Didn't God know eons ago, even before the earth and stars were born, that one day Barbara's mother would die, that her father would abandon her, that she would be taken in by an old man who was unable to raise her? Didn't God know that she would destroy herself in an orgy of sex and liquor and drugs?" Carmilla's fingers paused on one of the Bloomingdales packages buried in the pile of her clothes and money. She examined the shiny, shrinkwrapped carton, smiled, then sliced it open with one swift flick of her nail.

Two white stockings fluttered out, feathery, like wisps of fog.

Lauren cleared her throat. "But – Carmilla, Barbara Clovicky *didn't* self-destruct. You killed her." She watched the translucent nylons float down across Carmilla's wrist.

"Yes, Lauren, I did. But that's what makes the dilemma even more maddening. Didn't God also create me? Didn't He know that I would take Barbara's life?" Sitting there on the edge of the bed, she rolled one of the nylons up in her hands, dipped her foot inside, and slowly, very slowly, slid the stocking on, no whiter there than her already pale skin. "And if I hadn't, how much longer would Barbara have lived? How much more time had God already allotted her before a poisoned needle, or too much liquor, or a rusty blade in some back alley would have snuffed out her sad, useless life?"

Carmilla stretched out her leg and stroked the fabric, smoothing the stocking in place. Lauren watched, cheeks flushed, her breath steaming in the cold air, her eyes riveted on Carmilla's leg, her small foot, her tiny toes flexing under the nylon. She felt repulsed.

Felt queasy.

Felt warm.

She felt aroused.

"Lauren, to toy with these thoughts for one evening could be exasperating. But to wrestle with them for centuries is utter madness." Carmilla slowly slid a stocking on her other leg.

"How old are you, really?" Lauren asked. "Tell me the truth."

Carmilla flicked her hair away from her face and looked deep into Lauren's eyes.

"I was born in 1693."

Lauren gulped.

"I died when I was just a girl, really. In 1713, Lauren, many long years before this country you call home became a nation. I've roamed the world for nearly three hundred years."

Lauren started to tremble. She tried to back further away on the bed, but there was nowhere to go.

"No, precious, don't draw away from me," Carmilla said. "And please don't act surprised. I won't have it."

"Three hundred..." Lauren murmured. "You've lived for almost three hundred years."

"No, Lauren. I *lived* for some twenty years. Then I died. Since then?" Carmilla's dark eyes grew darker still. "*Lived* is not precisely correct. I'm not sure what is. But no, not 'lived'...not at all."

Lauren dragged her eyes away from Carmilla's pale legs. "Then, y-you are...you're...you *are* a vampire?" she said, revulsion oozing out of the word. "Is that it, Carmilla?" Revulsion. And intrigue. "You're a vampire?"

Carmilla appeared to ignored Lauren, evidently appraising the sparkle of the lamplight on her stockings.

"Carmilla? Look at me. Please tell me you're not. Laugh at me. Tell me I'm crazy for even saying anything so ridiculous. Tell me...you're not... a vampire."

"Oh, Lauren, but I am," Carmilla said, her head bowed, her hands clenched in her lap. "Of course I am."

Carmilla reached over and laid a cool hand on Lauren's. Their eyes locked. "I am. You knew I was. Your waking mind may not have wanted to accept it. But I think you knew all along, Lauren."

"No. No..." Lauren protested. But there was no conviction in her voice.

"Oh *yes*, Lauren. Yes. I can't read minds. But I *sense* many things, and I sensed much in you. Your heart and soul accepted all along what your logical, twentieth century mind would not. Oh, yes."

"No..."

"Yes. And I sensed more. Before we even met. Poor Barbara took me to that store, and there I saw you. I saw *you* that night, though you didn't see me. I knew then. I sensed your aching, your yearning for – *more*."

"More?"

"For 'more'. To me, it was as visible as the color of your eyes, the scent of your hair, the sound of your heart beating. A yearning for more, a longing for more than life could ever offer."

"No," Lauren said. "Now you're manipulating me again. You're just parroting back things I told you Tuesday night."

With that familiar, knowing smile, Carmilla shook her head. "I was *drawn* to you, Lauren. Drawn, because I sensed...a kinship. Yes, a genuine kindred spirit."

"Kindred spirit?" Lauren shot back. "Are you insane? *If* you are a... if you are what you say you are, if such a thing could even *be*, then it's certainly not me."

"Oh, really?"

"*Oh, really!* I could never be like you. I couldn't have taken Barbara

Clovicky's life. I wouldn't have let Mr. Houlder die. And that's the difference. I'll admit that all your witchy stuff has me hooked. But I'm human, Carmilla. And we don't kill."

Carmilla leapt forward and pinned Lauren against the headboard. "Lauren, if you could hear how naive you sound." A sneer curled the ends of her crimson lips. Her fangs gleamed there, all sharp and lethal, bare inches away.

"Never kill, Lauren? I watched your eyes when the wolves descended on the old man. I read fear in them, but I read more. Much more. I saw vindication, and sweet revenge."

"No –"

"Oh yes. Never kill, Lauren? Humans? See the death and torture and butchery that my eyes have seen, then you'd think otherwise." She grabbed Lauren's chin, squeezing harder as she spoke. "*Wampyr* were not riding in the vanguard of Napoleon's legions when they bled half of Europe dry. Wampyr didn't march a whole generation of the continent's youth into the bloody meatgrinder of The Great War, Wampyr didn't lock the iron doors on the gas chambers and the furnaces in the death camps. Wampyr didn't rain hellfire down on Warsaw or Rotterdam or London or Dresden. *Or* Hiroshima."

Her voice rose in anger. "Once my own era passed, I've mostly ignored the affairs of mankind. Politics, wars, news. But I know that Wampyr don't run rampant down the streets of your cities with guns and sharp knives, don't sell powdered poison to children. Or build terrifying engines of destruction, missiles and rockets and bombs that are almost beyond my ability to comprehend."

Indignation simmered in Carmilla's eyes. But then it faded, and she finally let go of Lauren's chin. Carmilla's whole body drooped. She leaned back, stared up at the ceiling, and just sighed again.

That sigh spoke volumes.

She slid off of Lauren. Crawled to edge of the bed, paused, then slowly headed for the bedroom door.

"No, Carmilla. Wait." Lauren jumped off the bed and grabbed the girl's hand. "What are you doing?"

"I was wrong to come here."

"Don't leave. Don't leave...*me*."

Carmilla looked back over her shoulder. "Lauren, you do know what you are saying. Do you truly understand the commitment you would have to make? It's more binding than any mortal vow. With no return. Lauren, if I stay –"

"Carmilla, please," Lauren whispered. "Please."
She pulled the vampire into her arms.

~

It commenced slowly, almost shyly, at first.

Lauren felt timid, even a little embarrassed. But she knew how magically cool and soft and good Carmilla felt beside her there on the bed, even though she wasn't sure of what to do.

But their lips met anyway, soft and velvety in the barest brush of a kiss. Carmilla shut off the nightstand lamp, drenching the room in moonlit darkness. Then she gently untied the sash on Lauren's robe, kissing her way down Lauren's shoulders, down her breasts, her belly, and lingering below. Lauren squirmed beneath her, pressing her body into those cold, red lips. She pressed herself against Carmilla's pale flesh, that immaculate, unblemished white skin painted lilac by the moonlight. She nuzzled into Carmilla's small breasts, nibbling at nipples colored an anemic pink, let her fingers wander down to the small tuft of darkness lurking between Carmilla's white thighs, and felt herself go all warm, and slick, all wet and eager when Carmilla's cool fingers fluttered between her legs. Lauren peeled her robe back further, then slipped it off altogether.

Carmilla's fragrance mingled with Lauren's, hovering around them with funereal scents of floral wreaths and fog, sticky sweet perfume and cemetery lawns. The vampire's nostrils flared. She sniffed the air and smiled.

A cool breeze still blew through the open window, licking at their skin as they clutched each other, as they twisted and tangled themselves in the sheets. The breeze was a cold whisper, just like their murmured sighs, just like the subtle, shimmery sounds of Carmilla's stockings sliding along Lauren's skin. Carmilla lifted Lauren's hair away from her neck and stroked her throat with those cold, cold fingers. Her dark eyes glimmered, from black to burgundy to fiery red.

She licked her lips.

Slowly, she lowered her head.

Two short, sharp fangs glinted in the moonlight. They poised just a breath away from Lauren's throat, where the pulse pounded beneath flushed skin, throbbing noisily in the quiet room, beating closer and closer to the needle point tips of Carmilla's teeth.

She kissed Lauren's throat, crimson lips on creamy skin, then pressed down, pressed harder, bit the soft flesh...

...And Lauren screamed.

It was a scream of pain.

A scream of pleasure.

A scream of surrender.

Rich, coppery aromas flooded the room. They flowed over Carmilla's hungry lips, filled her mouth and coursed down her throat with hot, red effervescence. And she drank.

She drank for a long time, her cool body clinging to Lauren's, their breasts pressed together, their hips grinding slowly, their legs coiled into knots. Lauren clutched the sheets in her hands and tugged at the blankets, squirming beneath the vampire, burying her head into the pillow and biting her lip because the pleasure was just too much, too intense, just too...

Finally, reluctantly, Carmilla pulled away and rolled over. Wet, red rivulets trickled down her chin and ran down her breasts. She looked deep into Lauren's eyes, past the arousal glazing them. Then Carmilla raised her own arm to her mouth, bared those bloodstained fangs again, and bit down on her wrist.

Blood bubbled out and dripped down her arm.

Lauren sat up in bed with a struggle. She took Carmilla's hand. Pulled that wet wound to her face.

She paused.

Some last indecision briefly crossed her face.

Just as quickly, it vanished.

Lauren pressed her lips to Carmilla's wrist.

She dabbed with her tongue at blood dribbling down Carmilla's pale arm.

Then she drank.

CHAPTER TWENTY THREE

"Want another, Steve?"

Steve Michaels picked away at the label on his beer, apparently lost in his own world. He looked up from the brown bottle. "No, I'm still working on this one, Nate." The foil paper was damp and mushy under Steve's fingers, and he continued to strip the label off the bottle. He'd been nursing the beer for half an hour.

Aside from Nate Stambaugh, who was loading cases of Stroh's into the cooler, The Moose's tap room was empty. Steve hadn't heard anyone puttering around in the market. And there wasn't much in the diner besides lunch's leftover grilled cheese and patty melt odors. Only two guys huddled over coffee cups at the counter.

Steve glanced at his watch. Four o'clock. Too early for the Friday after-work crowd, the good-time Charlies looking for a few shots before heading home to face the kids and the wife and a reheated plate of Hamburger Helper.

And that was just as well, since it looked like Nate was just about on his own today. And none too happy about it, by the way he grumbled to himself at the cooler door.

"Where's all the high priced help?" Steve asked, half regretting the question before he finished it. He wasn't really in the mood for conversation.

"Screw 'em, Steve. Screw 'em all."

"Dora's off?"

"Yep."

"Annie taking it easy?"

"Annie? Annie's taking it any way she can get it, if you ask me." Nate ambled off for another case out of the back, and Steve was happy to let him go.

He sipped his beer and made a sour face. It had gone flat long ago. Now it was warm too. He pushed it away.

"So what's with you anyway, Michaels?" Nate returned with another case for the cooler. "Old Cy pestering you about your wolves again?"

"No. I haven't seen Cy in days. Not since the storm hit, anyway."

Nate grabbed Steve's beer. "Gimme that thing. You're not drinking it anyway." He emptied the bottle in the metal sink behind the bar. "I'll get you a cup of coffee."

Nate returned with a steaming mug of his special short-on-help-days brew...hot, black mud that had been roasting on the Bun-O-Matic for hours. But the bitter flavor seemed to suit Steve.

"Say, Michaels, seen anymore of that pretty young thing you used to go around with years ago? Saw her round here a couple of times. Up from Chicago, right? Lori? Laura?"

"Lauren. Lauren Vestal."

"That's right, Johnny Vestal's kid. Got that place over east on, uhm –"

"Birch Lake."

"Right, Birch Lake. Heard you been sparking it up with her again. That what got you all in a funk, boy?"

"What funk?"

"Jesus, boy, what do you mean 'what funk'? You've been warming that stool half the goddamn afternoon. How come you're not out working anyway?"

"I took off, Nate." Steve gestured towards the window, and the parking lot beyond, where the plows had piled snow into six foot walls.

Nate nodded. "Yeah, but it's melting now, thank God. Pretty peculiar storm, though, wasn't it? So early in the season, I mean." He dropped the last Stroh's into the cooler and wiped his hands on his flannel. "Hell, the radio said it hit fifty seven this afternoon. Could be sixty five tomorrow. Regular Indian summer, huh? That oughta melt all this crap quick enough." Nate surveyed his empty tap room. "Bet there's still some folks snowed in. You think, Steve?"

"Count on it," Steve muttered.

"Come again?" Nate ambled over closer. "Say, what *are* you doing in here anyway? And who stuck the burr up your ass?"

"Nate, why don't you go pour some refills for those guys in the diner?"

"Screw 'em. They've been hanging around almost as long as you. Those truck drivers'll suck up a pot a coffee apiece for their fifty cents." Nate leaned his beefy arms on the counter across from Steve. "So what's the matter, your girlfriend go back to her big city friends? Left her big, handsome, northwoods sweety all alone with his trees and his wolves?"

"No, Lauren hasn't gone home yet. She's still up at her father's lodge. For your information, she's been snowed in."

"Oh." Nate wiped sweat off his face, and a teasing smile along with it. "Guess that is a problem. Is she okay?"

"I don't know. I hope so. But the road's still snowed over. I tried to get in earlier today, but I couldn't make it through."

"You did, huh? And when would that be?"

"Couple hours ago, I guess. Why?"

"So you're being all pissy just because you can't get into to see your sweetheart?"

"Nate —"

"No, listen to me. You see those guys over in the diner, dummy?" The two men were slipping off their stools and grabbing checks from the counter. They zipped up their parkas and headed towards the taproom. "What, are you blind, Michaels?"

"Nate, what are you talking about?"

"Can't you see the goddamned patches on their sleeves? Didn't you hear their trucks rumbling in before? Hell, I thought all you government guys knew each other."

The two men came to the bar and paid their fifty cent checks. And then Steve finally noticed the green and brown Gogebic County Public Works badges on their jackets. He shot a glance out into the parking lot: two, big orange dump trucks, with snow plows mounted on the fronts stared back at him, the curved plows shining in the afternoon sun like steel grins.

"Excuse me, guys, you're plowing the roads?" Steve asked.

"Yeah," one answered. "But don't go asking us to do your driveway or anything. People been asking us to do that all day. Our boss catches us doing that again, and we're dead."

"No," Steve shook his head. "No, I was just wondering where you're headed next? How are all the backroads doing?"

"Oh, we finally got ahead of the game yesterday," the other said. "Should be able to finish off the last of the fire roads and the boat landings by tomorrow. That is, if the snow doesn't all melt first. This has been the earliest I've ever seen a storm."

"Me too," Steve agreed. "So, like I was saying, where are you headed next?"

One driver pulled a notebook out of his parka. "Let's see, I'm going to clean out the pull-over at Sun Lake. He's going to finish off the road in to Marion Lake, then –"

"*Then* we drop these rigs back at the station and head home," the other fellow cut in.

"Nope, one more still." The driver scanned his notebook. "Yep, you plow out Birch Lake Road, and then we can knock off. Why?"

"Birch Lake? You mean it?" Steve hopped off his stool and started to pull his jacket on. "I've been trying to get in there. Tried earlier today, but I couldn't make it." He made for the door.

"Hold on, partner," the driver with the notebook said. "Don't be in such a hurry. It'll take us awhile before we get there. "Give us half an hour, hour. You'll get through okay, buddy." The two drivers grabbed handfulls of mints from the bowl by the cash register and left.

Nate stood behind the bar, smirking. "Yep, nobody wants to listen to ol' Nate. Yes sir..."

Steve smiled. He felt better than he'd felt in days. "Oh, shut up, Nate. And go brew some real coffee. I feel like a fresh cup all of a sudden."

—

Lauren stood before the mirror, toweling off her hair, her eyes glancing up at the glass, then quickly looking away. Her reflection was just as shocking now as it was when she first walked in.

She looked all drawn and pale. Not the beautiful, snow-white flawlessness of Carmilla's pale complexion. Instead, she just looked drained, sickly. Pallid, like she was coming down with something. Or more likely, as if she already did. But that wasn't what made her eyes turn away.

It was the marks.

The bite marks.

Those marks on her throat glared back at her from the mirror, big reddish-purple bruises, with little red punctures, right over the spot where her throat ached the most. But when she ran her hand over her skin, she felt nothing.

Nothing.

As if the wounds weren't even there. As if last night had only been another dream.

But it hadn't been a dream. It had been real.

Even though the power was back on in the lodge, Lauren ignored the blowdryer resting on the vanity. With her hair still stringy and damp, she climbed into a pair of jeans and slipped on a white shirt, not even noticing she'd buttoned it wrong.

She didn't bother to check on Carmilla.

Lauren knew she'd still be sleeping, lying there in her parents' room, still tangled up in the sheets, her white face still stained with red streaks, with *blood*, with Lauren's own blood. She would still be sleeping there, sleeping without any heartbeat or even the slightest trace of a breath, sleeping there safe in the shadows behind the drawn blinds. It was still daytime. Still, but not for much longer.

Lauren felt her pulse quicken, just thinking about the sunset. About the evening approaching.

About the night.

She wandered downstairs, aimless and lazy, still feeling sick, feeling tired. Kind of weak. Kind of...

Her stomach rumbled, but the sight of the leftovers in the fridge made her queasy. She drank a glass of water by the sink, squinting when she looked out the window at the backyard, where the sun still perched along the tops of the evergreens. It made her uncomfortable, and she stepped back to the center of the kitchen to drain her glass. She watched little flecks of iron and copper swirling at the bottom, as if she'd never noticed them before in the lodge's well water. The water tasted metallic, and she shivered. It reminded her of something else. Of another taste in her mouth.

Her mouth.

Her lips.

Her tongue, lapping at...

Her stomach rumbled again. Lauren filled her waterglass with the very last of the wine she could scrounge from the refrigerator, and left the room.

If her eyes squinted at the kitchen window, they actually watered when she stepped out onto the front porch. The lodge shielded the sun, casting a long shadow across the front yard that stretched halfway to the lake. But the lawn was still a vast sea of white, glaring in patches where the sun crept over the lodge's roof. Water had pooled in hollows left by the drifts. And some bushes over by the pier had already shed their dusting of snow. Even the waves appeared to be washing the snowcrust off the beach.

Lauren stared at the yard and the lake for the longest time, oddly transfixed by the way the shadows slowly groped across the snow. She could actually see them move. By the time her eyes finally adjusted to the outdoors light, it was already fading.

She stared, sipping her wine, curling her bare toes into the last of the melting snow on the porch, staring at the driveway, staring at the...

The driveway was clear.

Wet sand and gravel sparkled in patches where the sunshine warmed it all day. Plowed snow formed four foot canyon walls on each side of the driveway. Her Escort sat off on the side, still stuck in a snowdrift, but even that was melting. It wouldn't take much to get it out now. That is, if it was even running after being buried in the snow for three days.

Lauren leaned against the porch banister and sucked in a deep breath of the fresh air. She wasn't dressed to be out here. No shoes, no socks, just her jeans and her misbuttoned shirt. But the breeze felt nice on her face. It blew her hair back and soothed the soreness in her throat.

The sunlit patches disappeared fast now. Bright blue sky deepened into indigo, and she knew it would be purple – then black – in no time at all.

Night was coming again. And that made her eager. The thought made her pulse race. It made her waxen face flush, made her nipples tingle, made her squeeze her legs together.

But her ears pricked up: She slipped off the banister. The roar of an engine and crunching gravel echoed from deep in the woods, heading her way.

A dark green Jeep Cherokee crested the hill and splashed down the road into the driveway.

Steve Michaels pulled up and shut off the Jeep. He hesitated inside, then climbed out, doing a double-take at Lauren's half-buried Escort.

"Should be fun getting your car out of that snowbank," he said with a smile, sauntering up to the porch.

"Steve, what are you doing here?"

"Oh, just in the area. I wanted to pop in on Cy and see if the old coot made it through the storm okay."

Lauren's grip tightened on her glass. "And did you?"

"Actually, no. Maybe I'll check in with him on the way back. Don't worry, he's seen more than a few storms in his time." Steve leaned against the other banister across from Lauren. "But who cares about Cy. How are *you* doing?"

"Me? I'm fine, Steve. Just fine." She fiddled with the her shirt collar, pulling it up over her throat.

"So, what do you say I get your car dug out? Got a shovel in the back of the Jeep."

"No thanks, I'll get it later."

"Sure?"

"I said *no*, Steve." Lauren fussed with her hair, draping it around her throat like a scarf. "Really, Steve, it's nice of you to offer, but I can take care of it myself. Anyway, I don't think I'm going anywhere today. And the snow will probably melt by tomorrow."

Steve shrugged. "Okay. Well then, how about we get a bite tonight? Or something. Maybe a drink?"

"You want a drink? Lauren held her glass out to him. "I've got some wine here."

"No. Thanks." Steve screwed up his face, puzzled. "No, I meant, wouldn't you like to get together before you head back home?"

"Well, I haven't actually decided when I'm going. I have to think about that."

"Okay, Lauren. I just thought it would be nice to get together. I mean, I had a real nice time Monday night. And I thought you did too, and..." *Don't push*, Steve thought, *give her room, don't pressure her.*

Lauren looked away, guilty eyes shielded under her bangs. "Monday night? Right, Monday night." She backed in to the open doorway. "Look, Steve – about Monday. I'm not so sure Monday night should have happened."

"Lauren, what do you mean?" Steve followed her into the lodge. "I thought Monday night was just perfect. Or almost, that is, until the end. Look, Lauren, we said a lot of things Monday night, and if you feel I was moving too fast for you – okay, I understand. But why are you just blowing me off now? What did I do? What changed?"

Lauren kept backing into the hallway, determined to put some distance between them. *He smelled so good.* A real 'man' scent, all rugged and outdoorsy, with just a hint of musky sweat oozing off his skin.

She wanted to fling him on the floor, wanted to lick his salty skin all over. Wanted to...

No.

"Lauren, what went wrong? Was I the only one thinking we really had something going here, that we could pick up where we left off years ago? What did I –"

"Steve, please!" Lauren backed right into the wall.

"Lauren, what's happening with you? You don't look so good, you –"

"Oh, thanks a lot," she shot back, acid voiced.

"That's not what I mean. You look beautiful. Like always. You've always looked beautiful to me. I just mean you look kind of – sick. Are you feeling okay?" Steve reached towards her, but she edged away.

"Steve, I'm fine. Really. You don't have to worry about me. I don't *want* you worrying about me."

"Lauren –"

"Steve, please. Why don't you just go? Won't you please just go?"

"No, Lauren. Not like this. I can't leave things this way."

"Steve –" Lauren paused. She heard something upstairs. A door creaking.

A barely there squeak of a floorboard.

"Steve, please." Lauren sounded urgent now. "Just go, will you? *Now.* I mean it."

"But, Lauren –"

"Lauren?"

That voice.

That musical, mystical voice lilted down from the top of the stairs. Lauren watched Steve turn to the stairway, his eyes widening. Slowly, she turned around too.

"Lauren? I didn't know we had a guest." Carmilla stood there at the top of the stairs, wearing Lauren's robe half-on and half-off, with the sash untied.

Steve jerked his head back to Lauren, as if it was a struggle to look away from the figure at the top of the stairs. "Lauren, who –"

"Ah, Lauren," Carmilla cooed, dancing lightly down the steps. "Could this be your friend – oh, what is the name, now – Steven? Yes, that's it. Steven Michaels, I believe." With each step, the white robe fluttered open, revealing her even whiter skin.

Lauren's pallid cheeks blushed as many shades of red as they could manage. She tried to edge in front of Steve as Carmilla reached out to greet him.

"Mr. Michaels, how very nice to meet you." Carmilla extended her hand.

Steve ignored the gesture. He glared at Lauren, confusion, anger and hurt scrolling over his face.

"Lauren has told me all about you." Carmilla dropped her hand, but slid her other arm around Lauren's waist. She pulled Lauren close, all fawning and coquettish, her voice sticky sweet. "Why, he's every bit as charming as you told me. No – more so, I should say." Carmilla pecked Lauren on the cheek.

Steve fumbled for something to say. "Lauren?" It was all he could muster.

Carmilla stroked one of her long, pale fingers across Lauren's cheek. "You should have called me. You should have told me we had a guest. I would have come down immediately. *Had I known.*" Her last words oozed accusation.

"Well, uhm – Steve just popped in for a minute to see if we – that is, if I was doing okay. I mean, the snow and all."

"How very chivalrous, Mr. Michaels."

"Yes, but he was just leaving." Lauren wriggled out of Carmilla's arms. "Sorry you couldn't stay, Steve."

"Huh? Lauren, what –" But Lauren was already guiding Steve back out the hallway.

"Nonsense," Carmilla said. "Surely you can stay for a while, no? Perhaps you'd like to share a drink with us?"

"Carmilla, *no!*" Lauren said, but it was almost a shout. "No," she said more calmly. "Really, I think it would be best if Steve was on his way. Now."

She pushed Steve into the doorway. He looked back over his shoulder at the strange girl, sensing something lethal beneath her sugary voice, something dangerous behind that pretty face. Carmilla smiled back at him, all red lips and glistening teeth. He thought of a cobra, just before its hood extended. Steve blinked before he looked away, thinking for just a second that he saw the girl's eyes flash hot red.

Lauren pushed him again, right out onto the porch.

Carmilla whirled around and pranced back up the stairs, the white robe fluttering at her sides like little wings. She stopped halfway, and turned back to them, still smiling that wicked grin. "Perhaps we'll meet again, Mr. Michaels." She hovered there in the growing shadows, all pale and white and nearly naked. Her smile faded. "Then we may have a chance to share that drink."

Carmilla disappeared up the staircase.

"Lauren, what the hell...?"

But Lauren was all shoves and pushes, forcing Steve off the porch. "Couldn't you just go," she cried. "Couldn't you just go when I asked you to?"

"Lauren, who was that?"

"No one, Steve. A friend, okay? Just a friend of mine. She's – she's just a little weird. Stopped up for a visit, and got stuck here because of the storm."

"But –"

"*Go!*" Tears ran down her cheeks. Her voice cracked. "Just go, Steve. Forget about me, please."

Lauren pushed Steve away and ran back inside. Before he could say anything else, she slammed the door shut.

Steve stomped off to his car. He stopped – turned back. Stopped again, thought better of it, and made for the Jeep.

Inside the lodge, Lauren slid down along the door as she listened to his boots splashing through the puddles. She crumpled to the foyer floor when she heard the Cherokee roar to life and pull away.

Lauren wiped the tears off her cheeks and ran to the living room window. Steve's Jeep vanished over the rise and into the woods, his headlights flickering between the trees. Then they were swallowed up in the growing darkness too.

She waved a weak goodbye that Steve would never see, thinking that when she slammed that front door shut, she closed the door on a lot more than just Steve Michaels.

She stayed there at the window a long time, watching the moon rise over the trees, and the night fall over the woods. Then a cool hand fell on her shoulder. Lauren didn't turn around.

"You're angry with me," Carmilla said, pressing close into Lauren's back. "And you're upset. Is it your Mr. Michaels?"

Lauren spun around. "What the hell were you doing inviting him to stay? I was trying to get him to leave."

"I'm sorry," Carmilla said. "I...I misunderstood."

"Carmilla, *not Steve*," Lauren shot back angrily. "Okay? Not Steve. Promise?"

"Of course, Lauren. As you wish."

"No, I really mean it. Not Steve Michaels. Swear?"

Carmilla smiled and held up her hand. "I swear." She stood there in that robe, still untied and dangling wide open. Her breasts teased at Lauren's shirt. Carmilla wrapped her arms around Lauren and drew her close. "But there's more, no?" she said. "What is wrong, Lauren? Are you feeling – regrets?"

"No. At least, I don't think I am."

"It can be very difficult. Letting go. I warned you."

"No, that's not it. It's just – I feel so weird inside. Like my whole body's boiling over. Like I could burst."

Lauren stepped away from the window, and from Carmilla. "I can *feel* things. I can tell where the moon is in the sky right now. I felt the sun on my face before, and it almost burned. And my throat – it aches so much."

Carmilla nodded from across the living room.

"I *smelled* Steve," Lauren went on. "I mean, I really smelled him. I could almost taste him. And I wanted...wanted to..."

"Yes, Lauren. I know."

"And I look different. I look horrible, like I'm sick. I feel the pain in my throat where you...and the wounds – I can see them in the mirror. But there's nothing there." She rubbed her neck. "Nothing."

Carmilla shrugged her shoulders.

"Carmilla, am I...am I a vampire now? Like you?" Lauren held her breath. She wasn't sure what answer she wanted to hear.

Carmilla said nothing. In fact, she looked away for a moment. Then, finally, she answered.

"No."

Lauren exhaled a deep breath, a curious, mixed up sound of both relief and disappointment.

"I'm not? But last night? We...you –"

"It is not that simple, Lauren."

"So, what's happening inside of me? What's going to happen next? Will I –"

"Lauren!" Carmilla shouted. "Lauren, I don't know."

"You don't know?"

"No, I don't. This isn't science. Lauren, this is magic. My dark magic." Carmilla shrugged her shoulders. "We'll just have to see."

"Carmilla, what are we going to do? We can't stay here forever. Where will we go?"

"I don't know, Lauren. But you're right. It would be dangerous to remain here, as much as I like this little cottage. And these woods." Carmilla glided across the room and pulled Lauren back into her arms. "These hills, these lakes and trees...they are so different from the city. So different from most of the places I have stayed in America. They remind me of Europe." She kissed Lauren's brow. "They remind me of home."

A glimmer of red flashed in Carmilla's eyes. She smiled, her fangs poking right into her lips.

"Home, Lauren."

CHAPTER TWENTY FOUR

Cold November winds buffeted the lodge, tugging at the shutters and rattling the shingles. The wind lashed sleet against the windows, an icy rain mixed with flurries that cloaked everything in milky grey – the beach, the lake and even the front yard, where the last snow piles from the freak storm that fell a week ago were melting into wet grass.

Johnathan Vestal stared out the lodge's living room window, squinting through the sleet, his eyes riveted on the driveway. He'd been there at the window for half an hour now. Finally he gave up and paced back and forth across the living room.

"Johnny, sit down, will you?" Colonel Clovicky said from his easy chair by the fire. "You make me nervous." The Colonel set aside his newspaper, tapped an ash off his cigar into the ashtray on the endtable, and exhaled a cloud of blue smoke that circled around him like a halo.

But Lauren's father kept on pacing, pausing just long enough to pour himself another scotch from the bottle on the mantle. He downed the drink in one gulp, then started pacing again.

"Johnny, please, sit down."

"Colonel, how can I sit down? How can I sit still for a minute? How can you?"

"Well, there's nothing you can do till he gets back anyway."

Johnathan reached for the bottle again. "I know. But I'm going crazy just hanging around the lodge. We should be out there doing something."

"Out 'there'? Out where, Johnny? Look, just sit down here by the fire and try to get your mind off of things for a while." The old man stuck his newspaper in Johnathan's face. "Why don't you read the paper. Pretty interesting stuff."

Lauren's father put the scotch back on the mantle and took the newspaper. He plopped down on the sofa, trying to ignore the pile of papers spread out on the coffeetable in front of him: Lauren's drawings and watercolors. When he first saw them after he and the Colonel arrived at the lodge yesterday, he thought they were pretty things, actually. Until he'd looked at them closer. Until he noticed the peculiar, naked figure and that haunting face peering out from behind a tree, or veiled in shadows in each and every one. And until he saw the Colonel's reaction when the old man recognized *that face.*

Johnathan scanned the Gogebic County News' front page, looking at headlines and photos, but not really reading. It was the usual stuff; pictures of bowhunters beaming proudly next to a trophy buck, an update on this year's cranberry harvest, a slanted article against the DNR's proposed fishing regulations for the next season.

Then his eyes fixed on an article below the fold. The one with the small photo of a pretty girl, an out-of-date looking picture, probably taken from a high school yearbook.

The one with the caption, Anna Marie Riordan.

WATERSMEET WAITRESS FOUND DEAD

Anna Marie 'Annie' Riordan of Watersmeet, Michigan
was discovered dead in her trailer north of town
Monday afternoon by her employer, Mr. Nathan
Stambaugh, owner of The Moose,
also in Watersmeet. Gogebic County Sheriff's
police arrived at 2:27 P.M. in response to Mr. Stambaugh's
911 call, and found Ms. Riordan hanging in her
closet, an apparent suicide. The Sheriff's department
offered no further details, pending an
investigation...

Lauren's father dropped the newspaper on the floor, and looked back up at the bottle of scotch on the mantle. But before he could get off the couch to reach for it, the front door opened.

Steve Michaels stepped in.

"Ah, you're back, Mr. Michaels," the Colonel said, half rising from his chair. "So much for 'Indian Summer', eh?"

Steve slipped off his sleet soaked parka and stomped water off his boots. He made straight for the fireplace. "Not ten days ago we got socked in by the blizzard from hell," Steve said, warming his hands over the fire.

"Three days ago it was back in the sixties. Now this."

The numbness gone from his hands, Steve helped himself to a scotch and sipped it while the fire nibbled away at the dampness in his bones. He nodded towards the Gogebic County News lying on the floor by Lauren's father. "Seen that, have you?"

"What?" Johnathan Vestal took a moment to register. He followed Steve's glance down to the paper. "Oh, you mean the waitress?"

"Right. Annie Riordan," Steve said. "I stopped in The Moose on the way to Eagle River today. Talked to Nate. Pretty goddamned awful."

Colonel Clovicky puffed away on his cigar, enveloping himself and a whole corner of the living room with a thickening haze. "You knew that girl?"

"Annie? Sure, I knew Annie," Steve said. "Nate's about as tough as they come around here, but when he told me how he found Annie hanging there in this tiny little hole of a closet, a footstool kicked over by her feet..." Steve shuddered and took a big gulp from his scotch. "Hung herself with a piece of blue plastic clothesline, Nate said. Said Annie's face was as blue as that line was."

Steve wandered over to the window and stared out at the sleet pelting his Cherokee, parked beside Lauren's father's rental sedan. Right where Lauren's Escort had been snowed under from that crazy storm. But Lauren's car had been gone for days now.

"They found a note, too," Steve said. "It's not in the paper, but they did. I guess Annie was involved with someone. Or more than just 'involved'. Nate said he figured she was up to something, because she hadn't shown up for work for a couple of days, and Annie was always pretty reliable. The way Nate tells it, whoever Annie was shacked up with this time must've dumped her. Just left. Drove her nuts, I guess. You know, crazy stuff, '*There's no point in living alone like this...you promised, you promised...*' Anyway, that's what Nate figures from her note, and the sheriff grabbed that from him real quick. Nobody seems to know who Annie was with."

Steve emptied his glass and left the window. Crossing the lodge's living room, he glanced down at Lauren's drawings and watercolors on the coffeetable, seemed to sneer at them, and fell into the sofa with a tired sigh.

"Well, Mr. Michaels," the Colonel said, "It's a bad business all around. I wouldn't be surprised to find out that it's connected to our problems. So let's focus on our own dilemma. You know, when Johnny called me with your story, and actually said that – that *name*, well, I just dropped the phone. No, I really did. Fell right out of my hands. Thought

I was going to have a coronary." The old man smiled and looked at his smoking cigar. "You know, the old ticker isn't what it used to be. Anyway, once we got your message, we couldn't get up here fast enough. So the big question now is, where exactly did they go?"

"No, Colonel," Lauren's father cut in, "the question I'm still stuck on is *why*? Why did this girl, who may or may not have been responsible for your niece's death, get hooked up with my Lauren? Can we really be dealing with the same person? The coincidence is almost too much to accept."

"Maybe Lauren and Mr. Clovicky's niece were friends after all," Steve offered.

"No, I've talked to Lauren about Barbara," Johnathan said. "They didn't hang out together. And the Colonel never mentioned seeing them together. Just that one time, when I asked Lauren to look Barbara up. And that was a long time ago." He shook his head dramatically. "No, they just didn't run in the same crowd. No offense, Colonel."

"None taken, Johnny. But I'm not sure how or why this Carmilla creature and Lauren got hooked up really *is* the issue. What we're going to do about it now is what's on my mind."

"Mine too," Steve said.

The Colonel nodded, and twirled the cigar in his mouth. "Well, Mr. Michaels, we owe you a lot. You're the one who alerted Johnny here to the danger his daughter was actually in. Out of curiosity, why did you wait so long to let him know?"

Steve jerked his head up and glared at the old man. "Oh, I was supposed to know that Lauren was making friends with a psychokiller, is that it? Or the way Mr. Vestal tells me, you think she's some kind of monster. Look, I don't know about all your theories, old man. And I don't know anything about your niece. All I know is that I'm really worried about Lauren. No matter what the real story is." He leaped off the sofa and stomped across the room. As he passed the coffeetable and the pile of Lauren's drawings, that white face stared back at him again from the pictures, mocking him with that dark smile. He grabbed a handful of the sketches and flung them in the fireplace.

"I'm sorry," he said as the drawings burned. "It's just that this whole thing is so crazy. I thought that Lauren and I...that we...and now this *girl*. I mean, could the two of them really...?"

Lauren's father said nothing. The Colonel puffed away on his cigar.

"So, what did you fellows find around here?" Steve finally asked.

"Not much," the Colonel said. "More or less what you told Johnny about when you called him. The place is a mess. Dishes in the sink, food spoiling in the kitchen, wine bottles everywhere. Half packed suitcases upstairs, the beds unmade."

Steve nodded. "You can see why I called Mr. Vestal. When I came by here a couple days ago and found Lauren's car gone, the front door open, and then...well, it was obvious she'd left in a hurry."

"It doesn't make any sense," Johnathan said.

"None of this does, Johnny."

"No, I mean the mess. The door left opened. That's just not Lauren. She was always a responsible kid." Lauren's father turned to Steve. "I drove over to Cy Houlder's shack this afternoon. Thought I'd see if he knew anything. He *is* supposed to be looking after the place, you know. But he wasn't around."

"No," Steve said. "Actually no one's seen old Cy since before the storm. Must be on a bender back in the woods."

The Colonel had smoked his cigar down to a butt, and stamped it out in the ashtray. "Gentlemen, down to business. What did you find out today, Mr. Michaels?"

"Well, if you and Mr. Vestal had flown in to Eagle River instead of Rhinelander yesterday, we'd have already answered one question. I found Lauren's car there."

"Where?" her father asked. "Is she –"

"Just her car," Steve said. "It's parked at the Eagle River Airport. As it happens, I know someone who works there. One of the guys on my crew, his wife works in the little travel agency office in the terminal."

"Travel agency?" Johnathan said. "In that little airport? All that flies in to Eagle River are puddle jumpers. That's why we came into Rhinelander yesterday."

"Still, they have a travel agency," Steve said. "Those puddle jumpers can get you to Madison and Milwaukee. Even Chicago, if you don't mind stopping in every town downstate on the way."

"About Lauren's car, Mr. Michaels," the Colonel interrupted.

"Right. My guy's wife told me it had been there for days. That's where they left it."

"They?"

"'They, Colonel. Lauren's new friend was with her when they left."

"Left for where?"

"See if you can make sense out of it. I sure can't," Steve said. "They bought tickets to Chicago –"

"So Lauren went home," her father said.

Steve shook his head. "I don't think so, Mr. Vestal. They bought tickets to Chicago. Then my guy's wife booked them a flight to New York. Then to St. John's in NewFoundland, then to *Iceland*, if you can believe it. From there to Glasgow, Glasgow to London. London to Berlin. And from Berlin to Vienna."

The Colonel digested Steve's words, patting his pockets for another cigar. Lauren's father went back to the scotch on the mantle, downed one, poured another, then took to pacing the living room. "Glasgow, London, Berlin. Iceland, for chrissakes. I don't get it. And ending in Vienna."

Steve shrugged his shoulders. "That's what she told me. It may not make sense, but if it wasn't for my guy's wife, we wouldn't even know that." He turned to the Colonel. "No question it was them. She described them to me. Remembered both of them real well. Said that Lauren looked like she was stoned out of her mind. And that this 'Carmilla' just gave her the chills. She paid for everything. *Cash.* But, for what it's worth, her ticket was made out for a 'Mircalla', not Carmilla."

The Colonel nodded and grinned. "C-a-r-m-i-l... M-i-r-c-a-l-l-a," he murmured. He turned to Lauren's father. "Remember what I told you, Johnny? The anagrams? Now do you start to believe me?"

Johnathan clutched his glass, shaking his head. "No. I don't know. This is all just too strange. I can't –"

"Oh, one other thing," Steve said. "The travel agent told me that they fussed back and forth forever over the flights. This wasn't the only itinerary she tried for them. She could have booked nonstops from Chicago to any one of those destinations. But this Carmilla was all hung up on departure and arrival times. Even though the flights they ended up booking had them laid over at almost every stop." Steve looked back and forth between the two men, saw that Lauren's father looked more confused than himself, and then focused on Colonel Clovicky. "Does any of this mean anything to you?"

The Colonel's grin widened, and he started to chuckle. It was a chilling sound. "Mean anything? Mean anything, Mr. Michaels? What it means is *proof.*"

"With all due respect, no more of your witchcraft mumbo-jumbo, please."

The Colonel hefted himself out of the easy chair and began to pace as well, his old legs striding with unexpected and anxious energy. "No, young man, say what you want. But don't you get it? It's so obvious. 'Carmilla' – if that's what her real name is – wants to return to Europe. Somewhere in Austria is my guess."

"Yes. So?" Steve asked.

"So they had to take a peculiar route. They had to take all those different flights. Have all those extra layovers."

Lauren's father halted his own pacing and finished his drink. He shared the same lost look Steve had on his face. "Why?" they both asked.

The Colonel chuckled again. "So they wouldn't have to be out in the daytime, gentlemen. So they could fly only at night."

PART FOUR

CHAPTER TWENTY FIVE

"Hey, come away from the window," Rolf said, his lips rubbery from too much beer. "Come and drink your wine."

Lauren ignored him. She continued to stare out the fingerprinted window panes of this dingy, sixth floor suite, *Die Gast-Statten Rubersdorf's* finest. Which wasn't saying much.

She gazed out across the rooftops and through the prickly maze of chimneys, down to the dark ribbon of the River Mur winding through the center of Graz. But even the Mur seemed to twist away down below, as if the river didn't want to dirty its banks along the seedier side of the city. Lauren pressed her ear against the glass, listened intently to the wind whistling at the chinks in the window frames.

It would snow tonight, she decided.

Maybe only flurries. It was March after all, a little late for snow, even for Austria. She thought it might rain earlier this evening; there had been a whiff of spring in the evening air. But, no, now she was sure it would snow.

How she knew was something Lauren hadn't figured out yet.

"Lauren, listen to Rolf," Carmilla called from across the dimly lit hotel room. "We agreed to come up to Rolf and Martin's for a drink," Carmilla giggled. "So, let's have our drink." The two German college boys, Rolf and Martin, chortled drunkenly along with her.

Lauren tore herself away from the window.

It was like that these days.

She could lapse so easily into a daze, fixate on the most insignificant, everyday things. Study a leaf for long minutes, watch an icicle melt in the moonlight for an hour. Stare at the clouds rolling by in the sky all night, till Carmilla would have to drag her inside.

Lauren joined the others and picked up her wine. Tilting the glass, she barely wet her lips, while she peered over the rim to survey the room: a gloomy, cramped, little parlor, flanked by doors that presumably led to two separate and equally cramped bedrooms. The Gast-Statten's best, she guessed, curling her lip inside the glass at the offensive color of the beigy-brown walls and the browner carpet. Apparently Rolf and Martin's Austrian holiday was on a tight budget.

Rolf lolled on a sofa that had gone out of style before Lauren was born. He chugged on a bottle of warm, dark beer and slammed it down on a coffeetable cluttered with still more empty bottles.

Across the parlor, Carmilla lounged on an occasional chair that was worn into an unknown color. She ran those long, pale fingers of hers through Martin's blond hair, and he just sprawled on the floor at her feet, leaning against Carmilla's legs with his eyes closed, a stupid smile plastered on his boyish face, a half empty bottle of that same brown beer ready to slip out of his hand.

"Lauren, sit next to me," Rolf urged, patting the sofa and raising a puff of mildew smelling dust. "You're not going to act all shy and virginal now, are you? Carmilla, is she?"

"Oh, don't ask me, Rolf," Carmilla said, laughing. "Perhaps Lauren *is* a virgin. Or perhaps she's wondering if *you* are? Now wouldn't that be wicked, Lauren?"

Rolf grabbed Lauren's wrist and pulled her down on the sofa. For just a moment, she considered ripping his arm out of its socket, handing it back to Rolf, and politely telling these boys goodnight.

The urge passed.

Rolf reached around her shoulder, pulled her close and planted a sloppy kiss on Lauren's cheek. "There, this is better, isn't it?" he said, slurring his words. Lauren shifted away and straightened her black skirt.

Rolf and Martin, a regular Bavarian Bill-And-Ted's-Excellent-Alpine-Adventure, Lauren thought to herself as she primly crossed her legs. But Rolf squeezed her even tighter when he heard the hissing sound her stockings made when they rubbed together. The two Munich boys seemed so silly, their German so ponderous from too much beer and a curious affectation that almost sounded like laid back Southern California accents.

College boys, Lauren thought, her red lips curling into a smile when Rolf's hand settled on her knee. German college boys, but still college boys.

She could understand them, their German, that is. Or, most of what they said, at any rate. It didn't seem strange any longer. In fact, even Carmilla rarely spoke English with her anymore. It started almost as soon as they set foot in Austria, back in November.

"Well Martin, this parlor's very...charming," Carmilla said. "But wouldn't you like to show me *your* room?"

Yes, Carmilla was anxious, Lauren thought.

"Huh?" was all the boy could manage. Martin had tried to outdrink Rolf in the nightclub down on Welsbach-Strasse, while Lauren and Carmilla had watched them with quiet amusement, nursing their own glasses. And he still chugged on a beer all the way back to the hotel. Now his chin was slipping down to his chest.

Carmilla sighed. She stood up from the ugly easy chair, a tall, mono-chromatic swath of black...her long dark hair, too-short dress, shoes, nylons – all black. Only her pale, white face and throat strayed from the dark pallette. But in the parlor's dingy half-light, her face was veiled in shadows under her wavy bangs.

"Come on, Martin." Carmilla hoisted the boy to his feet and ushered him through the door to his little bedroom. She turned back and winked at Lauren, a brief flash of red sparkling in her eyes before the door closed.

Rolf's hand kept inching up Lauren's thigh. "So, are all American women as shy as you are? Your friend is so much younger, but she's not so timid."

"Oh, Carmilla's not as young as she looks, Rolf."

"Well, maybe so, but both of you are the most beautiful women Martin and I have ever seen. Or did I tell you that already?" His fingers slipped under the hem of Lauren's skirt.

"Only about a hundred times, Rolf. But that's okay. As long as you really mean it. I'd hate to think you were only saying it to –"

"Oh, I do mean it, Lauren. I do," he murmured, his fingers pushing their way between her thighs. "So tell me, are American women ashamed to be seen strolling through hotel lobbies with men? Or do they only make love in the back seats of cars – at the...the 'drive-in'?" His nuzzled his face in Lauren's hair till his beer-drenched tongue lapped at her ear. Rolf's fingers kept climbing like a spider under her skirt. They found the waist-band of her pantihose, crawled inside, wiggled around on her belly, then plunged lower.

Busy as he was, Rolf couldn't see Lauren's face in the poorly lit parlor.

He couldn't see her wicked smile, or the subtle flicker of orange sparks dancing in her eyes. He never noticed back in the dark jazz club, or even here in this dim little room, that her skin was whiter than the finest, unblemished ivory. And even if he had, the swelling in his jeans probably would have convinced him that it was just a trick of the light.

Bed springs squeaked from behind Martin's closed door. Rolf giggled, a drunken, annoying, adolescent giggle.

Lauren pulled Rolf's hand out from under her skirt. He was ready to protest, but she turned to him and smiled. Pecked him on the mouth with a quick, cool kiss. Then raised his damp fingers to her face, sniffed them and sighed melodramatically. She licked his fingertips.

"Aren't you going to show me your bedroom too, Rolf?"

Rolf leaped off the sofa, tripped over the coffeetable and sent the empty beer bottles rolling to the floor. He took Lauren's hand and led her to his room.

Barely inside the doorway, she spun him around, pinning Rolf against the wall and mashing her cool, red lips against his. Lauren slipped her tongue between his teeth and let it dance inside Rolf's astonished mouth. She kicked the door shut with her heel.

Rolf groped along the wall behind him for the light switch, but she grabbed his hand and shoved it inside her blouse instead. Lauren arched her back, pressing her breast into his palm.

She felt his heart pounding. Felt him panting. Felt the hard bulge growing between his legs. Lauren slipped out of their embrace, leaving Rolf against the wall, his arms hovering in the air where she'd stood a moment earlier.

He stumbled through the dark to his bed. Lauren followed. But as he turned to reach for her again, she threw Rolf on the mattress and pulled at his shirt, fabric shredding and buttons flying into the darkness. She could see his face clearly, even by the weak, grey city light stealing in through the windows. She saw the surprise in his eyes, the eager arousal churning behind them, the confusion. The glimpses of worry and boyish machismo, the question nagging at his drunken head...*who was seducing who here?*

Lauren undid Rolf's belt. Unzipped his jeans and yanked them off his legs. She gripped his little-boy-white cotton briefs, tugged, and they shredded in her hands. Hovering over his waist, she hiked up her black skirt. Rolf reached for her swaying hips, but she brushed his hands away. Instead, she reached behind her and slipped off her shoes, tossed them off the bed, then wiggled and twisted out of her nylons. One stocking leg still dangled from her foot when Lauren eased herself on top of Rolf's erection.

He slid right into her, too eager, too drunk, too excited to notice how cool her wetness felt, how icy her skin was against his. A few quick thrusts and Rolf came, moaning and bobbing beneath her.

As he finished his last, squeeky voiced grunt, she leaned over to the table beside the bed.

She flicked on the light.

Lauren flicked on the harsh, white, unshaded light, and chuckled while Rolf's blurry eyes adjusted to the brightness. Laughed as they widened in shock, and then fear.

Rolf stared up at Lauren's face. Her new face, white as fresh-fallen snow, pale as glacial ice. Framed in a glistening halo of honey wheat hair, all unearthly beautiful.

More beautiful, and more frightening than anyone – anything – Rolf had ever seen. More beautiful than Lauren could ever have been in life. Blandly blue eyes magically darkened into a perilously deep indigo, only now the irises burned bright red. A mouth that once perched in idle mediocrity between her nose and her chin was all rich, red lust now, crimson with sin and sex and desire, damp and glistening as her tongue licked across the edge of her lips.

Those red lips parted.

Lustrous, pearlescent teeth glinted in the harsh light. Especially the two fangs. The two, short, young vampire fangs, the fangs descending towards the tender flesh of Rolf's neck.

The boy's mouth fell open. A cracked, little wheeze of a scream breezed out of his throat. But before he could muster another, Lauren clamped her hand over his mouth and held on tight, while he pounded his arms and kicked his legs on the mattress.

She lowered her cold mouth to Rolf's throat. Tickled her sensitive fangs along the tingly skin, then bit down.

Hard.

Two jets of hot, red blood spurted out. She let the burning liquid spill down Rolf's neck, and lapped it up greedily with her tongue as it trickled down. Then Lauren fastened her mouth on his throat, and sucked contentedly, noisily.

Eventually, Rolf's muffled screams quieted. His flailing arms lay still and dangled off the side of the bed. Wide, terror-filled eyes rolled back in his head, and he just went limp, succumbing to the strange and wickedly wonderful sensation.

Lauren felt the numbing cold that lingered in her every limb and every joint fade away once Rolf's blood simmered in her throat. Of all the dark magic of her new life, of all the wondrous and frightening sensations of being a vampire, this was the most intense.

The pure, sensual abandon of drinking human blood.

The blood burned its way down her throat, warmed her belly with a sweet fire, and the heat swarmed through her head, seeped through her arms and her legs, all the way into her fingers and her toes.

Lauren almost cried. It felt that good.

It was a struggle, but finally she tore herself loose. Her fangs pulled out of the boy's throat with a little *pop*.

She eased off Rolf and sat beside him on the bed. She stroked his hair, ran her finger along his still bleeding throat. She kissed his cheek, tasting his sweat. It was human, salty, good. But nothing tasted like the blood. Once Lauren tasted her first blood as a vampire, nothing, not the finest wine, not the rarest champagne, could ever satisfy.

Rolf's heart still pounded in Lauren's ears. Fainter, slower, but still beating. Asleep or unconscious, she wiped the last of the blood off his neck and flicked off the lamp, plunging the bedroom back into darkness. Lauren hopped off the bed and headed for Rolf's little bathroom, still trailing her nylons from one foot.

The bathroom was all broken tiles, mildew and rust. Rolf's dirty laundry was heaped by the tub. She rinsed off her hands and face, watching the red stained water spiral down the drain. She didn't bother to look up at the mirror. Not because the sight of her blood smeared mouth would have shocked her. But only because she'd already learned all about that little bit of magic.

There'd be no reflection anyway.

Back in Rolf's bedroom, Lauren plopped down on the bed, and wrestled with her tangled stockings. She smiled to herself when she heard a gentle rapping on the door.

Carmilla peeked in. Red ribbons streaked her chin, bright drops of blood still glistened wetly on her small, porcelain breasts where her dress hung open.

"Everyone asleep in here?" Carmilla said.

"Yes, Carmilla. Rolf seems unable to keep up with me. And I always thought that boys his age were in their prime." Carmilla snickered and fell on the bed. She curled up like a kitten beside Lauren.

"And Martin? Resting comfortably, Carmilla?"

"Oh yes. Quite a surprise, actually. Woke right up and got all randy the moment the bedroom door closed. I'm thinking that some of that sleepy, drunken behavior was just an act. You don't think he was trying to lure me into his bedroom for sex, do you, Lauren?", she laughed. "I hate it so when men are insincere."

Carmilla stretched out across the bed, shoving Rolf aside. "Twisted little fellow, actually. Martin wanted to wear my clothes before we 'did it', as he put it."

"Sounds perverse," Lauren said, still untangling her nylons. "But interesting, I guess. So did you let him?"

Carmilla smiled and sat up. She slid close to Lauren.

"No, I'm sorry to say. I'm afraid I...*did it* before we got to that." She leaned over and kissed Lauren's lips. "Mmmmm," she murmured. "I can still taste Rolf. Very sweet." She dabbed at the edge of Lauren's mouth. "Missed a drop, darling," she said, and wiped away a bloody, red smudge.

Carmilla climbed off the bed and pranced to the window. "Look, Lauren. It's snowing. You said it might rain before. But it's snowing."

Lauren grunted at the knotted pantihose, gave up and ripped them into shreds.

"Hurry up, Lauren. I want to go home. This snow looks like the season's last gasp, but I don't trust old man winter to say goodbye lightly." Carmilla skipped out of the room, then poked her head back in. "And you know what terrible things can happen in snowstorms." Then she was gone.

Lauren found her shoes flung in opposite corners of the room. She slipped them on, then planted a goodbye kiss on Rolf's unconscious lips.

Back in the parlor, Lauren located her purse and tossed her black leather trenchcoat over her arm. "Ready?"

"Ready. Let's go home."

They opened the door and stepped into *Die Gast-Statten Rubersdorf's* dingy hallway. Lauren and Carmilla took one last look back inside the little hotel room. They shook their heads simultaneously.

"Boys!" they both hissed, and then ran away down the dark hallway.

⁓

The sleek, black Mercedes station wagon sped down the two lane highway, doing an easy 130 km even on the slick asphalt. Snow flurries speckled the windshield and added a wet shine to the pavement. There was a light dusting of white powder on the roadside, but nothing more. Winter really had given up, it seemed.

Lauren steered effortlessly with one finger. With her other hand she fiddled with the radio. If there was one thing missing in Austria, she concluded, it was a decent radio station. Frustrated, she flicked the radio off.

It was just as well. Carmilla wasn't particularly fond of the radio. Or recorded music of any kind. Or most modern technology, for that matter.

So many things that Lauren took for granted as a part of everyday existence, Carmilla found unsettling. Intimidating, even.

Lauren focused on the road. E57/59 ran south out of Graz and out into the Styrian countryside, mostly thick woodlands that occasionally opened up for a little patch of farmland, or dotted here and there by lakes. Actually, it looked a lot like the Michigan U.P. to Lauren's eyes. Except that the Calcerous Alps always loomed up all pale blue and snow capped along the horizon. She shifted in her seat to get comfortable for the long drive home.

They'd bought the Mercedes only a few weeks ago.

It was Lauren's idea to buy a car. At first Carmilla was reluctant. But Lauren brooded and harangued her about the hassles with taxis and limo drivers, till Carmilla finally relented.

When they first entered the Mercedes dealership in the pristine Graz suburbs, Lauren made a beeline straight for a shiny, red, two seat convertible. But Carmilla insisted on the station wagon, pointing out the advantages of a sturdy roof and a long cargo bay to stretch out in. Should the need ever arise. "I've slept in trunks before, precious, and believe me, it wasn't comfortable at all."

The salesman pretended he didn't hear.

He always did his well-mannered best to ignore the customers' eccentricities. Dark sunglasses on a March evening, dressed head to toe in black? Measuring the sleeping room in the back of one model versus another? Rock musicians, he surmised. What was the difference, he'd sold cars to movie stars and drug dealers and terrorists. These two weren't any stranger. Well, not much.

When the gleaming, black cruiser rolled out of the showroom and under the streetlamps, Lauren was as giddy as a teenager getting her first set of wheels. Even Carmilla couldn't help but be pleased.

Now as the Mercedes glided down the highway, Lauren glanced over at Carmilla, fiddling with a maze of buttons and trying to recline her seat. Once she figured it out, Carmilla unbuttoned her coat, fussed with her dress, stretched her long legs out and rested her feet on the dashboard. The orange dashboard lights reflected on Carmilla's face, on her neck, on her hands, on her white skin. It reminded Lauren of how she looked naked by firelight.

"You look comfortable."

"I am," Carmilla yawned, stretching like a cat. She wiggled out of her coat and settled back into the plush leather seat. As she did, Lauren reached over and ran her hand along Carmilla's cool thigh.

"Shouldn't you keep both hands on the steering wheel?"

"Mmmmmm. No."

Carmilla plucked Lauren's hand off her leg and placed it back on the wheel. "Well, I'd rather you did, Lauren. I don't fancy myself careening off the road. Or being staked by a fencepost."

"Yes, ma'am," Lauren answered sarcastically.

They drove on for a while in silence, just listening to the hum of the powerful engine and the sound of the pavement speeding by under their wheels.

"Happy?" Carmilla asked.

"Hhmm?" Lauren was concentrating on the road.

"Are you happy, Lauren?" Carmilla dabbed at a red stain on her stockings.

"What kind of a question is that? Of course I'm happy. Deliriously happy. You know that."

Carmilla shrugged. "Oh, just all the changes you've gone through. And in such a short time."

"I'm happy, Carmilla. Very happy."

"But?"

"But, nothing." The Mercedes quickly ate up another mile. Then Lauren finished her thought. "I'll admit, it's all a little overwhelming sometimes."

"Yes," Carmilla nodded. "I imagine it would be. I can barely recall my own youth. It is so very long ago. Now that I'm back here in Austria, and seeing how much has changed...it makes it seem like even longer."

She crossed one long leg over the other, still stretching them out on the dashboard. "But sometimes I detect a trace of remorse, Lauren. Some small regrets? A melancholy that can't be brushed away with a kiss or a hug? You miss your life, don't you?"

Lauren thought a moment before answering. "Sure. Sometimes. Sure, I do." She winked at Carmilla. "Sometimes I miss my glamorous career as a minimum wage sales clerk at Bloomingdales. And there's times I miss jockeying for a seat on a crowded bus, with some old creep sitting across the aisle from me, so he can try to peek up my dress."

Carmilla nodded, chuckling softly. She got the point, but Lauren persisted.

"Sometimes I miss going out on blind dates with losers, and then having to split the check with them, and then still finding myself wishing they would call for days afterwards and getting all depressed because I'm stuck at home alone with a tub of ice cream and the TV on a Saturday night. I miss my incredibly opulent apartment – oh, didn't I tell you – it's all your fault I had to cancel that Architectural Digest photo spread they were going to do on my place. And I miss microwaving lo-cal seafood pasta dinners every night, till I'm so sick of them I actually find myself looking forward to a Twinkie. Of course I miss having to go on a crash diet so I can fit in some stupid dress I bought that won't fit because I ate the damn Twinkies. I miss running short on cash when my bills come due, and having the credit card companies calling me at work. I really miss having my period, and having to skip dessert so I'll have enough extra cash to pick up a box of tampons and still have enough for bus fare."

Lauren patted Carmilla's shoulder. "Oh yeah, I miss it all. Lots."

Carmilla's laughter quieted, and they drove on some more.

"But it may not always be like this, Lauren. It may not always be quite this...*fun*. Things change. Remember, I've seen more than you. And I know that bad times inevitably follow after the good."

Carmilla looked at Lauren, all serious now. "Things can get rough and inhospitable. When the priests and the shamans and the self-righteous have you on the run, when they come after you with their icons and their crosses and their Holy Water and their stakes and fire. I know, Lauren. I have been through it before. Many times."

"Carmilla, get real, will you?"

Carmilla winced.

"Seriously, as old and wise as you are, sometimes you can be so out of touch," Lauren said. "Stakes and holy water? This is the twentieth century. Sorry, but nothing like that's going to happen. We don't have to worry, because *we-don't-exist*. No one believes in us. No one *really* believes in vampires. I know I didn't."

"This isn't America," Carmilla said gravely.

Lauren shook her head. "Austria isn't that different from America. The buildings are older, that's all. But the people are pretty much the same. They just all talk funny."

"I hope you're right." Carmilla wasn't convinced.

Their exit approached. Lauren flicked on her turn signal, headed down the exit ramp and onto a windy road through hillier and more wooded country.

"Okay," Lauren admitted, "At first, I was pretty scared. And I confess there were a few moments when I was really tempted to just bolt and run. Though I suppose you could have tracked me down if you wanted to. I mean, after we'd..."

E57/59 vanished behind them in the dark. "When we first left

Watersmeet," Lauren said. "When we flew into Chicago, and went to my apartment to get my passport. That was hard. Leaving behind all my things. All my precious little things, all the things I'd scrimped and saved and slaved for. Just walking away from all of my artwork. All of my books, and my tapes and music and clothes and – okay, it *was* hard to let go. When we walked out of my apartment, closing that door felt like – like, closing the lid on my coffin. Like I really was dying – or already dead."

Lauren watched the twisting road ahead of them, but her eyes had a far-away look. "And those next couple nights – well, that's when I really got cold feet. Sleeping with you in that awful maintenance shed by the airport in Iceland. It was so cold, so lonely and filthy. Then London? Hiding in the basement in Heathrow. I woke up long before you did and just wandered around the airport, crying. Then Berlin...why security didn't hawl me in, I'll never know. Skulking around in the subway until our plane was ready to leave. You sleeping all day in that scummy little alcove by the tracks. I mean, there were *rats* crawling on you, Carmilla. I was just about ready to see how close I could get to the good old U.S. of A. on my flimsy credit line. I even thought of calling my father, begging for money. And I've never done that."

"But it did get better after that, Lauren," Carmilla said. "Once we arrived in Austria."

"Much better. You took me to that little inn outside Vienna. I had a bath, finally."

"Yes, I thought you'd never leave that tub."

Lauren nodded, remembering. "And then we made love. Really made love, and it was wonderful, Carmilla. Truly wonderful. And then..."

"And then?"

"And then, you killed me."

"Yes," Carmilla sighed. "Then I killed you."

"Carmilla, you say it so – sad. Like you're the one with regrets. I think it's just been so long, you can't remember what it feels like. What it's like to change. What it's been like for me."

Lauren remembered, and it excited her. She didn't even notice her foot pressing down harder on the accelerator. "To wake up that next night, Carmilla, with everything all changed. Knowing – *knowing* I was dead. But...not dead. And everything I saw, and everything I heard, and felt and smelled, everything I tasted was – different. Better. Special. More intense."

Carmilla smiled. 'Yes, Vienna was...fun."

Lauren turned the Mercedes off the highway onto a narrow, cobble-stoned lane. The headlights bounced off a canopy of evergreens and leafless willows.

Carmilla opened her window and sniffed the air. Flurries dusted her cheek and lay there without melting. "Do you remember that arrogant Russian arms dealer in Der Karlplattz? Oh, how he cried, like a child, when he first saw your fangs."

Lauren nodded. "And the two bellboys – naked, except for those ridiculous little hats."

"Oh, and the limousine chauffeur," Carmilla said, laughing. "How he almost drove off –"

"Yes, yes and those four co-eds. All prim and virginal."

"Right, they actually stood in line, waiting for one another to be bled. Waiting and playing with themselves while they watched and –"

"And we left them in their room, naked and drunk and smeared with their own blood..."

"But starting an orgy of their own, as I recall."

The Mercedes drove past tall, iron gates flanking the entrance to their driveway. It wound along a gravel path, and Lauren eased it to a stop by the front door. She shut the motor off.

Carmilla and Lauren turned to one another and shared devious smiles. *"Remember the nuns?"*

CHAPTER TWENTY SIX

They left the Mercedes in the driveway, with the flurries dusting the gleaming black paint as they walked towards the front door. Carmilla hesitated on the first step. "I'm going for a walk. Care to join me?"

Lauren shrugged her shoulders. "I was going to paint for a while. But if you really –"

"No, paint. Please. I love the one you've been working on. You should finish it."

Lauren smiled. "Thanks. Maybe I will tonight. You can see when you get back."

Carmilla turned and started back down the driveway.

"Where are you going?" Lauren asked.

"For a walk. I told you."

"No, I mean *where?*"

"Oh, no where in particular. I just want to watch the snow fall. This will be the last before spring, I'm sure. I'll miss it."

"Carmilla, you're not going back *there* again, are you?"

"Again?"

"Again," Lauren said. "You've poked around those old ruins for three nights this week. I thought you promised me you'd stay away?"

"I suppose I did," Carmilla pouted. "But Lauren, it was my home."

Lauren just shook her head. "It's not healthy. Picking around old vaults. Digging holes. You could get hurt, you know."

"Styria is my land, Lauren. Karnstein is my home. I need to do this." Carmilla scampered back across the driveway. She hopped up the first step, where Lauren still stood shaking her head. Carmilla kissed her on the cheek. "Don't be angry with me. There – there's a smile, now. I won't be gone long." She spun around and headed across the lawn, her topcoat flapping in the breeze like giant black wings.

Lauren stayed on the steps, watching Carmilla till she vanished into the trees that circled the grounds. Tall, thick evergreens, just like at the lodge. Once the flurries and darkness completely swallowed Carmilla's silhouette, Lauren went inside. She made straight for her studio, not even bothering to change from her dressy clothes. She had lots of clothes now.

The studio was in a turreted corner up on the third floor, a spacious, round room with wide windows all around. It was the perfect room for an artist. All day the room literally glowed with an abundance of bright, natural light.

Not that Lauren had ever seen it in the daylight.

The rich smells of linseed oil and pigments filled the room. Tubes of paint were piled on a table next to a huge palette gobbed with smears of titanium white and pthalo blue, vermillion and umber. Dirty brushes soaked in jars of turpentine, and boxes of fresh ones lay next to the palette. She squeezed out fresh dollops of paint, grabbed a handful of brushes – all the tools and materials she could ever want, but could never have afforded. All the time in the world to paint, all the time in the world...

Lauren slid her stool in front of the easel and hopped on top. She slipped her pumps off and curled her toes around the rungs of the stool, then stared at the nearly finished canvas on the easel, with only the moon's glow shining in through the studio windows to light the dark room.

It was more than enough light for her eyes.

It was a painting of Carmilla. Carmilla, sitting naked and pale porcelain white beside the pond behind their house, with the moon peeking over the evergreens bordering the water. Carmilla's dark hair draped her bare shoulders, her dark eyes were shadowed caves beneath her bangs. Her red lips a crimson slash on a white face, that familiar choker circling her throat.

With a fragile fantail brush, Lauren softened the edges of still-wet patches of color she'd laid in last night. She daubed some highlights on the moon, deepened the night shadows behind the trees. On a whim, she dipped a small, pointed sable into the alizarin crimson on her palette, and added a tiny, red droplet at the edge of Carmilla's smiling mouth.

She paused to study what she'd done. Slid off the stool and stared at the painting from across the room. Compared it to dozens of others stacked against the walls: portraits of Carmilla lying in bed, Carmilla dancing in the trees, Carmilla with her eyes closed in sleep, Carmilla with her dark eyes flaming red. Carmilla grinning wickedly, pearly fangs poking over her lips.

Lauren nodded. The painting looked good. They all looked good.

She considered popping in a CD. Though she'd bought an elaborate stereo system for this room, she only played it when Carmilla was out.

No, no music tonight, she decided, and wandered over to the window, content to hear the sad song the wind made when it howled against the house's old masonry. Content to stare at the pretty pictures the wind painted in the darkness outside, swirling the streams of flurries in the sky.

It looked cold out there.

But no colder than it was inside. Neither Lauren or Carmilla could remember to turn the heat on. Sometimes they lit fires, but mostly just for fun. Lauren learned early on that artificial heat couldn't warm her cold flesh. She was dead now, after all. Dead, or something darkly like it, and only one thing could ever warm that gnawing, numbing chill that lingered in her bones and her skin. But for now she felt fine. For now she felt a pleasant, fuzzy tingle inside. Rolf's blood still ran hot inside her veins.

For now.

'Are you happy, Lauren?'

She stared out the windows, scanning the night sky and the gentle flurries billowing over the grounds.

'Are you happy, Lauren...you miss your life, don't you?'

That's what Carmilla had asked on the way home from Graz. Are you happy? She stared out at the night, stared and thought...was she?

Yes, she was. She was happy.

As happy as she was during those first nights in Vienna, it wasn't until they chose this house out in the rural hill country south of Graz that she felt truly at ease with what had happened. With what she had become.

Lauren adored this house.

When Carmilla announced that they'd be leaving Vienna for Graz, Lauren detected her friend's anxiousness. And her apprehension. Carmilla left Austria nearly eighty years ago. So much had changed: the end of one war and the sheer horror of the one that followed. Years of demolition and reconstruction and modernization. Carmilla had been heartbroken to see the glass and steel obscenities poking up in downtown Graz, the fast food restaurants and supermarkets lining the highways in the suburbs. She grew dead silent and stayed that way for days.

And then they went to Karnstein.

Lauren kept warning her. If the old village and the family's castle had already been in ruins a century ago, there wasn't much hope that they'd still be standing. Carmilla was the last of the Karnsteins, after all, or so she'd told Lauren.

It took a fistful of extra shillings to convince the limousine driver to take the overgrown road off the main highway. It took Carmilla's forceful glare to keep him prodding the car through the ruts and the rocks. When their headlights finally pierced the darkness cloaking the Karnstein valley, Carmilla pressed her face against the window, her eyes wide in disbelief.

When they reached the spot where Castle Karnstein once stood, she slid back in her seat and began to cry.

The village had virtually disappeared, now just hollowed out holes where houses might once have stood. Bits of crumbled foundations. A stone fence here, a crumbled hearth there, a patch of brick paving stone poking up through snow and dried weeds and catching the headlights' glare.

But the castle...

The castle was worse. Only later did they learn that it had been commandeered by the SS in the war. American bombers eventually decimated what was left of the ghost town. Russian troops leveled the castle on their way towards Graz. And whatever they left intact, vengeful mobs dismantled and demolished after the war...the young ones determined to obliterate the evidence of Austria's shame...and a few of the old ones – the very old – joining in to cleanse any memories of the even older evils that might still lurk in that cursed fortress.

Carmilla wouldn't even get out of the limousine. She cried in the back seat all the way back to Graz.

But they returned. Just two nights later, in fact.

Returned to meet a nervous middle aged woman, a realtor from Graz, who drove them around to several houses for sale in the area. She kept her distance from the two pale beauties who dressed all in black, wore sunglasses at night, and giggled like teenagers when they strode arm in arm into each house. She tried not to listen to their conversations as they weighed the pros and cons of one house over another. She didn't want to know.

But the realtor changed her tune when Carmilla suddenly pronounced this house as the one. And offered the woman a generous amount well over the asking price. To be paid in cash. Plus a little something extra for all her trouble...there would have to be some peculiarities with the title. And the deed. As little paperwork as possible.

The realtor got over her misgivings about making deals with the devil as she figured her commission on her pocket calculator.

The house had been built between the wars by a wealthy Graz merchant who meant to raise his family in the country. But the owners simply disappeared shortly after the Anschluss. Jews perhaps, or politically

undesirable, or they just said the wrong word to a party member. No one
knew. The building was held in trust by Graz solicitors since. And the last
family that had leased the old place had fled a year before, complaining
about the bleak atmosphere the nearby Karnstein ruins cast over the
whole area.

'Are you happy, Lauren?'

Happy?

Yes, she thought.

Deliriously happy.

The exotic beauty of her new nighttime world, the enhanced senses
to really experience it. The passion she shared with her vampire lover. And
of course, the blood.

Deliriously happy. It was all so utterly unnatural. So...*supernatural.*
It was magic.

And yet...

Yet, it was *dark* magic, all the same. Lauren couldn't ignore the
intensity of the desire she had for the blood. She couldn't pretend that she
never noticed how hard it was, how very, very hard it was to drink only
enough. She couldn't deny the uncontrollable urges that arose when she
drank, when her lips caressed warm flesh, when her fangs broke the skin
above a pulsing, blood filled vein. It was like an animal had been
unleashed inside her, something cold and vicious and predatorial.
Something that made her want to...

No.

"I could never do that," she said out loud. Her words echoed off the
studio's stone walls. "Never."

Lauren stepped away from the window and picked up a brush.
She held it poised over the canvas for a moment, then put it back down on
the palette.

The painting was done.

Carmilla's face stared back at her from the easel, shining in still fresh
oil paint.

It was a good painting. Like the others she'd done since they moved
in here, it was infinitely better than anything she'd ever done before. In
her real life.

No, she thought as she scooped up her brushes and dropped them in
a jar of turpentine, *this* was her real life now.

It was late. In another hour, perhaps an hour and a half, the eastern
horizon would begin to brighten. Already Lauren felt a familiar lethargy
creeping into her limbs.

She left the studio and headed for their bedroom, one of six in the rambling old house. It had some sixteen rooms, more than the two of them could ever use, and each as huge as their bedroom. Generous, big rooms with ornate fireplaces and wide window seats that made comfortable perches for surveying the expansive grounds, or fixating on the moon and the stars and clouds, as Lauren so often did.

There were tall, beamed ceilings, arched and trimmed doorways, artfully carved stonework everywhere. And stained glass insets at the sides of each window that lent a somber, funereal touch to the whole house.

In the adjoining bathroom, Lauren washed up and brushed her teeth, watching some last traces of red color the water swirling down the drain. She stuffed her clothes into the hamper, which was overflowing with dirty laundry. Monday was laundry day; Lauren had to remember to leave the baskets of clothes down in the kitchen for the laundress and the dry cleaner to pick up. And remember to carefully lock the dead bolt on the door that led from the kitchen to the rest of the house before going to bed Monday morning.

It was up to her to remember those things. Carmilla had no mind for them. She always had to be reminded to close the windows, to lock the doors, that the laundress came on Mondays, the maids on Tuesdays and Thursdays.

Lauren smiled to herself, wondering how Carmilla ever got along without her. She still smiled while she walked over to the bedroom window. Holding onto the thick, protective drapes that hung at its side, Lauren lazily ran a brush through her honey colored hair, and gazed out across the lawn. Past the garden that would sprout soon with spring's arrival, past the pond, to the thick wall of trees that sprouted up along the edge of their little estate. Those tall evergreens were the beginnings of a wide band of forest that ran between their house and the ruins of the village of Karnstein...and the tumbled down remains of Castle Karnstein.

She saw a little figure appear at the edge of the woods. Carmilla skipped along down there like a schoolgirl on holiday, arms flung wide, shoes held in each hand, merrily kicking up the light dusting of snow flurries with her feet.

Lauren left the window and dressed for bed. All buttoned up in black silk pajamas, she grabbed her book off the nightstand, a beautifully illustrated monograph on the nineteenth century German painter, Caspar David Freiderich. His bleak, alpine landscapes and studies of gothic ruins always interested her. They'd acquired a special appeal lately.

Lauren was under the covers and struggling with the German text when she heard the front door open and shut, a loud boom that echoed through the whole house. Then – Carmilla's light step prancing up the staircase.

"Carmilla, did you lock the front door?" she hollered.

The steps paused, then retraced themselves back down the stairs. Lauren listened for the two click-click's of the locks, then Carmilla's feet racing back up the stairs.

"Still struggling with that book?" Carmilla asked when she flitted into the bedroom.

Lauren shrugged. "I can't explain why it was so easy to pick up German. I never was particularly good with languages. But then, there's a lot I can't explain, isn't there?"

Carmilla smiled as she lay something heavy down on the dresser. Something big, square and metallic. She pulled her dress up over her head and dropped it on the floor, then padded off to the bathroom.

"But speaking German is one thing," Lauren called to her, hearing the faucet squeak and water pouring noisily into the bathtub. "Reading German, now that's something different altogether."

"Austrian, Lauren. Austrian."

"Same thing, Carmilla."

Carmilla poked her head out the bathroom doorway. "Well, the Germans seem to think so sometimes." Her head darted back in. The faucets shut off.

Lauren sat up in the bed, trying to see what Carmilla dropped on the dresser. "It's a bit late for a bath, don't you think?" Loud splashing was Carmilla's answer.

Lauren put down her book and slid off the enormous bed. The thing on the dresser was big, heavy looking. Rectangular. A thick slab of metal, a foot and a half by two. Bent, rusty spikes dangled loosely in holes at each of the four corners. It looked old, worn. Dented, dirty and scorched.

She turned it over.

Read the inscription.

COUNTESS MIRCALLA KARNSTEIN
1693 – 1713

Lauren dropped the slab on the dresser and backed away. She bumped right into Carmilla, who was patting herself down now with a thick towel. Water droplets sparkled like diamonds on her white marble skin.

"Carmilla, what is this?"

But Carmilla didn't answer. Instead, she traced one long finger around the pitted, scorched edge of the slab, evidently lost for the moment in her own thoughts of times long gone.

"Carmilla?"

"*This,* Lauren, is from my tomb."

"So, you were poking around in the ruins again. Don't you know how dangerous that is? Why do you keep going back there?"

"Don't be cross with me." Carmilla dropped her towel and slipped her arm around Lauren's waist. "To you, the past is just 'history'. To you, my stories of the old days are just that – stories. But the threat of stakes and torches and crosses, the fear of the priests' and peasants' bloody butchery – those are real memories for me, Lauren. I fled from my home when your own country fought its Civil War, fled with the nauseous fumes of the shaman's Holy Water burning my eyes and nose."

Carmilla leaned against the dresser, but her eyes bored into Lauren's. "Why return to the ruins of Karnstein? Why? To find out if things may have...changed. If the passage of time, the crumbling of belief, the crisis of faith that has plagued mortals since I walked there last has changed anything. If the old ways still have power over me. I *need* to go back, Lauren. I need to see it all for myself. They're more than just 'ruins'. They are the ruins of my past life."

"Carmilla, you ask *me* whether *I'm* happy. Aren't you happy? Happy with me? Why do you need to dwell on the past?"

"It's not simply 'the past', Lauren. It's *my* past. Every inch of ground in this forgotten corner of the world is my world. The land is stained by the blood of my family, my ancestors. By our blood, and the blood we've shed."

Carmilla took Lauren's chin in her hand and looked still deeper in her eyes. "You're from the New World. Your roots don't run so deep. You're young still. You've never yet felt the pain and the loneliness of exile."

Lauren stared at the metal tombstone. "1693 – 1713." She shook her head. "It's almost unbelievable. Even knowing all that I know now." She leaned her head on Carmilla's shoulder. "I mean, I know in my mind – I know intellectually that you died so long ago. But..." She blushed, a barely there pale pink coloring her pale cheeks. But when I look at you, I just see a young girl. Younger than me. Barely out of her teens."

Lauren slipped out of Carmilla's embrace. "It makes me feel silly."

"Don't, Lauren. It's not silly. Sometimes I am only twenty years old. Inside." She picked up the slab and stood it on a shelf perched over their bed. Carmilla stared at it for a moment. Then turned back to Lauren.

"*You* make me feel young again, Lauren." Then she climbed on the big bed and patted the space beside her, smiling.

"I can't think of you as *Mircalla*," Lauren said as she climbed in next to Carmilla. "I know that's your birth name, you've told me. But to me, you'll always be Carmilla."

"I've used many names over the years. But Carmilla – it suits me, best. It's the name you know me by. I *am* Carmilla." She kissed Lauren softly on the lips.

They kissed again, open mouthed and more intensely. Pearly fangs clinked together as they nibbled at each others' lips.

—

They made love.

It was leisurely, and very sweet. All lazy and languorous, as dawn's imminent approach slowed their limbs with fatigue.

When they were finished, Lauren slipped back into her pajamas and slid off the bed. Her steps were slow and sleepy as she trudged to the window and closed the thick curtains tight.

Carmilla welcomed her back to the bed with open arms. They nestled together and felt the familiar stupor uncontrollably overtaking them.

"I really am happy, Carmilla."

"I know, Lauren. I know."

"I love all the changes. All my new senses. I love this new life. I love the blood. I didn't think I would. I thought it would frighten me, repulse me. But it doesn't. I love the blood."

Carmilla pulled the blanket over them.

Lauren whispered to Carmilla's sleepy face, "I really do adore being a vampire. It sounds insane to say that out loud – to hear myself actually say those words. *I adore being a vampire.* But I really do."

Carmilla nodded, her eyes already closing.

"I love Austria, I love Styria, I love our home, Carmilla. I love lying here in bed with you, feeling your cool skin against mine. I love *you*, Carmilla."

"And I love you, my darling," Carmilla whispered back.

"I love everything about it...everything. But..." Lauren looked into Carmilla's gently closing eyes. "But I couldn't kill, Carmilla. I could never, ever kill. You know that don't you?"

"Perhaps you'll never want to, Lauren. Let's hope you never *need* to."

Sleep finally commanded Lauren's lips to stillness. Her words faded just as dawn's light crept up to their curtained window. The deep sleep of the undead overtook her, but she still murmured, "I could never kill..."

CHAPTER TWENTY SEVEN

"Steve, why don't you look this form over before I sign it." Johnathan Vestal scanned the three page certificate, nodding periodically as if he really understood it.

It was in Austrian, after all.

"Look, I think I have it all filled in properly," Lauren's father said as he slid the document across the desk to Steve. "But give it a once-over, will you? That okay with you, Mr. Scheurenberg?"

"Of course, of course, Herr Vestal. I will have the bills of lading photocopied, as you requested." Scheurenberg disappeared in a flurry of nods and bows.

"Looks okay to me, Mr. Vestal," Steve said, shrugging his shoulders. "Sure is one hell of an impersonal thing, isn't it? Someone's whole life reduced down to a three-part carbonless form." He slid it back in front of Lauren's father and looked away, scanning the room. It was all painted in grey, cold clinical grey. Chilly as the room was, the drab color scheme made it seem so much colder.

But it was pretty much what he expected in the basement of a mortuary.

"*Ach*, so – everything is in order, gentlemen?" Scheurenberg reappeared with a sheaf of papers and handed them to Johnathan Vestal. "Here is the receipt for the private hearse to Vienna, here are the papers to cover air transport and repatriation to the United States via Austrian Airlines out of Schwechat Airport. And I believe I've already given you copies of all the paperwork that will cover transport from JFK in New York City to Chicago, Illinois."

Johnathan took the papers and stuffed them in his briefcase.

"So, gentlemen – Herr Vestal, Herr Michaels – I think that takes care of everything? Will there be anything else?" Their business concluded, and Johnathan's check already handed over, the undertaker appeared to want them to leave so he could be about his business. But it was the nature of his profession; he was too polite to shoo them out.

Steve shoved his chair away from the desk. He glanced out the window, where a grey spring rain poured down relentlessly on the streets of Graz. It was as depressing out there as it was in Scheurenberg's mortuary. "Could we have a few minutes alone, here?"

"But of course. My sincerest apologies. Please, take all the time you want. I will be in my office, if you need me." Scheurenberg vanished again.

Steve turned away from the rain spattered window and approached a long, stainless steel table. A big metal box rested on top. He stared at it for a long time. "Guess we weren't much help, were we?" he muttered, shaking his head.

"Steve, there was nothing we could have done," Lauren's father said. "This whole idea was insane. Absolutely nuts. I should have known from the beginning."

"If only I'd gotten here sooner," Steve said. "If only I hadn't wasted so much time in Innsbruck. Then, maybe –"

"No, I don't think that would have mattered. I really don't. Come on, Steve. Let's go."

Johnathan Vestal locked his briefcase and came up beside Steve at the table. He patted the cold metal box. "Goodbye old friend. You fought the good fight, really you did." He stepped back, stood at attention, and saluted. Then left the room.

Steve followed behind him. But he paused at the doorway, and gave one last look at the Colonel's air transport casket resting on that stainless steel table. "I didn't really know you, Mr. Clovicky. And to be honest, most of the time I did, I thought you were a little crazy. But I swear, I'll do my best to find her. I'll do my best to avenge your niece's death. And yours. I'm still not convinced, but if there really is any truth to what you wanted us to believe, I'll finish things, or die trying. I promise."

～

The dining room in the Hotel *Auenbreuger Platz* was famous throughout Graz for the chef's way with veal and its renowned wine cellar. And the best of both sat on Johnathan's and Steve's table. But the *kalbsbraten* on their plates was untouched. The wine was another matter.

Lauren's father emptied his glass, then emptied another bottle when he refilled it. He knocked downed that glass in a gulp and waved for service.

The tuxedoed waiter bustled over to their table and saw their uneaten dinners. *"Was ist los? Das kalbsbraten, nein gut?"*

"Das ist in ordnung," Steve managed in the smattering of German he'd picked up over the last few months. "It's fine, fine. *Danke schon."*

Lauren's father pointed at the empty wine bottle. The waiter nodded and took their plates.

Johnathan stared at his empty glass. "Well, here's to the Colonel." He raised the glass in a toast and drained the few drops that dribbled out. "To come all this way. To try so hard. To spend all this time, and then to just pop off like that. All alone in a hotel room, in some old two-bit tourist trap, and in a backwater province in Austria. From a heart attack, for chrissakes."

"Well, he's at peace now," Steve offered.

"At peace? Hell, he's not at peace. He died leaving a job undone. That wouldn't have sat well with the Colonel. No, sir, not well at all. At least, not the Colonel I knew." Lauren's father looked around the dining room, wondering when the waiter would return with that other bottle of wine.

"Here, take mine." Steve slid his glass across the table. "So, Mr. Vestal, now that the Colonel's dead, and his body's on its way back home, I suppose you feel a little vindicated. About his idea of splitting up, I mean."

Lauren's father shook his head again; he'd been doing that a lot lately. There'd been so much to shake his head at since his world turned upside-down back in the fall. "No, I'm not looking for 'vindication', Steve. Maybe the old man was right. We covered a lot more ground, and a lot faster by splitting up. The Colonel staying in Vienna and using it like a base of operations probably worked as well as anything else we would have tried. Hell, we've been to every police station and consulate, every nightclub and hotel and airport in this whole goddamned country. Lord knows, I didn't turn up anything in Salzburg or Trieste. And you didn't have any luck in Innsbruck. Or Bregenz."

"No. No, I didn't," Steve said. "But I still can't help feeling that the Colonel *did*. That he turned up some kind of information. Or maybe even saw them. Why else would he leave Vienna in such a hurry, and head here to Graz? Do you still have his note?"

Johnathan smirked. "Note? Yes, I have his 'note'. The coroner let me keep it, along with his other things."

"Well, don't you think it means anything? Don't you think it shows that he really was on to something?"

"Steve, that note –" Johnathan shook his head some more. He fished in his pocket and retrieved a crumbled piece of hotel stationary. "Right, the Colonel's last will and testament, right here in my hands. The big clue, the big treasure map that'll lead us straight to Lauren and this mythical 'Carmilla'." He flung the note on the table.

Steve picked up the paper and looked at it. One word – just one word was all the Colonel managed before the massive coronary hit his chest like a sledge hammer. The hotel maid found him the next morning, splayed out on the floor, with the pen still clutched in his cold hand. The 'note' was smashed underneath.

And on that note, just that one word: *They're...*

"In the first place, Mr. Vestal, Carmilla isn't a 'mythical' creature. I know. I met her. I never said I believed all the Colonel's crazy ideas about what she's supposed to be. But there was something about her that wasn't – right. Not normal. And in the second place, I *do* think that the Colonel was onto something. I believe he saw them – your daughter and Carmilla. Maybe right here in Graz. Why else would he be starting a note with 'They're...'?"

The waiter returned with another bottle of wine. He refilled Lauren's father's glass and left the bottle on the table along with their bill.

"Steve, it doesn't mean a thing. Or it could mean a thousand things. '*They're* here in Graz and everything's fine.' '*They're* dead, and there's no hope.' '*They're* all out of cigars in the lobby – be back in half an hour.' The note means nothing."

"But, Mr. Vestal, why would he have told us to head to Graz? You said he sounded urgent."

Johnathan snorted from behind his glass. "He's sounded 'urgent' ever since he first told me about his niece. Face it Steve, the old man was losing it. Don't get me wrong – I loved him. He was my best friend. But he was certifiable."

"But –"

"*Vampires, Steve?* Vampires? The Colonel believed his niece was killed by a goddamned vampire. Bela Lugosi, Count Dracula – Jesus, Steve – capes and fangs and coffins? Steve, please...the Hinsdale police and the DuPage County Coroner laughed him off, and maybe we should have too."

"So, you don't believe the Colonel's crazy ideas," Steve said. "I told you, I never said I did either. But *you* never saw this Carmilla."

Lauren's father slammed his glass down on the table. "No, I didn't. But tell me this, Steve, what if we *do* find her? Find the both of them? What the hell are you going to do, then, huh? Pound a stake into this Carmilla's chest? Are you? Do you think I'm going to do something like that to my own daughter?"

"I don't know!" Steve yelled back. The diners at the *Auenbreuger Platz'* adjacent tables all looked their way. 'More rude Americans,' they thought as they returned to their meals.

"I don't know, Mr. Vestal. But that doesn't mean I can just give up. Can you?"

Lauren's father didn't answer. Instead, he refilled his glass, drained it, refilled it again.

"Well, can you? Can you give up on finding out what happened to Lauren? To your own daughter?"

"Steve, I've been thinking." Lauren's father looked away from the table as he spoke. "I'm not sure I feel right about the Colonel's remains flying back to the States alone. I talked to his attorney and his executor before I came down for dinner." He fidgeted with his glass. "I'm flying back to the U.S. tonight."

Steve nodded. "Well, we can pick up where –"

"Steve, I'm not coming back."

Steve saw it coming, but hearing it out loud still stunned him into silence.

"Look, my business is falling apart back there. If I don't set things straight – and quick – there won't be a business to come back to. Nothing.

Steve just kept nodding.

"Anyway, Steve, what are we accomplishing here? Nothing. The death of an old man, that's all we've accomplished."

"Mr. Vestal, she's your daughter."

"Don't you think I'm aware of that? But she's also an adult. Look, I don't like the sound of this character you found her with at the lodge. And it doesn't exactly please me to discover that Lauren might like...well, that she might not be the girl I thought she was. Just the thought...Jesus, I picture her mother spinning in her grave. Who knows, maybe if she lived? But Lauren abandoned her apartment. She dumped her car, quit her job. Left the damn country. Disappeared. And there's no trace of her here in Austria, at least nothing we've been able to find. Face it, Steve. She doesn't want to be found."

"But, Mr. Vestal, the Colonel's note," Steve persisted. "I just know we're getting close. It's like – like I can feel her nearby. Like Lauren's right around the corner."

"Steve, give her up."

Lauren's father focused his bleary eyes on the check. Then he pulled out his wallet and left a wad of Austrian bills on the table.

"I'm going home, Steve." He drained a last glassful, and got up. "I'm going to try and pick up the pieces of my life. I'm going to stop chasing after ghosts and fairy tales." He steadied himself and headed out of the dining room.

"Mr. Vestal," Steve called, "What should I tell Lauren when I find her? What do you want me to say? That you were too busy? Had an important meeting?"

Johnathan Vestal halted as Steve's words stabbed his back. He paused for a moment, then continued out of the dining room, muttering over his shoulder, "Go home Steve."

~

"*Jawohl, Fraulein,* I will have your purchases delivered to this address, happily."

The blue-haired old clerk could hardly contain herself. Carmilla flitted into the little boutique only twenty minutes earlier, and quickly picked out half a dozen new outfits for herself and Lauren, without a glance at a single price tag. The clerk had been suspicious at first, but when she saw the roll of bills her peculiar looking customer pulled out of her purse, she quickly changed her tune. This one sale was good for a hundred schilling commission, for sure.

Marking each purchase down on her pad, the clerk wondered if the *backerei* down the street would still be open after the shoppe closed. She planned to celebrate and treat herself and her cat to the biggest, sweetest, flakiest strudel Graz could offer.

"And delivery only in the evening, Fraulein? Not a problem, I assure you. Shall we telephone ahead?"

"No," Carmilla said, fingering some scarves on the counter. "There is no – that is, there have been problems with the phones. Just arrive in the evening, and that will be fine."

The old clerk tagged each item and piled them behind the desk. Carmilla sauntered over and picked up her change. She was getting better at remembering all these countless mortal practicalities; Lauren's persistent teasing at work. The girl would have her balancing a checkbook someday.

She stuffed the bills and coins into her purse, and gave another look at one of the items the clerk folded on the counter – a pretty, white cotton peasant blouse. Belled sleeved, with a lace-up front, very chicly faux-antique. The clerk saw her lingering over the blouse. "Yes, it *is* beautiful, isn't it? That embroidery on the cuffs and collar, that's real Lienze crafts-manship, right from the Tyrol. All our apparel is 100% domestic made."

Carmilla nodded, not really listening, instead picturing Lauren in the blouse.

"*Fraulein* has someone special? Your *junge-freund,* perhaps?"

"Yes, there is someone special."

"Well, that blouse will be sure to turn his head, especially on you. You'll see. It was made for you. It goes so well with your..." Now what? The clerk stammered. "It goes so well with your...color."

Carmilla smiled. "I'll take this one with me, please."

"Oh, but *Fraulein,* the rain! That lovely blouse will be soaked before you reach the street."

Carmilla looked the clerk in the eye.

The clerk shivered. "Of course. As you wish." She placed the blouse in a tissue lined box, shaking her head and tsk-tsk'ing all the while.

Box in hand, Carmilla closed the shoppe door behind her, smiling at the quaint sound of the jingling door bell. She liked that little shoppe, even the chatty, old clerk – just like some fawning auntie, all hair-sprayed, girdled and powder cheeked. She'd have to return sometime with Lauren.

Carmilla huddled in the doorway, pulling the hood up on her trench-coat. The old woman was right enough about the rain. It had been pour-ing all evening, a constant, driving rain that filled pond-sized puddles at every curb. It would be a wet spring, she concluded.

She tucked the package under her coat as best she could, then dashed out into the downpour. Lauren would be scouring the bookstores along *Auenbreugestrassen.* She'd have to be dragged bodily out of them, as usual. And at that, with an armload of new art books for each of them to lug back to the car.

Then, perhaps, a quiet cocktail in the piano lounge in the *Hotel Auenbreuger-Platz.* A nice, dark table in the back, by the windows over-looking the patio. Perhaps an opportunity for some extra amusement might present itself there, before they made their way home.

Carmilla smiled to herself as she ran, happily splashing down the street. She couldn't wait to find Lauren. Couldn't wait to show her the little present.

All in all, it was bound to be another wonderful night. Just like all the others since she and Lauren returned to Austria. Carmilla kicked her way through a puddle, laughing when the people scurrying past jumped away from her splash.

Rounding the corner onto *Auenbreugestrassen,* she swerved around drenched, late-night shoppers with their faces tucked into soaked collars, newspapers folded over their heads. She ran down booksellers row, glancing in the shoppe windows, looking for Lauren.

The *Auenbreugestrassen* was a wide boulevard with shoppes lining one side, a park and hotel on the other. She passed all of Lauren's favorite haunts, but there was no sign of her. Carmilla squinted, straining to see through the sifting, grey sheets of rain, dodging around couples huddled under umbrellas.

Then, in the middle of the next block, directly across the street from the Hotel *Auenbreuger-Platz*...was that Lauren? Carmilla drew closer.

It *was* Lauren.

Lauren, standing there in the rain, with her coat over her arm and soaked to the bone. Her sweater hung limp, wet and drooping almost to her knees. Lauren's hair was soaked to a wet, dark brown and plastered against her pale face. A shopping bag lay by her feet. Several books spilled out onto the sidewalk, their pages already water-logged.

"Lauren?"

Carmilla ran up behind her, and tapped Lauren playfully on the shoulder. Then jumped around to the other side. But Lauren didn't flinch. Didn't even look.

"Lauren?" She didn't answer. She just stood there in the rain, staring across the street.

Staring at the hotel.

"Lauren, what is it? Look at you, your clothes are soaked."

Lauren began to mutter nonsense. "No...No, no. Not here. Not you, no..."

Carmilla grabbed her and gave her a shake. "Lauren, what is it?"

Lauren raised one arm, and pointed across the street.

"The hotel? What about it?"

"No...no, no," Lauren continued. "It can't be. No..."

Carmilla looked across the street. A few people milled around under the canopy in front of the hotel. A doorman stood there in his period livery, umbrella ready. Nothing unusual. There was a taxi parked in front, with its windshield wipers fighting a losing battle against the relentless rainfall.

A middle-aged man hurriedly tossed suitcases into the back seat. Something about him...

Then there was another fellow, following behind that man. Younger, but familiar also. No coat, no umbrella, the pelting rain speckling his navy blazer a darker blue. The younger man yelled at the first. No – pleaded with him, leaning into the back door of the taxi and arguing with the older man, who seemed determined to ignore him.

Carmilla tried to blot out all the other street noise, the cars and the buses and the voices of the people running by in the rain. She focused her ears across the street...

"*You can't do this! You can't go. She's your daughter, for God's sake!*"

"*Look, let me know if you need any money to get home. I'll have it wired over.*"

"*I don't want your damn money!*"

"*Fine. Take my advice, then. You're a good guy. I wish it could have worked out with you and my daughter. But that's all over now. Go home. Go home, Steve.*"

Lauren's knees buckled. Carmilla scooped her into her arms.

"Steve," Lauren mumbled, shaking her head in disbelief. "Steve?"

Carmilla divided her attention between Lauren, just dead weight in her arms, and the scene across the street.

"Fine. Go, damn it. Go," Steve yelled at the taxi. He slammed the back door shut, and the taxi sped away, disappearing into the rain.

Lauren struggled in Carmilla's arms. "Steve? Dad? No – how could they – no..."

Carmilla looked back across the street. Lauren's Mr. Michaels still stood there in front of the hotel, his clothes drenched, glaring at the empty curb where the taxi had been. Finally he turned and pushed past the guests huddled under the canopy, shoving his way back into the Hotel *Auenbreuger-Platz*.

"Daddy?" Lauren mumbled. "Dad, you made it after all! The lodge wouldn't be the same without you. I knew you'd come..."

Carmilla hissed.

Cold steam puffed out from her lips, and her eyes flashed bright red. "Come, Lauren. Let's get you home."

She scooped up Lauren's soaked books and half-walked, half-carried Lauren back to the car. Lauren rambled all the way. Carmilla got her in the front seat, then dug through Lauren's purse. She found the keys, gazed at the glowing buttons and lights and gauges. Reluctantly, Carmilla pulled the Mercedes out into the rain-snarled traffic.

CHAPTER TWENTY EIGHT

Leaves cluttered the shore of the pond.

Even though the night air was still warm, a breeze blew down out of the mountains, warning that autumn would soon be descending on the Styrian heights. That breeze blew gently, just enough to make the grass tremble, enough to tickle the colored leaves on the trees, enough to flick them off their branches. Just enough to ripple the surface of the pond.

Lauren preferred it that way. Preferred the pond rippled by a breeze, or even better, churned up all blue-grey and choppy by gusty winds. Then she felt more at ease sitting on the shore, gazing down on the water.

Because then she couldn't see her reflection. The reflection that wasn't even there. It was easy enough to ignore in the mirrorless house. But nature had its own way of insistently reminding her that she was no longer a part of the normal world.

Lauren rolled up the cuff of her white shirt. She stretched her arm as far as she could, trying to reach the last water lily the pond would offer for the season. She leaned out over the pond till the ripples almost caressed her face, her hair dipping into the water.

No, the wind blew the lily away. She couldn't reach it. Too bad; with the temperatures falling a little each night, the delicate flower had only a few days left. At least it could have spent them in a precious vase on her dresser.

But that was a selfish way to think, wasn't it? She sat back on the shore and rolled her sleeve down over her arm. Selfish?

Selfish is what she was, Lauren thought. It defined her. What could be more selfish than drinking someone's blood? What could be more selfish than a vampire? Who could be more selfish than herself, than Lauren Vestal?

She said it out loud, "Lauren Vestal."

It sounded so peculiar. She hadn't thought of herself that way – by that full name – in a long time. No, Lauren Vestal was some other person. A dead person. Dead, since November of last year. Now, she was just – Lauren.

She wiped her wet hands on her bluejeans. Sniffed the air, nostrils flaring like a fox. The breeze was kicking up a little stronger now. More leaves fluttered down from the branches hanging over the pond.

Yes, she thought, Lauren *Vestal* died almost a year ago now, just as autumn was giving way to winter.

But she came back to haunt her, didn't she?

Back in the early spring.

On a rainy boulevard in Graz.

Hearing the sound of delicate footfalls across the grass, Lauren looked up from the pond. Carmilla appeared between the evergreens, heading this way across the night-shadowed lawn.

"*Guten abend,* Lauren."

"Hi."

"You were already outside when I awoke."

"I wanted some fresh air." Lauren didn't get up. She continued to watch the leaves dancing on the waves.

"So, are you sure that you don't want to come into Graz with me tonight?"

"No, you go, Carmilla. I'm not in the mood."

They said nothing for awhile. Just listened to the wind rising. Lauren sitting by the edge of the pond. Carmilla standing behind her.

Finally Lauren turned around and glanced at Carmilla. "You look nice tonight. Cute outfit. New?"

"Yes, it is," Carmilla said. "I bought one for you too." She wore a black tuxedo: suitcoat with silk lapels, black pants with satin side stripes. Shiny black cummerbund around her waist, and a ruffled white shirt tucked inside. Even black patent leather shoes. All carefully retailored for her slender, girlish frame. "It's hanging in your closet. I'm sure it will fit. Why don't you go try it on? Maybe it will put you in the mood to go out."

"No, I don't think so." Lauren turned back to the pond. "I was going to stay home."

"Are you painting tonight?"

Lauren shrugged her shoulders. "I don't know. Maybe I'll just read a little. Listen to some music."

Carmilla crouched beside her, laying her pale hand on Lauren's shoulder. "You haven't painted in weeks. You've left one canvas half-finished on the easel. Your brushes have dried and stiffened with old paint. It's not like you."

Lauren watched a leaf flutter down. She caught it in her hand. "Oh? What exactly *is* like me?"

Carmilla frowned, the tips of her fangs peering out over her lower lip. She stood up abruptly. "Well, if you're just going to be contrary..." She turned to go. Then turned back. "Lauren, I am sorry about your father. I have no more idea than you do how he found his way to Graz. I assume he was looking for you. And I'm sorry about your friend, too. But I won't lie to you and say I'm sorry that they didn't find you. Find us."

She knelt next to Lauren. "Are you? Do you wish they *had* found us? And what if they had? What would you say? What would you do? What would you expect *me* to do? You cannot go home, Lauren. You cannot turn back the clock, pretend it's this time last year. You cannot undo what has been done. What you *wanted*."

Lauren didn't answer. She just played with the leaf she'd caught.

Carmilla sighed, and shook Lauren's shoulders. "Come now, *liebling*, don't be cross. You've been wallowing in this malaise since the spring. The beautiful summer nights pass you by, while you mope around the house. Why, you only go out with me once a week now, if that. And only when hunger compels you." She wagged her finger in Lauren's face. "It's not healthy."

Lauren shrugged. "I went with you last Friday."

"Ah, yes. Last Friday. Five thousand schillings in your purse, and you bought nothing. Didn't browse in any of your favorite haunts, nothing. Two handsome, young violinists begging to serenade us in their suite, and what did you do? A brief little sip. Barely enough to redden your lips. Then left us, to go wandering the streets by yourself all night. May I remind you, I had my hands full with those two rascals after you left."

Lauren smiled in spite of herself, picturing Carmilla drinking from one of the Graz Symphony fiddlers while the other rode her like a hobby horse, and plucked his violin at the same time.

"Now that's what I wanted to see, Lauren. That pretty smile. Those lovely, young fangs of yours. You have them for a reason, you know. Come, now. Run into the house and get dressed. We'll both go out formal tonight. I have a box for the symphony. Perhaps my friends from the string section could pay us a visit there? And then, a little aperitif afterwards?"

Carmilla made it sound so tempting. Lauren's mouth tingled. Maybe she should...

The wind kicked up again, a strong gust skittering across the pond and knocking leaves off the trees like confetti. They fell into Lauren's lap and on her shoulders, landed on her hair and stuck there like a garland.

Autumn.

Sometimes it seemed like only yesterday that she drove her Escort through the fall colored Michigan countryside, filled with anticipation, eager for adventure.

But other times, it seemed like a lifetime ago. And that's what it really was, wasn't it? A lifetime ago.

Her lifetime.

"No. You go, Carmilla, please. I wouldn't be much fun tonight anyway. I don't want to spoil it for you."

Carmilla opened her mouth to protest. But she was interrupted by the sound of a car's engine rumbling through the gates of their estate, and bright headlights streaking across the lawn from the driveway.

"Please, Carmilla, go ahead. Your limousine's here."

"No, I'll stay here with you, Lauren. We can talk. Perhaps we can – "

"Don't be silly. We'll talk when you get back. You can cheer me up with some naughty stories about you and your private string section." Lauren got up and led Carmilla back towards the driveway.

She watched the limousine pull away with Carmilla waving goodbye through the rear window. Lauren waved back, until the car disappeared through the gates.

She hadn't meant to be difficult. It wasn't just petulance; she really was stuck in a foul, listless mood, and had been for some time. It had been growing on her ever since the spring, when she saw her father and Steve in Graz.

And bit by bit, she found herself thinking about her old life again. And questioning her new one. There was something so very, very wrong about it all. As spring turned into summer, it began to gnaw at her more and more.

And now that summer was fading away, she was trapped in a malaise, just like Carmilla said. The wild abandon of those first few months was all forgotten. Each night she woke with a feeling of melancholy, painfully aware that an eternity of these nights lay ahead of her.

Lauren left the driveway, ambling around the grounds, content for the moment with the feel of the wind on her skin. She watched clusters of leaves flutter through the air and collect in the grass. Listened to a thousand little sounds, the dark music of the night.

She came around the side of the house to the garden patio. It was a mess, as it had been for weeks.

Carmilla had been as ambitious lately as Lauren had once been with her painting. She never seemed to tire of poking around the ruins of Karnstein. The patio was cluttered with wash basins, garden hoses, scrub brushes and dirty work gloves.

Night after night, Carmilla returned with some new treasure she'd unearthed from beneath the fallen walls of Castle Karnstein. A whole chest one night, stuffed with decaying old gowns that crumbled into dust in their hands. A remnant of an ancient tapestry that hung in the front parlor now. Scorched and torn paintings of her long dead ancestors...for all Lauren knew, they could have been Carmilla's own siblings. She just cleaned them up, hung them up, filling the house like a museum.

Vases and jewelry, furniture she sent to Graz for restoration. Statues and knickknacks, books with faded pages.

But Carmilla seemed proudest of the weaponry.

She brought back long, notched swords engraved with old Germanic runes, and shields with battered heralds. Vicious looking pikes and lances, rusty flintlocks and muskets with broken stocks. Carmilla arranged them around the walls in their bedroom – a huge Karnstein war lance dangled right over their bed. The room began to look like a seventeenth century armory. With each addition, Carmilla would regale Lauren with tales of battles and bloodshed and heroism from the nobler days of the Karnstein lineage. From prouder periods in Austria's history. The stories were so vivid, so real, Lauren wondered if Carmilla herself had wielded some of those weapons three centuries ago.

Continuing around the house, Lauren pictured the pleading look on Carmilla's face back by the pond. Maybe she *should* just run upstairs and try on that tuxedo hanging in the closet? The Mercedes sat all shiny, gassed up and ready in the garage. It could overtake Carmilla's limo halfway to Graz. They'd be lounging in their box at the symphony by eight.

Maybe an evening under the sheets with a handsome fiddler was just the thing to turn melancholy back to serenity. From there, the path back to happiness might not seem so long.

And there was always...always...Lauren imagined the taste of sweetly mellow, young blood on her lips.

She came full circle back to the driveway, and lingered there indecisively, pawing her tennis shoes into the grass. If she went, it would please Carmilla endlessly...

Suddenly, the murmur of an engine somewhere nearby caught

Lauren's attention. She pricked up her ears and listened.

Somewhere just outside the gates?

Behind the fence that surrounded the estate, headlights flashed on. A hundred yards away, a car crept forward, pausing between the tall stone gateposts, then slowly rolling in. Its lights blinded Lauren's sensitive eyes.

For a moment she started to smile. Had Carmilla returned? Changed her mind, decided to surprise her and stay home for the night? Or, perhaps returned to plead with Lauren one last time to join her in Graz? Lauren decided she'd have that tux on so fast that Carmilla would barely have time to get out of the car. They'd make that eight o'clock curtain, for sure.

But the blinding lights crawled down the driveway so slowly. So tentatively.

Suspiciously.

As they drew closer, Lauren knew it wasn't the limousine at all. Once the car turned a little, she could see it was just a non-descript, grey sedan.

She backed toward the house.

The engine stopped.

The car door opened.

She thought about all of Carmilla's sinister warnings, all the silly things she'd laughed at. About priests and self-righteous villagers and vengeful parents. About scalding Holy Water and torches and wooden stakes.

Lauren ran up the front steps. Then turned and looked back. She had to grip the iron railing to keep her legs from buckling.

"Lauren?"

It was Steve.

~

"No! No, no, no – NO! This is insane," Lauren stomped back and forth across the parlor, shouting. "You shouldn't be here. You can't stay."

Steve sat on the sofa, doing his very best to appear calm. But it was all he could do to keep himself from grabbing her, to keep himself from pulling Lauren into his arms and hugging her until she melted.

But when he approached her outside, Lauren fled into the house. And when he reached for her in the foyer, she ran in here.

"Steve, what are you doing here?" She was crying now. "Why did you come? Why now?"

"Why now?" Steve asked. "I only tracked you down to this house a couple days ago. I've shadowed the place since. I saw the limousine pull away earlier. I thought –"

"You have to go."

Steve got up from the couch and walked towards her. Lauren backed away from him, till she was cornered against the wall.

"Lauren, are you that upset to see me? Really?"

"Yes! Go now, Steve. Please."

So close.

He was so close. An armlength away. One lunge, and...

So close.

So very, very close. Lauren could smell his familiar after-shave. The sweat on his tanned skin. His sweet, musky aroma, all rich with fresh air and cleanness.

But she smelled more.

She smelled it pumping in his veins. Smelled it flowing in his arteries. Bubbling in millions of capillaries.

Just one leap...

"Please, Steve," she cried, "Please, go. *Now.*"

He stepped back. Lauren looked so – different. Pallid, thin, almost sickly. Her eyes seemed deeper, darker, devastating. Her lips were shiny red, like they were caked with lip gloss, but they weren't, were they?

Lauren looked like a ghost.

She looked dead.

She looked more beautiful than ever.

"Do you really want me to go, Lauren?"

She slumped to the floor on weak knees. "Yes. Please. Go. Don't come back here, Steve. Not ever."

"Okay. I'll go," he said, turning away and making for the doorway.

"Noooooo..." Lauren stumbled across the stone floor, latched on to Steve's legs and hung there. "No, don't go." She clung to his jeans, sobbing. *His smell. The smell of love and blood and sex and love and blood and...*

Steve pulled her up off the floor and wrapped Lauren in his arms. "I never thought I'd see you again. I hoped, but I –"

"Steve, how did you find me? How long –"

"I've been in Austria since mid-November. Be a year pretty soon, now. Searching for you."

"Why? How?"

"We split up. Took different parts of the –"

"We?"

"Well, the Colonel thought –"

"Mr. Clovicky? Barbara's uncle is here in Austria?" Lauren pictured a dog-eared, spiral notebook diary. Imagined a blooddrained, naked corpse splayed out in a messy teenager's bedroom.

"Well, he was here. He's dead –"

Carmilla?

" – died of a heart attack in the spring. Right near here, in Graz," Steve said, still holding her tight. "And I guess that was about the last straw for your father, Lauren."

"My father." Lauren raised her face from Steve's chest. "I know. He left."

"You know?"

"I saw you. I saw you yelling at Dad when he got into a cab in front of a hotel. On *Auenbreugestrassen.*" She sounded all far away now. "It was raining. You should have had an umbrella..."

Steve grabbed her chin and turned her head to face him. He stared into those eyes, those blue-no-black-no-blue eyes, felt himself drowning in those dark pools, felt confused. "You saw us? You knew I was here? Lauren, why didn't you –"

"Steve, I couldn't. I couldn't reveal...I couldn't let you see me. The way that I am."

"Okay, you're ill. I can see that. What the hell has that witch got you on? Drugs? Is that it? Lauren, we can get help. There's nothing so bad that we can't work it out."

"No, Steve." Lauren slipped out of his arms. "It's not like that. Nothing like that at all. You'd never understand."

"Lauren, I don't care what it is. Give me a chance. Help me understand."

Lauren raked her fingers through her hair, shook her head furiously. "Steve –"

"No, try me! So, this Carmilla character's got you all twisted up. Mind games. Hypnosis. Whatever. That's okay. What is it, some kind of cult? Like devil stuff? Is that what she's into? It's all right, we can –"

Lauren screamed.

The sound shook the window panes. Steve clamped his hands over his ears.

"It's not like that," she shouted. "*She's* not like that. You'd never understand. None of it."

"Lauren, please –"

"Oh, this was stupid." She beat her fists on her thighs while she paced up and down the floor. "Stupid, stupid, stupid!" Suddenly she stopped. "No, I was right before. You better go. Go, now. I *want* you to go."

Her impossibly loud scream still echoed in Steve's ears. A tingly feeling crept us his spine. Somewhere deep down inside, a part of him whispered *Go-go-GO.*

But here she was, after all the wondering and all the searching halfway across the globe, here she was. Lauren, right here, just across the room. Lauren, in the flesh.

"No, Lauren."

Steve took a step towards her, his arms held out. "I'm not going, Lauren. I searched for you almost since the day you left Watersmeet. I let you go once, remember? The snow storm?" He took another tentative step closer, and Lauren backed away. "I wanted you to stay at my place that night. But I let you go." He came closer still, just a step away now. Lauren didn't move.

"I never should have let you go that night, Lauren. Now I've found you, I'll never let you go again as long as I live."

Lauren melted into his arms.

﹏

Lauren's clothes fell off one by one all the way upstairs to her bedroom. Once inside, she tore Steve's off, and threw him on the bed. Overhead, Carmilla's lances and shields shook on their mountings when he landed.

If he was surprised by her eagerness, if he noticed her strength when she leaped up on top of him, if Steve acknowledged how strange she really looked, or just how cool her naked skin felt against his, then he didn't let on. Or, at least, it didn't stop him.

Lauren straddled him and crushed their lips together in a long, hard, urgent kiss. A kiss that had to make up for almost a year of lost kisses.

With her long fingers clawing through his hair, her long legs locked around his, Steve didn't care. He didn't care about Lauren's father abandoning him in Austria, or the Colonel's lonely, pointless death. He didn't care about the old man's crazy notions, or give a damn about his pathetic niece.

He didn't care, because Lauren was here, now, in his arms, kissing him, loving him. He didn't care because right now Lauren looked more beautiful than anything he could imagine. Pale skinned, dark eyed, red mouthed beautiful. Sinfully beautiful. When she lowered herself onto him, and he felt her moistness envelop him, he didn't give a goddamn what her story was, because they'd work it out. They could work anything out.

Somehow. Some way.

Lauren closed her eyes and shook her head, rocking up and down on him, sucking in his heat, drinking in the sweet, sweet smells of his hair and his skin and his sweat and his sex. She raked her hair, mashed her breasts, clawed his skin, pounded on his chest.

But she felt it coming, felt the raw, cold hunger rising uncontrollably, insistently, rising up out of her belly just as her climax warmed. Felt her eyes start to burn red till she couldn't keep them closed anymore and her lids popped open. Felt her mouth water, drooling with dark, ugly desire and hunger and thirst, till it fell open, and her tongue slid out, glistening and wet and flicking at her lips.

And at her teeth.

At the tips of her sharp, sinister little fangs.

She growled.

Growled low and unearthly and vulpine vicious with hunger. Growled with the thirst for blood. Growled till it was a roar, and thrust her face at Steve.

His eyes widened with the final recognition.

An alarm sounded in his brain.

A voice in his head screaming *vampire, vampire, vampire, vampire...*

Months of indecision and skepticism and denial faded as Lauren flung his chin to the side and growled again all low and guttural. Her eyes flamed hellish red, her nostrils flared, cold steam puffed out.

Vampire, vampire, vampire, the screeching continued in Steve's head, as he felt her icy cold lips brush against his throat, felt the sharp tips of her fangs dent his flesh. Felt them press down harder.

Felt Lauren bite down hard.

Felt his blood ooze out into her cold, cold mouth, felt her sucking. Felt Lauren Vestal drinking his blood. Felt it till he couldn't feel anything at all, till his limbs grew numb and he went all faint from weakness and pain and pleasure.

He heard her, heard those grotesquely wet, slurping, sucking sounds till his hearing just faded, just gave out and all he could hear was that screeching alarm inside his head still going *vampire, vampire, vampire.*

Then his vision blurred, and the cold, dark room got hazy and indistinct, and the swords and the shields and lances stuck up on the walls all began to quiver like a mirage, then fade altogether.

The last thing Steve Michaels knew was just that voice in his head still going *vampire, vampire, vampire,* till even that faded away into utter silence, and everything just went black.

CHAPTER TWENTY NINE

"Kurt, just let me out here, will you, dear?"

The uniformed chauffeur punched the intercom to the rear seat. "Here, Madame? But it's quite a way to your gate yet."

"I know, but it's such a lovely night," Carmilla said. "Please, Kurt."

"But Madame, it's gone quite chilly. The walk down your driveway alone –"

"Kurt, please stop."

The driver nodded and eased the black limousine over to the side of the road. Carmilla knocked on the smoked glass partition, and handed him a hundred schilling note. "There, Kurt. A little something extra just for you."

"*Danke.* Please don't hesitate to ask for me next time."

She glanced at his handsome face and the splash of blonde hair falling out from under his chauffeur's cap. "I'll remember that, Kurt." And then she was gone.

Carmilla skipped along the side of the road, swinging her little purse at her side. The symphony tonight was Schubert's Symphony No. 8, the 'Unfinished', and the performance was fine, but she just couldn't concentrate on the music. Instead, she brooded over Lauren. So when the intermission came, she forgot all about her two young violinists and left the Graz auditorium.

Carmilla flung her purse over her shoulder, crouched, then leaped right over the iron fence. She landed on all fours, but was up and skipping along again instantly. She headed across the wooded grounds towards the back of the house.

Scampering across the patio on tip-toes, she tried to be as quiet as possible. There was a mischievous gleam in her dark eyes.

The back door was locked, of course. Lauren was always double-checking the locks. She was good about that sort of thing. But Carmilla was determined to surprise Lauren in the middle of her melancholy mood.

She tried the lock once more, shrugged, then gripped the handle in her slender white hand and twisted hard. The tumblers crunched, brass and steel screeched, the handle bent. She stepped into the house.

No music blared on that detestable stereo.

There were no videotapes playing on Lauren's television with noisy car chases and gunfire. The entire house was as quiet as a chapel.

Surprising Lauren might be harder than she'd planned during the long drive back from Graz.

Carmilla slipped out of her patent leather flats and tucked them under her arm. She crept up the hallway towards the front of the house. But when she turned into the front foyer, Carmilla stopped cold.

The front door hung open.

A few leaves scattered across the marble tile. They blew around in the night breeze, rustling over Lauren's tennis shoes, lying there on the floor by the stairs.

"Lauren?"

No answer.

Still tip-toeing, Carmilla shut the front door quietly. She looked in the parlor.

Empty.

Turned to the stairway.

And smiled.

She picked up Lauren's bluejeans from the bottom of the first stair.

So, she planned to surprise Lauren, and all the while Lauren had decided to do the same for her. Dear, sweet Lauren.

Carmilla crept up the stairs, stockinged feet whispering across the cold stone. Four steps up she grabbed Lauren's shirt. Halfway, she picked up Lauren's bra. Near the top of the stairs she collected Lauren's little white panties.

Carmilla turned down the upstairs hallway, pausing to add Lauren's socks to her pile. "A pleasant little invitation you've laid out for me, Lauren," she whispered to herself. "Though I'd just as soon have unwrapped your 'present' myself."

At the end of the hallway, the bedroom door was open a crack. No light shined from inside. It appeared to be as dark in there as it was in the hallway. Perhaps Lauren heard her come in? Carmilla wondered how quietly she could slip out of the tuxedo here in the hallway. Thought about the cuff links and snaps and suspenders, and the sensitivity of a vampire's ears. She changed her mind.

"Don't start without me, precious," Carmilla whispered to the dark hallway. Her dark eyes gleamed with excitement while she crept up to the bedroom door. She slowly pushed it open, barely able to keep from giggling.

She stepped in.

Her smile faded instantly.

She dropped her shoes and Lauren's clothes on the floor.

Inside, Lauren turned around on the bed, her still glowing eyes all crazed, all wide with fear and revulsion. Tears cascaded down her cheeks. Blood, painted black in the darkness, smeared her lips and dribbled down her chin.

"Lauren – *was it –*"

Lauren lifted her hands to her face. Two bloody hands. She stared at them – then at Carmilla – then back at her hands.

She screamed.

Carmilla ran to the bed. Lauren's naked body was tangled in blood stained sheets. She straddled a naked man. A naked man with his eyes closed, with his throat all torn and bruised and bloody. A naked man with a vaguely familiar scent. With a familiar face.

Recognition lit Carmilla's eyes; it was Lauren's friend from America.

"*Ca-Car-Carmil-mil-la,*" Lauren stammered. "What have I done? Oh God, oh my God, what have I done? Steve, Steve..."

Carmilla leaped on the bed and pulled her off Steve Michaels. She wrapped Lauren in her arms. "It's all right, *leibling,* everything is all right." But Lauren groaned and cried at the same time, her whole body shaking uncontrollably. "Everything will be fine, Lauren, everything."

"Carmilla, he – he came here, and – and I – oh God, oh sweet Jesus, what have I done?"

Carmilla winced at each of Lauren's heavenly pleas. "Precious, I am sorry. So very, very sorry. But he shouldn't have come here."

"I told him. I told him that, but he just wouldn't..." Lauren untangled the sheets, looked down at Steve, saw the blood pooling below the wound in his throat. "Oh Steve, Steve, I'm sorry." She gagged and threw a bloody hand over her mouth.

Carmilla tried to calm Lauren, her magical voice a litany of soothing words, her cool hands all gentle caresses. But inside she seethed at the stupid mortal who'd invaded their fragile little world.

"Come, Lauren. Let me clean you off." She lifted Lauren off the bed and helped her towards the bathroom. "It will be all right. Come now, precious."

But only halfway there, Carmilla halted.

Stiffened.

Hissed — her ears pricking up right through her dark hair. She began to turn her head, but it felt like it was turning in slow-motion.

"Carmilla, what's —"

Silk sheets rustled behind them.

Carmilla loosened her grip on Lauren.

Metal clinked against the wall over the bed.

Lauren slipped out of Carmilla's arms, her wet, bloodied hands grappling for a hold on the tuxedo sleeve.

The bedframe creaked.

"Run!" Carmilla screamed, flinging Lauren across the room. Carmilla spun around.

Spun, just as Steve lunged off the bed, his hands gripping a Karnstein war-lance that hung proudly on the wall just a moment before.

Carmilla wheeled just in time.

Just in time to meet the sharp point of the lance.

"Die, God damn you!" Steve shouted.

He threw his whole weight behind the lance, ripping through Carmilla's shirt, through flesh and breast-bone and flesh again. The lance thrust out of her back, poking out of the black tuxedo with an obscene burst of dark blood. Steve fell on the lance with the last of his strength, driving it — and Carmilla — down to the floor.

"No," Lauren screamed. "Noooooo!"

She dove across the room, plunging to the floor by Carmilla's side. Blood bubbled up around the buried lance, soaking the white tuxedo shirt all dark red and wet. More gushed out of Carmilla's mouth. Arms flailed in the air, struggling to grasp the lance, her legs jerked and slapped the floor.

"No! Carmilla, no!" Lauren screamed. But Carmilla didn't answer. Grotesque, wet gurgling sounds were all that passed her lips. The muscles in her throat flexed beneath the thin ribbon of her black choker. The glow in her eyes faded from red to a dim, bloody burgundy. Then it was gone altogether.

"*Carmilla!*" Lauren shrieked. Her cry thundered off the stone walls, shook the windows, slammed the door shut. "Don't die, Carmilla. Please, don't leave me!"

But Carmilla's hands slipped off the lance and fell to her sides. Her flopping legs stilled. Her lids slowly closed over vacant, black eyes. Her head dropped limply to the floor.

Steve hefted himself up on one arm, then he crawled towards the bed. "Lauren," he groaned, "We did it. You – you're free now." He tried to pull himself up on the bed, one hand on the bedpost, the other grasping for the sheet. But the silk just slid off the mattress. His bloody hand slipped off the post. He tumbled back to the floor.

"We did it, Lauren," he croaked. "We did –"

Lauren screamed again. A terrifying, long wail of a scream, a banshee howl all bitter with dark anguish. Her eyes kaleidoscoped back and forth from mortal blue to dead black to glowing vampire red. Her lips curled back over her gums.

She crawled away from Carmilla's body. Crawled across the floor towards Steve. Crawled naked and bloody and sobbing like a wounded animal, red-stained drool glistening at the tips of her bared fangs.

Lauren grabbed Steve by the shoulders, picked him up in effortless rage and spun him around to face her. She shoved him against the bed, flung his head back, and sank her fangs into his throat.

And she drank.

She drank with rage. She drank in fury. She drank for vengeance.

She drank whatever last blood lingered in Steve's body, shaking her head back and forth like a hungry panther, ripping his throat wide open.

She bit and mauled and sucked until Steve's weak arms stopped pawing the air, until his heart just stopped. Till his confused, terrified eyes went glassy, then froze.

Steve's lifeless body lay limp in her arms. Lauren looked into his empty eyes and screamed one last time. She laid him down, gently now. Just laid him down on the floor.

Then Lauren crawled back across the cold stone floor, back through the slippery red smears of mingled mortal and vampire blood.

Back to Carmilla.

CHAPTER THIRTY

It would be the very last of the beautiful Styrian edelweiss for the year. Gathering even this meager bouquet took far too long. The night was speeding by. Lauren knelt down and set the small white flowers on a dirt and stone mound. She lay her pale hand on top.

"I'm sorry. I truly am sorry." She wiped a single tear off her cheek. Just one. She already cried a river of tears last night.

A bitterly cold wind gusted up. A cold wind on a moonless night, a cold autumn wind that whistled between the stones that made the crude grave. It had no marker. The wind fluttered the edelweiss petals, then flipped the little bouquet over. The flowers rolled off the grave and blew away across the grass.

But a slender, long fingered hand reached out and caught the bouquet.

Slow, cautious steps carried the edelweiss back to the grave. They were laid back on top of the stones with a sigh, and a wince of pain.

"So you have buried him."

"Yes," Lauren said. "I can't very well arrange anything official, now can I?"

"No. I suppose you can't."

Lauren stood up and dusted off the knees of her jeans. "But in a way, I think he'd almost like it here. You can hear the waves lapping in the pond. The evergreens are tall enough here. You can even smell the pine sap. It's not Michigan, but..."

Carmilla reached out to her, but Lauren stepped away. Even that simple gesture made Carmilla's chest scream with pain.

The ugly wound still throbbed beneath her white robe. But the gash began to close the very moment Lauren pulled the Karnstein warlance out last night. Now it was a swollen, purple bruise perched just above her pale breast. By sunrise, the swelling would be gone. In days, even the bruise would vanish. But for now, the pain was no different than what a mortal might feel. And she only had her own dark magic for sutures and anesthesia.

Carmilla never asked to challenge the old legends. But they'd proven themselves remarkably true. Just the silly superstitions from another age? Garlic, wafers, Holy Water? Cleansing fire, axes gripped in righteous hands?

A wooden stake, made of ash, the same tree-flesh that made Christ's cross. And wielded in the name of God by hands fired with faith and belief.

The metal lance wounded her sorely. But kill her?

No. Evidently dark eternity still beckoned.

She didn't ask why. If the cruel God and his uncaring heavens saw fit to spare her, she didn't pretend to understand. But He'd made her. He'd allowed her to roam the earth for nearly three hundred years.

There had to be a purpose...

"Lauren?" Carmilla's eyes fell on the small satchel at Lauren's feet. "What is that?"

Lauren picked up the bag and slung it over her shoulder. Another gust of wind whipped her hair across her face. She shivered and zipped up her jacket. Not that it could keep out the cold. The cold was *inside*. The cold would always be inside.

"Lauren, what are you doing?"

Lauren looked back across the lawn at the house. Their house. Their *home*. Her books. Her studio. Her paintings.

"I'm leaving."

"Leaving?" Carmilla stepped closer, winced, but Lauren backed away. "Leaving for where? Why?"

"I'm not like you, Carmilla. I can't pretend that last night never happened." Lauren pointed down at the grave. "I can't pretend that Steve isn't dead. That his body isn't lying right here, in a dirt hole, with a pile of rocks for a tombstone. I can't pretend that I didn't kill him."

"No, you can't," Carmilla said. "Nor should you. But you also can't pretend that you are something you're not. You are *wampyr*, Lauren. Running away from what happened won't change that."

"No," Lauren said. "I know that."

Tears welled up in Carmilla's dark eyes. "Then what will you do? Where will you go?"

"I don't know. Anywhere. But away from here." Lauren turned away.

"Away from you."

"Why?"

"Because you made me what I am."

"You wanted it. You know that."

"Maybe I did. But it was wrong. I was wrong. It never should have happened. Maybe then Steve would still be safe, still be alive."

Lauren took a tentative step away. "Carmilla, I shouldn't *be*. You shouldn't be. We shouldn't exist. There's no place in the world for monsters like us."

"Perhaps not, Lauren. But here we are."

Lauren started to walk away. She couldn't listen to Carmilla's voice anymore. It still had that same seductive allure that it had on her mortal ears. All soft and supplicative and rationalizing.

The rationalizing lure of evil.

The wind whipped Carmilla's white robe open, baring that vicious bruise. She tried to follow, clutching her breast, gritting her sharp teeth. "Lauren, please!" But Lauren just walked on, heading towards the gate.

"You don't understand how hard it will be," Carmilla called. "You'll go mad. Mad with loneliness. Mad with grief over last night. You'll go mad and walk into the sun one morning."

"No, I don't think so," Lauren said over her shoulder, still walking. "I don't think I'd have the courage to do that."

"Lauren, our home. Our life here together..." But Lauren was little more than a shadow now, floating through the gates.

"Lauren, I love you!"

Lauren stopped.

She didn't turn around. Couldn't turn around. Couldn't risk looking at Carmilla once more. Couldn't bear to let Carmilla see the sadness in her eyes. See the love in her eyes, the love she couldn't hide.

She didn't turn around. But she did speak.

"Carmilla...I hate you."

And then Lauren vanished into the darkness.

Carmilla stood there, just staring. The wind grew colder still. She shivered, and closed her robe.

A soft sprinkling of Alpine snow began to fall.

CHAPTER THIRTY ONE

Leisel Gertener hunched over the little round table, her clean, nordic face hidden under a mop of blonde hair and buried deep in a thick book. She turned the page, made some notes on a tablet, and then took a sip from her wineglass. That sip emptied the glass. She'd been nursing it for over an hour now.

The small tavern on a non-too-prosperous backstreet near the Ammerenplatz was really much too dark for reading or notetaking anyway.

But it was quiet, and the house wine was only seventy five *groschen* a glass. Leisel's pathetic paycheck didn't allow much room for sipping flavored coffees with the smart and the hip in Graz' better clubs and fancy coffeehouses. So dark as it was, this tiny tavern would have to do. At least it was always warmer here than back in her cold water flat near the warehouse district.

And Leisel considered it as good a place as any to concentrate on her writing. This was her first novel, and the fact that all of her short stories were still only earning rejection slips didn't deter her for a moment. If her friends called her presumptuous for embarking on so ambitious a project this soon after graduation, well...they were all still clerking in stores, just like her.

She lifted the glass to her lips again. Oh, yes. It was empty.

A waiter appeared at her table. *"Mehr rotwein?"* he asked.

The writing was going well tonight. She wanted to stay. And the snow was falling so heavy outside.

Leisel opened her second-hand shop purse.

Empty.

"Momentan – nichts," she replied, shaking her head. The waiter

snatched her empty glass and whisked away to the even darker back of the tavern. Leisel snapped her purse closed and returned to her book and her notepad.

She felt something behind her.

Or felt...*someone.*

Leisel felt eyes staring at her back. She turned around.

That girl.

That same, strange girl. Leisel noticed her before. Here in this same tavern, but other places as well. How could she not? The girl was...well, strange looking. Peculiar, wearing those dark sunglasses every night Leisel saw her. Very pretty, though.

No, not just pretty, really.

Beautiful. Almost unnaturally so. Just the slender sort of beauty Helmut had dumped her for, only two short months ago. That still hurt.

The dark haired girl eased around the table. She held two glasses of red wine. "May I?"

Leisel shrugged her shoulders. "Sure. Why not?"

The girl sat down and slid one of the wines across the table. "You looked like you could use another."

"*Danke.*"

She slipped her dark sunglasses off, revealing even darker eyes. Those eyes...

"My name is Leisel. Leisel Gertener."

"I know."

Leisel raised her eyebrows from behind her glass. "Oh?" She put her pen down and sipped at her wine. "And you?"

The girl leaned in close. Those dark eyes seemed to sparkle and dance in her pale face. Her red lips glistened, parting to reveal hints of pearly white teeth lurking inside.

"My name?" She paused, as if she were actually trying to remember. Then she slid a pale hand across the table and patted Leisel's.

"My name is – Carmilla."

"...And to this hour the image of Carmilla returns to memory...and often from a reverie I have started, fancying I heard the light step of Carmilla at the drawing room door."

Joseph Sheridan LeFanu
1872

AUTHOR'S NOTE

So, why Joseph Sheridan LeFanu's *Carmilla?*
Perhaps the more appropriate question would be, why not *Carmilla?*
For some reason, LeFanu's female vampire – considered by many in horror circles to be *the* preeminent literary female vampire – has intrigued filmmakers while managing to elude horror novelists much more astutely than she escaped her pursuers in the original novella itself.

When so many critics regard *Carmilla* as one of the three formative works (*The Vampyre, Carmilla, Dracula*) in the development of the vampire literary canon, it's just plain odd that modern writers have ignored it. It's certainly appeared in enough anthologies; after all, public domain vampire stories are the anchors of 'classic vampire collections'. Its influence on fellow Irishman Bram Stoker's *Dracula* is self-evident: it was *Carmilla* that plopped the vampire myth down where readers seem to like it best – Central Europe – and not Greece (Byron/Polidori), England (James Malcolm Rymer's 1847 *Varney The Vampyre*) or Venice (Theophile Gautier's 1836 *La Mort Amoureuse*). It was *Carmilla* that introduced the Central and Eastern European folklore, as LeFanu found it in Dom Augustin Calmet's *A Treatise On The Apparitions Of Spirits, And On The Vampires Or Revenants Of Hungary, Romania, Etc.,* including the preferred method for dispatching vampires with a stake through the heart and decapitation, the vampire's unnatural strength, the infectious nature of the vampire's bite, and much more. And it was *Carmilla* that Stoker paid homage to in the excised first chapter of Dracula, later published as *Dracula's Guest*, in which Jonathan Harker has a small hint of what he's heading for in Transylvania, when he narrowly escapes death while lying at the foot of the tomb of a revenant Countess from 'Gratz".

Joseph Thomas Sheridan LeFanu (1814 – 1873) was the proprietor and editor of the Dublin University Magazine, a dabbler in conservative Protestant Irish politics, and much more notably, a prodigious writer of supernatural fiction. Note: that's *supernatural* fiction, because unlike so many 19th century Gothic stories, LeFanu's tales frequently neglected to explain the frightening occurrences away with convenient, if implausible, natural causes, plots and schemes, masquerades, etc. Starting in 1838, LeFanu published several story collections, novels and various short works, largely ghost stories or brooding Gothics of one sort or another.

Unquestionably, his strongest work appeared in the story collection *In A Glass Darkly*, published the year before he died. The collection takes its name from St. Paul in the New Testament (1 Corinthians, Verse 12), and is presented as the collected papers of one Dr. Martin Hesselius, a German 'metaphysician', and possible model for Stoker's Van Helsing. The best known – and the just plain best – story in the collection is the last: *Carmilla.*

Carmilla is narrated by an English girl Laura, who lives happily, if in isolation, with her father (her mother having passed away) in a remote schloss in Styria, not far from the ruined and deserted village of Karnstein. Laura expects a visit from Bertha Rheinfeldt, niece and ward of family friend General Speilsdorf. But news arrives that Bertha has suddenly died from mysterious causes. Soon after, a coach overturns on the road in front of Laura's schloss, and they take in the injured passenger, Carmilla, a lovely young girl who, despite her many strange and morbid ways, eventually seduces Laura, and slowly vampirizes her, nipping at Laura's breasts at night and drinking her blood. Laura takes ill, doctors are summoned, Carmilla vanishes, and the old General arrives just in time to reveal precisely how his niece died: at the hand of one 'Millarca', who insinuated herself into the Speilsdorf household and slowly drained the blood from poor Bertha, then vanished. Worse: Millarca/Carmilla is actually 'Mircalla', the last Countess Karnstein, dead some hundred and fifty years. Aided by a Baron Vordenburg and various clerics, they all converge on Karnstein, locate the Countess' tomb, where they find Carmilla's undead body bathed in blood. She is staked in the heart, decapitated, her body burned. But even as Laura finishes her tale, she acknowledges that she still feels haunted by Carmilla, and sometimes fancies she hears "the light step of Carmilla at the drawing-room door".

Oh, there's much, much more. Like many 19th century Gothics, there are more subplots and character cameos than most readers can digest. Laura dreamt of Carmilla as a child. Carmilla finagles her way into house-holds with the help of an unidentified "Comtesse", who introduces herself as Carmilla's mother and then disappears. When the coach overturns in front of Laura's schloss to disgorge Carmilla, the mother's there again, along with a mysterious turbaned black woman, and evil looking coachmen. None of them reappear. Laura's mother is supposedly related to the Karnstein's. Carmilla appears in Laura's room at night in the form of giant black cat, then transforms into her human form at the last moment. There's the Baron Vordenburg, who pops up right at the end, and turns out to be the descendant of a man who was one of the mortal Countess Mircalla's lovers (and presumably a very bad one, since she switched to the fairer sex in her new existence). To say nothing about the whole business of Carmilla's anagrammatic names. LeFanu, like many of his contemporaries, didn't agonize over tossing all kinds of narrative flotsam into his stories, but then, that was before computers, when editing and rewrites were a pain.

But perhaps we should be grateful. Like the loose narrative threads and veiled hints of the past in Stoker's *Dracula*, LeFanu's sometimes cumbersome plot devices can all be the starting points of modern writers' new takes on his immortal tale.

Bypass the pointless subplots, ignore implausible coincidences, and Carmilla remains the most atmospheric and sensually macabre story, long or short, in 19th century vampire literature. If you've never read it, and still consider yourself a fan of the vampire genre, shame on you (sorry, watching the Hammer films doesn't count). If you've read this novel, go back and re-read *Carmilla*, and savor the richness of the roots that drove everything from Stoker to Rice. Don't analyze, just enjoy. *Carmilla* has suffered the indignities of countless Freudian/psycho-sexual analysis, feminist/lesbian socio-political interpretations (that, despite it having been written by a man) and of all things, has been frequently portrayed as some sort of allegory about Irish Protestantism, Anti-Irish Catholicism, land ownership and anti-English sentiment. Right.

So forgive this writer's hubris for simply trying to pay homage to one of the finest tales in all of vampire literature.

Oh yes...all those subplots and character cameos that could work as the basis of modern writers' new takes on the Carmilla character? Well, who says this one novel covered everything *this* writer has to say about the languid, pale, blood drinking Countess of Karnstein?

Kyle Marffin

THE NEW VOICES IN HORROR

Night Prayers   *by P. D. Cacek*

Bram Stoker Award winner P. D. Cacek's NIGHT PRAYERS is a wryly witty romp that turns the conventions of traditional vampire fiction inside out. You'll meet Allison Garret - thirtysomething, biological clock loudly ticking and perpetually unlucky in love - who wakes up in a seedy motel room after a three day binge...as a vampire without a clue about how to survive! In a rollicking tour through the seamy underbelly of L.A., Allison hooks up with a Bible-thumping streetcorner preacher, and it will take more than prayers to save them both from the clutches of a catty coven of strip club vampire vixens.

ISBN 1-891946-01-3
5.5 x 8.5 trade pb, 224 pg $15.95 US ($19.50 CAN)

The Darkest Thirst - A Vampire Anthology

Sixteen disturbing tales, from some of horror's most exciting writers, that explore the undead's darkest desires for redemption, lust, power, revenge...and blood. Includes stories by familiar horror names and emerging new talents:

Michael J. Arruda	Stirling Davenport	Barb Hendee
Julie Anne Parks	Edo van Belkom	Robert Devereaux
Paul McMahon	Rick R. Reed	Sue Burke
d.g.k. Goldberg	Kyle Marffin	Thomas J. Strauch
Margaret L. Carter	Scott T. Goudsward	Deborah Markus
	William R. Trotter	

ISBN 1-891946-00-5
5.5 x 8.5 trade pb, 256 pg $15.95 US ($19.50 CAN)